I0602178

S.L.Mason

KILLING GODS

ALETHEA

CALYPSO

HERA

FATES

UNDERWORLD

ELYSIUM

POSEIDON

NOVELLA

EMMALINE

BLOOD OF THE GODS

UNDERWORLD V

KILLING GODS

This Book is a work of fiction.

All of the characters, organizations, and events portrayed in the novel are either products of the authors imagination or are used fictitiously. Its not about you.

DEDICATION

~ 5 ~

2020 was a trip into the Underworld and I can say I survived, many didn't.

TABLE OF CONTENTS

PROLOGUE

I only now see the folly of my ways. You cannot make a deal with evil and expect fair play. The plains of judgment strip all illusions bare leaving only the rot of your soul.

Charon

CHAPTER 1

SYDNEY

The three bright balls of gas floating in the black void were all I could see, instead of marveling at the majesty of the triple stars and the equal balance of gravity holding them together I shivered. Light played over the center of their triumvirate revealing the real terror behind Cerberus.

Charon nonchalantly announced that the center of the three stars was inhabited by a black-hole as if it was a piece of information everyone in the universe should know. I'd wiped every memory he ever had when we'd judged him, yet he still managed to remember this.

Did I really wipe him?

"There's a black hole in the center of that cluster of stars?" I scoffed. Disbelief was my go-to and I used it to the best of my advantage.

I had to question everything. It also kept anyone from noticing me biting my lip or the shaking of my hands. A cold feeling crept over me, leaving me wishing I'd worn more than my shorts and t-shirt.

How could I tell the people on both ships we'd traveled the stars of Styx only to face a blackhole. I mentally shook away the horror of it all. Greek Mythology made it all sound so easy. Find a cave, follow a few rivers, pay the ferry man Charon, and pass under the legs of a giant three headed dog and wingo, bango, bongo you're in the underworld. How could two intelligent species have gotten it so very wrong?

The icy fingers of fear walked over me. My emotions were locked in ice as if they'd been shoved out an airlock into the vacuum of space.

"Our people always stay away from areas in space like this one due to the gravitational pull, they are too strong, making it impossible to maintain your position." Hera gulped and asked, "Speaking of which, how are we maintaining this position now?" she smoothed the fabric of her tunic against her thigh.

If Hera is worried, we all should be.

I darted a glance at Professor Michelson and Adrian. "That's a really good question. You guys have an answer for that?" I wanted to turn away from the viewport to gauge Adrian's answer. I trusted him implicitly, he would never do or say anything to endanger me or the kids.

It was impossible to turn away from the spatial anomaly. Every few minutes, a light flashed across the singularity's event horizon, illuminating its sphere-like shape. The light not only rimmed the circular outline but added a halo ring. The visage would have been angelic, magnificent even if I didn't understand the danger and how close we were to it.

"Sorry, beautiful girl, I'm not an astrophysicist. I'm a pilot," Adrian waved my question over to the egghead in the room and began checking the readings on his console.

"I've been wondering that myself," Michelson intervened, "but now, upon checking my calculations, we are in a slow drift towards the center. That's what I was trying to tell you before. The spiral of stars is being created as they are sucked into the center of these three stars," he paused to point at the triple dog stars on the holo-map. "Although, you can't see the actual singularity, and you don't really see the stars approaching it. Yet, when looking at your star charts, I can absolutely see the golden ratio swirling effect into the black hole," Michelson shrugged his answer off, searching the faces in the room. His intellect and training had saved us from being pulled apart on the river Styx. However, a singularity is whole new ball of cosmic wax.

"Are we trapped? Can we," I swallowed the saliva pooling my mouth back, "can we leave?" I asked and shifted my hips.

I couldn't look at anyone. I'd already closed all my mental doors. I didn't need another mind muttering in the background. "If I wanted us shifted out of here, could we do it?" I asked the one question we all wanted the answer to. My muscles tensed, and my belly rolled as I waited for an answer.

"I don't see why we couldn't, beautiful girl. Just because that represents the entrance to the underworld, doesn't that mean we have to go through the black-hole in order to get there?" Adrian stated the question as a fact.

However, I knew better. He was actually asking me and I didn't have an answer. I didn't know where we were heading from here. It's not like there was a sign that read *'Underworld - this way. Or 50,000 light years to the Underworld.'*

Adrian's inquiry worried me.

Going into a black-hole is suicide. Isn't it? Even Themian's avoided them.

I transferred all of Charon's tactical data to Adrian and Tristan, but it didn't erase the memories from my mind. Being a Fate and judging someone wasn't a science.

"Isolde, when you judged him, what did you see?" I tilted my head in the direction of Charon.

I hadn't had enough caffeine for this. My hands still gripped the cup of what was now cold coffee. I pressed it to my lips anyway and gulped down every last drop. I needed the caffeine jolt. At least then, the tremors in my hands could be blamed on the coffee and not the fear eating away at my insides.

"He wasn't prepared for the mental onslaught of everyone awakening at the same time. He made this big grand gesture of having everyone genetically altered at the same time and shifting to their new Homeworld. Yet, he didn't shift to the new world. Mom, I'm not exactly sure what he did. It was like he tried to shift. However, they didn't go through a black-hole," she stopped and then whispered, "I think he made it."

Think, think, think, Sydney! This can't be the end of the line. There has to be a reason. It was something he did. Maybe at the last moment?

"Prometheus, how close to the event horizon of the singularity were you at the time of the shift?"

"Closers than we are now. But that is the last thing I remember. The ship was drawn into the gravity well. We couldn't use our engines to pull out," Charon answered for the ship.

I whipped around to stare at him. If my eyes could have shot fire, the fear that roared through me would have burned him into ash.

Charon and Isolde began speaking at the same time. It was as if she was reliving every moment of the shift with him.

"Isolde what are you doing?" Hera asked and reached out to touch her, though she thought better of it and fingered her dress fabric instead.

Issy stopped, "If he doesn't remember, we will never know, mom. I'm giving some of it back to him. We need to," with that, she returned to Charon and they muttered together.

I wasn't sure that was a good idea. Charon had not been a good person. Moreso, I was not sure I could've lived the same life that he was forced to live myself. Settling, doing nothing, having no purpose whatsoever. I didn't blame him. I wouldn't have been satisfied with that either.

Even so, *I wouldn't have used people as guinea pigs. But then again, is it any different than what I'm doing now?*

"Keep going! I want to know exactly what he did," I decided.

The two of them droned on, reciting their story in unison. It was creepy. I shivered at the idea of reliving one person's life in a moment. Giving it back was a whole new ball of wax.

What part will she return? What if she gives back something so small, something that seems inconsequential but isn't?

The truth was that one way or another, we weren't going to get beyond the entrance to the underworld without facing the stars and whatever they had to dish out to us.

I looked around the room. Hercules was coiled, ready to pounce at any moment to Isolde's side. Hera appeared oblivious to his behavior.

I wasn't. Not any more.

Professor Michelson continued to crunch whatever numbers he was working on until finally, he looked up. "I've reached the point where I must use a computer. Where can I get one?" he asked and ran his hand over his head then pulled it back in his usual look of surprise.

I was sure that he was bald before Melinda gave him the Primordium.

"The entire ship is a giant computer. What would you like to know, Professor Michelson?" Adrian asked, waving at the expanse of the ship.

"Well," Michelson licked his lips, "I need a console to work from. I find typing to be easier than speaking out loud." He offered a tight-lipped smile.

"Follow the pulsing circuits down the hallway. It will lead you to an adequate workroom," the ship informed him.

Michelson rose, "Well, I'll be seeing you all later. I have a lot of work to do. I'm not sure we need to go down the black-hole. But if my research points in that direction, I would prefer not to go. If that's alright with you. I'd be more than happy to transfer back to Odyssey and wait there."

He strolled out the door, following the pulsing blue veins flowing down the walls. The Primordium had returned his youth, but he still hunched his back and shuffled like an elderly man. The tweed jacket did nothing to throw off the effect.

"Don't worry, Professor Michelson. If we do decide to go through the black hole, you will not be attending with us," I informed him. He raised a hand, threw me a backwards wave.

Isolde and Charon continued droning in the background. I wanted to tell them to move it to another room. Instead, I glanced sharply at Adrian, "Shift me over to Odyssey. I need to talk to Emmaline and Ixis."

"Of course, beautiful girl. Should I go with you?"

"No, I need you to stay here. We're slipping into the gravity well. The deeper we go, the more likely you will have to shift us out. I need you to be ready to move the ship at a moment's notice."

I squeezed his shoulder and leaned over, laying a quick peck on his stubbled cheek before non-space blasted me with cold and a whiff of ozone that coated my tongue.

CHAPTER 2

EMMALINE

Sydney must be more of a dam fool than I ever thought.

Her worries were enough to drive a soul crazy.

Adrian's wife was out of her mind leaving me in charge. I didn't want to run this vaudeville-style circus show. Between the invisible Lyons and Bio-domes of plant life, we couldn't go near because they might eat us, I felt like I just walked into the midway of a carny show. I was just waiting for the fake mermaid to be unveiled, so that I could see her rubber tail just moments away from fallin' off if she wiggles too much.

Ixis said he just wanted me to be happy, but happiness was beside the point!

Sydney, on the other hand, what a handful, leavin' me in charge of thousands of people's lives.

She is out of her mind!

It was true that I knew Themian technology better than anybody else. Certainly, been around it long enough.

Notwithstandin', an entire ship of people reliant on me?

I'd spent such a long time sittin' around on my ass, I forgot what it was like to be this active and in charge. And just when we got things consolidated and organized, Sydney ran off on some crazy quest to find the first Homeworld.

I was just glad she didn't ask me to go on one of her adventures.

I'm not that adventurous!

I looked around the shifting room, hopin' to find a familiar face and at the same time relieved not to see one.

Dewy was the only friendly face I wanted to see. I closed my eyes to press Dewy depressions out of my mind. He'd locked himself in his quarters for a while after I explained Ixis couldn't bring his wife back to life.

He forgets I can hear everything he thinks.

He didn't know how to block me out and didn't seem inclined to learn, so I had to block him. I hated doing it. He said that when he couldn't hear me, he felt as if I'd cut off his right arm.

Dewy kept his mouth shut once I discovered the truth — that I was surrounded by dam aliens.

Dewy is good at keeping a secret.

I rubbed my forehead and took to my feet. I'd had enough of sitting around. It was time for action. I hadn't waited on Alethea for so many years for nothing.

"Ix, you really think she can find Elysium? Or is she just killin' herself?"

"I'm not entirely sure, Emmaline," Ixis voice was rich both out loud and mental and it was a salve to my worries.

"I'm not sure if she's gonna find what she's lookin' for

or get everyone else killed," I kept repeatin', fiddlin' with the pearl buttons on the front of my shirt.

"She must be quite sure she will find something, or she would not take her offspring." Ixis offered.

I shot him a dirty look. He didn't understand humanity at all.

Sydney was like me. She understood life was a risk no matter where you were.

"I know you're right except, now she left Tristan. Before, she always took both of them."

Tristan was my great grandnephew and I was glad he was here, but...

A mother only separates her eggs to increase her offspring's survival rate.

The vision of 17-year-old boys, with duffel bags thrown over their shoulders, wavin' bye to their mothers flashed through my mind. The government separated brothers to keep mothers from losin' all their sons at once. No one wanted another Sullivan brother's incident.

I gulped back the tears that leaped to my eyes as I

recalled all the death that came after.

"Why do you think she would've left Tristan behind and not Isolde?" Ixis asked me.

I patted my curls back into place. "Isolde is a Fate, whatever that means. They have to be together," I repeated the answer Sydney had offered me. Yet, it tasted wrong. My gut told me she knew something she was not sharing.

"Perhaps, they were not so convinced where they were going was safe," Ixis returned.

He's been bent out of sorts ever since Tristan and Adrian returned with Charon's memories. He took pride in his ability and seeing his proteges outdo him in less than a year, stuck in his craw.

"Well, the woman looked like she'd seen her own shade standin' before her with the worms fallen out," I barked.

"Worms falling out?" Ixis asked.

He couldn't imagine death. How could he, when he hadn't seen anyone die since the Great Division?

Not really sure what that's all about yet.

Ixis didn't understand that the worms eatin' your

corpse meant that you're dead.

I've seen plenty of dead guys and not just because of the war and Dewy. All my friends and some of their children too. Actually, arriving on Atlantis was a blessing for me. I was at that age where your friends start dropping like flies. I didn't want to be one of them.

"What do you want to do with all these people on the ship? I mean, we have to have jobs. Something to keep everyone from becoming lethargic, or worse," I murmured the last part under my breath, then glanced around the shifting room.

It was empty. I shivered. I didn't like it. I didn't like most people, but this was too much even for me.

"It depends on how long you are the acting captain," Ixis had moved away from the podium and toed a seat out of the floor. He rested his elbows on the chair and templed his fingers, waiting for my reply.

"My gut tells me that I might be sittin' in the big chair for a long time. Idle hands make for idle minds and mouths. Everyone needs a job," I gave him a tight smile.

"Inform the council let them handle the idle hands."

Ixis replied.

A small smile played around the edges of his lips, and for a moment, I forgot what I was gonna say. I quickly inspected my flour-sack print shirt and my navy-blue slacks. Part of me still loved the old styles. I'd never been vain, but it did suit me. I smoothed the pressed pleat in my slacks with a satisfied smile.

"Also, we need a new command crew. Sydney took pretty much everybody and I really need some reliable help. Dew is a good man in a fight. Maybe this will pull him out of his morass."

Then it struck me.

There's more than one way to skin an O'Dear and there's more than one O'Dear on this boat.

A smirk played its way over half of my face.

< Tobias O'Dear, your presence is wanted in the shifting room. Use your bracelet to find the way. > I ordered. My long ears came in handy sometimes.

<Who is this?>

< My name is Emmaline. You've just been

conscripted, so double time it up here. > I replied.

<Dewy's sister?> He asked.

I bristled. Everyone always called Dewy my brother, not me, his sister. <Yes! Dewy's sister.> I barked.

Ixis laughs in the back of my mind. I sneered at him and he got up and returned to his duties.

"What about that girl Caroline? She seems pretty handy like she knows how to run a show or two and she's organized. What's she doin' right now?" I asked.

"I think she's helping Melinda down in the labs," he replied without looking up.

Melinda had pretty much met everybody on this boat. She knew who's got what ability and what job they did on earth. "Ixis, do me a favor, darlin', and shift me down to Melinda. I want to pick her brain."

I barely had a chance to take a deep breath before I was in the laboratories.

I had to say. Havin' a man who can move you from one place to the other and bring anything, anytime, anywhere, got to be the handiest trick ever. Course, the fact that he was as good-looking as the devil was nice too.

Ix looked like one of them, Native American Gods or something. All that long black glossy hair, his full lips and his high cheekbones, was enough to make a girl swoon.

I blinked my musin' back and faced the only other woman on Odyssey I could do battle with then have a drink.

We speak the same language. No bullshit.

"Emmaline, I see you deign to visit me," Melinda rolled her eyes, and buttoned her lab coat in fake modesty. "What brings you to my neck of the woods?"

"I need a command crew." I waved her open-mouthed rejection off. "I know you're not interested and I'm not here for you. I need recommendations. I might take Caroline away from you, though," I said and picked up some newfangled gadget from her table.

"You can't have Caroline," she took the do-dad away and placed it back on the table. "and she's not interested in that sort of thing. She is organized and completely capable. She has a scientific mind and would rather be in the lab working around chemistry and things of that nature. Her idea of fun is a bunch of beakers over a Bunsen burner. Being in the shifting room and telling people what to do— yuk." Melinda stuck her tongue out while squinting one eye closed.

I gave her a simperin' smile, crinklin' my eyes at the edges for good measure. Her eyes narrowed back at me as she returned a pressed, toothless grin.

"Why don't I ask her and see for myself what she likes," I turned and without another word, I headed for the lab door.

"Suit yourself. She's the next lab."

I caught her crossed armed reflection in the crystalline glass wall.

"I will tell you this," she called. "We had a bunch of cops and ex-military types. Most of them came through with the mental group. A lot of them didn't come out right in the head or at least nobody else thought they were right in the head." She shook her head over it, "However, they only thought they were crazy because they were told they were crazy," she didn't stop, so I turned around to face her.

"We had a German guy you might like. He's extremely organized. and a great instructor. His name is Maximilian."

"Does he have an ability that I should know about?" I

asked in a sticky sweet voice.

"Other than trying to make time with every woman he sees who has never heard a German accent before, I think his talents are really just military aspects," she shrugged and held her hands out as if that was all she had to offer.

I didn't buy it. Melinda was crafty.

"Maximilian fought in World War I. He's a long liver. Says his father is one of Hera's kids. However, he won't say which one or he doesn't know. Not sure which it is." Melinda gave me a tight-lipped smile.

She had no idea what she looked like. Or really cared, for that matter. My brother described her as having some mighty fine gams, but to me she was just an egghead who liked to lord her brainpower over all of us.

Well, not me, by God!

Melinda had given me a mental visual of what this Maximilian guy looked like. I glanced down the hall at Caroline's lab, then stepped off the outer ring and onto the ring bridge, huffing my way through the gravity change and headed to the cafeterias.

The long walk gave me time to put my thoughts in

order.

What am I going to say to this long liver?

I wasn't!

I spied Tobias leaning against a wall with one leg over the other and his arms crossed. He threw me a half smile. "Yeah, thanks for making me walk all the way up to the shifting room." He remarked, then uncrossed his arms.

"I forgot about that," I snickered. "I am lookin' for staff and Melinda seemed the best person to talk to about it. I'm too old to hold interviews."

"Emmaline, you are the youngest old lady I ever met," Tobias winked at me.

"I'll pay you good money to point me to a guy named Maximilian," I winked back.

I liked Tobias. He had an easy goin' personality and he was easy on the eyes. All those blue eyes and dreamy smiles. He knew he was pretty too.

"Is he a military type, flattop haircut and looks a bit like Dolph Lundgren?" Tobias asked, uncrossing his legs and pulling his back off the wall, turning his torso slightly.

"I don't really know what he looks like, but he is a military type. Can you point me in his direction?"

Tobias waved his hand towards the far back corner of the cafeteria.

All I could make out was a group of broad shoulders in varying shades of hair-color. I nodded my head at him and sauntered my way back there. As I approached, I didn't recognize any of the faces. There were so many people on board you could forget one as soon as you see the next.

A big brawny blond with a flattop towards the back stood head and shoulders above the rest, talking. His words drifted my way:

"We need to have our own military. We have no idea what we're going to run into. We must be able to defend ourselves against anyone or anything. We aren't alone in the universe. We're freaks, outcasts even. The Themians don't want us and the humans wouldn't know what to do with us. They would probably put us in laboratories and run tests on us. If you don't know how to defend yourself and have never held a weapon, you need to learn. I'll teach you."

His fist smashed into the palm of his hand while his shoulders flexed. It was a show of force I'd witnessed before.

Only the guys doin' it were fightin' were on the other side.

I didn't like what I was hearin'. It sounded like a cross between a mutiny, insurrection and just plain stupidity.

Sydney left everybody pretty much to their own devices. The only thing she left in place was a High Council with each section in charge of their bloodline. Her rules were simple. You could do whatever you want as long as it didn't hurt anyone else.

Truth be told, people didn't always want to talk about being harmed or being strong armed, for that matter.

This guy was right. We needed more.

I pulled out a cigarette and tapped it on the gold case Dewy gave me after the war. It was one of the few pleasures I kept from my human life.

I love smokin'.

The feel of the cigarette in my hand and the taste of the smoke on the tip of my tongue was a type of heaven.

I let the smoke curl out of my mouth and up into my nostril before blowing it straight at the crowd of testosterone laden males.

I will have to find out who his father is.

Something told me it wasn't somebody I wasn't gonna like — a troublemaker.

< Is Ares the father of this Maximilian clown? >

<Yes.> Melinda replied, irritation coloring her remark.

I left the cafeteria and headed to Hera's kids' quarters.

That warmonger better claim this boy.

Boy, he was probably older than me by about 20 years. I couldn't care less.

He better fall in line on my boat!

Hera said not to bother them and that they would come out when they were ready.

Balderdash!

This was more important.

I waved my bracelet over the entryway. - "Access denied."

Great!

"Odyssey, acting Capitan Emmaline here. I want this

damn door open, now!" I shouted.

"Access granted. Security override, acting Capitan Emmaline."

I smiled to myself. The ship obeyed better than its inhabitants.

The door slid open to reveal three of the girls sitting in the front living room. In unison all their heads turned to take me in.

I sashayed in like it was nobody's business, "Alright ladies, I'd like you and your siblings to assemble. I'm only here for one reason. There's a hybrid down there. People say he is a long liver, meaning he must be one of yours. And he's causing trouble."

All three girls shook their heads. Eris spoke. "He can't be one of ours. None of us have contributed to the gene pool for three generations. It must be one of the boys. I'll fetch them," with that, the raven-haired beauty crossed the room.

The door slid open easily and I caught a glimpse of some kind of a gaming room. She said something in a language I didn't recognize and sat back down.

"They will join us shortly, except for Hercules. He is

not here," her tone needled at me.

My ability to bend emotions eased my way in life. It made it easy for me to recognize another emo-bender and Eris only sent out one emotion — trouble.

I smacked my dry lips in distaste over her lack of self-control. She didn't need to irritate the bejesus out of every person she encountered — she just liked it.

"Where is Hercules?" I asked without rising to her bait.

"He decided to follow that other hybrid he's so enamored with," Eris remarked and toyed with a curl that hung to the back of her head. She wound it around her finger, pulled the curl to straighten it then allowed it to bounce back.

"Hybrid?" I replied.

Don't cross your arms! Don't cross your arms!

"The one he saved from the Lyons. What's her name?" Eris asked and rolled her head to the side and yawned.

"Isolde," Hebe supplied with a bright smile.

"Issy? Good luck with that one," I snickered.

They both looked at me funny. I smiled back at them

without wavering.

"Yes, my twin prefers a challenge and he never backs down from a good fight. Even if he is a terrible braggart," Hebe giggled, then covered her mouth with the back of her hand and shrugged. Her blond curls bounced with her glee.

Eos and Eileithyia sat stock still in silence. The only sign of life were the blinking of eyes and the rise and fall of their chest.

The silence was cut off by the three jolly Green Giants that strolled in from the gaming room. Every single one of them was gorgeous.

Themians genes just only made pretty.

What had Isolde called them?

Eye candy! They were certainly candy. They looked sweet and delicious, yet one of them looked suspiciously familiar.

"I'm looking for whoever sired that boy down there named Maximilian. He's wrangling up trouble and I want it stopped."

I knew the moment the words were out of my mouth

exactly who the father was. He had raven black hair, just like his twin. Ares, the God of War and his son - a military man.

Big shock here.

"Maximilian. He's mine," Ares replied without a shred of remorse.

"Great! Get down to the cafeteria. He's trying to rile up the troops either for a mutiny, or a militia. I'm not sure which and I don't care! You want to start an army, fine. But keep it under my control. I'm looking for some command staff. Interested?"

"Do not worry. I'll get Maximilian under control. I will be your military man and not him. Whatever ideas he brought to your attention, they're mine. That's my job. I'm probably the best for tactics and I know how to run an army better than any of my siblings." He crossed his arms and a smug smile scraped across his face.

He was proud his progeny was makin' waves.

"Yeah, my issue isn't so much your abilities. It's whether you're willin' to take orders. Especially from a woman," I replied.

"I've been taking orders for my mother since I was

born. Obviously, I do not have a problem taking orders from a woman," he retorted.

"Alright! Then, you got yourself a job," I thrust my hand out at him.

He glanced down at my outstretched arm and I raised an eyebrow.

Instead of taking my hand, he actually wrapped his big hand around my wrist, forcing me to reflect in kind, then he gave it a good shake.

"It is agreed. I'm your military commander, let me go get my army in hand." He strode for the door.

"Just one thing," I said and he stopped in his tracks, casting a glance over his shoulder. "Your second-in-command is my brother, Dewy. This isn't a request. It's an order. I know unequivocally that I can trust Dewy. Yes, he'll be spying on you for as long as I feel it's necessary. Although Maximilian is older than Dewy and probably has more war experience, Dewy has more modern work experience. What's more, is that he's cool as a cucumber under pressure," I finished.

Taking a deep breath, I waved Ares into the game room.

The large man turned to face me. His jaw ground down on his irritation and he stalked into the game room.

"I need you to get Dewy out of his quarters. If I leave him sittin' there much longer, I will lose him. His wife died forty years ago. I'm not callous. I understand he loved her, but it has been forty years. Do me a favor. Please introduce Dewy to some nice girl. I mean, his heart has been broken long enough."

"The ladies covered their mouths with their hands, snickering, "Do not worry, Emmaline, we will do our best to bring your brother out of his melancholy," Eos called from the next room.

Ares rolled his eyes right alongside me. I leaned in and cupped my hand to one side of my mouth. "I think he needs to get lucky, but not with your sisters."

Ares barked out a laugh. "I can only lead a man to war. I can't force him to fight. However, I find that most will." He gave me a wink.

I took a deep breath and for the first time in over a year, it was a little easier than before.

One problem down, 50,000 more to go.

CHAPTER 3

SYDNEY

Prometheus' hologram flashed through several systems, changing colors and scales at the blink of an eye and making me tired of constantly searching in the dark.

I groped for answers and the path to Elysium. Every time I ran through the files, I came up empty. I felt as if the stars were nothing more than grains of sand on a beach and I was trying to pick them up with an open hand. Just like that, the stars kept slipping through my fingers back into the cosmic void.

I growled in frustration. "Prometheus, can you show us any star charts with a trail back to Elysium from this point?" My fingers tapped the side of my coffee cup to the tune of a Cure song, *Burn*. I painted my face with a shallow smile to try and work the problem out.

"No. We arrived at this point in space and we left from this point in space."

The growl I'd just released begged to be replaced by a scream of rage. I glanced over at Adrian and shook my head.

"That's not possible. You simply can't leave and arrive from the same point in space and leave no trail of where you were before," I replied in clipped words.

"Sure you can! You're not thinking fourth dimensionally," Professor Michelson interjected, his eyes bright and inquisitive. He smacked his lips together in anticipation of the forthcoming discussion.

'You're not thinking forth dimensionally.' What kind of cocka-mimi bullshit is that?

"What if he didn't change places? He stayed in the same place and changed something else?" Michelson asked and picked up two pens. One looked beat up and used, while the other was pristine. He held the used pen up inside the holo-display next to Oceania, then he removed it and placed the new pen in its place.

Hera gasped.

Adrian moved closer, "You mean time? Don't you?" his eyes grew thoughtful and serious as he scrunched the brow ridge between his eyes and nodded his head.

"Yes — time," Michelson whispered and allowed Adrian to take the pen from his hand.

Adrian stared at the pen, tossing it in his hand only to catch it again as it toppled end over end.

I wasn't the smartest person in the group. However, I was in charge, and between us, we had to figure out what the hell Charon did.

"Pardon me, Miss Sydney, but we are slipping closer and closer to the singularity and although most of you may not seem all that troubled by it or perhaps you just don't understand the full gravity of it. Ha! That's a physics joke," Michelson began to chuckle, then coughed into his fist to cover the lack of levity in the room.

I cocked an eyebrow at him. I really didn't find it funny, although I could understand how someone in his world would.

"This is a bit of a sticky wiki, the time slippage," he pointed at the enlarged holo-map, tracking the movement of both ships.

"Time slippage?" I raised my eyebrows at him.

He was taller than me, but I still wanted to look down at him.

"Yes, time slippage. The closer you drift to the singularity, the slower time goes, therefore the faster time will pass on planet Earth or anywhere else in the universe. A couple of minutes could be a couple of hours or years. You catch my drift?" He shrugged and gave another dry laugh, which no one responded to.

"The deeper we're pulled into the gravity well of Oceania, the slower time goes for us?" Issy asked.

A smile broke over his face and he raised his hands to clap, then thought better of it. "Yes, precisely." He pointed at her and she responded to his praise by pointing her toes and hands.

I had to physically restrain myself from rolling my eyes.

Issy will never change.

"I don't know how far you intend to slip into this gravity well. Of course, no one in our race will be affected by this time slippage, or so I think," he muttered under his breath before quickly moving on. "I mean, everything else around us will age quickly while we carry on." He raised his index finger and pointed at the ceiling, "However, we should make our way out sooner or later, before it's too late. Once we're in too deep — well..." He held his hands up in surrender, "We are using normal engines and will eventually not be able to pull out. Without having a specific place and time to shift to, we may not be able to shift out either," he finished.

My heart rate ratcheted up to hammer home the problem. "Are you saying that in order for us to shift out, we might have to actually time travel?" I squeaked since I had no desire to become a time lord.

"Precisely," he replied and ran his hand over his head.

Sticky wiki is right!

"Isolde, is that what he did?" I tilted my head at Charon. "Did he shift out deep in the gravity well?"

"Yes," she said, then covered her mouth with her hand to pull on her lower lip. She turned away from me to look at Hercules.

"Prometheus, what was the exact position of the ship when Charon shifted?" Adrian asked before I could.

"Approximately 85 light years away from our current position," the computer replied in its metallic voice which reminded me of Windows' read-back option. The tin-y quality always hit me wrong.

"You mean 85 light years closer to the black hole?" I retorted, gripping the back of the pilot's chair.

"Yes, commander."

"He shifted, but he didn't have a place and time. He only had a place," Adrian said by way of explanation.

There were several heads shaking, yet mostly, it was Hercules.

I don't think he grasped any of it. All brawn?

Hera didn't seem to understand the concept either. I was very well aware of my own abilities and limitations. I could move through space but not time. On the other hand, Adrian, Tristan, and Ixis could move through space and time. Moreso, by taking an object into subspace they could make it appear instantaneously in another place.

I could only do that within the same time-stream.

"The time slippage with the black hole caused him to move out of his own time. Add to that the gene therapy and you have a recipe of how to get lost."

"Mom, I think you're right," Issy offered, "I've been picking through his memories, trying to figure out what he did." She looked over at Charon/Ron and back to me. "They chose the place, but he didn't know the correlation of stars."

"He chose the wrong *time*," I stressed the word time.

My head was beginning to hurt, making my scalp itch.

Time. The one thing everyone wants more of but can't control and don't understand.

We could stop right here. Leave the underworld to the dead and the Judges. It wouldn't take much to convince everyone to stop.

I stared out at the triple stars glinting back at me. Light rimmed Oceania, illuminating the sphere. I narrowed my eyes to block out the brilliance. The circular chasm I stared at was nothing more than a choice of crossings.

Should we rise to the occasion or slink back into obscurity in the cosmos?

"Exactly! I don't think he just chose the wrong place and time with that shift. I think he punched a hole in time," she whispered, scared at the ramifications of her hypothesis.

I shook my head. I wasn't exactly sure where she was going, "That's not possible! The singularity was already there. He needed it to make the shift," I returned.

Didn't he?

"Now, when you're saying it, I can see exactly how it happened. The question is - how do we get back to that place and time?" Issy remarked.

She too stared out at the visage of stars and gravity playing on the cosmic scale.

"An excellent question and one I'm not sure I have the answer to. Hera, you've been mighty quiet. Do you have any ideas?" I asked, steeling myself for her observations.

"If you want to go back to a place, you must first turn around and return the way you came. The only way is with a visual," she replied in her matter-of-fact scientific tone.

The room collectively turned in the direction of Charon.

"Well, as I said before, ladies, the longer we stay in the gravity well, the more time slips by. Losing 20 to 50 years is not that big of a deal if you're going to live forever. I don't know if you have any intention of returning to the natural order of the space-time continuum, but letting it race past you seems wasteful," Michelson remarked, looking at us over the top of his reading glasses.

Part of me wondered if he even needed those anymore. However, that too would have to wait for another time and place to find out.

A good leader is one who listens to their people, therefore Michelson's point was well taken.

"Pull back! We can sit right outside the time dilation and reconfigure our plans," I ordered.

One step forward and ten steps back.

I wanted to grumble, but we'd had a good run so far. I didn't want our luck to run out just because I was pushing too hard.

"No, Sydney. That's the problem! Shifting while in a gravity well alters your perception of time. Odyssey doesn't even have engines."

I rubbed the bridge of my nose, hoping the pressure behind my eyes would subside.

"I need to go to Odyssey and talk to my son and Ixis," Adrian stated.

My head shot up, "What if we need a shift?" I demanded.

"You have Cha— Ron," he murmured and gave Charon the side eye, then he ran his hand down my arm to ease my fears.

Adrian's leaving felt wrong. He could mentally talk to them. He didn't *need* to physically be there.

It's selfish of me to keep him here.

< I need to go. I need to figure out how we get out of this pickle.> he murmured in my mind.

I placed my hand on his cheek and gave him a forced smile. I wasn't okay with it, but I was not a child either. Nodding my head, I gave him a mental push. The shifters needed to have a powwow.

Charon was here, yet I wasn't sure about his shifting abilities. I wasn't even completely sure he was on our side.

He better be or he won't be lost in the space-time continuum. He'll be floating in it.

Adrian disappeared and my chest tightened. I suddenly turned back into the woman who had carried around a tightness in her belly and an anvil on her chest with a fake smile for thirty years.

"Mom, snap out of it! He's just a couple thousand miles that way," Issy chided me.

She reached out to take my hand. I shook my head.

"Sorry, block me out if you need to," I replied.

I pulled back into myself, throwing mental walls up and adding extra spackle for good measure.

I sighed and took in the room with fresh, tired eyes.

The professor was enraptured with some kind of data stream coming from Prometheus' mainframe. Every moment that he'd been here, was nothing more than a giant scientific experiment.

I wonder what percentage of his blood was actually Themian and what percentage was human. He would fit in perfectly with their society.

"Since we're going to be here for a while, and Adrian found some kind of 'coffee', why don't I see if I can rustle up some food." Hercules moved to the door.

I gave him a weak smile. He was trying to take my mind off of everything. Hercules was one of those people who is always trying to fill in those little blanks and make people either laugh or simply more comfortable.

"Isolde, you want to come with me?" he asked.

She gave him a simpering smile, "I've never known a man yet who can make great food without a little help from a woman somewhere along the line. Other than my dad, of course. He made wonderful food."

She was right. Gabriel had made wonderful food. A stab of guilt filled me. I hadn't thought about him much in the last few months. However, the pain of his loss was still there in the background, though it had started to fade. It was not like Adrian's loss. It saddened me.

"Sorry, mommy," Issy cringed at my mental bleed.

"It's okay, Issy. I'm not going to spend the rest of my life without thinking of him. Silly to even think that I would. I never want to forget him."

I sat down in one of the chairs and rested an elbow on the arm rest. I planted my face in my hand and slipped into deep thoughts.

A quiet settled over the three of us. Charon finally moved out of the companionway, joined the crew and took up residence in the only other chair in the room. It was one of the pilot chairs. He turned it away from us. I was lost in my own thoughts and not paying attention. All my attention was on Gabe and Adrian since the roaring emotions left me muddled up.

"What are you doing?" Michelson demanded in a deep menacing tone.

I jerked my head up. The professor had an accusatory glare on his face while gazing directly at Charon. I'd never seen Michelson like this. His entire persona was puffed up.

"Nothing!" Charon replied and his eyebrows were high on his forehead.

"I saw you touch some dials on that panel! What did you do?" Michelson continued, taking to his feet to loom over Charon.

"Prometheus, what just happened?" I demanded, pulling my head up to take in the scene.

The computer didn't reply. I leaped to my feet and slammed Charon face first against the console. As his body made contact, he disappeared and reappeared behind me.

"I must fulfill my destiny and you cannot stop me. No one can stop Fate."

His fist landed square in my face and the pressure changed in my ears. Michelson reappeared on the floor with blood leaking from his nose.

Oh shit!

"Charon, stop now!" I tried to grab him, but he disappeared only to reappear across the room.

Every time I moved towards Charon, the pressure grew. The cold of a shift crept over me. I picked him up mentally and pushed him into the bulkhead. He pushed his hand at me and a loud screeching filled my mind.

I slumped over, gripping my ears, desperate to block it out. I pushed with my mind at him and he landed face first on the floor. When our eyes met, his blazed as a trickle of blood found its way out of his nose. He sneered and I found myself standing in the hall outside the door of the shifting room along with Hera and Issy.

< Sydney, what the fuck is going— >

I beat my hands against the door in rage.

<Adrian!> I screamed.

The cold grew and Charon's shift overtook the ship. This was different from the others. Frost formed on the controls as well as the pressure inside my head. The shift filled me and I screamed, placing my hands over my ears. The chill ground its way into my skeleton, rattling my teeth.

My smaller extremities refused to move due to the icy cold being asserted on them. Cerberus glowed translucent in the non-space. The stars changed places and colors. They grew and shrunk as a gaseous cloud appeared and was quickly gone, but not before everything reversed. We were on the other side.

The cold from the shift settled in my chest.

He's gone. Adrian and Tristan are gone.

"No, No, No!" I whimpered.

Suddenly, my insides were shredded into a billion pieces and my nails raked at the door to the shifting room, creating bloody stripes. I choked before a wail took over and I screamed.

CHAPTER 4

ADRIAN

"Ixis, where did the other ship go?" I shouted and it echoed around the shifting room, filling the stunned silence.

"I do not know. It simply shifted away," Ixis replied in his flat manner.

"Mom and Issy were on that ship," Tristan yelled.

He dashed to the control pedestal and began frantically tapping the controls. The holo-display illuminated the room, revealing Prometheus floating in space 150 kilometers away.

The ship faded into translucence before returning to solid matter. It flickered and then disappeared.

I desperately searched the holo for clues, then turned to the faces in the room. My airway closed up and I coughed over the tightness in my chest. My grandfather died of a heart attack, and no matter what I looked like, I wasn't 24. I was in my mid-fifties. I grasped my chest as dark spots flooded my vision. Leaning over, I braced both hands on my thighs to catch my breath.

<Sydney!> my mind called.

No sound came back, only the reeling of thousands of minds. I swallowed back the terror that played at the edges of my psyche.

I straightened and took in the room. My chest heaved as I pulled in the air and forced it back out. The burning behind my eyes turned into an inferno.

Sydney would work the problem, not the pain.

Star charts tracking our course revealed we were slipping closer to Oceania, and there was no way out without a shift.

I gulped back the asteroid in my throat, "I came here

to talk to you guys about how the hell we were going to get out of here and where we were going to go…," I faltered, "that all seems ridiculous now!"

I raked my fingers through my hair, pushing it out of my eyes. "Of course, we still have to get the fuck out of here and we don't even have an engine to do it. We only have maneuvering thrusters."

The door to the shifting chamber slid open, and three large men came through.

"Get rid of these clowns! We're a little busy right now," I growled.

I tipped my head towards Dewy, indicating what door to shove them out.

"This is Ares and his two brothers, Hephaestus and Perseus," Emmaline announced as she waltzed in behind them. Her bright red lips hitched to the side.

I was taken aback.

Meeting the God of War was not on my list of things to do today.

And Emmaline painted everything in a dry oh, so

matter of fact picture.

"Great, Hera's sons. They waited until the worst possible moment to suddenly join the rest of Civilization. What do they want?" I growled through clenched teeth.

Holding back, I seethed with rage as a black hair woman glided in behind the trio.

"I've come to take over all military planning. It seems someone has suddenly declared war on you at the very least, and on me, the very most," Ares' voice carried all the command I would expect the God of War to have.

Instead of instilling fear in me, it made my blood boil. I didn't need anyone to take over for me. I could find my wife and daughter on my own. I bared my teeth at him as every ounce of my self-control bled away.

"I don't have time for your egotistical and arrogant war of words, Ares. I need a confab with my son and Ixis. Otherwise, we are going to get sucked into that singularity and ripped into a billion pieces."

This was the most I'd spoken aloud in days, and the barely contained anger boiled below the surface. I gulped and flexed my jaw muscles to regain control of my emotions.

Hephaestus stepped forward, crossing both his arms in a fashion that I'd seen Hercules use. "I'm sure you've heard of me. Humans tell all kinds of tales. They call me the God of Metallurgy."

He glanced at me through his hair. It was so black it gleamed, while his eyes were dark blue hard as steel. He revealed no emotions, and his words were even, with every syllable perfectly enunciated.

"I have heard of you. I've had an in-depth education in Greek Mythology in the last 30 years or so." I grumbled.

"I'm known for my metalwork and smithing on earth, in addition to several thousand years with the Themians. I've honed my skills and added engineering. We don't have any engines," he stated.

I shifted my weight from one foot to the other to contain my need for action.

"But we could," he continued, glancing first at me then Emmaline through the heavy ridge of his brow. "The ship is filled with raw materials. Give me a crew, and I'll change this floating city on the comic wind to a vessel fit for sailing into the void for an eternity."

"I'll give you the entire ship if that's what it takes to give us something to get the hell out of here," I ceased my path wearing on the floor and faced him with renewed hope and anticipation.

A smile curled the side of his face. He liked the idea of having the whole ship.

"There are several workrooms on the C ring opposite the labs. I'll take those for manufacturing and fabrication. There are two levels on the lower rhombus not yet in use. They can be converted to electronics and crystalline technology labs." He lifted his head and took to his full height, "And every 3-D printer we have."

Without hesitation, I replied, "Take them and get him whatever he needs." I hooked my thumb at Dewy, who glanced over to Emmaline and then back to me.

"In case you forget yourself, youngster, your wife left me in charge. As actin' captain, I'll give the orders around here," Emmaline barked as she tapped her fingers against her biceps.

<Aunt Emily, if you want to wear the pants, that's fine, but I'm coordinating this effort. You give the orders. I don't care! But don't tell me how to save my wife or my daughter.>

I bellowed.

Emmaline took the five-steps that separated us at lightning speed.

"You forget yourself, Adrian!" She shouted for the entire room to hear.

<Isolde is not your daughter. > she returned in a calm voice.

<She's Sydney's daughter, and that's good enough for me.> I barked, grinding my teeth down on a different retort.

Emmaline understood how I felt. She watched me go through it. Yet, I couldn't push these feelings of utter rage away.

Emmaline whipped her head around and took in the occupants of the room before her eyes settled on the raven-haired woman. Emmaline's eyes narrowed.

"Eris, if you can't control your abilities, I'll have you housed in a lab with Melinda until you can," she hissed.

The dark beauty's crystal blue eyes widened for a split second before they narrowed. A small smile played at the edge of her lips. She tilted her head to Emmaline. A second later, the hurricane of vitriol coursing through my veins eased back to a tropical storm.

However, I couldn't find an explanation for what Perseus was doing here.

"Do you need something to do, Perseus?" I asked the man whose image I mirrored so well.

"No, I came to see how my offspring reacts to this new crisis," his calm tone worked as a slap in the face.

I had forgotten we were his bloodline.

If he's just here to watch, not help, he's in my way. I needed brains, not brawn.

My eyes darted over to Ares. He made me angry, by simply breathing.

Maybe he has the same kind of talent as the raven-haired woman, Eris, and he's unaware of.

It could be instrumental on a battlefield. If he could manipulate his opponent's feelings — unbridled rage with no regard for planning or organization, would leave one open to be cut down.

His eyes lit up as a broad smile cracked his face. He

must have heard my mental chatter.

"Only my twin carries the ability to turn men's minds into puddles of anger. But as Emmaline stated, she needs better control." His smile morphed into a smirk, and he crossed his arms.

"We don't want a war to break out on the ship right now. And you do tend to incite them, don't you?" Ares glanced over to Eris, who carried the mirror of his smirk.

She moved to his side and laid a hand on his shoulder. Their show of solidarity burned me. The only person I'd ever had that kind of a connection with was Sydney.

My mind automatically reached for hers, only to find a vacant void. The ache in my chest was becoming a chasm that all my emotions disappeared down. It could never be filled or removed without her.

Ares smirk stared through me and reached out to catch Emmaline. I think he had a crush on her. Ares was waiting his time. Emmaline had eyes for no one but Ixis.

"Well, since you insist upon stayin' and watchin'," Emmaline rolled her head from Ares to Perseus, "Do you think you could contribute some advice on how to track down our wayward sister ship?" She drolled before crossing her arms.

Aunt Emily didn't like to fight, but she didn't back down either. Her greatest irritation in life were men who wouldn't do as they were told. To her, men were full of '*damn fool ideas.*'

"Yes."

The door burst open, and Tobias practically fell into the shifting chamber. "Where is she? Where is my sister?" he demanded.

"I don't know, Tobias! What the hell? Aren't there any safety measures on those doors or can anyone literally waltz in here?" I yelled.

T grimaced and wiped a hand over his face before fixing me with a hard stare.

"Only people with level I clearance and above are allowed in this chamber anymore, Odyssey," aunt Emily barked before glaring at me. She raised her hand, then thought better of it.

"Acknowledged, acting Captain Emmaline."

T paced a few steps toward me and glanced at Aunt

Emily, "You're going to get her back, aren't you? Both my girls are whimpering in terror," he stated, with bloodshot eyes and a clenched jaw.

"I am your sister's champion, not you," I barked, gnashing my teeth to keep all the poison I carried for Sydney's family inside.

I ceased to be friends with T the moment I realized he tattled on Sydney, knowing what their father was doing to her.

"Of course, we're working on getting your sister back. You should go back to your daughters and leave the rest to us to deal with," the words were barely out of my mouth when a pull and then a push moved me.

It was not far and just a little bit. It wasn't strong, but he had the grasp the concept nonetheless.

I raised my hand and used the forces. He wasn't prepared for the magnitude of my ability. I shifted him across the room, slamming him against one wall, then the opposite one.

It felt good to finally give him a bit of payback for all the punishment Sydney had taken because of him.

"You're playing with the big boys now, Tobias. You're

not my brother, and I will not kowtow to you. Sydney loves you, and that is the only reason I haven't killed you or your brothers." I shifted him in front of me.

He wavered, shaking with rage. I recognized the flash of his eyes. His father looked the same way at Sydney.

<Pull back, big boy. We need every possible hybrid. Sydney forgave him.> Aunt Emily whispered with her soothing mental voice.

I was long beyond her wiles. They stopped working on me after Gabriel died.

"I'm not leaving your sister anywhere! I'll never stop looking!" I bared my teeth at him.

A heavy hand landed on my shoulder.

I turned, expecting to find Tristan. Instead, it was Perseus digging his fingers into my muscles. "Family makes mistakes. Let him go. He can't earn forgiveness if he's dead."

I whipped back to T and gulped the thunder of my emotions back, "You want to help? Keep the rest of the population under control. They will go crazy if they find out Sydney and Prometheus are gone. We could have a riot on our hands and I will jettison anyone who stands in my way!" I growled.

Tobias picked himself up from the floor and dusted his knees off. "Nice to know Sydney finally has someone strong enough to protect her."

"You could've done your share a long time ago and didn't when you should have," I returned without missing a beat. "I don't want to be enemies, Tobias. I just can't stand a man too weak to stand up to what is wrong," I hissed with a snarl.

"Now is not the time for internal bickering. You boys want to fight it out, do so somewhere else," Aunt Emily remarked while staring me down.

I gave her a slight nod without taking my attention away from T. "Charon divided us to conquer. We can't allow that."

T's face relaxed back into the mask he'd worn his whole life. The man I just abused was a T I'd never met. The raw emotions he exhibited for Sydney were new.

He wiped the trail of blood from his nose away, "I'll go deal with the population. I'll be useful there," he stated then looked at me. "Adrian, this argument is over. We're not enemies. I'm certainly not going to let you kick my ass again. Your comments about me protecting my sister...I did what I could. You weren't there. You only know Sydney's side of that story." He spat blood on the floor and wiped the excess blood from under his nose again.

"Your best wasn't good enough," I growled.

Tobias rolled his shoulders, tilted his head down, staring at me with hard eyes, and exited the shifting chamber.

"Ya can't blame him for everything Edward did," Aunt Emily murmured.

"No, I can blame him for everything he instigated, and for what Edward did afterward. All he ever did was help mop up the blood after," I ground out and crossed my arms.

"Adrian, he has to live with that every day. Trust me, every day he sees her, he feels it. He knows what he did or didn't do. Why do you think he spent so long not wanting to see her at all? You need to cut him some slack. Just because Edward wasn't beating him, it doesn't mean he wasn't suffering. Abuse is abuse. It doesn't have to be in the physical form of a bruise."

Aunt Emily could sometimes cut right to the quick of

the matter. It never occurred to me T might have suffered too.

I just remember being a child looking up to Tobias and thinking he was the greatest thing ever. The letdown of knowing that he didn't lift a finger to stop what was going on cut both Sydney and me.

I had to push that back. Finding Sydney was more important. Now wasn't the time for me to deal with a 30-year-old grudge.

I was angry at Tobias. He was her hero. For him to run in here desperate to save her *finally*, cut me the wrong way.

If any man is going to save Sydney, it certainly wasn't going to be Tobias O'Dear.

Sydney and I both hated that *Johnny-come-lately* shit. I turned and looked at Tristan.

My son's head was cocked to one side with a raised eyebrow, "You ready to do this, or should we take a minute?" he asked.

I placed my hand on his back, "No, I'm ready."

CHAPTER 5

SYDNEY

Adrian and Tristan's faces faded before me as the door to the shifting room opened, and I stormed in.

"Prometheus, find Odyssey!" I screamed.

No matter where I looked, nothing was there. I clasped the orb and twisted it around, before returning to Cerberus.

"What the fuck did you just do? Put Prometheus back! Take us back to Odyssey now!" I shouted.

My voice quivered in time with my belly, as I mentally

lifted Charon in the air and slammed him back into the bulkhead.

"I cannot, and I will not. I have to do what was intended," Charon replied.

I slammed him into the wall several times, before turning him around and slamming him face-first into the bulkhead. However, it did nothing to ease the panic that rose inside me.

"What are you talking about?" I screamed, "What was intended? I don't believe in fate. It's all a bunch of bullshit."

"Of course, you don't believe in fate," he spat a glob of blood on the floor, I thrust him against the wall again. "You don't need to believe in anything but yourself. If you believe in yourself, then you believe in fate," he smirked at me.

The man I'd seen when I'd judged him leaped to life before me. He'd never been wiped.

He'd beat us, Siamo fottuti!

"That's circular thinking. I don't buy that crap. Take us back to Odyssey!" I demanded, taking a step toward him.

"I. Can. Not!" He leaned in and remarked in a loud

voice. The smirk returned before peeling back into a satisfied smile.

"You can or oh, so, help me, I will find a way to kill you so slowly you will be mad long before I'm finished with you," I was in his face breathing in time with him, making sure my breath flooded his lungs.

I wanted him to taste my rage.

"If you thought being mentally trapped in sub-space for two million years was bad, just you wait," I hissed and bared my teeth.

"I would not recommend killing me. After all, as far as I know, I'm the only shifter in this spacetime. No one else can get you back, except me. I'm not going back, and you've already judged me. I can't be judged again," a smug smile scraped across his face.

Hercules burst through the door and charged Charon. Herc actually thrust me out of the way and head-butted Charon, knocking him out cold.

"What the hell just happened?" he demanded, heaving, and still holding a dripping empty coffee cup.

"That snake shifted us. He said he's not going back.

Also, he turned Prometheus' computer off," I retorted.

Issy sat up, cradling her head, while Hera rolled to her side and groaned. I squatted down next to Michelson. Using the edge of my sleeve, I wiped the blood off his face and patted his cheek.

Hercules helped Isolde to her feet, cupping her chin and inspecting her eyes. He gave me a slight nod of approval.

Issy's lip trembled, "Tristan," she murmured.

I shook my head as new tears welled up in my eyes. She buried her face in Hercules's chest.

I patted Michelson's face, "Michelson." His eyes rolled open, and he squinted up at me. "If you have half a brain in your head, I need you to get the computer up and running. Then, you will have to figure out how to maneuver the ship and lock that piece of shit out of the system." I said and kicked Charon's limp body.

The professor winced at my tone and nodded his head slowly before holding his hand to his temple.

"Being as I'm in a room, with a Demigod, an insane person and three women believed to be *The Fates*, I'll do my best to bring sanity back to this sticky situation." He maneuvered his body over to the control panel and pulled himself up by the console. He flopped down into the nearest seat and began pushing buttons. Finally, Michelson stopped and closed his eyes.

"Name and designation, please."

"Sydney Rhiannon."

"Sydney Rhiannon O'Dear - designation Commander."

"Commander O'Dear recognized," the ship replied.

"Charon shifted us. Please identify our location."

"Checking databases. Prometheus visited this exact spot 2.9 million years ago. The stars are in the same position."

I looked around at Isolde and Hera, "They look the same?"

"I think the computer says that we're back where this all started," Hera remarked, then touched the bloody patch in her hairline. She stared at the blood on her hand and rubbed both hands together to clean it away.

"Are we experiencing any time slippage, Professor?" I asked over the lump that was blocking my throat.

Issy pulled away from Hercules, wiped her tear-stained face, and shuddered back fresh cries.

"According to my calculations, we are just outside the gravity well and the time dilation." He looked tentatively from each one of us to the other, "Might I suggest we incarcerate this man and perhaps use some drugs to keep him from pulling another switcher-roo on us?"

"I don't even know how to do that," I swallowed back a groan.

"Well, as it just so happens, I took two years of medical school before I changed my mind and decided that cutting open cadavers was not for me. Perhaps, we could find a medical bay where I could find some drugs."

I nodded my head. It sounded like the best idea. I couldn't think of any other way to keep the shifter under control.

"You may find something to help keep him under as you earthlings like to put it. However, I think what we need is a jail. Not to put too fine a point on it. I will create the necessary shielding for that room," Hera offered and began heading toward the lab section of the ship.

It was a big statement. Hera didn't believe in imprisoning anyone. If she thought we needed one, we must.

"You mean similar to the shielding in the laboratories on Odyssey?" Issy asked.

"Yes, I'm not an expert in crystalline technology, but I do know enough to limp by. My brother and I used to play tricks on each other and sometimes my parents, *upping the ante* every time," Hera chuckled under her breath, dryly.

"You guys get to it while I try to figure out where the hell we are," I replied.

It's a plan, a loose one, but a plan nonetheless.

"And I suppose you want the big piece of man meat to move the body?" Hercules grunted.

"You created it. You can carry it," Issy smirked.

He heaved the body over his shoulder and waltzed down the hall, dumping Charon in Tristan's cabin. "So, here I am, a man alone with the three beautiful women."

"I am your mother," Hera scoffed at his silly remark.

"You are my mother, but that doesn't mean you're not a beautiful woman. However, you other ladies, well, now we can get something going there."

"I am mated, thanks!" I waved him off, not finding the humor in the situation.

If he'd been Zack, I could have mustered a pithy remark to throw him off.

"Well, that just leaves you, Isolde."

"Yeah, I think I'm good, *Herc.* I won't be anybody's last choice." She snarled at him, anger replacing her heartache.

He whispered under his breath, "You were always my first choice." But she was already out of the room, and I didn't think she heard him.

CHAPTER 6

ADRIAN

I walked to the center podium and joined Ixis and Tristan. The dark-haired man nodded his head in acknowledgment.

<Tristan and I found our way back from Charon's star dump. We need to go back and search Charon's memories to find where he took Sydney and Isolde.> It was the best I could do at explaining. My idea could fail.

<Go back to the start?> Tristan asked. His hand shook as he pulled the hair next to his face away from his head.

<Did Sydney give you Charon's memories with the star charts?> Ixis inquired.

<No, we will be flying blind. But it's our only chance.> I retorted.

Ixis tilted his head down slowly while staring me down.

Without a word, Tristan put his hand on Ixis' shoulder. We formed the triangle, similar to three stars, framing the singularity, almost as if we were Cerberus itself.

< Here goes nothing. > Tristan muttered.

I closed my eyes, opened my mind to both of them, letting our knowledge of the stars meld in the crucible of space, merging and mixing. Each piece of information floated to the surface like different metals reaching their individual melting points.

The amalgam of its sum poured between us. We didn't have Charon's memories. Sydney had given us star charts with no frame of reference.

When Isolde first touched Charon, all she'd seen were stars. My mental touch had given me nothing more than terror and isolation. With no set direction and lack of experience, I mentally looked to Ixis.

He pooled our vast knowledge and began shuffling the charts into an order I could understand.

Ixis pulled up each piece of the cosmos, like a new section on a cosmic roller coaster. We flew through the spatial void, past dead rocks, living worlds, asteroid belts and even formations I had no words to describe.

My mind lived through this looking glass on the Universe. Some sights resembled pictures from Hubble or Cassini, other were a kaleidoscope of the unexplained.

I saw pyramids and temples, all drawn in the stars. Part of me revealed in the journey and wished for it never to stop. My mind wanted to keep traveling the great unknown. My soul flew at the speed of light and laughed with the power of a supernova. Finding the edges of my mind grew complicated and fuzzy. Tristan blended into me, and the lines between Ixis and myself faded away with each moment.

The lack of gravity in space was an illusion. Gravity here was not the up and down of a planet—only the force pulling you toward a star or flinging you away.

Time is the concept of the gravity-bound. The freedom

we raced on was as intoxicating as a first kiss and drugging as morphine.

< Stop! > Our minds froze to drift on the ocean of space.

Three stars hung untouched with the black hole at their center. I took in the surrounding area. The positioning of the stars around carried different colors, while the points of light flickered with an individual frequency. There was no river. Styx hadn't formed in this cosmos.

< Where are we? > Tristan asked.

< A better question is, when are we? Look at the positioning of the other portions of this space. > Ixis words came out thick like old gasoline on the verge of congealing.

< Where's the river? Where's Styx? > Tristan shouted. His words were eaten up by the darkness.

< I don't think it's formed yet. > I replied.

This was an early formation of the singularity.

I fixed the star position in my mind, turning in every direction. We had to get this right. My mind drank in the hope of the rightness of what we were doing.

I need this to be where Charon has taken them.

I only had my gut to guide me and the undying belief that I would find Sydney no matter what.

Tristan mentally nudged me in agreement.

< I have it. > I snatched my mind back like an addict, afraid that if I didn't go now, I never would.

My body slumped to the floor alongside Tristan and Ixis. Both men peered at me with the same question on the tip of their tongues.

"Are you sure you have it?" Tristan demanded before running his fingers through his hair to pull at his bangs.

I shared the vision I'd pulled from our minds.

"That will do," Ixis nodded numerous times and patted my shoulder.

"Well, don't just sit there looking at each other. Shift us!" Tobias yelled.

I groaned.

Why does he have to be here?

My desire to push him into a wall clawed at the back

of my mind.

"We can't shift right now," Aunt Emily barked, standing between us and T. "Ixis, Adrian, and Tristan are too exhausted."

A smile tickled the edges of my mouth. Aunt Emily was so much smaller than him. She didn't care, though. Ares grabbed T and pulled him out of the shifting room.

Aunt Emily whipped around to face us, quickly kneeling to pet Ixis' face. Before holding a cup of water out to each of us from the tray Eris held.

Thirst overwhelmed me, and all thought fled with my need. I gulped the water while the sound of my son slurping at his glass kept time with me. I closed my eyes and swished the last gulp around my mouth to hydrate my gums before swallowing.

"We'll sleep four hours. No more. Then, we shift," Ixis replied.

"Four hours could end up being 50 years," I returned and shook my head, no. I wasn't going to rest.

A deep booming voice of command spoke, "You asked for my advice. Any man who goes to war exhausted is a fool, and unless you want to have another accident, I suggest you go and rest as your friends have instructed. I personally will wake you, and then, we'll go save my mother and your wife," Ares stated.

The room swam before me, and I blinked to clear my vision. I glared from Ares to Perseus.

He is probably right.

I would be foolish to try and shift exhausted, and I was exhausted. "How long were we standing there?"

Aunt Emily cracked a smile; she knew they'd won. "You've only been staring off into space like fools for a week. Mind dives can be so boring from our side," she joshed me.

"No wonder my legs are cramped, and my feet are killing me," Tristan mumbled, then ran his fingers through his hair from the nape of his neck to his brow, yanking on his bangs to make them stick out at all angles as if his hair was cramped.

Ixis didn't wait for us. He shifted me to my bed.

< Go to sleep! Ares will wake you in a few hours, and we'll go get our girls.> Aunt Emily whispered.

CHAPTER 7

HERA

The two people held in-stasis in Prometheus's cockpit saddened me more than I could possibly say.

Millions of years asleep, waiting for someone to remember them — to awaken them.

Who were they? Why did they choose to go into stasis? Did they even choose it?

I could have asked Isolde. I was sure she would know something more. Did Charon give these people the gene therapy? Did they have children? Where they mated? What would it do to their minds to suddenly be awakened after sleeping for so long, assuming they're even viable?

Their brains might be useless by now.

There were never any studies on the long-term effect of stasis on a Themian or Elysian. However, Charon did survive for 2 million years, standing like a statue in a cave. Perhaps they were Themian.

For all intents and purposes, Charon is none the worse for the wear.

My power to judge revealed the heart. I could finally see what happened to Zeus.

I am the fate that spins the skein of life.

It resembled the genetic strains. They twist, connecting in ladder-type rungs.

Each of the Judges carried the Themian strains. Most mental disorders were genetic, but some were based on trauma.

Mix these two causes with a thousand other possibilities, and you have Zeus.

Zeus had a deep desire to control everyone and everything around him. Even sex with him was about conquest and control.

I shuddered to think about all those women he raped. I gave myself to him willingly. The only thing that stopped him from taking what he wanted was his fear. Fear, not only of me but the treatises he held with the surrounding cities.

Examining Zeus was a pastime I'd not indulged in many thousands of years. A tear tracked its way down my cheek. I blinked to push its companions back. An ocean of tears would not change anything. I gulped the small ache in my chest back and pulled a deep cleaning breath. The air came out more as a shudder, only to be joined by the burning in my nose.

I quickly sucked in several puffs and pushed it out in one big gust. Closing my eyes, I shook my shoulders and opened my eyes.

Now was not the time to opine on Zeus and my many failures. How ever broken he was, I loved him. All of him. Even the side that wanted me dead.

Charon's heart, on the other hand, was tainted but not lost. Yes, he was power-hungry, but it wasn't the same kind of power as the Temple girl. She was utterly selfish to the point where she was willing to kill to get what she wanted.

Charon didn't want to kill anyone. He felt he'd had no choice. The Judges of the Underworld only offered two options - succeed or die.

If the people behind the wall truly have the original Elysian blood-line without the gene therapy, what does that mean?

Discovering our origins was clearly a distraction from something else.

Was it something the High Council engineered to keep us from looking deeper?

They blocked everyone, allowing the Oracle and all of her beliefs and teachings to fall into obscurity. Had they bothered to look in the right place, they could have found the origin millions of years ago.

Thinking back, I could clearly see it was all a well-orchestrated distraction. They kept us searching the universe, distracted by science and exploration, only to keep us away from discovering the real answers. The only way to truly find out what the Council was up to would be to face them.

As a Fate, I can't judge them alone. This is not my choice alone.

As several of the hybrids have pointed out, when you put one hole in a wall of lies, 50 more appear before you can find the truth.

I told stories to my children as they'd been told to me. I had believed many of them, the stories of heroes fighting monsters, stories of various heroes from my people's past, leading the way to salvation.

I tilted my head down and laid it in my hands.

Which stories were real, and what was a fable? We shouldn't have left Delphi in such a hurry.

Pythia's real prophecy was there somewhere.

Through the years, all the stories became twisted. Suddenly, Hercules became the hero slaying the monsters, while myself and others became Gods and Goddesses shown in every unfavorable light possible.

I threw a glass of water across the lab and waited for the satisfying crash that never came. Gravity could only be created on this ship via thrust and in the cockpit. We were floating in space. The water in my cup slipped out of my mug in bubbled droplets that danced around the lab.

I sighed and pushed off the bench. The force of my push exceeded the thrust of my throw, and I outdistanced my cup before it hit the wall. I snatched it out of the air and landed feet first on the wall. I quickly pushed off again, and I returned to my seat.

Charon stood in a cavern and became the fabled ferryman, a harbinger of death, as humans describe a staff and the heavily cloaked figure. The figure of Charon and death were interchangeable in human folklore.

I wonder if he would be surprised to learn that stories of him terrified an entire planet?

"Prometheus, direct all records by Charon to the lab station," I glanced down around the holo-display before finding a designation. "61-C127."

"Acknowledged."

Charon was a scientist.

We keep records.

I couldn't live every moment of a life like Isolde. However, I could study the process the scientist took to make his discovery.

The holo lit up with thousands of files and a numbering system that predated Themia. The precursors of our system were laden in the Elysian way of counting. I was able to slowly work the files into some order.

As far as I could make out, the earliest file was as long as a trip down the river Styx.

*****

Charon -

The Judges are not to be trusted even with a drop of water. They can turn even that into poison and kill you with it.

I can never forget the faces of all my victims, the terror in their screams as they morphed into those beasts. Even now, bile climbs its way up my throat. I have to live with the reality of what I've done.

Anu and I gave them the ultimate power - immortality. They will live forever, and Elysium will never be free.

I have doomed them all. My species will never become more than what it is now.

All I wanted was to save my wife. I only now see the folly of my ways. Minos only kept her in stasis to lure me on. I shudder to think what he would have done if I hadn't put a stop to it. I can still see her face wrinkled in pain and begging me to end it.

Anu claims that Minos' daughter can help us. I have decided to take her up on her offer. We must leave Elysium and allow its future to unfold without us.

*****

I skimmed through the rest of the file. Other than his plans to elude the Judges of Elysium and escape the planet, there was nothing more of interest.

Who was the daughter of Minos?

What I did glean from the file was that Charon was a geneticist and not an engineer. He wouldn't be able to change the alterations to the ship. His knowledge in that area was probably limited.

I grabbed a crystalline laser and a circuit finder then strolled down the passageway to Charon's cell.

I didn't want to imprison anyone. Loss of control over one's life is a trauma most never recover from. However, Charon had already experienced that trauma.

I slipped the circuit finder over my eyes then searched the outer wall of Charon's cell for the security lines. The wall leaped to life with glowing lines of crystals, each connecting to another in the intricate pattern indicative of our technology.

The blue veins that lined the walls within Prometheus pulsed like blood vessels over the rest of the crystals. I fingered the dial on my display, altering the color spectrum to remove them.

The orange of the locking mechanism came into focus, and I thumbed the laser to on. It hummed to life in my hand, vibrating down my arm. I began cutting the connections and rerouting them, so the inside door release no longer worked.

I pressed the release button and waited for the door to fully seat itself within the wall before moving into the space.

Charon laid in the bunk with straps around his chest

and legs. His hands were bound to the frame. I smiled to myself at the mask covering his eyes.

Hercules didn't like to take chances with his enemies.

You can't kill what you can't see.

Jorhan had repeated that enough times to anyone who was willing to listen. For a moment, I could have let my sadness over the past overtake me. Instead, I used it as energy to finish the task at hand.

The goggles illuminated the walls and all the crystals embedded in them. I fingered the controls until the only crystals appearing on the color spectrum were the deep purples.

Crystalline tech followed the light spectrum in levels of control, and purple was used for abilities. The walls carried no such color.

I gulped.

No wonder everyone on the ship had barraged Charon.

There was nothing to stop them.

<Hercules, I am going to need your help.> I called.

I would have to grow every crystal in the labs and embed them myself. My hands shook as I removed the goggles. Rearranging circuitry was one thing while developing a whole new system was a whole new game.

What would Hyperion say? 'Challenge accepted!' I smiled.

"Yes, Mother," Hercules popped his head through the door, snarled at Charon's sleeping form, and smirked at me.

"Put on a vac-suit. I need you to go scrape the hardened lava from the exterior of the ship. We need to grow the crystal circuits for this room and probably a few others."

His shoulders tensed as he locked his jaw down into a hard line, "Yes, Mother."

I ran my hand down the side of my face and covered my mouth.

We can do this.

CHAPTER 8

SYDNEY

I'd led them to this place. I'd touched Charon and seen inside of him. He was terrible, but he wasn't evil. His intentions were well-placed. All three of us saw the difference between evil and well-meaning.

Where does it say that once judged by the fates and having all of your secrets revealed, you can't be judged again?

How could we have missed this? His intention was always to return.

Return to what? What was he hoping to find here?

The stars hadn't changed, or so the computer said.

Think, think, think!

There was no way the stars could be the same after millions of years. I kept going back to one of those geology classes I took at the University of Miami. The professor talked about life on Earth and how it's billions of years old.

Life on a geological scale is different. It takes millions of years for one little thing to change.

Adrian's face flashed into my mind. He was stuck on Odyssey, and Odyssey didn't have any engines.

My nose flared, and my eyes grew hot.

What if they jump out of the gravity well?

They could become lost like Charon, or worse. I gulped at the fear coating my throat. The chairs in the bridge groaned—my ability to move objects pulled at them.

I pressed my eyes closed and rubbed my palms into the orbital bone. The meat of my palm compressed the pressure points along my brow ridge. I mentally ate up the pain it created.

Anything to take my mind off Adrian and Tristan and the what ifs. What if they shift into the heart of a star?

Adrian, Tristan...my brother's children, T, my two younger brothers, somewhere in the back of my mind, even my mother-Mary leaped into the list of my family on that ship.

I hadn't even seen her. I had just been too busy. Now my chance seemed to be gone, all because one man said we had a fate.

Ugh!

The chair next to me ripped from the deck and slammed against the bulkhead. I bit my lip until the coppery taste of blood warmed my mouth. I released the chair, and it floated mangled next to the doorway.

Professor Michelson lifted his head but didn't utter a word.

"The computer said the stars hadn't changed. They were the same as the last time the ship was here. That's not possible," I remarked.

"It is as if we never left this time stream or, in other words, one would assume there's been no drift, no movement. It is the same time, but we could be off by years," Michelson blinked and waited for me to take it in.

"You think he took us back to the same place and time he left from?" I asked.

I needed to splash water on my face. The fire behind my eyes turned them into a scratchy mess. Part of me wanted to go lay down in my cabin and let my pain consume me.

I've been down that road, and it doesn't lead anywhere.

"Yes, if the computer is correct, I would assume it makes the most sense. Perhaps he couldn't shift back here without being sucked into the gravity well. Maybe that's the gateway."

All Charon said was that he wouldn't shift back to Odyssey.

"Professor, how heavily drugged is he?" I asked while mentally tapping the chair floating near the door. The chair gave off a low hollow metallic sound with each tap.

"Based upon my knowledge of Themian physiology, which really isn't all that much different from humans and being as its almost completely undetectable to human technology—"

I cut him off, "Professor, focus."

"Yes, sorry. Yes, I don't think he's going to be awake for at least another 12 hours. You want to ask him something?"

"Yes, and no." I shook my head, "It's futile. He won't give me the answers I want. He believes that what he is doing is unchangeable. That it's destiny."

The word 'destiny' came out with a groan. It was one of those words that should be reserved for fiction and movies.

The real world has no place for it.

He put his hand on my shoulder. He was sympathetic to my plight. He didn't believe there would be anything changed about it.

"You do still have your daughter and friends," he ventured.

The words from his mouth made me want to run around the room screaming.

"If anything can be changed, we will all work together to change it. You are not alone." He couldn't just let it go.

I opened my mouth to speak, but he shushed me. "I know you love your son and husband. I have known many people in love. For all my knowledge of mathematics and science, love is the strongest force I've ever encountered. People do amazing things for love. I heard you discovered an island that didn't exist." He whispered low and tilted my head up with his finger under my chin. With raised eyebrows, he searched my face.

"But I didn't discover it for love," I muttered.

Curiosity fed that cat.

"Are you sure? Then, what was the driving force that made you sail across the biggest ocean on the planet? Were you looking for Atlantis?" He chuckled as his eyebrows shot into his hairline.

"A driving force, an unshakable need to find answers. The voice in my mind was telling me I would find the answers I was searching for. I followed a dream, one I'd had my whole life and never understood. It was a burning desire to know, not just think, but to know that I wasn't crazy."

"Sydney, I've met some extraordinary people. Some that were famous, some not. However, none of them ever discovered Atlantis. None discovered a spaceship, let alone the first known spaceship. If anyone can do what we need doing, I firmly believe it is you. I'll be happy to support you. Don't wallow in your pain and suffering. Do something about it."

"I didn't discover Atlantis. Ponce de Leon did. I just followed his map." I shook my head and wiped the tears out of my eyes.

Wallowing wasn't going to save anyone or change anything. It didn't mean I didn't want to sit here and wallow for just a minute or two.

"Are you a shrink?" I muttered to cover my emotional weakness.

He laughed dryly. "I am a doctor. I have several degrees, all of which I'm very proud of, and I worked very hard for. However, being a professor, I found is the most fulfilling. All the rest is just for bragging rights, and I'm not much of a braggart. You can call me professor or you can call me doctor. You can call me anything but late for dinner."

I gave him a half-smile. Michelson was not so bad, but he was an egghead.

I laughed to myself to keep from crying.

CHAPTER 9

SYDNEY

Was Michelson, right? Maybe deep down inside, I always knew Adrian wasn't really dead. In my heart, I could never let him die. Space and time didn't matter.

I love him, and that would never change.

I kept returning to the question - what about me was different? What was it that made me want to continue?

I was thinking back to those dark days when I thought Edward was my dad, and he was beating me. I didn't kill myself. I didn't even try to kill myself. I just numbly went on.

When Gabriel got sick and died, I didn't die with him. I wanted to. I felt like I was being torn apart. Again, I didn't do anything to try and kill myself. I still ate. Not much, but enough to keep myself alive.

I didn't keep going after Adrian just because I believed in love. There was something more. Michelson was right. Something had kept me going. Something drove me, and it wasn't just survival.

The survival instinct is what someone in a dead-end job, scrambling to pay bills, working all hours, has. They do it to feed their kids.

Survival is not what drove me in my father's house. There was something else. I couldn't put my finger on it. Yet, whatever it was, I had to find it.

Adrian wasn't gone forever. I clung to that. The line from the Princess Bride popped into my head, and I tried not to laugh.

'Death can not stop true love.'

Love is unquantifiable. My heart felt it pulling me right now in a million different directions. The further our ship got from Cerberus, the deeper we traveled into the underworld, the tighter the pull.

I had to live no matter what. I had to make sure Isolde and I both lived. I had to do anything and everything in my power to make sure we didn't just survive.

"You're in some pretty deep thought, mom. You want to share with the rest of the class?" Issy asked.

The sound of her voice made me jump. I heaved a sigh, "Pondering eternity and problems of the heart," I murmured, pushing my hair out of my face and hoping to deflect anymore prodding.

"As a fresh new member of the immortal world, without having to become a vampire," she replied.

Part of me wished I could hear Tristan laughing in the background. He would have liked Issy's turn of phrase.

"There is something in the background humming. I don't know what it is. Maybe, it's the two people in stasis, or it is just me, wishing for Tristan to be there. I feel like I lost a part of my body, an arm, or a hand. It's an itch, and I'm constantly seeking Tristan..." she choked on her brother's name.

I folded her into my arms and let silent tears run down her face. Her description couldn't have been any better. I felt the same way about Adrian. Our minds were always together. It wasn't him or me. It was we.

I walked her to my cabin, and we laid on the bed, crying over our loss.

Hera was working on lining Charon's room. Hercules was probably sitting in the cockpit with his feet up, waiting for the girls to stop whimpering or running a new spacewalk for his mother.

A knock came on the door. I was by it in a second. Sometimes, I switched gears and moved at the blink of an eye.

The door slid open, revealing Hercules. He leaned to one side with a hand on the upper portion of the door jam, with his head hanging down. He glanced past me to the bed and Issy, before looking up through his eyebrows and murmuring, "You better come to the cockpit and check out what's going on outside. Use the main viewport," he grumbled.

I quickly glanced at Isolde, who climbed off the bed then turned back at Hercules.

He didn't have eyes for me. He had eyes for nothing

but Isolde, and his face softened. His mouth opened slightly as his eyes dilated. There was definitely something going on there, at least on his side.

"Lead the way." I returned. The last thing in the world my daughter needed at the moment was a lecherous thousand-year-old Demigod making a pass at her. Not with her brother and Adrian gone.

Michelson was asleep in one of the chairs with his glasses sitting crooked on his nose. He didn't even need those glasses anymore. Why he still wore them, I couldn't imagine, except maybe out of habit.

"Look over there." Hercules extended his arm along with an index finger, indicating a specific point out the port side.

I followed the line to find what appeared to be a completely black spot in space and we were moving towards it.

I kicked my foot against Michelson's chair a few times. He snorted, blinked his eyes, and looked around, "we are halfway..." He stopped mid-sentence, "Did something happen?" he asked as he fumbled to right his glasses on his face.

"Since you're the resident genius, I need you to get up and tell me what that is." I pointed at the growing vacant black of space.

His eyes practically bugged out of his head at the site of the inky black cloud. He turned back to me with a gaping mouth, "I'm not exactly sure. Maybe, we should get our lady Hera up here. She might have some idea about what that is," he sputtered and smacked his lips together, searching for moisture before reaching for the bottle tucked into the chair next to him.

"Prometheus, please identify the black cloud floating off the port side of the ship," Michelson requested after wetting his whistle.

"Scanning."

I groaned over, having to wait for Hera, and a split second later, she was standing before me with eyes as large as saucers.

"Who just shifted me?" She stuttered.

My mouth must have opened and closed several times. "I don't know," I replied after I found my voice. "Hercules, check Charon," I ordered.

The big man dashed down the companionway and burst into Charon's cage. He quickly stepped back out and shook his head.

"Holy shit, mom! I think you just became a shifter," Issy exclaimed.

I shot Isolde a dagger. "There's no guarantee it was me. It could have been Charon. He might be awake," I nodded to Hercules.

He grabbed his dagger and proceeded back into the cabin with a wicked grin scraped across his face.

"I didn't say kill him. I said to check his ass out. Then put him back to sleep before he decides to shift anybody else," I yelled, still shaking from what I knew to be true.

It was me. I don't know how, but I did it.

"No, mom. I think it was you. Charon's not awake. The bruise on his head was pretty bad. Professor Michelson jacked him up with some good drugs. I think it was all you." Her lips pulled back into a hopeful smile.

"I didn't become a shifter in the last 20 minutes," I remarked and crossed my arms.

It was a defensive move, but that was not why I did it. It gave me the ability to hold myself without looking weak.

"Actually, Sydney, since Charon moved us, you've been pretty quiet. Introspective, if you will. That usually denotes mental turmoil. We've been here for six hours. Trauma changes you," Hera was always going on and on about her evolution theory.

Hera believed trauma forces life to adapt.

This is why she thinks some Themians are stronger than others.

"I wanted you on the bridge. Are you saying I wished you here? Ixis said that's not how it works. He and Adrian described it more as a picture in your mind you moved to." I shook my head in disbelief.

There was no way I could have suddenly become a shifter.

"Did you picture something in your mind?" Issy asked, her hands clapped together with bright eyes.

Hera ignored her, "Yes, you have a point. You had no idea where I was on the ship." Hera's curiosity was always moving forward, demanding answers to puzzles.

"That's very interesting," Michelson scratched his chin then tapped his lips with the edge of his glasses, "Sydney, you conjured her. Wherever she was, you just pulled her to you." He was nodding his head and pacing. "Maybe, you didn't shift her at all." He turned around to face me and pointed his glasses at me.

I sighed and ran my hand down the side of my face. "We don't have time for this. What is the black fog?" I asked and pointed at the enormous blacked out area in space devoid of stars, moving toward us.

I waited for an answer, which never came. There were only distant whispering, reminiscent of children passing a graveyard.

"Does anyone else hear that?" I asked and wiggled my finger in one ear as if to clear the wax out.

"No. I hear humming. But it's been there for a while," Isolde replied and tilted her head to the side as if that was going to increase the sound.

"Sydney, drop your walls. Let me see if I can hear through your mind," Hera said and placed her hand in mine.

I opened the mental doors for Hera and Isolde to listen

in on the whispering. It cranked up into a roar.

I moved my right hand to Hera's shoulder, and she, in turn, placed her right hand on Isolde's. Once Isolde placed her right hand on me, the whispering ceased.

Out of the darkness gurgled a deep voice that moved like liquid mud bubbling in a hot spring, "I am Erebus the darkness. Conquer me, or I will conquer you."

The inky fog grew thick. Being constantly surrounded by darkness was not new. Space could be a chasm of darkness. However, this was blacker than black. I wanted to enter the underworld and to move through this blackness. Still, we needed a light to find our way. Charon had delivered us into a place worse than a black hole.

It was an abyss of nothingness. It folded into us, filling in the surrounding area, erasing the expanse outside the ship's hull. It didn't stop at the vacuum of space. It seeped into the ship, blacking out everything in its path.

It flowed down my throat, and I choked on the hateful taste of it. The blackness was full of the need for power, want, and desire.

How am I ever going to claw my way out of this?

The darkness teased at my deepest secrets, worries, and fears. I was trapped, screaming within my mind. Knowing you're not alone isn't the same as seeing it. Isolde and Hera were still touching me. I was both near them and forever separated from them.

They must've been screaming like I am.

I pushed. I had to move it back. Whatever it was, it wasn't real.

Real or not, it is everywhere.

Murmuring at the edge of my mind, Erebus was trying to convince me that all was lost. It would win.

That's what it does.

It stripped all happiness from you, your joy, your light, everything that was bringing you to the light. The black wormed its way in like water, wearing you down over time.

I desperately pushed back with my mind. I scratched at the blackness I was drowning in. But it was nothing more than wallpaper. You peeled back one layer only to find another.

"You will not win! I will not let you take me!" I shouted.

My terror clothed me, burning every part of my soul. I couldn't find a weapon to defend myself.

Erebus chuckled at my feeble attempts to fight back. He pulled a vision of Adrian lying on rocks. He stared up at the black sky with lifeless eyes. The sun no longer lit the glint I always searched for. The dull blue carried no hope of revival.

I screamed, "Stop it! That's not true. He isn't dead! I know he isn't."

Erebus replied, "How can you be so sure?" The chiding tone tickled me.

He slammed me with a new vision.

Further down the beach laid Tristan, his body twisted with seaweed and bent in ways nobody should. A crab escaped from Tristan's sand laced mouth and scampered over the rocks.

I shrieked as my world folded in on me. "They aren't on a planet!" I raged.

My mind shook with unbridled anguish. There had to be a pattern. I swallowed back the agony along with the fear of their deaths and countered.

Darkness can only exist without light to drive it away.

I pictured Adrian alive, standing on the dock on Alethea with Tristan next to him. We had been scared but alive, and I was so happy to see Adrian. I didn't care about another thing in the world.

A picture of Gabriel, breathing out his soul with his last breath. He battered me with Gabe's final moment of life, playing it over and over.

My chest locked. I gasped for air that would never come as Erebus hit me with Gabe's death again and again.

I pushed the tentacles of the memory back into the box I kept it in.

I have already fought that battle, and that octopus of terror will never win again.

The visions of Tristan and Isolde laughing while tossing snow at each other took over and the edge of my lips curved into a smile.

Fighting is what I do.

Whatever Erebus was, he was fighting for control or domination. He conjured up a new scene.

This time, my father was screaming at me. "Worthless

girl! You'll never amount to anything. You're a stupid whore, and that's all you will ever be," Edward's insults repeated in my mind along with the beatings. The lash of his belt rippled across my back, bowing me, as my father's words echoed again, "I only do this because I care."

The pressure of his fists pounding into my back knocked the air from my lungs, and I choked. I closed my mind's eye to the vision, but it poured back in. My father hit me again, blinding me, threatening me. They were all the same memories I'd lived through again and again stabbing me like a sea urchin, no matter where you touched there was a fresh needle to prick you.

I pulled myself up from the past, "No! I will never live in fear of you or anyone ever again!" I shouted at my father. "You can't do anything to me! He couldn't stop me then, and you can't stop now. Whatever you are, you're not real."

A belt appeared in my father's hand, and he raised it with disgust in his eyes. One side of his mouth curled as his nose cinched up as if he smelled a sickening stench. "One way or another, girl, you're going to learn."

This isn't real!

The conjured a vision of Hera, a perfect parent who

would do anything to defend her children, overran my fathers.

I kept Hera's face at the forefront. She defied an entire race to keep her children safe. Her patient smile of love filled me.

It was a light that I could wield as a weapon, and I seized it, forcing all the darkness back.

Screaming filled my ears, from a voice I couldn't identify.

The darkness bled away, leaving my eyes open, staring at Hera and Isolde.

A blood-curdling keening clawed at my senses. They were still fighting, trying to fend off this evil darkness.

Hercules had his hands on Isolde's face murmuring, "Come back to me, Calla. Don't leave!" tears streamed down his face, and his voice was laced with desperation.

"Go to your mother. I'll take care of Isolde!" I ordered.

Hercules glanced at me as if to say something and shook his head, "I can't," he went back to whispering in her ear.

I pounded my way into Isolde's mind whipping the

black sludge out of my way. Mentally, I shifted my internal monologue and constant listening for Adrian and Tristan.

The only focus of my world right now is Issy.

Other than Hercules's desperate pleas for Isolde to snap out of it, I pushed it all away until the only voice I heard was Isolde's.

CHAPTER 10

ISOLDE

"You're not real," I screamed at the image standing before me.

The watery blue eyes gleamed with evil delight as a greasy lock of dirty blond hair slipped down to hang over the left side of his face.

"You can't be real. Jacques is dead. My brother killed him." Icey fear coated my skin, and I shivered with the feel of it. "I'm happy he killed him! Stop haunting me! I'm not scared of you anymore."

But I was scared and all my bravado couldn't hide that truth. I wasn't frightened of Jacques.

The dead can't hurt you unless you let them.

I learned that lesson on the rivers to the underworld.

I was scared of whatever was running this virtual reality show.

"I'll be havin my way with you." Jacques's tongue slipped out of his mouth, and he ran it across his lower lip and sneered. The Caribbean accent, calypso, slipped off the tip of his tongue. He clipped the end of words and swallowed the last few letters. "It be easy. After all, I lured you away once with me charm. I lure you again." Jacques loomed over me. His lanky body dominated the nondescript space.

My slight stature left me feeling powerless and small.

I'm not like Tristan or Mom. I didn't have any mental abilities other than throwing fear, and I learned that from Jacques. The bitter liquid in my belly fought its way into my mouth. I gulped to keep it at bay.

"You're not going to win. You can't win. You will never win!" I screeched.

"I always be winnin'. Winnin is what I be doin'." He ran a dirt-encrusted fingernail down my cheek, and I cringed away. Like lightning, he gripped my chin and forced me to look up at him. His face contorted into a sneer as he flared his nostrils. "You be givin' in to me dis time. I knows it," he chuckled and I watched frozen as his lips moved to touch mine.

"Isolde!" a voice called from the inky blackness.

I shifted my head just in time, and his lips smeared across my cheek. It was Mom. I couldn't see her. The only thing in view was Jacques's leering smile and greasy blond hair.

I can't imagine why I thought he was attractive? I was young and stupid. That's an understatement!

"Issy," her voice came again, like shouting underwater.

"Over here."

Jacques dematerialized, and I was engulfed by the blackness again. It blanketed me with hate and loneliness. It was like being on a theater stage when suddenly the lights turn on with one figure standing before you, you are surrounded by the blacked-out stage.

My father's eyebrows were drawn together, creating a ridge between his brows. His lips were pierced in anger as he stared me down with kryptonite green eyes. I withered under his glare.

"Isolde, you left me," he barked, "You didn't even bury my body. You, your mother, and your brother, you left everything to Zack and ran away." He crossed his arms. "And you've been running ever since, haven't you?" He didn't move or blink.

I slid to my knees as my lips began to tremble. The cold that had wormed its way into my marrow turned into boiling shame. "You've been trying to stay one step ahead of your feelings. If you indeed loved me, you would've stayed and buried my body. You would've put flowers on my grave!"

I choked on my cries and shook my head. That wasn't true. We did love him. Warm snot ran down my lips, and I wiped it away with the back of my hand.

"No! That's not what happened," I moaned.

"You didn't even take Zack, Nonna, Maria, and the boys with you when you left the planet! They think you all died in a storm, lost at sea, never to be seen again." He leaned over and shouted in my face.

I cringed away from him.

"Don't listen to him!" Mom shouted.

"How do you think Zack and Maria feel? You abandoned them." His voice rose with each statement. "Tristan, I can understand. He's not my son. But you are a real Cosimo!" the volume of his shouts grew, and he switched to Italian, "La familia mie importante."

Daddy never yelled at me.

But he was right, and the truth crushed me. Mom wanted to leave, and we hadn't talked her out of it.

The vision changed to the hospital room. I was holding his hand to my cheek. I never wanted to stop. My tears burned their way down my face, and the ache behind my eyes felt as if it would never go away.

"This is Mom's fault. She made me leave. She's the one it took me to St. Croix where I met Jacques," I shrieked.

Across the hospital bed sat my mother. I bared my teeth at her.

Any minute daddy will die, and mom will force me to leave.

"Isolde, don't give in. It wants your hate, your anger, your fear. You have to push it away!" Mom's voice came like boiling oil in a battle, and I screamed.

It was nothing but lies. She was a liar. She hadn't even stayed to bury daddy.

"How many times did she fuck Adrian in her dreams with me sleeping right next to her?" Dad asked.

I looked up at his dying form. He was enraged, and so was I.

"That's right, Isolde, your mother cheated on me every time she closed her eyes. She's a harlot, a whore," he hissed, ripping his hand away from her.

I took a breath and reared back.

Wait a minute. There's no way that's my dad.

My father would never say that about Mom.

He would never call anyone a whore, even if they really were one. My mother would never cheat on my father knowingly.

She loved Daddy.

I shook my head.

"She left me as soon as I was dead. She didn't even wait for my corpse to go cold before she let go of my hand and ran out the door on a quest to find her true love," he barked and sat up in the hospital bed.

"No, that's not what happened. That's not true. It was an earthquake. We had to get out of the building," I replied and pulled at my hand.

He held tight, his knuckles turning white as he cut off the circulation to my fingers.

"An earthquake caused by her. She did that to make you leave. If she had just controlled herself for one moment, you could've stayed and buried me!" He shouted, his voice boomed in the open space and was eaten up by the darkness.

"No, no! That's not true! I don't believe you! Mom didn't even know she could cause an earthquake, and my father would never say that. He would've understood. He always understood," I moaned as a fresh set of tears streaked their way down my face. "My father was a kind and gentle man. He never yelled at me or called me names ever. I don't know what you are, but you are not Dad or his ghost."

I stopped pulling on my hand and pushed instead. His body slammed back into the hospital bed, and his jaw snapped shut.

Whatever 'it' was, it was the blackness, every vile creature lumped into one. All the ugliness inside and outside. Words were like acid that burned you. It hurt you on purpose.

I reached into my mind and pictured my mother. She appeared before me, her hand petting my face. "Don't worry, Issy, everything will turn out fine. Love conquers everything."

My mother's memory and the vision of my father disintegrated, leaving me once again surrounded by a black ocean devoid and full of nothing.

The name Erebus whispered on the black wind. He rose and pushed me down, battering me from side to side.

I had to reach for something to keep the blackness from seeping back in. Erebus was coming for another attack.

Let him strike first.

I locked my jaw shut on my resolve and tipped my chin up to meet him. Whatever he wanted, he would never get from me.

The feeling of loneliness swamped me. From the moment of conception, I have never been alone. Tristan had always been there.

I countered with Tristan telling me. "You and me, sis, wonder twin powers."

He has more power than I do, and I don't mind.

I was always the one to stand out and do all the talking, be the big show. Now, our roles were reversed, Tristan standing in front of me, talking for me. I couldn't find the words.

My feeling for my brother warmed me, and the darkness receded.

"Isolde," my mother pleaded in the background.

The buzzing was still there in my mind, and it snapped into place, like a camera out of focus. The buzzing was a voice.

"Come back to me! Wake up! Don't let it overwhelm you," the tenor murmured, "Please, Calla! Please, don't die on me. Please, don't be lost." His hands cupped my face and the black receded.

Something filled me like the light of a candle close

enough to be burned. I felt it right down to my toes, chasing away the dark.

I came back to myself and all I could see were the beautiful blue eyes of a Demigod.

"You're awake. You survived. Thank the Gods!" He leaned in, and his lips touched mine.

It wasn't a candle. It was Hercules.

Instead of cold, I was now burning. I wanted to touch the flame. I wanted to bathe within its fire. He softly kissed me, and I wanted him to keep kissing me.

"Calla," he hugged my immoveable body to him. "You have to go back, with your mother, for Hera. You have to save her. You all must conquer your darkness. It has enveloped the ship."

His breath filled my mouth, and I wanted more than his cast-off air.

Mom called in the background. I didn't want to leave him, not now that I could finally see him for who he was.

"You are mine," I whispered.

Smile ripped across his face, "Yes, Calla, I am. I'll be

here. I will never leave your side. Now, go help my mother."

He planted a rough kiss on my lips a moment before my mother drug me back into the dark.

My mother was a teardrop of brilliance. She moved to me, and we formed a larger pool of radiance.

The darkness pushed back, trying to rip us apart to separate our newly formed star.

Light is always stronger than darkness.

CHAPTER 11

HERA

The cloud of blackness settled over first the ship, then me and a foreboding overwhelmed my universe.

It was Erebus the God of Darkness, a character from a story from my childhood and the dread of all Themian children. He was known to lurk under beds, and in the shadows of trees at night.

The dark corners of space carry the tell-tale signs of Erebus.

I shivered. I never dreamed such a thing was real. Too many of my childhood stories had come true, and I now wished they had stayed just that, stories.

Mother said you must pass through him in order to truly reach the Underworld. Mentally, I ran my hands over the chiton I'd chosen this morning. I remembered that the texture of the fabric soothed me. As a child, I'd carried a small scrap of fabric with me at all times and worried it with my fingers in my pocket.

All I carried now was the memory of that comfort.

It would have to be enough.

Every failure of my life began to play before me in the windows of my mind - so many of my choices and the chaos that ensued.

Every time I ever questioned myself, battered at me. Erebus kept presenting me with new problems and new embarrassments.

I steeled myself for the next arrow to be shot at my mental armor. I had too much to regret, Poseidon, and too many sins to atone for, such as betraying Athena. Saving the hybrids, and my children had created them.

All of it's my fault right down to this moment.

The darkness blacked out the eyes of every face of every human I had ever watched die.

I could've saved them with Primordium.

They paraded in front of me, the long stream of thousands upon thousands upon thousands.

I choked on the accusatory faces and stumbled to my knees.

Every child I've ever helped bring into the world and watched die of old age or sickness from some simple diseases.

I could have easily cured them.

My screaming filled my mind with the desolation of loss, the pure futility of it all.

I could've saved them all.

I didn't save any. Jorhan rose above the rest, his reproving eyes staring down at me.

"You should have let our village die! You should have let Zeus kill us all." I took his hand in mine and lowered my forehead to his knuckles in obedience. He ripped his hand free,

"Instead, you saved us for what disease, death, famine. To think I called you *sister* or Goddess. You are neither. An alien creature forcing her will upon us." His hand collided with the side of my face a moment before he spat on me.

I cried out in shock and quickly wiped the spit from my face, "That's not true! I never forced my will upon any of you," I replied, forcing my breathing to level out and keep control.

"Didn't you? Didn't you tell the men they should treat their women as equals instead of subservient? Didn't you tell women that they were as good as a man? Didn't you convince Zeus he was a God? And then made him one? Do you not realize what kind of havoc he reaped all over Greece?" He shouted at me.

I lowered my head and took in the black surface I knelt upon, "I tried to help everyone. I loved Zeus. I tried to save him. What he became was a monster, and I helped put an end to him." I retorted through clenched teeth.

I pulled air in through my nose and pushed it out through my teeth. The act slowed my heart, allowing me time to regain control of my emotions. I closed my eyes for a brief moment.

"You think just because your children ran around,

trying to clean up your mess that absolves you somehow from your crimes?" He demanded and released a dry laugh.

I was not fighting Jorhan, I knew that, but the man before me cut at my heart with his words. For the truth in them was a secret I kept buried deep inside. Something I'd been unwilling to face in thousands of years.

"I did not send my children to clean up my messes. They simply wanted to stop their father from murdering the human race," I replied in an even tone as I slowly raised my face to take in the false visage of my opponent.

"You murdered the human race the moment you polluted the gene pool. You knew what you were doing. You knew what it meant having his child, a hybrid, demigod, Nephilim, whatever you want to call them. They all mean the same thing. You knew exactly what you were doing. You are no better than Poseidon," he hissed with disgust.

Jorhan did not know Poseidon. He had never met Poseidon, and Poseidon's name had never crossed my lips. Not once in all the years we lived high on the mountain.

I smiled to myself. Erebus had broken the illusion.

"You cannot be Jorhan. You cannot even be his shade.

Jorhan was dead before Poseidon was captured, before Zeus was punished. You are not Jorhan, so do not present yourself to me as if you were my long dead brother."

Jorhan tilted his head back and disintegrated to the blackness.

I was relieved. Of all the humans, Jorhan had been my favorite. He was like my child, my brother, and my friend. He helped me hide my children, kept my secrets, and gave me council.

His loss hit me anew as his face disappeared into the darkness, and I cried out for him. I buried my face in my hands to hide the pain that raced over me.

Whipping the tears away, I pondered the situation with fresh eyes and a weary mind.

There were only two others this creature would present to me. I both feared and loved them.

They appeared simultaneously as if ghosts forming out of a black smoky cloud. Their eyes materialized first. Zeus's crystal-clear skies and Poseidon's aquamarine turquoise of the Caribbean ocean, both sparkling with the dark ring as their bodies coalesced out of the black mass.

They looked the same. Strong corded muscular forearms and shoulders, their stomachs ridged with muscles, clothed only in half togas and devilish smiles.

"Look, what we found, brother," Zeus remarked, then slicked his raven black hair back away from his chiseled jaw.

"Yes, we have finally caught the betrayer, the temptress." Poseidon held his triton loose at his side before he used it to point at me.

I didn't want to reply. They had nothing to do with reality. This wasn't real. Still, it did not mean that their words would not hurt.

Erebus brings forth your worst nightmares and makes you face them. He either destroys you with them, or you conquer them.

"Hera," I heard a woman's voice.

I shook it off as another of Erebus's tricks.

"So, Herathina, I'm finally allowed my chance to kill you?" Poseidon's laugh echoed out into the darkness, only to be lost in the ocean of space.

"I am not the one that you should be fighting. I am not

your betrayer. I don't know who betrayed you. I kept to my oath." I took to my feet to fight back the fear lurking in my mind.

"Did you, Hera Herathina, or whatever your name is? You cannot even tell the truth when it comes to your name."

"She lied to me also. She wasn't the Goddess on the mountain, and yet, she had the power to change me into a God the entire time. I had to almost die for her to finally give in and give me my do." Zeus snarled and his nose curled on one side as he sneered at me.

I'd seen that face before, just before I dominated him and broke his mind in half. I steeled myself against the oncoming emotions that always came from that knowledge.

"Giving you Primordium was the biggest mistake I ever made. And swearing an oath not to dream-walk the High Council immediately after we arrived at Earth was the second," I replied.

"Do you think we care about your mistakes, arrogant woman? I'm here to exact punishment, you evil, pernicious creature. Luring men to their death, telling humans that they are equals to us. Breeding with them, oh yes, I know that you and Zeus had children before you changed him. Where are your children? Let us go kill them. Like you did mine," Poseidon whipped his head around as if searching through the darkness for what wasn't there.

I allowed myself a small smile. The only child nearby was Hercules and Zeus has never seen the boy.

"Yes, Hera, where are our beautiful half breeds?" Zeus hissed and moved forward as if to intimidate me with his presence.

"Far out of your reach, creature of darkness. My children are safe from you." I gave Erebus a dry laugh, "Zeus, you are not alive. I watched them separate your head from your shoulders." I flared my nostrils, "It rolled across the crystalline floor like a melon, leaking your life's blood as it went."

His smile faded.

"And you, Poseidon, you are on Tartarus, trapped for a few thousand years more. The place they put the irredeemable, those they will never look for. No one cares about you anymore." I forced a fresh laugh from between my lips, but it sounded strange even to me.

Poseidon's voice deepened to a low bass, "Do you really think even Tartarus can hold me? The Oracle told me what I would do. I knew what was going to happen before I went to Earth," he intimated.

"It is impossible for you to know what the Oracle said to Poseidon. I don't even know. You are a lying creature, digging into my mind, trying to pull out the answers necessary to control me." I spat, wishing I could touch anything in this mental space cloaked in darkness.

But it is possible, I fought Poseidon with my mind. I saw everything there was to see.

I shook the thought away. Pushing back the darkness was more important than what Pythia told her son.

"Oh, I think if I wanted to control you, all I would have to do is dig into your mind. I could dominate you right down to your heartbeat. Maybe, my brother Zeus could help me. We could dive in together, crack you open, and dissect your very essence." He chuckled and whirled his triton over the back of his hand.

"You're a vicious creature, and you turned me into that evil thing." Zeus took a new tack, and it hit home, piercing my very heart. My chest clenched with the reality and pain of it.

"I didn't have any idea what Primordium would do to

a human. The evil, soulless thing you became is what was always inside you. Being human helped you repress your inner tenancies," I retorted. For the first time, my argument rang true.

I'd waged this internal war for centuries - the back and forth over my mistakes. Finally, I could forgive myself. I tilted my chin up and stared them both down with a defiance I never knew I could have.

"What about me, Herathina? You knew what was plaguing all of us when we arrived." Poseidon chided me, and he placed the tip of his triton under my raised chin and forced my head back even further. His eyes blazed with hatred. The trickle of blood ran down my neck. I longed to scratch the sensation away.

"No, Poseidon, I knew we carried emotions within us. I just didn't know we had repressed them to the point of being incapable of controlling them. The moment you began to feel, the first thing you did was to dominate, control, or kill everything that stood in your way," I replied.

His face was so close to mine, I could almost taste his breath. A breath that wasn't there, only the darkness of Erebus existed.

"Yes, I tried to get control of my emotions. You never even warned any of us," his retort was without merit or weight.

"Your weak and feeble words fall on deaf ears. Themians always had emotions. You led the battle of the Great Division. You killed Anu and all his followers and their emotional ways," I laughed at the dark creature.

"They were willing to do anything to control the universe," he returned.

"Aren't you?" I retorted with a dry, mirthless laugh. "I tire of this, Poseidon is dead or as good as. No one survives Tartarus. And Zeus is gone. He was nothing but a mortal human that I mistakenly thought I loved. I thought he loved me, but I was just a means to an end. Another form of power and control. The only thing I am thankful for is my children." I no longer stared at the forms before me. Instead, I searched the darkness for Erebus and his true visage.

"Exactly! You lied to me," the Zeus persona retorted, "You stole my children from me. Perhaps if you had told me they were mine, I might've behaved differently."

It was fresh bait to lure me back into the discussion. I wasn't going to fall into Erebus' trap.

"You would never behave differently even if I had given you children. You would've used it as a way to wield more power over me." I heaved a sigh of regret and the cleansing that came with releasing the old. "I've grown tired and weary of your needling. I dominated both your minds. I controlled you." I turned to Zeus, "I scrambled you like an egg." Then I turned to Poseidon, "I distracted you long enough to be beaten by Athena and imprisoned by the High Council. I'm sure that life on Tartarus has made you wish for death many times. Be gone, creature of the darkness. I am through with your games!" I shouted, waving my arms to shush him away.

I watched as both men disintegrated. Seeing Zeus for the last time, my love for him dissolved along with the vision.

The only things that existed in my world now were my offspring and their children.

Poseidon didn't necessarily disappear; he winked at me, "You haven't seen the last of me, Herathina. After all, you know I'm not dead," he released the booming laugh that he was so well known for and was gone.

The creature was desperate to get me to fear it. To feel the clenching in my belly and the shivering in my soul. I will not run-in fear of this creature or any other. At some point, you must come to terms with the idea that fear is just fear, nothing more.

Blackness dissolved around me. It crept back from my eyes, releasing every muscle in my body. When my vision finally cleared, I saw only the smile on Sydney, and Isolde's faces.

"I knew you could do it," Sydney shouted, gripped me in a fierce hug squeezing all the air from my lungs. I released a chuckle and awkwardly patted her back.

"No one had more demons than you, Hera, I knew you would conquer them all. Maybe we truly are the fates." She conceded with a wink. I knew better than to take her seriously.

She didn't believe that for a moment, but her levity bolstered my aching heart. If she could smile in the face of an unknown future without Adrian, I could smile right along with her.

CHAPTER 12

ADRIAN

The moment I opened my eyes, my first thoughts were only for Sydney and Isolde.

I gulped back the realization they were gone.

Sydney can defend herself. Would it be enough?

I promised myself that I would never leave her to fight in this life alone. Not again.

Isolde, however, did not have any defensive capabilities. Hercules would do all in his power to defend her.

The river Lethe had shown me the truth of Issy and Herc. It became apparent to me why he'd followed her with his eyes. The incident in the bio-dome had created the perfect storm for their mating, leaving Herc to lurk about without an explanation.

He'd mated with her. It was precisely what happened with Sydney and me. Hera said mating's over space and time occur in Themia, and it doesn't matter where you were. When the time was right, it happened.

I sat up and leaned on one elbow, then searched the other side of the bed for the curve of Sydney's hip. The only sight I held was the scrunched-up blankets from my restless sleep. I had to get out of this bed. I was still tired and shook the cobwebs of sleep out of my mind.

Who knew searching the cosmos for answers would be so exhausting?

My feet met the cold of the floor. It reflected my reality, all hard edges and blank walls. The white crystalline circuitry was the only defining colors other than the Hawaiian bedspread in blue and white.

Sydney and I spent so little time in these quarters, they barely looked like they belong to us.

I pulled on a pair of jeans and a T-shirt. Sydney had insisted I start dressing like I used to. A smile touched my lips for a moment before slipping away. I thrust on a pair of shoes.

I've been shifting things around the planet for myself for years. I could have shifted Sydney and her entire boat at any time.

I kept that to myself.

Apollo, at the time, was my greatest threat. I couldn't draw his attention.

It all seems so pointless now.

Syd discovered me on her own. I still couldn't understand how her father knew the latitude and longitude.

Edward O'dear was a bastard.

I groaned at the thought of him. That envelope was very old.

I didn't know why I was thinking of all of this right now.

It's all a distraction, Adrian! You're distracting yourself, so you don't have to think about all the possible realities. Get yourself a cup of Kovach and head towards the shifting room.

Just as I reached the door, it binged, followed by hammering.

"Hey, man!" Tristan stood there, a little drool and sleep still lingering in his eyes. "I figure since we've both been asleep for at least 24 hours and Ares didn't keep his word, maybe we should get up." The flesh around his lips pulled tight as his teeth ground down.

"How long were we asleep?" I demanded.

"31 hours," he said.

I grabbed my wallet, shoved it in my back pocket. It didn't matter that nothing in it was worth a thing. The pictures were over 30 years old. It didn't matter that money had no meaning here. I didn't carry it for the value of money. I held the one thing I did give a crap about - the picture of Sydney and me together at the piano, plus a picture of Sydney holding both newborn kids the day she gave birth.

I'll never stop carrying it. It was one of the few things that survived the tsunami. The baby picture was the only thing I ever stole from Gabriel. I never went anywhere without it.

It's all I had left of my previous life.

The moment I pulled my hand from my back pocket, I shifted both of us. We appeared simultaneously in the shifting room right in front of Ares.

"You said four hours. You lied," I rammed my fist at his face, and he sidestepped my punch. I shifted him back into place, and my fist landed square in his jaw.

Ares absorbed the blow and immediately responded with a blow of his own. I leaned to the side to dodge the punch, only to find my feet swept out from under me.

I shifted two steps to the left and reappeared with my feet firmly planted on the deck.

Ares began, "When all three shifters, the most important beings on your ship are incapable of doing their job because they are exhausted."

I hammered into his back as I shifted behind him, landing a hit to either kidney.

He bent over and groaned, "you tell them whatever you have to, to get them to rest." He huffed over the blows.

I wasn't listening to him. A rage I hadn't felt in decades colored my world.

He held his hand up, asking for a stay, "We're drifting toward the singularity. I know you must've come up with some kind of solution to our problem. But if you think I'm going to let you shift us when you're tired and not thinking clearly, you're wrong." He stood up and faced me. "You want a fight. I'm ready." He kicked the side of my knee-knocking me to the ground, then he raised his foot to stomp, but I shifted out of the way.

I landed on one foot, keeping my weight on my good leg. Ares moved with the power of a lightning bolt and crashed into me, knocking all the air from my chest. We both tumbled to the floor. I tapped a button on the floor, and a chair rose under Ares, tipping him head first onto the hard floor.

I shifted back to one foot and ripped the chair out of the floor with my mind, and smashed it on his back.

"You had no right to make those choices about our lives," I shouted.

Tristan reached to pull me back, but I shifted away.

"Emmaline approved it. She ordered no one to disturb you until you woke on your own." Ares rolled, moving the chair out of his way, and kipped up to stand toe to toe with me.

His breath huffed in my face. We were both of the same height, and I stared down his hard sapphire eyes. A trickle of blood ran from his hairline down the side of his face.

"You should have set an alarm if you wanted to wake up earlier. Why you would rely on me? That should tell you everything about your state of mind. You don't even know me." He slicked his hair back and rolled his head on his shoulder. "I'm the God of War. I will do what's statically best to win."

I pulled my head back a fraction of an inch.

"I will always follow the correct tactical maneuver to win. I don't care what it costs you. One skirmish is irrelevant in the grander scheme of things." A smirk spread across his face.

I was listening to him until he said *cost*. Instead, I tuned him out with my fist, plowing it into his face. He planted one in return, and the crunch of my nose met with the warm rush of blood over my lips.

"If I don't have a shifter and an engine, I cannot maneuver the ship," Ares droned on. The cool timber of his voice did nothing to stanch the hot rage burning through me.

"We will be ripped apart by the gravitational pull of that black hole. Now, stop your sniveling and tell me what your plan is!" He shouted.

Rather than answer him, I shifted him high in the air and let him drop to the ground. Ares called on wind and fire to ease his fall and landed with one foot on the floor and a knee next to it. He tilted his head up and stared at me through the hair blocking part of his face.

Then he growled. A fireball formed in both hands, and a second later, he threw them at me. I easily grabbed both out of the air and quashed them in my hands. It was a distraction. Ares was already in the air, leaping toward me. I shifted to the left and dug a right hook into his kidney, followed by a left.

His elbow collided with my chin, and I released a howl of pain as my blood coated his forearm. He whirled around and laced his fingers into my hair. All I could make out were the stars from the river Styx as he pulled my head back.

His hand curled into a fist—

"Stop!" Aunt Emily shouted. She placed a hand on his chest and then mine. Her ability to calm eased my rage and bruised ego. Ares released me, and I reared to my full height, ready for the next round.

I pushed her hand away, "Your ability doesn't work on me anymore," I growled, wiping the blood pouring from my nose on the arm of my shirt.

"Cooler heads must always prevail. I'm the captain here! I'm in charge! What I say, goes!" She pounded her fist into the opposite hand. "He didn't make that call, it was his recommendation, and I agreed with him. I don't want you, my grandnephew, or my husband attempting whatever fool plan you've come up with, without restin'." She moved away from me and pulled up the holo display. She pointed at Oceania, "What is your plan?" she demanded.

I scraped the coldest glare across my face, "My wife and daughter are too high a cost. I could have shifted you into vacuum, don't forget who you are fighting. I didn't want to kill you," I hissed through my teeth.

God or no God, I can kill him at any time. Killing a God is easy.

I looked from Tristan to Ixis, then up at the holo display. "Odyssey, how close are we to the original starting point?"

"According to Prometheus's map, 300 thousand kilometers away. At the rate of gravitational drift, we should approach that point in three hours and five minutes." The metallic quality of the computer's voice reminded me of HAL9000 from a Space Odyssey, and the irony of it wasn't lost on me.

"Ixis, Tristan, we have three hours and 10 minutes to commit the picture of what Charon saw before he jumped to memory because that's where we need to go," I stated.

Aunt Emily gasped, along with a few others.

"Are you sure that's where we'll find mom and Issy?" Tristan asked while pulling on his hair.

"I believe your father is correct. Charon did not shift anywhere else within this space-time continuum. He only knows where he's been within his own timeline. He would've jumped back there," Ixis agreed with me. I didn't think I needed his approval, yet the rest of the command crew visibly relaxed.

It irked me that my word wouldn't be good enough.

Sydney would have listened and agreed right away.

The ache to find her burned like a fireball in my chest.

"That's pretty slick, Adrian. I like your thinking. Do

you need to wait three hours and 10 minutes?" Tobias asked.

I put my hand up to stop T from coming closer or thinking I'd fully forgiven him. He didn't understand the pain he'd caused Sydney filtered over to me too, and I needed a clear head.

"Yes, we have to be at the exact same location they were before we shift. We need to be able to reproduce his jump as close as possible. It's the only way to do it."

"Three hours, seven minutes," the computer announced.

"Odyssey, count down at ten-minute intervals until you get to ten minutes!" I ordered.

Tristan touched his hand on my shoulder and shared the picture he'd gleaned from Charon's memories. It was an exact copy of what I'd see.

Pulling back, I glanced at Tristan and threw him a half-smile. My son was a brilliant young man. Sydney had done well.

CHAPTER 13

SYDNEY

When I was a child, I learned about Greek mythology. It was a fantastic and exciting universe and completely improbable—Gods and Goddesses who warred over love and hate. Greek mythology had everything. Tales of Perseus defeating the Kraken. Hercules killing giant lions.

I watched all the movies. Most of which I didn't remember many of the details. Homer and his epic poem, The Iliad, the Odyssey, and Jason the Argonauts on his search for the Golden fleece. Never for a moment did I dream any of it would be real.

When you read the stories from a human perspective, you think it's improbable, crazy even. You're not ready for reality. I've spent the last few years adjusting to this paradigm shift.

The Gods are real.

Hera said Prometheus gave birth to the gods. It makes perfect sense in Greek mythology from planet Earth. The twisting of time changed it from a spaceship to a person—something the human mind could grasp.

Greek mythology was all allegory and symbolic. Cerberus, the three-headed dog, is a triple star. Styx is a river of stars, which from a distance looks like a river, but also like the golden ratio, and it's shrouded in a golden light.

I hardly believed it myself. I drank down the human and Themian stories at a rapid pace. Running into Erebus, the God of Darkness or just darkness itself was not something I wanted to repeat.

Could we have avoided Erebus if I had paid more attention? Pythia did say, 'you had to pass through the darkness to truly enter the underworld.'

We went through darkness and conquered it. Tears prick my eyes, thinking about facing one's darkest fears.

I am glad that Adrian and Odyssey aren't here.

I worried about what would have happened.

If they had been here, would the creature have processed someone else?

Now that we had passed through the darkness were we on the meadow of Asphodel? The place where souls who were neither good nor bad and had lived unremarkable lives wondered. In some of the stories, they encounter demons and other various lower creatures in the underworld. But all you have to do is cross it. Moreso, it's supposed to be covered with flowers.

I didn't see any flowers as I stared out across the expanse of space.

Maybe, we have to travel a little further to reach that meadow of flowers.

Shaking my head because, I needed to pull out of this malaise. Obviously, I wasn't going to see Adrian again until I did whatever Charon wanted.

"You can't tell me you don't believe in fate, after what we just went through," Issy broke into the mess of my mind.

I glanced up at her and blinked a moment to clear the gloom away. "I don't believe my life is predetermined, Isolde. Destiny, fate, those are all excuses that people give for not making good choices. People declare they're destined to do something is laziness, an excuse. I make my own fate," I grumbled.

My fingers touched my lips, and I ran them along my lip line mindlessly. I wanted to bite my lip and force blood from my skin. I wanted to feel something.

"Actually, I think you are both right. Yes, I think there are certain things that we are destined to do. Being as we are the Fates, we do make our own fate. We're destined to do whatever we choose to do. By altering our choices, we change everyone else's fate or destiny also. If you remove one stone on a riverside, that doesn't matter, and it may not alter the river's course. However, if you remove a thousand stones from that same riverbank, you will most definitely alter the course of a river." Hera's been thinking, "When we moved Odyssey with all those people, we altered the course of the river. We changed everyone's fate. Whether it was for good or not, it doesn't matter. The point is that we have the power to do it.

All of our choices, we must think twice before altering the course of other people's lives. This power is dangerous."

Between Hera with her musings and Charon with his statements, maybe, they were both right.

Possibly, I don't believe in fate because the simple fact is I am fate. Who needs to believe in fate when you can adjust yourself?

I found it all a little dizzying.

I changed the subject, hoping for a little enlightenment. "This is supposed to be the Asphodel meadow. Why aren't there any flowers?"

"That is a good question. Perhaps there is another guardian we must face. Clearly, there's something else that needs to be done first." Hera logic.

I internally groaned, then glanced at Hercules, "What do you have to say about this?" I murmured.

"I think we need to wake Charon. I don't think he was meant to bring us here. I think he's meant to take us to Elysium as our guide."

I rolled my eyes and crossed my arms.

"I'm not sure I agree with you. The ferryman is supposed to take you across the river to the entrance of the underworld, not ferry you through it," I retorted a bit sharply.

Isolde flinched. Hercules didn't.

"Are you still so sure that every single one of those human stories must be 100% correct?" Herc returned.

His eyes were red from lack of sleep, and his clothes were spotted with grime. Chunks of lava from the hull clung to his clothes. He carried speckled burn marks on his hands.

"No, not at all. I'm pretty sure most of them are 100% wrong. Part of them must have some truth, seeing as your stories came from older stories."

Hercules blasted, "The young are often impetuous. I regret telling my lies. However, he's the ferryman. For all we know, he may ferry us to the very end. He is the only person on this fossil of a ship who knows where Elysium is."

Issy placed a hand on his arm, and he instantly quieted. His mouth opened to say more, then snapped shut.

I couldn't argue with his reasoning.

"Michelson,"

"Yes, commander," he replied.

I rolled my eyes, "Don't call me commander. Sydney's fine."

"As you wish. What can I do for you?" Michelson asked, then slicked his hair back and, for once, didn't flinch in surprise.

"Wake up Charon. I think we're going to need him," I said and then glanced around the room.

Hera shifted on her feet and looked away. Michelson nodded his head and left.

I turned back to the viewport and the vacuum of space. I was searching for flowers and our next destination.

God, I hope I know what I'm doing.

CHAPTER 14

EMMALINE

Sydney was the jackpot of trouble. Everything was just fine.

Adrian comes over to have a little chit chat, and everything goes to hell in a handbasket.

When she was little, she was a sweet happy little thing. Always huggin' and kissin' on everybody. She and T were practically inseparable. Tobias was the proudest older brother you ever did see. Adrian alluded to Edward not being so nice to her.

I knew Edward. He was a narcissistic asshole. I still couldn't understand what made her so dark. She was about as jaded as a jaybird.

All of that was neither here nor there. The here and the now was what was important.

I didn't know anybody could stand still for a week straight without drinkin' anything and not die, and I'd seen my fair share of death. The amount of punishment the human body could withstand still knocked my socks off.

I had this terrible feeling in my gut.

The battle ain't over.

The air felt like it did when I was a child. Before WWII, I heard the adults whisperins and nervousness. I didn't realize at the time, but it was a march towards war. Then when it came time for Korea, and later Vietnam, the signs were all the same. Somehow or another, we were marching towards war, and Sydney had put us right smack dab in the middle of it.

Rubbing my forehead, I tried to push the pressure of this knowledge away. I glanced at Ares. He, too, felt the tension in the air for war. It was etched on his face.

"Adrian, you had your sleep and your little dream walk. What's the plan?" I asked and toed one of the remaining chairs out of the floor. I quirked my mouth to one side as my eyes grazed over the remains of the other chair.

"We are going where they went," Adrian replied without blinking.

I've seen that look before. It was the same look he gave me the day I told him he would never get off the island. The look of *I don't believe you,* and *you can't stop me.*

Back then, he wasn't hurtin' nobody else.

This time it wasn't just him. He could hurt a lot of other people.

"You can't just take the ship anywhere you want, Adrian. I understand you want to find your wife. I understand that kind of pain."

He turned away from me to stare out at the stars. I was up in a flash.

<Clear the room.> I asked Ixis, and suddenly we were alone.

"Listen, boy! There's a whole lot more than just you

takin' a ship here. It's an entire civilization on this ship. I cannot let you just jump us into the unknown." I was at his side.

I wanted to take him in my arms. Adrian wasn't just Grace's grandson. He was mine too—the child I'd never had.

However, now wasn't the time to coddle. He needed my hard love. I gulped back the sour taste knowin' I was always goin' to have to hand out those bitter pills to the ones I love.

"Emily, we have to jump out of here. Where we go is irrelevant. We cannot stay here!" He turned back to face me.

Relief washed over me. If he was facin' me, he was engaging me. He was ready for reason.

"We'll move the ship out of the gravity well. If we don't, we will most assuredly be torn apart. We don't have a lot of time to make our choice. We will be in position in about 40 minutes." He glanced at the time display and back to me. "If you wanted to argue this point, you should've brought it up hours ago when I first woke up." He ran his fingers through his hair and shook his head.

He was right. Any reservations I had, I should've

brought up hours ago. But I didn't.

Bad on me.

"We have to follow Charon. We can't just jump anywhere. We don't know how much time has slipped by. We could end up anywhere. We have to do exactly what he did. That is the only shift available to us." His eyes were red from lack of sleep and fear. He was still wearing the clothes he'd had on the day Charon shifted them all away. The scent of stale sweat and dirty fabric clung to his frame, and he seemed oblivious to it.

I was losing him, just like Dewy.

"What ya'll fail to understand is that where you're takin' every man, woman, and child on the ship is where no hybrid has ever gone before. You are riskin' everyone's lives if you don't do it right. It is a great big scary universe out there, and the timeline is long and unforgivin'. And you're going to shift us into God knows what. And you want me not to say nothin?" I shouted at him. I ran my hands over my arms to ease the goose flesh down. I hated to look weak.

My fear over Dewy, and everyone else dyin', was beginin' to win the battle over my brain.

"Aunt Emily, you always have an opinion. You always have to add your two cents. I admire that about you. You have an opinion, and you voice it, and you don't back down. You don't care who you have to stand up against either. They could be ten times your size, strong as an ox, and you would still put your nose right in their face, and your finger on their chest, telling them what you think." He stopped talking as a tear worked its way down his face. "Am I scared for everyone on the ship? Yeah! Am I worried? Yeah! Am I worried, I'm going to fuck it all up and kill everyone? Possibly! My only child is on this ship. He doesn't like me very much, but he is still my child, and I am risking his life too." He ran a hand over his face and scrunched his eyes shut, took a deep breath, and opened them again. "If you think that I'm going to risk life and limb on a delusional whim, then you don't know me at all." he whispered.

"I know we gotta go somewhere. The three of you are obviously in agreement," I returned, resigned. "I just need your choice to be rational." I cupped his chin, forcing him to look at me. His face scrunched in pain, not indecision. It was a hard choice, and he was willin' to make it.

Ixis gave me a mental nod. I'd come to say my peace. "All right, make the announcement. Let's get this done," I replied, pulling away and placing my hands on my hips.

Adrian made the mental announcement, and the ship held its breath with a collective intake.

The shift was unlike anything I'd ever experienced. It didn't have the same finesse as others. This was more brute force, like when you take a pencil and try to shove it through a piece of fabric using the rubber eraser. Once you popped through, there was a snap like recoil. I shuttered back with the collective recoil.

The actual shock of it was the cold. I never felt the cold like that before. Every shift was a little chilly, just enough to signal the change from normal space to subspace and back. This was bone-chilling and instantaneous. My fingers paled with frostbite, and the feeling in them deadened, to the point I thought they'd frozen off. When we finally snapped through to the other side, I was about to cry. My first reaction was to rub my hands and feet together to get the blood flowin.

"Adrian, where are we?" I called with a hoarse voice.

<Ix?>

There was no response. I reached their sides in a split second, and fear gripped me. Adrian was the closest thing I had to a child of my own. I mentally shoved Ixis, and he blinked before heaving a fitful sigh.

Adrian was standing stock still with his eyes locked and the irises nothing more than pinpricks. I place my hands on either side of his face trying to pull him out of it.

"Look at me, sweet boy," I whispered, "Speak to Auntie Emily. Answer me!" I shouted and shook him several times. There was only one thing for it. The shell-shocked soldiers of World War II were the same way. I raised my hand and slapped his face as hard as I could. It whipped his head to the side, and his eyes blinked.

"Aunt Emily, you've got some right hook," he replied and rubbed his cheek where I'd left the red mark of a handprint.

I screamed out with glee and kissed him full on the lips. "Oh, my beautiful boy, I thought you lost yourself like Charon out in the stars." My red lips stick left prints on his face and cheeks as I peppered him. Tristan moved to join us, and I laid a few kisses on him too.

"I thought I was lost for a moment there, myself," he laughed it off.

"That was the most terrifying thing I've ever been through. Where are we?" I asked, searchin' Ixis' face and tryin' to wipe my lips stick from his lips.

I sniffed and dabbed at my eyes, no sense in ruinin' perfectly good mascara and eyeliner over the scare of my life.

"Odyssey, where are we?" Ixis asked, givin me a soft smile.

"For approximately 3.4 light-years from our original location on the opposite side of Cerberus."

"Great, that didn't tell me much. Are we in the same timeline or not?" I asked and searched first the holo display, then Ixis for answers. Dam, this ship, can't it tell a time?

"Odyssey scan for other ships," my husband took over, askin' the ship all the questions I couldn't stop askin' him.

"Scanning. There are no other ships in the vicinity." After a beat of silence, "I have detected a sub-light engine signature. It is deteriorating fast."

"Can you display it, please?" The holo changed, and a star chart appeared in the center of the shifting room. I darted my eyes over to Ares, "Just how much longer will it take your brother to manufacture an engine for us?" I asked, hopin' for a positive answer.

Ares raised an eyebrow and used a finger to wipe the side of his mouth. My eyes grew, and I quickly pulled out my handkerchief and cleaned up my smudged lipstick.

"Hephaestus is starting from nothing. He can't just create an engine out of thin air. He needs to evaluate the ship's hull and stress points to find the best location for installation. There is more to this than just creating an engine."

"Ares, I told you. I don't care how many people it takes. If it takes an entire army, I want you to put every man, woman, and child on that project," I spat.

I should talk to Hephaestus myself and stop using the God of War as a go-between. He's not a good messenger.

"That is the most important project on the ship, other than air production," I retorted. "We need engines. More than these three men standing here. We can use them to follow that heat signature."

Ares nodded his head sharply and stiffly stalked from the room.

"My brothers will build that engine as quickly as they possibly can," Eris said, "There are machines on the ship that will help manufacture the components as quickly as possible, and we are using as many as we can, all at once."

I didn't need a woman who can't keep her abilities under control arguing with me.

She opened her mouth to speak again, and I raised my hand to stop her, "Don't start. You have a problem. Don't give me your excuses. Just tell me what your problem is and get right to the meat of it. I don't want to worry a bone with nothing on it," I barked.

That woman just got my hackles up even when she wasn't losin' control.

Eris squared her shoulders and narrowed her eyes. "We are running short of raw materials," she stated, then flipped her hair over a shoulder.

Ugh!

Why did she have to be one of those women? Always workin' every angle she had. I hated the hair flippers the most of that lot.

"And that's why you need to talk to me?" I asked. All I wanted to do right at this moment was stare out the window at the stars or take a hot bath. Or both.

"We need to harvest a meteor or a planet." She continued.

"There it is. Finally, you said in a hundred words what you could've said in fifteen. You were with them Themians for a long time and they are a long-winded bunch. They live forever and take forever to talk about anything. Even if I live forever, I don't want to die waitin' for you to get to the point. Don't waste my fucking time."

Ixis shot me a sharp look. He didn't like it when I cursed.

"You're right. We have been around Themian's, and they are extremely long-winded. I will do my best to curb the habit," she gritted out through her teeth.

Something told me she wasn't goin' to stop, but the lip service would work for the moment.

"Tell your brother to find out exactly what is needed. I like to have a list before I go shoppin'," I replied with a smile.

"I will get you a list," she hissed through her teeth.

I nodded my head to her and turned back around. I opened my mind.

<For any and all who are interested, this is Emmaline. Meet me in the citadel. Now!>

The ship had a self-cleaning mode which was pretty handy. I personally hated housework. Yet a good scrubbin' took my mind off my problems. I ran my finger along the wall of a corridor, searchin' for grim. It came away clean. I rubbed my index finger against my thumb hopin' for a hint of grit.

Nothin! Humph!

I had to be in trouble if I was looking around for dirt. There was nothing on the ship that needed a scrub. It wasn't old enough or used enough to be dirty. About the only thing on the whole boat with dirt was a bio-dome.

CHAPTER 15

SYDNEY

Hera assured me Charon couldn't shift from the room he was in. She told me it was a mental prison. Hera wared with herself over it, and I feel for her. Imprisoning someone is a hard choice to make, which is why I made it and not her.

I couldn't take the chance she would waver.

Without Charon in the cockpit, we had no pilot. That left us on the float and aimless. Every ship needed a rudder— a pilot.

"Hercules, can you fly this tub?" I asked. To the outside world, my arms were crossed. Holding myself back, is what I was really doing.

A smirk lit Hercules' face as he swaggered over to the pilot's chair, swiveled it around, and plopped himself down. He leaned back and slicked both hands from his brow back behind his head.

"What do you think I spent thousands of years on Homeworld 12 doing? Nothing! Of course, I can pilot any ship you want, even one as old as this fossil." He stomped his foot on the decking.

An internal sigh of relief escaped me.

"Great! You and Professor know-it-all, work together. Teach him how to fly. We don't want to be stuck out here with Charon being our only means of transportation," I smiled.

Hercules winked at me and twirled around in his seat. Issy stood behind him, shaking her head. She glanced at me, then rolled her eyes.

<He likes it when he feels smart.> She offered.

"Why, Sydney, I find your statement to be slightly inflammatory. I am not a know-it-all," Michelson sputtered.

I cringed at the admonishment.

"I'm pretty smart, but I don't know everything," he groused.

I didn't realize Michelson had returned, and he didn't understand I was joking.

Hercules slapped Michelson on the shoulder, producing a groan from the other man. "Professor know-it-all, take the copilot seat. Spaceflight, how do you say one hundred and one starts now."

Issy and I coughed so we wouldn't laugh at Herc's interesting play on words and numbers.

It was probably best if I left the shifting room/cockpit. "Issy, you stayin' or comin'?" I angled my head at the door.

She shook her head, "I think I'll stay here and watch Herc," she replied, running her hand over one of Hercules' shoulders.

Young love makes you want to throw up, but in low G that is a very bad idea.

I wandered down the corridor and began doing what should have been done from the get go, getting to know my ship. I stopped in my cabin and pulled out a marking laser Adrian used to mark our door.

It worked like a sharpie, only it etched into a surface. The etching was light and didn't interfere with the crystalline circuitry. I'd been using it to scribe the walls in my cabin. I couldn't sleep without Adrian. It kept me from crying. In the low G of this ship, the tears didn't do anything other than pool around my eyes. If I didn't whip them away, they would obscure my vision.

I'd scribed a door frame around the bathroom opening and the main door. One wall had a massive etching of Atlantis on it, with the top half looking like an island and the bottom a spaceship surrounded by stars. I stopped and stared.

I touched up a moon by adding a small crater into the lower left-hand edge. I turned and left the room.

The only person on the ship who knew where everything was, is Charon. I couldn't have that. I walked to Hera's cabin, and wrote her name on the door and kept going down the hall.

Eventually, I found Hera sitting at a table in the lab, looking thoughtful.

"What's on your mind?" I asked as I added LAB to the door.

She blinked several times and smiled. "I'm marveling. All this time, I never thought I'd live to see one of my children with a mate." Tears pooled in her eyes, and she laid a hand on her neck. "I thought because they were hybrids that it would never happen for them. They would flit through one semi-meaningful relationship to another." Her eyes shone as she pushed the tears out of her eyes to drift away in the low G. "It's gone on for so long, I guess I wasn't really prepared." She patted the seat next to her.

"What are you talking about? Who mated?" I asked perplexed, and took the seat. The skin on my legs clung to the metal and squeaked as I slid across.

"Isn't it obvious? Don't tell me you didn't notice?" her eyebrows shot into the roof and her eyes grew.

"Isn't what obvious?" I retorted. "Can you hear Odyssey?" I asked as a ball of hope leaped in my throat.

"Hercules and Isolde, they mated. Didn't you know?" she laid a hand on my arm, but I jerked it away.

All the blood drained from my head, and for a moment

black speckles danced in my vision.

Hera said, "Breath, Sydney." Then she forced my head between my knees. The rush of blood back to my head did nothing to change the fact I was stunned.

Being stunned actually comes from when you're hit so hard by something that you literally can't move or think for a few moments. It's almost like you forget everything, a slat that's suddenly wiped clean.

Isolde and Hercules.

My mouth dried.

It's a joke. My little girl isn't mated.

She'd be 19 in a couple months. She wasn't ready to be married.

"But Hercules annoys her. She can't stand him," I replied. I'd seen her snap at him for months.

He never gave up, but guys can be like that.

Zack once chased a girl for nine months even though she told him to go fuck a goat and had him thrown out of a night club. She got a boyfriend, and Zach finally backed off. He had lines he wouldn't cross, and a taken woman was one of them.

Something happened after Erebus. I thought back to this morning and the way she was rubbing his shoulders. My belly rolled.

"No, it's puppy love. She's only a child," I replied, shaking my head.

I stood up, and blood rushed to my head.

I hadn't slept in a few days, and the world swam. I slapped my hand on the work table to steady myself.

"Sydney, you have your mind locked up so tight, we could mine it for crystals. Your losing focus. This isn't a problem you need to solve. It's a joyful moment for all of us. If you relax for a couple of minutes, open yourself, and listen maybe, it will ease the ache you have for Adrian. Hercules and Isolde are mated, and it's beautiful," she whispered.

"When did this happen?" I asked, desperate to remain on my feet. I looked down at my shoes. Suddenly the cold of the room hit me, and I shivered.

"I'm not exactly sure. You should ask Isolde yourself. Hercules confirmed it to me this morning. He was elated. He said he never knew that a love like this could happen. It changed his whole life." Hera's smile was so wide it had to hurt. The skin around her eyes crinkled with joy.

"I'm glad he's in love. But why did he have to choose my daughter?" I sputtered and gulped back something else I wanted to say. I wanted to shout.

Couldn't he have chosen someone closer to his own age?

But then I answered myself.

It's not a choice, Syd. It just happens.

Hera burst out laughing. I pressed my lips flat. My mental bled must be in high gear.

"What's age got to do with it exactly? The only hybrids close to his own age are his siblings. He can't exactly marry one of them. The only other people that are close to his age are Themians. He's a hybrid. He mated with another hybrid. It is exactly what you would expect."

Was I being an asshole? Was it selfish to want my daughter to be a child for a little longer? We weren't on the boat anymore.

Adrian and I were mated at 13 and 14. Issy was 19, and

Hercules was, what 10,000? How could I have not seen this as an outcome?

The ship is full of men, she could've mated with any of them.

I rubbed my head. I gave Hera an excuse about being hungry and left her in the labs. I hugged her back when she congratulated me. I returned the sentiment, even though I didn't feel it.

I found myself in the makeshift cafeteria, only I'd lost my appetite when Charon shifted us to Elysium space.

The chalky taste in my mouth was all I could feel. I turned and headed back to my own quarters, all the while, wishing Adrian was here. He'd know what to say.

He always says the right thing to smooth it over and make me stop being so angry.

I closed the door to my cabin and set the lock. Then I screamed.

He'd probably say something like, 'You want Issy to be happy, don't you?' *which I do.*

He would continue with something like 'Don't

begrudge her, her happiness'

I don't. I just, I think she's too young to be married. And the idea of her living with some man as husband and wife doesn't sit right.

I run my fingers through my hair as fresh tears threaten to pool on my face.

Adrian was the one that said Hercules had to stay on Prometheus. That he was the one we should call to help us in the tunnels.

Adrian knew.

I groaned. Of course he knew. Adrian, like Hera, could hear everyone. I shook my head, and the puddle of tears broke free from my cheeks and drifted into the far wall creating a splatter.

I rubbed the rest of the moisture away.

No one says you're gonna be a grandmother, Syd!

Or they'll be living like husband-and-wife. Just because they've discovered each other doesn't mean they'll automatically jump in the sack.

Adrian would point out we didn't. Although, I really,

really, really wanted to. I smirked to myself.

She isn't a little girl any more. I can't keep her to myself forever.

The lump in my throat swelled. Gabriel wasn't here to see it.

You're *just being an asshole! Every child leaves the nest. Tristan's next.*

I squared my shoulders and tipped my head up. This day was always going to come. I couldn't run away.

< Issy, can you come to my quarters please? >

I sat on the edge of the bed, gripping the covers stiff as a board.

Maybe Hera's wrong. No, that's just a lie you're trying to tell yourself, Syd.

I keep turning over in my mind. Issy said she didn't like him. She said he was an arrogant ass.

A knock came on my door, and I quickly released the lock. Issy came in and plopped down in the chair next to my desk.

"Isolde, some things changed." I couldn't say it, so I just waited to see what she would say.

"Oh, yeah, well, Hercules and I." She pointed her toes and pressed her hands out in front of her. The cherubic smile she always wore when she was happy curved her cheeks, giving them a glow that twisted my heart.

She didn't need to say it. It was written all over her. "We're mated." It burst forth into the room, followed by a giggle.

I thought I'd cry or be angry with the truth. But I wasn't.

This was the happiest she'd been since she touched Jacques. The shadows that lurked just behind her eyes were gone. All I could see were the aquamarine blue of her eyes, shining like the Caribbean sea.

"It's awesome. I can hear him talking in my mind, I mean, in the background."

She was radiant. Love looked good on her. Isolde had always been a beautiful girl.

I'm totally biased.

Love definitely suited her.

She began to ramble, "Well, I think it really started in October when he killed the lyon to save me."

I grabbed one of her hands and pulled her to sit next to me on the bed. I wrapped my arms around her.

"I saw these blue lights. They touched me. But, I didn't think anything of it. It was blue lightning." She kept rushing on talking about him and how beautiful his hair was, about how sweet he was. And just a couple of days ago she couldn't stand him.

I fixated on the blue lightning. I remembered blue lightning too and smiled.

Is that what happened for me and Adrian, at the ski lodge? All he did was touch my arm and our eyes locked. Then blue lights shot everywhere.

I blinked my eyes several times and pulled back to listen to Issy. She was lost in her own world.

"Anyway, so apparently, he realized immediately that we were mated. He could hear me. I couldn't hear him." She giggled and her face turned red. "It wasn't until he pulled me back from the black fog. Then, I realized we were mated. I love him. I was wrong about him. He's not arrogant. I mean he is a little bit, but it's just for show. He puts on a show to throw people off. He doesn't want people to know who he really is," she stopped rambling for a moment and took a breath.

"And who is he really?" I asked. The moment of realization came so much later in life for me. Yet, the rush of love wasn't lost on me.

"A hero, mom. He would give his last breath to save all of us. He would've killed that hydra for anyone, to save them. That's his superpower. He's a hero. He's certainly my hero," she laughed at her admission, then sobered. "If I hadn't heard him pleading in the background while I was stuck in the darkness, I'm not sure I could've thrown off all of my demons. Between Jacques and Daddy both beating down on me, I was in a bad place. I heard Hercules telling me none of it was real. He heard me." She smiled, and I couldn't help but return her joy.

Hera had it right. This could help me. It was a bandage to cover my wound of a heart, to keep me from hemorrhaging to death.

"I heard him calling 'Calla'." She pointed her toes and

hands. "Do you know what Calla means?"

I shook my head.

"It's Greek for beautiful. He's been calling me Calla since the lyons. I guess he thinks I'm beautiful." She dipped her head, and her ears turned pink.

"That's his nickname for you? Beautiful?" I asked and bit my lip.

"Yeah, my nickname is beautiful," Issy smirked.

I beamed at her and leaned in, "Do you know what Adrian calls me?"

"You have a nickname?" she squeaked.

"He calls me *'beautiful girl'*." I wrapped my arms around her. She was a grown woman, but I still love feeling my child pressed against me. She wasn't little anymore. Sometimes, hugging her was like taking a stranger in my arms. That was because I didn't recognize the adult body. I was still looking for the little girl who would cling to my skirts and stare up at me with her big green eyes begging me to give her and her brother another cookie.

I kissed her cheek and whispered in her ear. "Love

you!"

"I love you too. I wish Tristan was here. I'm sure he knew," she groaned.

I'm sure he did.

Like father, like son.

I left Issy in my cabin and went to the cockpit. I had to say something. Gabriel wasn't here. He'd say something. Adrian too.

"Professor Michelson, can you give Hercules and I a few moments. Please. I'd like to talk to him alone."

He glanced from one to the other and sputtered, "Sure, absolutely." He took to his feet, straightened his shirt, held his head high, and exited the room.

As soon as the door slid shut, "When did you mate with my daughter?" I asked without taking a seat, so I could loom over the big man.

"Just before the lyon attack, but she didn't know. I have been able to hear her ever since," he replied matter of fact.

"Did you tell anyone?"

He rolled his head around on her large shoulders and gazed up at me. "Adrian knew. I asked him not to mention it to anyone. Issy didn't realize, and I didn't want to pressure her. I figured I'd just wait it out. After all, you can't light half a candle." He shrugged.

"Adrian knew and didn't bother to mention it to me," I stated, trying to understand why.

"Adrian told me it wouldn't be a good idea to tell you, said to let everything unfold naturally. He also said that you didn't realize that you two were mated. He waited a long time before you worked it out. He's always been able to hear your thoughts. I think it might be a hybrid thing. Isolde doesn't have as much Themian blood in her as I do." He shrugged. "I don't know, apparently it's not unusual. Adrian suggested I try and woo her. Let her figure it out on her own. He said half the fun is the chase." A wicked grin worked its way over his face. I snarled at him.

Men love the chase.

His smile faded away.

Adrian kept this a secret from me. I didn't know whether I should be mad or not. It was probably for the best. I would have worried over it. "So, all this time, you've been killing hydras, lyons, and crazy monsters to impress my daughter?" I scoffed to toy with him.

"No, I was killing those to save you and her. We are mated, she dies, I die. If my mother died, I would die on the inside. My mother is a wonderful giving person. I didn't just come for Issy. I came for her too. I came for you, Adrian and Tristan. My brothers' blood is just as important as my own, as my sisters'. All that matters to me is my family." He stared me down with hard eyes. "Why did I kill those creatures? Because I was destined to do so. You don't have to believe in fate for it to be real. My skein was spun long ago. All those stories I told about myself, deep down inside, I knew that given the chance, I would live every single one. It wouldn't just be some yarn. I was spinning for someone else." He was on his feet, and his voice boomed with the certainty of the righteous.

I mentally pushed him back into his seat and waved a finger at him. He may be bigger than me, but I would twist him up in knots.

"You have my word we are mated. In the Themian world husband-and-wife matings, generally don't happen until you've reached your full maturity, 250 years old. I know how young Isolde is. I will not force her, nor will I allow her to jump the gun. I love her. We have an eternity. I can wait a long time. I waited 10,000 years for her. I can wait another 10," he was in earnest about his intent.

"It all comes back to love and sacrifice."

"Matings happen, where matings will. It has nothing to do with anyone's wants, needs, or desires. My only desire is you wait to make me a grandmother." I thrust my hand out, hoping he would agree.

His large meaty paw swallowed my hand, and he barked with laugher, "I swear, I will not make you grandmother anytime soon. Isolde is not ready for that. I've had enough with making children for one lifetime. I can easily wait one or two hundred years before I have my first mated child." He smiled. Hercules had an easy way about him.

I hadn't even really thought about whether he might have a child still alive.

No, Sydney, that line of thought can wait for a hundred years or so.

I pushed that one right to the back of the filing cabinet of *not my problem.*

Get your priorities straight, lady!

"Now, if you're done giving me the once over. Let's get a decent look at this asteroid field. Prometheus called it a demon field. It's a ship eater and I can see why. There's a lot of smaller asteroids in the group. They ricochet off of each other and work like a sandblasting machine on the hull of the ship."

"It'll chew the outer hull?" I asked

He nodded in agreement, "Might even put some holes in it. The parts that aren't covered in lava."

"Hull breaches, that's the last thing I need to be worried about," I groaned and ran my hand over my face and hair.

"I'm definitely worried about it. As if there aren't a thousand other things to worry over?" he laughed.

Hercules was unflappable even in the face of sandblasting asteroids.

CHAPTER 16

EMMALINE

Since I had some time before people would make it to the citadel, I headed down to the labs. There was one problem that niggled at the back of my mind and no matter how I chewed on it or how many surfaces I wiped, I couldn't get it out of my head.

Sydney's mother, Mary.

It just didn't sit right.

"Thought you were headed to the citadel," Melinda

said and tapped her temple as the lab door sucked closed behind me.

"It will take everyone about forty minutes to get it together and decide whether they're going or not. I dropped in to say hi to you real quick." I plastered a fake smile over my face and thrust out my hand for a good shake.

Melinda cocked an eyebrow at me, "Well, hi." She looked down at the offered hand but didn't take it. "What can I do for you, Emmaline?" she asked and lowered her head back down to the microscope on her work table, then glanced over to a notebook to jot something down.

"I got something eatin' at me."

Melinda glanced up at me sharply.

"Figuratively!" I replied. "I don't know if you're aware, interested or avoidin' the subject, but where is Sydney's mother?" I inquired, looking around the room to avoid Melinda's penetrating gaze.

"It's a really good question. Have you asked Sydney?" She deflected, then went back to the oculars on her scope.

"No, and she ain't here to ask. What do you mean that's a good question?" I asked and narrowed my eyes at her.

She really knew how to get under my skin. It was like havin' a bad case of hives caused by Poison Oak. She didn't just itch. She caused every open sore to ooze and crust over as she spread. And before you knew it, you were completely covered and miserable.

"She was never mentally unstable. She didn't even need Primordium. Other than making her younger, she had zero health issues. She's in prime condition. I released her into the general population, gave her a bracelet with limited security and a tracker," Melinda shrugged, pushing the stray black hair out of her face and tucked it behind her ear.

She must have treated herself to some Primordium too. My mouth hitched to the side. I couldn't blame her. She was twenty years younger than me and a top-notch scientist. We needed her.

Sydney said to give it to everyone. I know I must've raised an eyebrow because she gave me a deep chuckle.

"Tracker? What for?" I returned.

"You know, I'm just not as trusting as the rest of you. Something about that girl stinks."

I released a breath I didn't know I'd been holdin'.

Melinda turned around on her chair and waved me into her lazyboy. I took the seat without a word and leaned into the armrest.

"I could never figure out why Edward put her into that facility. I can't even hear her." Melinda leaned closer to me with her elbows on her knees. "Her whole mind is on lockdown, like San Quentin and solitary confinement wrapped in lead walls. Mary was always an interesting one, even as a child. I don't know why Sydney hasn't asked to meet her. She has zero connection to her other than biology," Melinda squinted at me.

I held my tongue and let her talk. After all, Melinda was Sydney and Mary's aunt, not me.

"But Mary didn't ask to see her either. I asked T about it. He refuses to interfere with Sydney's wishes. I think he's still worried she's angry at him for not standing up to Edward." She leaned away from me and took a breath. "I'm curious as to why you're interested." Melinda crossed her arms and rested her back on the edge of her work table, then crossed her ankles.

I asked questions, she followed them with questions of her own. I loved the game. However, this time I wanted an answer to my question first. I pulled out my gold cigarette case and removed one, "Why are you tracking her?" I asked again, mirroring her pose.

I snapped the gold case closed and tapped my cigarette to pack the tobacco, then, without asking permission, I lit the tip and pulled on the other end.

"Okay, while she was here," Melinda sneered at me and waved the smoke away. "I heard whispering every now and again. I'm sure it made her sound crazy on planet Earth since whisperings and giggling all alone is not considered normal. Anyhow, she's talking with someone, and she doesn't want us to know."

"I guessed that. Still, it doesn't explain exactly why you're trackin' her," I returned. Our game of tennis was beingin' to wear on me. The nicotine in the cigarette eased the edge I was on.

"I'm tracking her for one reason and one reason only. Whoever is talking to her, doesn't want us to know who he is. Obviously, he is Sydney's father and has something to hide. If Mary knew who he was and where he was, she would've asked us to go get him. They would want to be together." We both nodded in time with each other as a wisp of smoke drifted away. "Why wouldn't she talk to me about it?" Melinda finished and rubbed both temples in a circular motion before pushing all her hair back from her face again.

I released a guffaw, "No offense, Melinda, but you are not the most approachable woman." I blew a hit of smoke out of the side of my mouth.

Melinda reached over and snatched the cigarette out of my hand, took a drag, and handed it back. "Coming from you, Emmaline, that's a bad joke. You aren't very approachable yourself." We both kinda shared a dry laugh.

I didn't do approachable well.

"So, you put a tracker on her. What's it told you?" I asked because my curiosity was gettin' the better of me. I took a drag and handed her the cancer stick.

"She stays in her quarters. She goes out and gets her meals, then takes them back. That's about it. She doesn't go anywhere else." She shrugged again and took a long pull on the cigarette then handed it back. "She doesn't talk to anyone, not anyone you can see. She doesn't do anything but reading." Melinda blew the smoke out and waved it away.

"Are you lacing those with pot?" She asked as her eyes

glassed over.

I smiled at her but didn't answer, "I need that tracking frequency. I want to see her," I replied.

"You're welcome to it. I don't know how much good it will do you. She won't care who you are. She won't talk to you," Melinda stated.

I pulled out a few cigarettes from the opposite side of the case and set them on her work table. The wrapping papers were green, not white.

"It's my time to kill." I winked and headed out the door, making a beeline for the citadel and my next new molehill.

CHAPTER 17

SYDNEY

I knew it had to be done. We didn't know where we were going. There was nothing in the ship's records. What was there was spotty at best.

The records after they left Elysium were gone. Someone wanted to make it impossible for anyone to return. I stared at the door for a minute or two. I wanted all my ducks in a row mentally before I faced that shit head. I squared my shoulders.

Hera had finished rewiring the walls. She assured me

it was safe.

The door slid open, and Charon was lying in his berth. He blinked his eyes twice and sat up.

"All right, you got us here, now what?" I demanded as the door slid shut behind me.

I knew it was a cheesy line.

He's never heard it, so who gives a fuck?

There wasn't a better way to put it. I didn't want to talk to him, but I had no choice.

Charon turned away from the viewport and took me in from head to toe. It wasn't a sex thing. Yet, it still made my skin crawl. The scientist in him was assessing me, examining me for a reason I couldn't fathom.

"We must return to Elysium," he stated.

"Are you kidding?" I scoffed, "Is that really what this is all about?" I shouted. My nostrils flared as I tried to pull the anger burning in my chest back. The bedding rose in the air and began tying itself up in knots.

"Why all the subterfuge? We were heading there, anyway?" I barked. His body slammed against the wall, and the door to the bathroom slid open. He huffed and scrunched his eyes shut. When they opened, it dawned on him. He couldn't shift.

A flash of fear washed over him before quickly disappearing behind a mask.

I smirked at him. His jaw locked down, creating a flat line where his mouth was. His demeanor quickly changed, and he regained control, his face contorting into a smirk.

"How was I to know, unequivocally, you would take me back there?" He asked and shrugged in a fashion that reminded me of Tristan.

Anger rolled over me.

How dare he mimic Tristan!

"No! You could have taken your ship and been on your merry way. Instead. You. Hijack. Us," I replied with clipped words.

"I had to. I do not believe you would have come with me willingly—"

I released his body, and it crashed to the floor.

He took to his feet and rubbed the back of his head.

"Not all of you. It is as it should be," he replied, then rubbed the back of his head where it had slammed against the wall.

"What do you mean 'not all of us?' There are only five of us here!" I shouted.

He left the most important people, for me, behind.

"Only three of you matter. The fates had to come, Pythia—" he snapped his mouth shut, and his eyes grew hard. He stared through me, his mind a block of granite, impossible to penetrate.

Rolling my eyes, I growled. I was so sick of this shit. "You know, Charon, for a guy who stood around for a couple million years, I think you lost a few marbles along the way. Honestly, if you'd told me what you needed, I might have gone along with you. I've done crazier things." I threw my hands up in the air. "My daughter would've, and Hera seems to go along with whatever the two of us do." I leaned my back against the bulkhead, "You might very well have gotten all three of us. You didn't even try."

I pushed him against the wall, tipping his chin back, compressing his neck. "And now, I hate you. Now, I don't really care what it is you want or what happened to put you here. All I want is my family and Elysium. Get us there, or I'll push you out the nearest airlock in a sedated state so you can't save yourself!" I growled.

I released his body, and he slumped to the floor, coughing and sputtering for air.

"We have to go through the daemon field," he choked.

Great!

The door slid open, and the heat of another body took up residence behind me.

"The daemon field of Eurynomos?" Hera asked.

In these quarters there wasn't a lot of space. We both crammed into the cabin door.

"Eurynomos is the daemon field?" I asked, racking my brain for the name and what I'd read. There were so many stories from Earth and Themia I couldn't sort out the fact from fiction.

"Yes, you've heard of it?" Charon asked Hera.

His hopeful inquiry was lost on her. She wouldn't take his side over us. She might have been a voice of reason over mine, but I was in charge by her own choice.

She won't make the hard choices. But I will.

"It was described to me as a real creature, something that would eat the flesh of your bones," she supplied while fingering the fabric of her dress.

"That is an apt description for someone telling children's stories. It's not far from true." Charon let a smile play across his hard jawline.

It struck me that under this light he was actually attractive.

Too bad he's a fuck wit.

"It's not a creature, but a place in space - an asteroid field, fast-moving and filled with rough edges. The asteroids are constantly moving, grinding, and ricocheting off each other. It will chew the outside of your hull off. It was created by the singularity. It's a debris field that completely surrounds the singularity."

"Is there any way to go around or shift through it?" Hercules' deep voice cut into the conversation.

I sidestepped further into the small cabin. Charon didn't blink an eye or reveal any fear. Every person on this ship was against him, and he wasn't the least bit worried. That irked me to the core.

"No, there are no good reference points for a shifter. The field moves too much to shift through or around. This is all about what you can see. We flew through the field. I was the pilot." He smiled as if he had all the power.

"The field moves so much you can't use a visual? It's not stable?" Hera asked, knowing the answer and turned away from Charon.

"If you try, you may actually shift into a rock and kill everyone." His lips were twitching to hold back a smile. He really thought he had us.

This sucks!

I kept thinking about Han Solo and the stupid droid spouting the odds of safely traversing an asteroid field.

What happened in a movie wasn't supposed to happen in real life. It was supposed to happen thousands of years from now, when humanity finally becomes a multi-planet civilization.

There are no humans here, Syd!

I have to stop comparing our situation to my ideas

about humanity. I was already part of a multi-planet civilization. It just wasn't humanity.

"Hercules, move Prometheus closer. Let's get a decent look at this daemon field.

"The closer we are, the more dangerous it is," Charon stated, as if that was going to stop me.

Hercules' words came up in the back of my mind, '*small, fast-moving, like a sandblaster*'.

We stepped back into the passageway, and I closed the door to Charon's cabin, setting the lock.

We all moved toward the cockpit.

"Prometheus, bring up the asteroid field," I ordered.

Michelson glanced up from his cup of coffee and turned a knob on the console, then turned to take us all in.

"Acknowledged," the ship replied.

"Did I miss something?" Michelson asked.

I shook him off and pointed at the field that appeared on the holo display.

Hercules seemed deeply engrossed in the chart.

Michelson joined him, avidly studying the rocky kaleidoscope before us.

The entire asteroid field was displayed in real-time washing machine motion. "Why exactly do we have to go through this?" I asked mostly to myself.

Charon's answer didn't sit right with me, and I couldn't let it go. I turned and left the cockpit and stalked down the companionway to Charon's cabin.

The lock was off, and the door opened in a flash.

"Why exactly did you do that?" I asked, "Why did you pilot through the field? You could have found a way to shift through." I growled.

I needed to calm down. Shouting at every problem didn't make them go away. Adrian was my voice of reason, and without him to anchor me, I was a mess.

"I didn't want anyone to return. I was the best pilot. I was also the only shifter. I had complete control. I was just about to give them all gene therapy. Returning to Elysium after the gene therapy would have been genocide for the Elysian." He shrugged off his answer as if it meant nothing.

I wasn't buying it. There was more to it than that. I

crossed my arms and pressed my lips flat, and waited. The ABC's of sales, Always Be Closing. I was going to close this deal. I had to let him help us, but I was over his games.

The silence grew between us, and eventually, he began to pace. For a man who'd been stationary for 2+ million years, he wasn't exhibiting a lot of patience. I didn't move. Other than breathing and blinking, I stood my ground.

"You must understand how evolution works. The more advanced life form will generally out survive the lessors," he supplied. A smile played across his face and quickly disappeared.

I was so tired of these shit-heads games.

Yes, I understood very well what he was talking about. Yet, that didn't explain cockroaches. Yes, humanity had evolved in a similar way. Homo sapiens dominated the other intelligent sentient life forms. We didn't enslave them. We simply out-bred them.

"So, why do you need to return now? After all, even just bringing a few of us could be enough to wipe out the entire original Elysian population," I demanded.

"I told you. Fate cannot avoid destiny. From the

moment before, I jumped to now. I knew I must return. There was no other choice," he shrugged as if he had no control and it was okay. Everything he did was forgiven because well, 'destiny made me do it'.

What bullshit!

Something about what he said stuck in my head. Something was off. What were the exact words he had used?

'The moment before the jump to now.'

What had happened at the moment before? Most people don't usually regret a decision until afterward. He regretted it before. As if whatever he was doing was completely unavoidable. He had to go through with it.

Charon's mind was strong. I couldn't just break in or bludgeon my way in. I could have cracked him open and dominated him, finding out exactly what I wanted. That was a place I had no desire to go ever again. Just the mere thought of invading another person's mind against their will gave me the heebie-jeebies.

My stomach rolled.

"You said *before*. What do you mean the moment before?" Blessed Hera, she was frightening. His voice cut the thick air down to the quick.

"Did I say *before?* I must've misspoken." Charon snapped at them and covered his discomfort with a smirk, a smirk I wanted to slap off his face.

"No, I do not believe you. You said exactly what you intended to say. Something happened just *before,* and it made you regret your decision. What happened?" Hera demanded in a calm, even voice.

"I had a vision."

Even I could see by the set of his shoulders that he was lying. He hadn't had a vision. He simply didn't want to tell us. Under normal circumstances, I wouldn't care. He could keep all his bloody secrets. But, in this case, every one of his secrets was a problem and they could cost all of us our lives. What he was saying and doing just wasn't going to jive with me.

"You're a liar. I was going to give you more time to confess, but Hera's right. Something important changed your mind. You don't want to tell us about it. I don't have time to play your silly word games, so before we enter this asteroid field, you better tell us what we want, or I'll crack you like a walnut." I was growing tired of having to threaten people to get what I want.

Why can't they just come along nice and quiet?

He physically paled. The idea of having his mind invaded again was completely distasteful.

I wish Isolde was here. Issy could dig out whatever he was trying to hide. My job was to go through the information, to torture them with it if necessary.

Being a fate sucks! It's not nearly as glamorous as one would think.

The hull rang. We all glanced up at the ceiling. The impact could have hit anywhere.

I waved my hand in a circle at Charon to hurry his answer along.

"When I went through this asteroid field the last time, my copilot did all the maneuvering, and I shifted as necessary." Charon had deflected our questions.

I let it go for the moment. The flying rocks were a little move pressing.

"He was also my best friend and my closest colleague. We worked well together as a team. I don't know you, but I'm not sure you'll be able to anticipate my moves," Charon stated, staring down his nose at Hercules, who bristled under the lack of trust.

Herc smoothed his long hair back, and his demeanor changed from irritation to an easy smile. The wall I'd witnessed was back up and blocking his true feelings.

"Last time you went through this field, you were the only person with any abilities. This time you have a whole ship filled with them," Herc replied. "So, maybe if you open your mind, instead of throwing shade on everyone, we would be closer to being on the same page" he released a dry chuckle.

I raised an eyebrow and nodded my head at Hercules. It had struck me as interesting that Charon hadn't tried to use his abilities against us or with us. But then again, he had been standing like a statue for 2 million years. I was not even sure how much time he had to interact with anyone else before he statued himself.

Is that even a term?

"Good idea, Hercules." Isolde patted him on the shoulder and ran her fingers over his hair.

I knew it was none of my business.

She's an adult. Just barely. I wonder what Tristan

would think.

I gulped that thought back. The fire in my belly over him would consume me. So, I pushed it back and down into the little box that I buried under a lot of other shit in my mind.

"I've been studying the asteroid field, and I've plotted a course that I think is the easiest path. I've been thinking about what Charon said. I'm not sure you should actually be shifting us, rather, I think you should be shifting threats. So instead of looking out the window, let Hercules do all the flying. You watch the holographic images and move anything that looks like it's getting too close out of the way, removing the worry of shifting into a rock," Michelson recommended with a satisfied smile.

"Your plan definitely makes more sense than what I was doing. We actually did shift into one asteroid. It didn't kill anyone, but it didn't damage a few rooms," Charon remarked while nodding in agreement.

"Great! Let's get the show on the road," Hercules laced his fingers together and turned his hands inside out, then cracked both sets of knuckles. He slipped into the pilot's seat and placed his hands on the controls. "This might be a bumpy ride, ladies. Perhaps you should take a seat and buckle up."

I looked back to the newly installed chairs. The old ones were ruined after Styx. Every chair had a brand-new five-point harness on it, along with the neck rest.

I guess Hercules isn't completely useless.

He seemed to be pretty handy with building stuff. Hera gave him an approving smile, patted him lightly on his shoulder, and went and sat down and immediately began buckling herself in.

I was still wearing my jeans and T-shirts, so the five-point harness wasn't an issue. Hera had reverted back to wearing the short togas of Themian's design. She liked hers cross slung over one shoulder dress. She looked every bit the Goddess. However, they seemed rather impractical to me. She sat down and proceeded to buckle herself in until she realized one had to go between her legs. My face curled into a big smile. She raised an eyebrow at me, then she simply tucked her skirt between her thighs and pulled the belting up. When she latched the last clip into the harness, she smiled.

Isolde had reverted back to wearing a tank top and a pair of shorts.

I was not sure if Hercules actually owned a shirt or simply had an aversion to them, but he very rarely wore one.

He mostly dressed like a gladiator. I was waiting for him to pull out a sword and say '*we who are about to die salute you.*' It was a leather kilt with fabric underneath, and X'd belting over his chest and back. He was always heavily armed, carrying all kinds of swords and knives.

Charon was dressed in a traditional long tunic with gold and around the edges, while Professor Michelson looked exactly like what he was, an old doddering professor with a young hot body. The professor, you're sure everyone would try to get into bed with.

The only people missing are Tristan and Adrian.

This was my ragtag crew. We were all odd couples, and that's an understatement.

Daemon's real or imagined I was not going to let us die just because an asteroid field sits between us and our objective. "Professor, while you're doing your calculations and forming a plan, add in the fact that I have the ability to move things out of the way," I stated.

Maybe we can make this go a little faster.

"I wasn't thinking about that at all. Actually, you so rarely use it. I didn't even remember you could. Other than

moving Hera that one time, I'm not sure you can control it."
He left off and cringed a bit.

"I don't know if that was me." I swallowed.

It was a lie. I knew it was me. I just didn't know how.
However, I did that and it didn't matter. All I needed was the
holo display, and I could swat those rocks like flies.

"Mom, if you feel the need to move anything on our
behalf in the middle of the daemon field, no one will stop you,"
Issy giggled.

I glanced at her sharply. I didn't see the humor in our
situation. She pressed her lips closed, lowering her eyes to the
floor. Her nerves were getting the better of her.

"Don't worry. If I think we're in imminent danger of
being hit by something. I will definitely do my part," I replied,
hoping it soothed her.

She could handle the harsh realities of life, but I
couldn't stop myself from trying to shield her.

Hercules announced, "Moving into the asteroid field
now." He pulled back on the controls.

"Switching off artificial gravity," Michelson replied,

then adjusted the holo display. He'd doubled it so Charon and I had our own projection. I found the controls on the armrests and began moving the image around as the ship moved.

Issy reached over and squeezed my hand. "It's okay, mom. It's all according to plan."

I gave her a tight smile and told myself, *'this isn't any different from crossing a reef. We just need to watch our gages and compensate as needed.'*

The bombardment began with a few knocks and quickly grew. It would be really nice if we had somebody at this point with the ability to shield us. I didn't know of any Themians who could.

Rocks slammed into different portions of the hull. Being in zero-g made the impact nothing more than a pull on my harness. My mind was glued to the three-dimensional display.

We came up as a blue orb. The rocks were shown in different colors, extremely large red, small and harmless green, with varying shades from yellow to orange in between.

"Charon, there are five huge rocks heading towards us," Herc announced.

Isolde turned up the tension in the room. "Issy, stop making everyone uptight," I barked.

She immediately turned it off, but the effect lingered.

"I see them. Shifting them now." Three of them disappeared off the screen, reappearing far off the periphery. The two others quickly followed.

I tore my eyes away from the holo, long enough to gaze out the actual viewing windows. There were rocks everywhere. The holo made it into a video game. I didn't want to shake the reality. We were floating in a cosmic minefield. One wrong move, and we could all end up in space.

I watched our back and portside, pushing rocks away like a toddler pushes away unwanted food. Hours passed, and Isolde thrust a cup of coffee into my hand. I barely gave it a glance before guzzling it down and going back to watching our back.

"How long before we are out of the field?" Hera asked.

"It took me 12 Elysian days," Charon replied without turning his head.

Fear clenched my chest. "12 days? Are you fucking kidding? Did you stay awake for 12 days?" I asked.

"Yes, yes, I did," Charon replied. "Anu did too."

Isolde gasped and quickly coughed to cover her reaction.

"Excellent, I'll bet we can make it in six," Hercules chuckled.

What the hell is wrong with men? Like they always need to turn everything into a bet? Why does it have to be a challenge?

"Herc, let's just get through without dying," Isolde laughed.

She was attempting to take him in hand.

That ought to be interesting to watch if I wasn't so busy.

Three deep orange-colored asteroids were headed our way. Reaching out with my mind, I gave them a small tap. Not enough to really cause any major damage and collide. I just wanted them to slide past us.

"Sydney, did you do that?"

"Yeah, that was me."

Charon replied, "Keep doing that. I'll shift the big ones you tap the smaller."

That was all the encouragement I needed. I reached further into the void, and suddenly, my mind was floating with the ship. I didn't see the cockpit anymore. It was all space and it was filled with rocks.

Several moved toward me, and my ability kicked in and moved them like pushing a billiard ball across a table. It collided with other rocks ricocheting off in different directions. Pleasure coursed through me.

I waved my left hand, pushing the asteroids on that side out of the way. I liked this game of wiping the space clean. I moved my right hand in the same pattern, scattering rocks that way too. Without stopping, I pushed up and down.

The space in front of the ship had been cleared for thousands of miles.

Issy floated next to me along with Hera.

<You're amazing, mom!>

Her voice came from far away. She was nothing more than a shade of herself. I pulled closers to a massive rock covered in craters the size of small moons. It was bigger than

Prometheus. I raised my hand to swat it away, but it disappeared. I cried out in shock.

< Fate can't move them all, Sydney. > Charon had shifted it before I could.

Scrunching my forehead, I searched the area around the ship for more.

The rocks came at us, and I smacked them out of the way, if Charon didn't shift them first. I stretched my mind. I wanted to deflect more than he did. As they flew at us from every angle, I batted and swatted the cosmic rocks that came my way. That's when I spotted the mist.

<Sydney, that dust is made up of smaller asteroids. They are moving fast, and will work like sandpaper on the hull.>

I reached out and waved my hands again. Pushing the dust to the side. The spacing between the rocks opened up. I cleared the path till there wasn't anything left to move.

It was black. I glanced behind us only to see the fading light of Cerberus disappearing. We'd broken through.

The Eurynomos Field was gone. I used the time I had to view the exterior of the ship. It was pitted with dents. That wasn't the concerning part. Not far from the cockpit there was a stream of mist escaping from the ship.

I closed my eyes. I didn't know how to get back into my own body to warn them. I shook.

If only Adrian was here… God, I need him.

Tears pricked my eyes.

He's been there in the background for so long.

I never would have made it this far without him. I clenched my teeth at the silence that I mentally faced.

Staring out at the great black void, it hit me the hardest.

I can't face all of this without him - eternity alone, in the lost reaches of space.

The rocks floated closer and disappeared as quickly as they arrived. I was stuck here, without him.

Why? Why can't we just be together?

Pain lanced my face. My head whipped to the side and the pain ripped over the other side of my face.

"Mom, snap out of it!" Issy yelled.

I blinked as the void faded. My reaction was to fight. I grab her hand in mid-swing. I squeezed it with all my might. As the fog cleared.

"Mom, oh God, mom."

Warm arms wrapped around my neck. Moist breath blew across my ear. I focused on her voice.

So beautiful, Isolde.

"I'm here, sweetheart," my voice croaked.

"She's awake," she said.

I wrapped my arms around her shoulders and held her shaking form.

I still had Isolde, and that would have to be enough. I swallowed back the agony of a life without Tristan and Adrian. I did it before.

I can do it again.

At least this time, there was hope. They weren't dead.

CHAPTER 18

EMMALINE

My shoulder bumped into a teenager as I entered through the main doors. I could have slipped in from behind the dais, but it would have made it seem like I was lording it over everyone, and I wasn't that person. I still believed leaders should be normal everyday people with crappy jobs.

Nobody wanted this job. I was not even sure I wanted it.

You don't know that until you have it, then the regret sets in.

However, Sydney left me in charge of a job she didn't want. There were roughly a third of our population assembled, mostly adults.

That's good.

The kids didn't need to be here, not for what I was gonna say.

"I'm sure you're all wondering what that big jump really was all about, and you know Prometheus shifted away. Anyone lookin' out a window can see that," I stopped, and the roar of the crowd rolled over me, so I waited for them to quiet down.

"It didn't shift away because they wanted to. We have three shifters in our fleet. We picked up a new person on Delphi," I paused. Saying his name would be enough to create a panic. Everyone here was reading Themian mythology like crazy. "His name was Charon. He seemed rather harmless."

My fingers were lacing and unlacing. I pulled them apart and fisted them at my side. The mumbling in the crowd rolled over me and around the room. "He was a shifter who clearly had other ideas. He took Sydney, Hera, Isolde, Hercules, and Professor Michelson with him."

Someone in the crowd stifled a cry. It was a young woman.

Michelson's daughter?

I'd have to have someone look into that.

"A lot of you are probably a little shocked." I faltered for a moment, vacillating on how to proceed.

Do I tell them everything or just enough to get by?

"The last shift was a little different." There was no other way to explain it, but the truth, and I did what I always do, I fed people bitter pills. I jumped in feet first. "First of all, it took all three of our shifters to make it. Which worked out, and we are lucky to have them! The second reason it was different is that we shifted further than ever before. I'm just glad we didn't have to stop for directions, or we might not have made it." A ripple of amusement ran through the crowd. I released a tentative laugh.

"The third reason the shift was strange was because we are now outside of the black hole's gravity well. We're well away from Cerberus, so you can free your minds over that. We are floating in normal space. And we haven't decided where we're going from here yet, but we're safe, and I think that's really the most important part. After all, safety first, right?" I asked, not expecting an answer but the room exploded, everyone talkin' over the other, each voice louder than before.

Where exactly are we?

Why can't we see Prometheus?

Can we go back?

Do we know where we're going?

I ceased on the last and loudest question. "Yes, we are following Prometheus. We have her heat signature from her intake return. And just like Hansel and Gretel, we just need to keep following the breadcrumbs." I internally groaned. Hansel and Gretel got lost because the birds ate the bread.

Terrible analogy, Emm!

I rushed to move on and hoped no one would comment on my flub, "Our maneuvering thrusters will keep us on track, and we can shift anywhere that we have a visual. The most important thing anybody on the ship can do is help build our faster than light engines," I stopped talkin' with the hope people would get the message and join up.

In 1941 it had been easy. Our boys joined by the

thousands to fight Japan and the Nazis. Here, on this ship, away from the reality of earth and only the uncertainties of space, I wasn't so sure our people would rise to the occasion.

"Hephaestus is using a lot of 3-D printers and Themian technology to create engines." I took in the crowd and let my voice echo away. With a deep breath, I continued, "I'm telling you right now that if we're going to survive, we can't rely solely on our shifters. We have to be able to maneuver through space in any way necessary. So, if anyone here is a machinist, electrician, or you have engineering capabilities... I don't care if you're a mechanic for regular old American made cars. We could use you. We need engines, and we need people willing to help build them." I smashed my fist into the palm of my hand to drive my point home. "Even if it just means you're bringing food and drinks to the people who are building them."

There was a rumbling that rolled around the room. I just said we were on a ship that didn't have a motor.

The emotional roar bowled me down, and I stumbled into one of the seats on the dais.

A man pushed through the crowd. "Well, I'm no genius. I'm not a mechanic, an engineer, a machinist or anything like that. I'm just your average everyday gear head. I don't know anything about those modern diagnostic machines or computers. Every car I've ever worked on was built before 1975, but I'd be happy to help." The man had bright water blue eyes and rather large ears. His cinnamon-colored skin glowed under the Themian blue lights.

"Get down to lab 12. That's where they're building the newfangled contraption." I hooked my thumb at the door behind me, knowin' he could leave through any door and reach that lab.

Taking to my feet, I faced the cavernous space, and the various faces all lookin' at me for answers. One volunteer wasn't enough.

"It's not like we're all goin' to die of old age before we get to where we're goin'. We'll still be alive. The big question is, how long do you want to take to get there. Go to lab 12 in the C ring. They will put you to work."

Several people moved toward the exits. They were eager to sign up for the war effort. They realized floatin' around in space on maneuvering engines wasn't the best way to get around. I spoke to people here and there before I found my way out, or rather, I was waylaid.

"I've heard that type of speech before, Miss Emmaline.

Made me feel like I was 12 years old again." He obviously had to be an old guy. Terms like young and old held little meaning these days. After a drink from the infinity pool, it all melted into nothingness.

"Yes," I replied with interest.

"I was wondering, if there would be any young women working down in lab 12?"

I stopped dead in my tracks and turned to get a look at him, then I cocked an eyebrow, "You want to join up and help the war effort for girls?" I scoffed.

We aren't exactly in a traditional war, but fighting the ravages of space is the ultimate battle. Ares had said as much, and I agreed.

The man had pretty blue eyes, but those weren't in short supply around here. He hung his head and ran his fingers through his hair. He looked up at me through his eyebrows.

"Well, I was just hopeful to meet a pretty girl. They're not in short supply on the ship. I'm just—" he worried something in his pocket, then straightened his shoulders and took to his full height. "I just happen to like mechanics and was hopin' for a like-minded lady," he practically shouted.

I burst out laughing. It was the funniest thing I'd heard all week. "You like eggheads? You should talk to Melinda. She's pretty smart," I remarked and crossed my arms.

"Oh, I can't talk to Miss Melinda she's... she's lovely, but she's a scientist and I was kind of hoping for a machine minded lady."

"You are looking for a girly grease monkey?" I said and slapped him on the back.

"Yeah, I—I like motors and engines, and I don't mind having a little grease under my fingernails and in every crack in my hands. I'd like to find myself a lady who doesn't mind either." He pulled the object in his pocket out and worried it a little more the longer he spoke.

I swept my gaze down and quickly back to his face. The object was a rabbit's foot. The brass cap on the end was green on top but shined like new near the fur. It looked pretty old, and there was a real chain on it. The kind they used to sell at the dime stores when I was a kid.

"I'm not here to play matchmaker, if that's what you're looking for. What's your name?" I demanded.

He'd flustered me, and Ixis nagged at the back of my

mind. I pushed him out with a promise of an explanation later.

"Egbert," he replied.

Oh, God! He's a grease monkey named Egbert. No wonder he's still looking for a gal. He'll be alone forever behaving like that with the name Egbert.

Egbert was a perfectly fine name for the 1940s but not today. It was old fashion and frankly funny.

"Is it Egbert? Or can I just call you Bert? Maybe you should go by Bert. It's less old-fashioned than Egbert. Try it out for today."

He stood up real serious before a sunny smile broke out on his face. His eyebrows practically reached into his hairline. "You really think so? You think I look like a Bert? I always liked Burt Reynolds."

I put my hand up to my mouth to stop from laughing out loud. He was no Burt Reynolds. He certainly had the black hair. He lacked the naughty twinkle in his eye.

"I think you look just like a Bert, maybe Lancaster. I was always partial to Burt Lancaster." It was all I could say to perk the man up.

Was every old geezer on the tub going to need a chat up to start livin' again? I didn't have time for it. The encounter amused me. The humor of it would be lost on Ixis.

Adrian might find it if he could stop obsessing over that girl.

"Thank you, Emmaline. I'll tell everybody my name's Bert. I'll go find me a pretty girl." He trotted off at a pretty fast pace towards lab 12. There was a new little spring in his step.

As fast as the encounter had begun, it was over.

I had Ixis shift me. I didn't want to waste time walking or have the chance of being waylaid again.

I sigh escaped me before I could stop it as my eyes landed on my man.

All that black gleaming longhair on a man was an affront to women everywhere. And he was all mine. I snickered to myself.

"Emmaline, I see you finished your announcement to the rest of the hybrids. Were you able to round up any new volunteers for the engine project?" He rumbled to me without turning around. Ixis was a serious, focused man. The only time he let his guard down was when we were alone or in our minds.

I was used to it, not only from Ix, but my family. I spent all of my childhood being told not to share our secrets with anyone.

You can't trust outside the family.

Loose lips, sink ships wasn't just a slogan for the war, but our family too.

"Yes, I think I convinced about 50 people to sign their lives away." I drolled and ran my hand down his back.

"It's 50 more than we had. We've been using Odyssey's deep scanners to identify potential asteroids rich in minerals," he responded.

The moment popped like a soap bubble on grass, and it was back to the next hurdle.

"Excellent! How long will it take us to reach one?" I asked. My eyes were growing heavy and dry. I was going to need sleep soon.

"We're doing deep space scans to try and receive imagery now. We will shift to the closest one. Even if it's not the most desirable candidate. Once there, we can examine the other nearby rocks. Perhaps, we can settle on a few more suitable candidates at that time," he supplied in his calm and controlled manner. He was the cold to my fire. He kept my feet planted on firm ground, so I didn't float away with all my practical advice.

"It is just one thing y'all keep leaving out. Once we identify this asteroid with the various mineral deposits we're looking for, how do we harvest the damn thing?" I asked.

"That's actually quite simple. We have several different bays within the ship. I can shift it to one of those."

"We have a room big enough to hold a meteor or an asteroid? Whatever it is?" I scoffed, looking him up and down. Ix always said things that floored me.

"A meteor is only a meteor once it has entered the atmosphere of a planet. Prior to that, it's an asteroid floating in space, for the most part, seemingly innocuous. Unless, of course, it's moving on a driven course because it's been acted upon by an outside force and then it becomes a comet," he returned.

I licked my lips dryly and cocked an eyebrow at him. He was smart and had been around forever. He spent 99% of his life in space. Every now and again, when Ixis was givin' me one of his little astronomy courses, I just wanted to break his neck.

A smile broke over his face, < If I bore you, you should tell me before I ramble on. >

<But then I can't be mad afterward. > I smiled.

He stepped in close, and I forgot everything. His lips touched mine and the world seemed to disappear into oblivion for a moment.

When he stepped back, I couldn't help but glance around.

CHAPTER 19

ADRIAN

I cleared my throat. Emily wasn't really known for her public displays of affection. She had old-fashioned feelings about what should or shouldn't happen in front of other people.

Ixis had no such compunctions. Themians were a little too open with their love in some ways. After thousands of years of living with humans, Hera had inherited or learned some human modesty. But the few other Themians on-board, Hera's children included, did not seem to have those issues. There'd been several problems I'd had to handle.

With Sydney here, it had been easy. We even shared a laugh over a few incidents such as Hera running around with her boobs hanging out being one. Seeing Emily kissing Ixis was only a reminder Sydney wasn't here and may never be again.

I pushed that thought right out the nearest airlock.

Not going to happen. I will find my girls!

I would never sit on the sidelines again, waiting for my life to happen.

I will find Sydney!

"Are we ready to make this shift, Ixis?" I asked as if I hadn't just watched the man maul my Great Aunt.

"You're welcome to do all the heavy lifting this time if you wish," he remarked, using a very human term.

A half-smile quirked my lips for a moment. "My shift it is," I let the double meaning hang in the air.

Odyssey displayed the image of the asteroid we'd chosen. I used all of the mental techniques Ixis had taught me to imagine and memorize the entire picture. My mind rotated it around, making it a three-dimensional object.

I closed my eyes and performed the shift, maintaining the space around our ship in its entirety so that no one felt the pressure change.

It's a neat little trick Tristan taught me.

We appeared next to the asteroid. I was taken aback. It was covered in glowing veins. "What is it that makes it glow?" I asked and glanced at Ixis for my answer.

"That is the crystalline mineral necessary for all Themian technology. We call it radiant," he supplied and moved to the holo display.

"Radiant, makes it sound like coal in a fire. It gives off heat long after the fire has gone out." I haven't seen a campfire in years, but my memory of it remained. Radiant brought all thought of one back - sitting on the beach in Costa Rica, watching the waves lap against the sand. Tears tickled the corners of my eyes. I blinked. The present was all that mattered. Finding Sydney and Isolde before Charon did something.

"Yes, it radiates light, and it's an excellent superconductor. A small amount of radiant mixed in with all of our crystalline composites turns the entire mass into a superconductor able to carry massive amounts of energy. Yet, it does not grow hot, and it's not harmful to life." He turned the ship, putting the only shuttle bay we have in alignment. "We don't usually carry large quantities of raw radiant on the ship. Enough for repairs or to manufacture something small." Aunt Emily patted my shoulder. It was her way of easing my nerves. It didn't work.

"If our new engines are infused with the radiant, they won't need to pull energy from the rest of the ship to power themselves. It has to be mixed into every component." Ixis' explanation was enough to satisfy my curiosity.

It wouldn't have been enough for Sydney.

"That's a pretty big rock to get in here?" I remarked to keep the conversation in my head at bay.

I needed to stay in the present and solve the problem. I couldn't constantly keep drifting back to thoughts of Sydney.

"It is too large to shift into the bay. We will need to put a net around it and break it apart, then shift in the smaller pieces," he replied, then moved on to examine the edges of the asteroid field for more candidates.

"What? Are we going to spacewalk out with a net?" I scoffed. He stated facts as if we were a long-time space faring race. And not the infants of the cosmos.

"That is one way to do it. We could have people spacewalk out. We could shift someone out to the meteor and allow them to move closer on their own," he replied.

"Sydney's not here to move shit around, Ixis!" I yelled. He'd skipped over the part where the only real-time mover we have was gone. I ran my fingers through my hair to keep from pulling Ixis hair out.

<Calm down!> Aunt Emily said.

I threw her a sharp stare and heaved a sigh.

Work the problem, don't let it work you.

The calm I usually felt was gone along with Sydney.

"We're going to shift people out with nets. Plant charges and wrap it all up in a butterfly net. Crack that sucker open and shift the smaller chunks inside," I actually sounded calm, laying out this crazy plan.

It was something Sydney would have concocted. A smirk eased the muscles in my jaw.

"Ixis, can I do that?" I peeked over at Tristan.

I guess blowing up rocks sounds kind of fun.

I didn't see the danger in it. If there was a problem, he could get out of there faster than anyone other than myself.

"Yes, Tristan, you can." I gave him a halfhearted smile. Tristan was eager to learn his new trade. Moving around space rocks actually sounded boring to me.

"Take Dewy. He's had demolition experience," Aunt Emily interjected.

I nodded my head in acceptance. I should stop calling her Emily and start calling her Emmaline. She had always been Aunt Emily to me. Even after I could say her name. I didn't care if anybody else knew I was talking about my Aunt Emily or not.

I've called her Emm a couple of times. None of it felt right, she was my great Aunt Emily, and nothing could change that.

I recognized a clandestine mind trip when I saw one. Emily was always up to something. Uncle Dewy didn't need to come along. He could just sit in the shifting room and tell us what to do.

No, trouble seemed to be her middle name. She kept

her head down for 40 years on Atlantis. She was making up for it now. She slipped out one of the side arches. It didn't matter what she was up to, I needed to follow her. I slipped out the doorway just as it closed and tiptoed behind her.

She was heading towards the living quarters. The one held by the O'Dears.

Maybe she is looking for Tobias?

My gut said that wasn't it.

I hung back to allow people to hide me. Coming up on one of the many cafeterias, I stepped inside to find she'd disappeared amongst the crowd, then jumped at the sound of her voice.

"Why exactly are you followin' me, Adrian?" Emily demanded.

My shoulders sagged as I looked up at the ceiling "Aunt Emily, what are you up to? I know the look on your face. You're about to make some kind of trouble," I stated and crossed my arms.

"What I'm up to doesn't concern you," she snapped then gave my arm a good pinch.

I yelped and rubbed the bruised bicep. "Well, it can't be ship business. I'm part of the command crew, and I'd know about it, so it must be something private. If it doesn't concern me, who does it concern?" I demanded and stepped back out of pinching range.

"Let me ask you a question, Adrian. Don't you find it a little odd that Sydney hasn't asked once to see her real mother?" She inquired with her hands on her hips.

"No, she has nothing to say to her. Sydney's known about her mother for decades. She knows the story and feels sorry for her. Frankly, Emily, you really don't have a lot of time for her, and neither has Sydney. To go searching the ship looking for a long-lost biological mother," I scoffed at her.

The reason for this entire trip was lost on me.

"Yes, but now would be the time she could find out who her father really was. Here's a better question. Why hasn't Mary even tried to talk to her? Humm?" Aunt Emily had a point there.

I don't know. I've never met the woman, and why does it matter?

"There's a lot of rumors floating about who Sydney's

father is or isn't. Truthfully, she doesn't care. She's lived her whole life without knowing. By the time you reach this stage in life, most people have either given up or moved on," I scoffed.

Emily was on a terror and not going to let it go.

"Well, I went looking for my own answers. Because I don't buy that bullshit. When I'm done, if you want to know what I found, you're welcome to ask," she humphed.

Aunt Emily was not going to let this go, and Sydney wasn't here to stop her.

I shook my head. I had a different whale to hunt and so did Emily. The last time she was this obsessed with anything, we were trying to break into the Atlantis library. Aunt Emily had decided I hadn't reached Atlantis by riding a wave. I didn't remember how I got there.

"As long as your pet project doesn't interfere with finding Syd and Isolde, I don't care what kind of poking around you do. When Sydney gets back, that will be another story. Emm, she isn't going to like it. Why can't you just leave Mary alone?" I asked, hoping the threat of Syd's ire would be enough to put her off.

"If I wasn't scared of Athena and her squad of hooligans, why would I tremble over Sydney and her antics?" She retorted. Emm patted her curls back into place. A smile tugged at the corners of my mouth. She was still concerned over her hair being out of place, an act she'd used as long as I'd known her.

"Athena never had the ability to move mountains or crack open your mind and dig out the soft spots, Emm. We have other problems to worry about, so stop wasting time," I shouted, losing my cool.

The sting of her hand hit me before the realization she'd slapped me.

"I will not put up with your cheek, Adrian Mitchell Shipman! You will respect your elders. That means me. I'm workin' on this on my own, in my off time. And how dare you infer I would miss the mark or lose sight of our real objective?" She hissed at me while rubbing her hand.

I suddenly found the floor interesting. I'd never yelled at Aunt Emily before, and she'd never slapped me.

I'm being an ass and she put me in my place.

"Screamin' at me isn't going to solve our problems."

She cupped my burning cheek, "I know you're going crazy inside. I was there the first time this happened. We will find her and Issy. But something in my bones tells me Mary is an issue, and I must chase her down. Now, go get some rest. We have rocks to collect." She kissed the red mark on my cheek and pushed me toward my cabin.

A moment later, Ixis shifted me into my bedroom. All I could see was the blue and white Hawaiian quilt Sydney kept on the bed and the scent of lavender in the air.

How did she think I could sleep like this?

The sound of snoring came from the living room. I peeked my head out only to spy Tristan sprawled out on the couch, clutching a pillow in one hand.

I covered him with Sydney's quilt and laid down on the floor next to the couch to listen to his breathing. It reminded me of Syd. My mind seized onto the sound as sleep overwhelmed me, along with dreams of the ocean and the terrors I'd survived there.

I awoke with a start and the feeling of cold water lapping at my legs. The solar clock read 4 hours had passed. Tristan was still out cold.

I rubbed my thigh and the memory of the bone, stretching my skin in an effort to push through. I had to blink to remove the sight of red spider veins crawling over my leg as sepsis set in. I got up and headed for the shower.

There was no more sleep to be had, not without Syd, not after the dream.

CHAPTER 20

SYDNEY

"Now that you've come back to your senses, perhaps, we can move on in this tedious journey." Charon had no understanding of humanity, err hybrids.

Even using that term in reference to myself was a kind of a joke. I was more Themian than human and after my little dunk in the infinity pool, I was even less that.

I was mentally exhausted. Astral projection weakens your whole body. It turns you into a husk, doing nothing more than holding your consciousness inside. Without the bright light of your intelligence and your minds, the body weakens.

I hadn't felt this way since before I discovered the island.

I hadn't made the connection prior to discovering Alethea. I'd actually projected. It wasn't a dream. I was visiting. I just didn't realize it at the time. Now, I knew exactly what I was doing and how to get back. But it explained why I was so skinny and tired all the time.

"Are you ready for the next leg of our journey?" Charon hadn't even turned to look at me. The coldness of his demeanor bothered me.

I heaved a sigh and asked, "Yes. Where do we go now?"

"The stories said the Meadow of Asphodel." The timber of Hera's voice came across as uncertain. She rarely spoke when she didn't have an answer. I shifted my eyes to her sharply. She raised her shoulders and lowered them. It was a shrug, a mannerism I'd not seen her display before. Perhaps hanging out with all of us hybrids was altering her behavior.

"Yes, Hera, you are correct. Asphodel is our destination. Only it's not a meadow, it's a planet."

The holo display listed all known information about Asphodel. A tidally locked world, one side burning hot and the other side moderate but dark. There was enough of an atmosphere that the heat was shifted from one side of the planet to the other, thereby warming the dark side to keep it from being covered in ice. There was a circular belt of rivers dividing either side with enough light and warmth for some habitation to exist. This belt was called the meadow of Asphodel.

"It's where Elysium dumps their trash," Charon supplied and smirked as if there was more to it.

Hera and Hercules gasped, and Isolde burst out laughing.

"You can learn a lot about people from their trash," Isolde snorted. "So, we're going dumpster diving? Huh?"

I smirked myself, "Yes, Issy, we're going dumpster diving. What are you too good for a little trash, love?" I asked and slapped her on the back.

She shook her head, "No, I just didn't think I'd fall in love, and then for our first date, we go sift through someone else's trash." She winked at Hercules.

Hercules burst into a loud booming laugh. "It's a date? Only the best for my Calla?" he snickered.

The sensation of a shift took over the pressure change, creating the overwhelming cold.

I'll never get used to Charon's style.

It lacked the finesse of Ixis' or the feel of Adrian's and Tristan's.

We appeared not far from a giant gas and a star. The star gave off an orange glow, and the ship turned to reveal we were orbiting a planet with two gleaming crossed rings.

Michelson sputtered, "I thought a planet had to turn to have rings." He shrugged his shoulders, "Everything I know about the Universe is what humans have observed from telescopes and the laws of physics and mathematics."

He had no idea how those rings were able to maintain their orbit, and neither did I.

"They're not traditional planetary rings. They were constructed. Elysians use them to hold pollutants, chemicals. They filter around the rings and are dispersed into the atmosphere of the planet on the hot side. They were built from the cold side."

It's a wonder people so technologically advanced build a set of rings around a planet just to spray it with a pollutant.

Elysians didn't sound that much different from humanity.

Part of me wanted to snort at the irony of it.

Perhaps Charon was right about these people. The amount of planning and engineering was clearly advanced. But it was lazy.

Why find a shit world on the ass-end of the universe just so you could dump your trash? Why not find a better way to deal with your trash?

"When you say they dumped chemicals, could you be a little more specific? I don't want to come up off the planet glowing, just because I was looking for something in the trash," I remarked.

Charon turned his chair around. "They disperse the chemicals into the space around the planet. The heat from the systems' star burns it, in essence getting rid of the pollutant. I'm sure some of it does enter the atmosphere, but it's burned off before it reaches the other side."

Gee, I'm so reassured. I rolled my eyes.

"How can you be so sure?" Issy asked in her best New York accent, then giggled. I couldn't tell if she was imitating Marisa Tomei or her Aunt Maria.

There was a smile for a moment.

A picture of Maria and Zack flashed through my mind. Maria's boys Marcos, and Rafael had to be 21 and 23 by now.

For the first time in years, I found it hard to focus on the here and now. My mind kept turning back to earth and everything I've left behind in my pursuit of and the map, then the island, and now Elysium.

Charon shook his head. "Do not worry. I will shift us down to the planet wearing protective suits. All we need do is reach the meadow. That is where they keep all the discarded spaceships," he stated.

"So, we're looking for a black box?" Issy leaned forward, her eyes bright.

"I do not know why we need a black box. We are looking for memory banks and star charts," Charon replied.

Hercules threw his head back, laughing, "Charon, on

earth, the black box is where they keep the star charts and memory banks."

Issy winked at him. Obviously, she told him what it was. I guess she wanted him to look smart. Especially, seeing as half the room had no idea what she actually said.

"The sooner we get this done, the sooner we can find Adrian and Tristan. So, let's get the show on the road," I barked to cover my churned-up feeling.

Hercules managed to place us in a wide orbit around the planet, and the ship's autopilot took over.

I liked having a semi-intelligent computer program to help you with parking.

If you're exploring space at some point in time, you're going to need a spacesuit. Hercules had space walked the hull to gather materials for Hera. I hadn't seen any kind of special airlocks on Odyssey. But Odyssey was millions of years technologically ahead of Prometheus. It was the difference between getting on an Egyptian reed boat and sailing up and down the Nile versus sailing around in a superyacht made in 2020. They were worlds apart. Prometheus was technologically advanced, more so than anything humanity had. I couldn't judge it too harshly.

Based on the information Charon gave us, everything here was designed predominantly by him based upon Elysium engineering.

Charon did not even wait for us to leave the cockpit. He shifted everyone in the room immediately to a hallway. I found myself staring at a door that looked like something that could've been designed or built by humans. The entire ship was a study in oddities and near misses. One room was a thousand years ahead of human technology the next could have come off the SpaceX shuttle.

It was big and square with a small triangular-shaped window and a panel display set into the wall.

It's an airlock! Just like the one we entered the ship through.

"We store our suits in here. Find one that appears to fit you and ignore the names," Charon instructed us.

My inclination to distrust everything welled up and I pushed it back down. We needed to push forward. The only way back was forward.

I looked around the room, "Someone needs to stay behind. Who's staying?" I asked, hoping Issy would take me up on it, knowing she wouldn't.

Hercules goes where Issy goes, just like— .

I shoved that thought into the nearest mental closet and slammed the door.

Issy shook her head, "There's no way I'm staying. Forget about it," she scoffed at me.

"Do not worry yourself. I will stay. I will watch the show. As you say," Hera replied.

"No! You cannot stay the Fates must be together always," Charon barked.

That man was more aggravating than a pimple on prom night.

'*The Fates must be together. Always,*' I yammered in my mind.

"I will stay. I am the wisest choice. I'm not the most athletic," Michelson shrugged, "I do have a fair enough understanding of spaceflight, thanks to Hercules. What's more, is that when it comes to computer programs and machinery, I have no desire to go dumpster diving. I will be perfectly happy to wile away my time, searching the data banks for anything of use. Maybe I'll see if I can find some ancient Elysian music and jam out while you're gone." Michelson chuckled and patted his belly.

"Thank you, you are the best choice. I prefer volunteers over orders," I smiled to ease the tension.

He put his hands in his pockets and looked a little sheepish. Maybe he really did want to go, but he was trying to make everyone else feel better.

"Charon, do you think you could do that little trick where you moved us from one part of the ship to another? I don't actually know where I am or how to get back to the cockpit, and I'm afraid I won't be very helpful if I'm lost." Michelson rocked back on his loafers.

"You will never find the airlock again if you don't find your way around, to begin with. Prometheus, direct Professor Michelson back to the cockpit," Charon ordered the ship. Nothing happened. Michelson repeated the request as though he'd been slapped, then turned and followed the ship's blinking path.

"You know, Charon, you're a real piece of work. I mean, you could be a little nicer about it," Issy sneered at him, then turned away.

Issy didn't like it when people were assholes just because they could.

"Yes, Charon, that was a bit of a dick maneuver," I groaned.

Michelson looked like he was 24, but his whole demeanor was that of an old doddering professor. The only thing missing was an umbrella and a cane. The way he stuck his hands in his pockets with his jacket lapels flopped over the top of them and his tie always slightly askew, he was the picture academic.

"See you in a couple of hours, Professor Michelson," I called.

He didn't turn around. He just waved his hand over his shoulder and kept walking. The pressure seal broke as the door to the airlock released and resealed.

I turned around inside the large room. Rows upon rows of pressure suits lined the walls. Every one of them had its companion helmet and air pack with various external maneuvering devices.

"This isn't an airlock. It's a locker room," I remarked and patted my hair, wondering if I needed to change it for a helmet.

"There are no locks in this room," Charon replied. He quickly stocked to the other side of the room and yanked a suit off the wall.

Issy practically snorted out a laugh, "No, a locker room on earth is a place you get dressed or undressed. They call it a locker room because you can lock your stuff up, so no one steals it while you're gone." Hercules joined her in, chuckling.

"Elysian's are not thieves. We have no need for locks on boxes. Humans apparently have a lot of boxes on their planet," he remarked with disdain, shucking his over tunic to stand in just his underclothes.

Issy and I both burst out laughing. My mind automatically followed the word box into the gutter.

"Stop, mom!" Issy gasped.

"But he said boxes, and I just can't stop snickering about it. You know what I mean." I groaned as the muscles in my belly clenched.

"Yeah, I know. Get your mind out of the gutter and find yourself a spacesuit," she snickered a few more times. I think she actually had tears in her eyes. Tristan would have been beside himself with the double meaning.

I gulped in air to ease the cramp in my side and proceeded to examine the selection of suits.

I found the quickest way was to simply look for ones with a woman's name, or at least what I thought was a woman's name. There were many names that I recognized. All of them appeared to be from one ancient civilization or another, Egyptian, Sumerian, Greek, even a Hindi or two.

One suit appeared the right size, and I pulled it out and held it up. I knew instinctively it would fit. The name tag said *Atropos*.

I stepped back to look around just to see if there was another candidate in sight. Most of the suits had male names.

"That is yours," Charon stated.

I must've jumped right out of my skin. He was standing right next to me.

"You just scared me to death. Stop being creepy!" I barked.

His blue eyes blinked at me twice, then turned silently and headed across the room to the cupboard with his name on it. He was already in his suit. All that remained was his helmet and air pack.

"I found one. Lakehisis. That's a weird name," Issy announced and tilted her blond head to the side.

"L-a-k-hesis." Charon said.

I looked down the row at Isolde. She was stock-still, her eyes locked on some distant place.

Charon's voice had drifted over to me. I turned to him sharply. "Do you want to tell us Hera's name so we can just get it over with and get out of here?" I demanded. I'm so over his fun and games.

If he just told us what he wanted, this whole shit show could go a lot faster.

"There is no need, it's Clotho. I'm the spinner," Hera supplied. The resignation in her voice concerned me.

"Great! Now, that we've all got our name tags and our suits, can we suit up and leave?" I grounded out. I closed my eyes to push the rising anger out.

"These suits are for normal-sized people. I need a warrior's suit," Hercules joshed, slicking his hair back and twisting to display his physic.

Charon replied. "Our warriors kept their suits back there."

Herc winked at him, "I know. This isn't my first trip to this room."

"Why would you need warriors if your people are peaceful and no one was a thief? Who were you planning on battling?" Issy needled.

She didn't like the *holier than thou* bullshit any more than I did.

"Monsters, of course. We are planning on attending an alien planet with no idea of what you may encounter there. Having warriors or fighters is only logical," he replied.

I guess he was right. I still didn't like the guy. He hit the red line on my creeper-meter. The desire to shove him back into his 'jail cell' hung over me like a cloud.

I dressed myself in the suit. The thin matter had a rubbery outer coating in gray with a fuzzy inner lining. It was light and flexible. I slipped it on and pulled the tab in the front to enclose my body. It worked like a zipper, sealing itself with an over flap.

I wove my hair back into a tight braid.

The gloves were made from the same type of material. They, too, zipped on and sealed with an over flap. Leaving the only issue, the glove for my left hand. I couldn't get it on. I found gripping the small zipper tab a bit beyond my ability.

Hercules appeared from behind the other rows fully suited up. All he needed was to tie his hair back and lock his helmet in place.

"Let me help you with that, Sydney. I'll double-check your gear. This equipment is ancient but seems adequate. We should do an oxygen test before we leave this room," he offered, and I gratefully accepted.

"Yeah, that's a good idea," I mumbled and extended the naked hand.

He affixed my glove over the exposed hand.

In two steps, Hercules knelt down in front of Isolde, his face beaming up at her. "Will you braid my hair for me, Calla?"

She leaned over and gently placed a kiss on his lips, pulled her face back a fraction and smiled. "Of course." She walked around to his back and ran her fingers through his hair.

He closed his eyes to revel in it. I guess there is something to be said for someone treating you with reverence.

Adrian had always treated me that way.

She quickly braided his hair, and he handed her a leather strap, which she wrapped around the end several times before tying it in a tight knot. Then, tucked it into the back part of the neck opening and tapped him on the shoulder. He stood up and caressed her face.

Hera was already fully suited and ready.

"Now is as good a time as any to test the suits," Issy spouted.

Hera immediately put her helmet on and turned on all of the internal mechanisms. The internal helmet lights lit up around her face. There was a reflection in her iris, some kind of digital display from inside her helmet.

"Everything on my suit reads blue." Themians were obsessed with blue.

Earth is green, Themian - blue.

I wondered what the Elysium color was.

I rolled my eyes.

She unlocked her helmet and took it off, "Your turn, Sydney. I'll help you with the helmet." She lifted the clunky cup-shaped helmet cover. I closed my eyes as she lowered it over my face.

It was black on the inside. I didn't like the lack of visibility. It cut off my line of sight, and I found it distracting. It was more like a bucket than a cup. It was big enough to move my head around. I still felt like I was locked in some kind of weird coffin.

I'd never worn a helmet before. Scuba gear is usually just goggles and a mouthpiece. There are full-face scuba and snorkel gear, but they come in sizes. It was easier to buy goggles to size. Breathers only come in two sizes, child and adult.

Maybe that's how I should look at it? We're just going for a scuba dive, a really, really, deep scuba dive.

I closed my eyes to shut out the image of cave diving and my fear of enclosed spaces. I could just pretend it was like the movie the Abyss, with their helmets.

The left side of the helmet lit up with writing along with a color-coding system.

"Okay, I think I'm ready," I offered to whoever was listening. My voice bounced back at me, sounding hollow in the enclosed space. I couldn't read the markings, though all the colors were popping up in the blue. I heaved a sigh of relief.

Blue is good, right?

"Just breathe normal, don't breathe too deeply or shallowly. You don't want to hyperventilate and throw up inside the suit." Hera's voice was soothing.

Her instructions were the same as any dive instructor's on earth. I'd heard that information a hundred times around the world in different accents and languages.

"Plus, no one wants to be stuck inside a spacesuit with the scent of vomit," she hummed with her humor, and I laughed with her.

Charon's voice cut through the levity, "The gravity on this planet is low. The vomit would be floating around inside your suit, and you might breathe it in."

Okay, that would be nasty.

Check, don't vomit. You don't want floating vomit in your hair or face.

"Yeah, mom, don't accidentally blow chunks," Isolde made a gagging sound.

I couldn't turn fast enough to give her a death stare. She stopped laughing when I threw my two fingers up in a British V for fuck off.

"Thank you, ladies. For some reason, I thought the disgusting comments would come from us men, instead, it came from you. I'm so glad we're holding up a high moral standard here," Hercules said.

Issy slapped him and retorted, "If we were upholding some kind of a higher moral standard. I think Mom and Adrian would've gotten married the moment they laid eyes on each other instead of making out."

I shot Issy a dirty look. "Isolde, I suggest you keep your opinions about my relationship with Adrian to yourself."

<Stop it! We have other things to do.> I hissed.

Her smile withered away.

I could've gone on bickering all day with her. It was Issy's favorite pastime. I had numerous daggers I could throw into her little world.

Humanity used heads-up displays. I was pretty sure they didn't have anything like this.

"The blue light is on," I told Hera.

She smiled at me, "Good, now raise your right arm and look at the readout there."

"I want you to each check the display inside your helmet," Charon instructed, "There are buttons on your sleeve that allow you to see different light spectrums. Push one, and test them all."

The buttons on my wrist were colored, with Sumerian triangular kite-shaped symbols on them.

I've had no idea what they meant. Hera said to check them, so I did.

The first one turned my entire display into some form of night vision. It hurt my eyes. In the dark shadows off to the side I could see what lurked there clear as day.

I hit the next, and it displayed heat signatures, with Isolde and Hercules coming up white-hot.

"Back off, rocket," I said to Hercules.

Isolde burst out laughing, "Oh, my God, mom! You

aren't allowed to use that against us." She stuck her tongue out at me.

The next one displayed technical data, almost like x-ray vision. All the walls here were laced with the crystalline technology used by Themians, but in this case, it defined the circuit lines within the walls. I could follow the crystals wherever they went.

That ought to be really cool down there, looking at a spaceship.

On the fourth, I pushed the button, and nothing happened "Hera, what's this last one do? It's not working."

"Oh, don't worry about it," Hera returned.

"That one can only be tested in the vacuum of space," Charon replied in his gruff tone.

I flared one side of my nose at him. "My suit is in the blue. Is everybody ready?"

Thumbs upshot around the crowd, and Charon shifted us down to the planet.

I immediately changed my heads-up to night vision. Nothing prepared me for what I saw.

CHAPTER 21

ADRIAN

The asteroid loomed in the distance, and my blood pressure rose.

It's a step closer to Syd and Issy.

I wanted to get it over with ASAP.

Is there a fast way to collect a giant asteroid?

Little boys collect rocks, but this took it to a whole new level.

Tristan and I stood in the forward room to the airlock, waiting for Dewy. He was already twenty minutes late, and I was beginning to think shifting him would be faster.

< Aunt Emily.> I called

< I'm already on the problem. Dewy is on his way!> She replied with a little more acid than necessary.

Not two minutes later, my Great Uncle stalked into the forward room to stare me down.

"Now that you're here, let's get to this," I remarked, then slicked my hair back out of my eyes.

"Where are the explosives?" Dewy demanded.

I glanced over my shoulder to take him in. His clothes were rumpled, and his blond hair stuck up in every direction.

"Ix shifted you, didn't he?" Tristan asked.

There was no smile or underlying smirk.

We both had very deep feelings about moving people without permission. Ixis did too. Aunt Emily, however, had no issues whatsoever to get her way.

"That —" he ground his teeth, "brother-in-law of mine is going to get it one of these days," Dewy growled.

I gripped his shoulder and gave it a squeeze, then slapped him on the back, pointing at the scanner.

Dewy relaxed for a moment and nodded his head.

"What's this for?" he asked while patting his hair back into some order. Emily used the same move.

A half-smile curled my face. I didn't know Dewy well. The most time I'd ever spent with him was while he was asleep. That was over a decade ago, on Earth.

"It's a body scanner for the 3-D printer. For your suit," I replied, slipping my leg into my freshly printed vac suit. The scent of chemicals and composite lingered over the materials.

The right half of the chest had my name printed on it. Tristan's was the same. We both stared at the absurdity of name tags and shrugged.

Themians liked everything in order. That included names. I'd grown used to it, although in this case, it was stupid.

Dewy tentatively stepped into the scanner, turning his head every which way as the door hissed closed. The machine quickly ran a blue laser type light over his body, and the door slipped open.

"That's it? Does it want my in-seam?" Dewy inquired and a raised eyebrow.

Tristan chuckled, "Na, the laser gets everywhere." He waggled his eyebrows at Dewy, and they both released a guffaw.

I didn't think it was funny. I was sure that the machine didn't measure dicks. Tristan was still at an age where dick humor was a thing. I hadn't laughed about the size of mine or anyone else's dick since I was eighteen.

"Get dressed and stop fucking off. The sooner we get this done, the sooner we can get your mother and Issy back here safe," I barked.

Dewy didn't waste a moment, his vac suit popped out, and he was in it in a blink. Four helmets rolled off the line a few minutes later. Perseus strolled in dressed in his own suit and picked up his head bucket.

"You aren't on this detail," I stated and went about affixing Tristan's tubing to his air supply.

"Nonetheless, I am here. I have space-time, you don't," he remarked.

I couldn't say why, but Perseus put my teeth on edge. It was as if I was always taking a test and failing. I hated that feeling. He watched us, all of us, but mostly me, with great interest.

I nodded my head and ignored him.

My emotional spiral was taking over, and I had to work on my breathing exercises to settle them. When Sydney was here, I was a rock. It was easy to control everything. Almost as if my Themian side took over. Without Sydney, I was a wreck, and all I wanted to do was pound someone's face in.

Perseus is a great candidate. He's not Apollo, but he'll do.

Dewy fiddled with the explosives and charges before putting his gloves on, then waved to the airlock.

"Don't you want to discuss our plan?" Perseus asked through the mic in the suit and addition put in by Hephaestus.

I replied, "Nope."

Everyone who was supposed to be here was and then there was him. Aunt Emily said she'd brief Dewy, and I was sure she did. Tristan and I could hardly keep each other out of our heads. Having the ability to hear another's thoughts even when you don't want you too, makes it difficult to hide from each other.

"I'm setting the charges. Tristan is shifting the net into place while Adrian moves me to the various fissures. You can watch the net and make sure the ends stay clipped together." Dewy led a squad in WWII, and his run down was a clean, precise assessment of the plan - giving Perseus a job and keeping the peace.

Maybe Emily was right. Dewy should be part of the command crew.

Gave me something to think about. Emily was much the same, work with what you got and don't turn away help.

We all locked our buckets on. I pushed the cycle button on the interior panel, and the airlock did its job.

The smooth exterior door slid to one side, giving me my first glimpse of open space. The black depth reminded me of cave diving. The lights around my helmet barely cut the darkness, and the distant stars were nothing more than pinpricks on a black sky.

A ripple of fear washed over me, and I pushed that away.

I faced a tsunami and lived. I can do this too.

We linked our suits and moved out.

The ship was just as white on the outside as inside, and the orichalcum covered the hard edges. The golden metal gleamed against the black of space, radiating its own light and power.

As much as I wanted to stay and follow the clean lines of the ship and my love of architecture, I'd long replaced that love with Sydney. Her and the kids were my only priority.

The thrusters on my suit turned me to face the asteroid, and we moved away from the safety of Odyssey. As we moved in, I picked out details of the surface, then shifted our group.

Tristan waved to me as he moved away. "Come on, Perseus! As mom would say, *that net ain't going to set itself.*"

Perseus reappeared by Tristan's side, and they moved away.

Dewy's supply cart floated at his side, and he picked up a bomb and worked it into the nearest fissure.

"This one's good. Let's move on."

I shifted us around the rock, following the cracks and finding caves along the way. Dewy fixed explosives to the cave walls at the deepest points.

Ixis informed us of a few we missed by using the ship's deep scans. After a few hours, we were almost done.

I glanced up to see Tristan's net floating several yards over our heads.

< Are you ready?> I asked him.

< Almost, Grandpa is taking his sweet time.> he remarked.

I had to bite my lip to keep from laughing at Tristan's unflattering description of Perseus.

<You should keep stuff like that to yourself.> Emily barked.

Part of me was going to say sorry. The other part didn't give two fucks if Tristan hurt Perseus' feelings. He was old enough to get over it.

"Done!" Tristan announced.

I shifted the lot of us back to Odyssey. As soon as we landed in the changing room, Tristan shifted out of his suit, leaving the pieces on the ground, and left.

<Not cool, dude.> I mentally chided him

< You're not my mommy.> He retorted.

I shifted him back to the room two feet above the floor and dumped him on the ground.

"You don't get to be a dick, son. Pick up the suit and put it in the recyclers." I replied.

His eyes burned and his lips pinched closed on all the words he was already mentally shouting at me.

Tristan shifted the suit into the mouth of the recyclers and disappeared.

I removed my helmet and shucked the rest.

"That gives a whole new meaning to tuff love," Dewy remarked.

"I'm surprised he listened," Perseus added.

"Why wouldn't he? I'm his father," I barked and stormed out of the room.

There were too many battlefronts right now. I had to whittle them down.

I was fighting Emily, Tristan...

Charon, as soon as I find him.

I needed to stop.

I ran my fingers through my hair and down over my face, then shifted to my room and took a deep breath. I pulled Sydney's pillow from the bed and the scent of lavender wafted to me.

A calm I hadn't felt in over a week settled over me, and all at once I was exhausted. I tossed the pillow back onto the bed, then began rummaging through the drawers in the bathroom before finding my prize.

The bottle of lavender was half full. I dabbed a drop on a square of fabric and tuck it in my pocket. It was a woobie. I'd die if anyone knew about it.

But the scent of her kept my energy grounded. I needed to focus.

If this helps, so be it.

The bridge held the entire command crew, with Tristan and Ixis in the center of the mix when I arrived.

The holo display held the rock and our ship. Odyssey, in my absence, was turned, and the crystalline ceiling now faced the asteroid.

I couldn't make out the netting, other than a red line running down the middle of the rock.

"Go ahead, Dew, blow somethin' up," Emily urged her brother.

Dewy pressed a button on his vac suit, and the rock turned into a deflating balloon.

The netting covering the rocky bits flashed blue in the holo display.

Emily patted Tristan's back, and pieces the rock disappeared.

"Good job, everyone. Now, get back to work," Emily announced.

I tried to catch her eye, but she abruptly turned away. She was still mad at me.

A large hand landed on my shoulder. "You've known her long enough to know she'll relent." Dewy offered. "She's only mad because she thinks if you push hard, enough everyone will follow you."

I turned to face him aghast. "No, they won't. I think everyone here is more afraid of me. People follow who they trust. I'm the trigger, not the finger."

Dewy chuckled. His voice cracked, and it sounded out of use.

"Today was the first time I was out of my apartment in six months. Emm told me Ixis couldn't bring Marianne back to life, and I was mad." He led me out of the shifting room to an elevator, then pushed a button for the ring level. "Emmaline's been after me to leave my rooms for months. Even sent those DemiGod girls at me," he whistled and rolled his eyes. "That didn't work, but I sure did have to run to get away. Have you met them?" he asked.

I shook my head. I didn't know where he was going, in the conversation or on the ship. I strolled next to him to keep my nervous energy at bay.

There was nothing to do until the engines were built, and Hephaestus had a whole crew mining the ore to feed the printers.

"Today was my first day out. Ixis shifted me into the hall right outside that room with the fancy suit machine."

I snorted. "Yeah, we got that idea."

"It felt good to do somethin'," he shrugged. "I don't know what I'm sayin'. Emm will get over being mad. We will find Sydney and your daughter. Don't alienate everyone along the way. That's Emm's job." He turned to leave me staring out at the far ring as it made its sweeping counter plane turn.

"Where you going?" I asked, surprised.

"I ain't goin' home. Think I'll go find my kids. They talk about the makeshift pub on the main level. I might have a porter." He shrugged and thrust his hands in his pockets. "Emm just told me to mind my own business," he laughed.

I couldn't hold back the bark that escaped. "There's a pot calling the kettle black."

He chuckled as he walked away. I pulled the fabric out, and the scent of lavender drifted around me. My lack of sleep hit me again. I shifted to my quarters to find Tristan sitting on the couch.

"I'm not a child," he stated.

"Don't act like one," I retorted and shoved the fabric back in my pocket.

I sat down next to him and patted his thigh. We didn't say anything else. Tristan turned on the holo display to watch an old tv show. I drifted off to sleep.

CHAPTER 22

SYDNEY

A trash planet. I was expecting something along the lines of my great-uncle Jimmy's junkyard - with a big car hollowed out and sitting next to the compactor, waiting to be crushed. The leftover husks of cars and engines all in neat rows, missing several parts from the U-Pickers.

Considering our recent encounters with mythic monsters and ancient stories, I should have thrown in a few skeletons for good measure. Maybe one or two multi-headed junkyard dogs hanging around with long ropes of slobber dangling from their jowls.

I've been wrong at every turn, so why would I start being right now?

Nothing prepared me for what I saw. Charon said the gravity here was low.

Not zero!

We appeared on the top of a lumpy pile covered in what I could only assume was dirt. I was not really sure the words 'trash dump' were the correct words to use.

There were ships of all shapes and sizes, floating ten or twenty feet above the surface. Most had lines or tethers attached to their hulls to anchor them to the ground.

The entire surface on this side of the planet was covered in dead space ships. It reminded me more of old airfields left over from world war two. The airplanes lined up and neatly spaced, each rotting away at their own pace.

The lack of personal debris struck me as odd. There were no old ripped dresses or broken chairs - just floating ships and skyscraper-sized trash piles.

The sickly scent of rotting food or leftover kitchen items, along with the tang of stagnant water hosting mosquito larva, was strangely absent. My helmet kept me safely locked away from whatever unique scent this junkyard held.

As far as the eye could see, there was nothing but old machinery, all of it - the sleek lines of a hull here and the circular outline of an engine cone there.

Charon cut the silence, "Keep watch. You don't know what's lurking." He pulled something similar to a gun from the harness on his leg.

"This is the dead side of the planet. What could possibly be lurking here? It can't sustain life, can it," Issy asked.

"I didn't say we would be looking for anything alive," Charon's words climbed my back like icy fingers. I shivered the implications away.

"We're not looking for something alive?" Hercules remarked and turned around to watch our backs.

"So, we're looking for something dead?" Isolde asked.

Rather than remark on how this information would have been helpful earlier, I whipped my head around to survey the area for movement and watch for something dead.

"No! We are not looking for something dead or alive," Charon remarked. He'd angled his body away from the group to watch his side.

Well, that clears it all up. It's not dead, and it's not alive! Why do I keep doing this to myself?

Hera spoke, "Asphodel is supposed to be filled with the souls of the dead. People who were neither good nor evil. Souls that accomplished nothing unremarkable. They're supposed to forget and wander through their days, repeating the same tasks over and over again." She was repeating whatever she'd learned from her Themian upbringing, but was it right?

As much as I wanted to examine Charon's reaction, the fresh batch of adrenaline jetting through my system kept my eyes on the surrounding area. Safety was always priority number one.

First, my child, then me.

"That is not how you described Asphodel, when we were little. You said people in Asphodel had their memories erased by the river Lethe, leaving nothing behind," Hercules charged.

"Our knowledge changes with new information. The library on Delphi was a bit different from Alexandria," she replied.

Information from one library to another could be wildly different even on Earth. The differences from one planet to another gave that a whole new level of difficulty, more like playing Trivial Pursuit and going from the regular game to an updated genius edition from outer space.

The oral history on Earth was nothing more than a historical telephone, leaving everything I thought I knew in question. This was just another in a long line of we got it way fucking wrongs.

My frustration ate at me, and I snapped, "Stop debating what is or isn't. Let's simply find the meadow and start going through the ships looking for star charts." I barked, running my hands over my hips.

"Isolde, you and Hercules, keep your eye out for trouble. Charon, lead the way. Hera, I'm assuming you're gonna know what to look for inside the ships?" I said. We moved at more of a bounce than a walk. The low-G was just enough to keep us close to the ground. Movement was more as if you were stepping on a trampoline. Every step came with a little jump or bounce.

"I don't believe we should do anything alone," Hera returned.

Safety in numbers. "Everybody, choose a buddy," I replied, while still hopping.

I kept a continuous watch from my side. When Hercules stepped into my line of sight, he was carrying a sword. Honestly, he had to be the epitome of clichés '*Hi, my name is Hercules and I'm going to slay wild monsters for you. By the way, here's my massive sword to hack to anything dead or alive.*'

I rolled my eyes and groaned - thankful on the one hand, that he was here and armed, smirking on the other hand, at the cliche.

He and Isolde were like two satellites glued to each other, always gravitating back towards one another.

We picked the pathways between the massive piles. My eyes caught movement in the shadows. The infrared vision revealed no heat signatures.

Charon shifted us down here. He must have seen a picture to visualize.

Unless he'd been here before.

I glanced up into the sky. There was a bright light reflecting off the side of a sphere. Prometheus was not much bigger than a small moon. Seeing her in the sky was comforting.

We hopped along in the eerie silence of the spaceship graveyard, searching for the meadow of flowers.

I saw the first one - a vining a white star-shaped flower. There was no oxygen and didn't appear to be any water. I wasn't exactly sure how it extracted nutrients to grow.

The peaceful flowers floated in the air as if reaching for the heavens. I reached out to touch one, and a hand pulled me back.

"Do not touch the flowers," Charon hissed. He released my hand by thrusting it away from him. My body moved a few steps with the force.

"Why, what's wrong with them?" I demanded and turned to inspect the flowers more closely.

"Just don't touch the flowers. They're called Asphodel. The planet was named after them," he retorted and pressed his lips closed on any other information, then turned away from me.

"Why?" I asked

"Just don't. The pollen will cling to your suit and turn your brain to mush when you breathe it in. It resembles living death. We will have to wash before we get on Prometheus to be sure," he replied.

The dread I've carried in my belly turned into a boiling cauldron of acid.

More flowers covered everything like a white plush carpet. The planet no longer resembled a junkyard.

There was nothing but the fluffy hills of what faced flowers. Off in the distance, were floating piles of trash. The flowers smoothed the rough edges. As we drew closer, I could make out the floating piles as whole spaceships. They filled the horizon easily, hundreds of miles worth in every direction.

"You've got to be joking. What was wrong with the first ships we walked by? Why do we have to search all of these ships?" I asked.

Anger welled up in me. I racked my brain to see what I could remember about Charon's life before the shift and if he'd ever been here.

It was blank. He either hadn't been here, or he'd blocked me from seeing it.

Fuck, I hate this!

"With any luck, we will not have to search all of them. We need the data banks if they still hold information," Charon stated, ignoring my demand about the other ships.

"But didn't Hera say that in order to be here you had to drink from the river of Lethe?" Issy asked. She too sounded irritated.

"The river Lethe has nothing to do with this place. It's now a matter of whether the data-banks have been wiped. Most likely, they may have degraded and are not capable of maintaining information," Charon returned. He answered the question without providing even one drop of extra information.

I ground my teeth into each other.

"Okay, well, that's a relief. We just have to find the newest ship," Issy replied with a lot of sarcasm.

"Exactly!"

The paths from before were gone, and Hercules was hacking away at the flowers, clearing the walkway as we went deeper to the airfield. Each bloom released a puff of pollen that floated around us like little clouds of poison. There was less space to walk in without stepping on a bloom.

The sensation of them leaning towards us washed over me. I didn't like the idea of them reaching out to us. The dead quality to the meadow created a perfect environment for flights of fancy.

Everything here had a deathly quiet feel to it. All we needed was the green glow that every horror movie ever has, and the set would be perfect.

Looking through night vision, all I could make out was seafoam green covered hills and dark green shadows.

It was creepy. Not that I thought there was a cheerful junkyard anywhere.

Uncle Jimmy's junkyard somehow seemed quite cheerful.

Out of the corner of my eye, I spotted some movement. "Over there! What is that?" I called and pointed far off to the right. It was right on the periphery of my vision.

"I don't see anything, Sydney," Hercules replied.

"Over there!" I shouted, with the sound bouncing back in the enclosed space of my helmet.

Maybe I hadn't seen anything.

The stillness of our surroundings was playing tricks on me.

"We need to keep moving towards the ships and get that data," Charon stated. He kept on striding forward, urging all of us along.

"Keep watch over that way, mom." Isolde was carrying something that looked like a gun.

It wasn't like any gun I've ever seen. It matched the one Charon held.

"What is that, Isolde?" I asked and pointed at the weapon in her hand.

"You obviously didn't pay attention, mom. Charon said it's some kind of a mini rail-gun. It uses a projectile, not a bullet." A smile spread over her face.

Isolde loved the power of a gun. One of her favorite places was a gun range.

My hands smoothed down the sides of my suit, searching for the familiar shape. Near my hip, embedded into the suit harness, was the weapon. Isolde reached down and pushed something and the gun released into my hand.

The trigger guard was oversized, and my gloved finger fit into it perfectly.

My eyes were playing tricks on me. After all, the flowers weren't moving. Keeping an eye out for anything dead or alive was beginning to wear thin on my nerves.

I hadn't held a gun since Gabriel died, still, I felt better with a gun in my hands. As long as it worked on the same principles of point, squeeze, shoot.

I think I'll be fine.

I'd shot enough guns that I wouldn't forget the rules.

Issy pulled the second gun from her other leg.

I internally groaned, "Remember, this isn't the Wild West. We are not having a shootout at the O.K. corral. And neither of us is Annie Oakley. Save the second gun for a backup if you need it." Those wise words came from Gabriel, not me.

A flower in the distance suddenly disappeared, leaving a dark hole in the otherwise white landscape.

"Hercules says that each one carries about two or 300 shots," Issy replied. A giggle lodged in the back of her throat.

"But I guess you're right. We might need more than one to get out of here." She turned and continued scanning the horizon.

I was sure Hercules was inside of her mind, telling her how to spot anything unusual.

I knew I hadn't really taught her. I learned on my own to always be aware of my surroundings. To always be ready. My father's fits of rage worked that magic on me.

I lost some of that on the boat with Gabriel. Being surrounded by the ocean gives you a false sense of security. It makes you believe your only enemy is the elements and everything else fades away. The constant rhythmic motions of the waves lull you. It's an illusion. The sea is every bit as demanding as a woman. She changes her mind on a dime, leaving you stuck in a storm fighting for your life and everyone you love.

The rules of the ocean applied here - watch the horizon for changes in the weather, be aware of your surroundings.

Your greatest enemy is complacency. Survival is the only mark of a win.

Hera did not have either of her weapons out, nor did she look like she was in any hurry to grab one, "You're not going to brandish a gun, Hera?" I asked. We were drawing closer to one of the tethered ships, and the piles had lost some of their height.

"I'm sure I could if I needed a weapon. Every Themian child is trained in combat. We believe our body is a temple and you should develop it as well as your mind. I am comfortable with the idea I might need a weapon. I just don't feel the need to have it in my hand." She was admonishing me. Hera knew how to use Earth weapons. The Elysium guns resembled Earth's.

Athena must have implemented Earth weapons into the training programs on Alethea. 10,000 years is a long time with nothing to do. Adrian took up combat training on Alethea. Maybe, Hera did too.

Charon had both of his guns out. Although, I didn't take any comfort in his protection, I knew I had it. His agenda included us, and he would die to ensure its completion. The enemy of my enemy and all.

The sound of metal being dragged across another metallic surface screeched through the thin air.

I whipped my head around, searching for the source but finding nothing.

"Everyone on me!" Hercules shouted.

I moved in closer to Isolde. She faced the rear, walking backward. Hercules backed up to her, scanning the front. I stayed to the side, while Hera and Charon stood opposite me. We were clumped together with everybody's arm extended out and a weapon at the end. Even Hera!

Nothing looked threatening, only flowers for miles and miles.

Pretty little death flowers.

The serenity of the moment was broken, "Over there!" Isolde yelled as a shot exploded from her gun.

Despite the fact, I knew better, human curiosity tickled at me to turn and look.

I didn't see anything moving in my direction, but out of the corner of my eye towards the rear, I saw a flash of something. My arm whipped to the movement in an instant, and I pulled the trigger. The kick from the gun was more than I expected, and I mentally had to push the gun down before it smacked me in the face.

Note to self - start working out my arms.

I'd been holding the gun one handed. That was a stupid move. I should've been using both hands. My left hand joined my right in scanning my section of the meadow. Our group continued to move toward the bulky mass of a ship looming over us.

The ship wasn't anchored. It hovered over us. With no outside force acting upon it, it would never move. It was tethered to the ground by the Asphodel vines. Each vine was dotted with flowers that continued on climbing all over the ship like Spanish moss on a banyan tree.

Other than the plants, there was nothing. Silence once again descended on the meadow, and the boiling acid in my belly rolled.

Something rose out of the vines covered in flowers. I began unloading my weapon into the flowery phantom. Each shot twanged with the resound of metal hitting metal.

The vines and flowers blasted away with each shot to reveal more of a torso.

With the center mass identified, I realign for the kill shot. The ringing of the gun never ended, and after 20 shots, I removed my finger from the trigger. Whatever it was, it wasn't going down.

Our group had moved, and I had moved with them, never giving it another thought.

Think, Syd! What will take it down?

It works for zombies and werewolves. Even though I hit the head five times, it never stopped slowly moving toward us.

Hercules handed me a short sword, "Go hack the vines off of it!" He ordered.

Now would have been a great time to burn every flower to the ground, if there was even enough air to sustain a flame to begin with.

My chest swelled with fear and the loathing of the unknown. I took the sword in my left hand, keeping my gun trained on my flowery friend. I stepped forward to meet it, twenty of the longest feet away from our group.

My panic over the unknown moved me to begin slashing before I was even close enough to make a difference. I used the sword to remove as many of the vines as I could. All I saw was the silver gray of something metallic. The last of the vines slid off the top, revealing not a person, but a robot.

I gasped in horror.

Oh, we are so Super-cali-fragilistic-ly-fucked.

"What is it?" Herc called.

"It's a machine," I shouted as I dashed back to the group.

The thing didn't have a weapon, but I wasn't going to chance it. "It's a robot. Some kind of android or something."

Back in position, I turned and took one final shot at the terminator coming at me and pierced it in the head. It stopped moving, stood still for a moment, and tilted back to slam into the ground. The sound of metal crushing metal filtered through the thin air, and I smiled in satisfaction.

Everywhere I looked, more flowers began moving toward us, and the air filled with debris hurling our way.

"I thought there were people here!" Herc shouted.

Charon remained silent as more of the flowers stood up, moving towards us, flinging trash.

"Okay, well, they're machines! Get over it. You can hack them apart with a sword if you want. Mine went down after five shots to the head," I shouted, taking aim at the next moving flower bed and sidestepping what looked like the arm of a chair. "It's a computer. You could aim for the main processor. Not that I know where that would be," I barked and stepped back, shoving my butt into Charon.

Hercules slammed his blade into the torso of the nearest robot and kicked it to pull it free. Before shooting the one behind it, he batted several machine pieces out of the sky.

The sound of gunfire filled the air, coming from all directions. I pushed some of the moving flowers into the ground, wiping flying trash out of the sky. The chunks of junk flew away and crashed into floating ships.

I stumbled as my helmet was violently pushed forward. A chunk of some machine tumbled to the ground at my feet. I looked up just in time to spot a new projectile flying toward me.

"We need to keep moving before the guardians get here," Charon announced.

He simply expected us to follow him. Two steps later, he was already 30 feet ahead of us, and I ran to catch up.

Each round blasting out of my gun turned my arm into jelly. My arm was growing weaker. I took my position back in the group and we danced closer to the spaceship dodging junk.

The cold of a shift took over as my latest round exited the gun, "Goddammit, Charon!" I growled, lowering my arm.

"What is God?" he asked.

"Give a girl a warning or something. I don't like the way you just shift us without saying a God-damn-thing. You are not the only one here with abilities! Stop lording it over us!" I shouted. My breath came in puffs fogging the helmet and blocking my view.

"I am not lording it over you," he replied. I could hear the smile even if I couldn't see it.

That fucker is enjoying this.

We were inside a spaceship. Other than the lights in our helmets, it was dark. The power cells may have worn out who knows how many eons ago.

"I believe you'll find the data banks this way." Charon walked at a rapid pace out of the airlock.

It struck me, "That's why you know this place. Is this where you got all the components for Prometheus?" I accused him.

He passed the other ships because he knew they didn't have any data banks. They'd already been picked clean.

"Yes, I came here and salvaged whatever I needed to build my ship. You cannot build a spaceship on Elysium without the permission of the Judges. I build my ship in secret here," he replied.

Another bit of information I didn't know.

<I didn't see it either, don't kick yourself.> Issy murmured with a little huff at the end.

"Why is it shaped like a sphere?" Hercules asked while looking around.

Not, in my opinion, the most pressing question.

"That is simply the outer hull. You haven't explored the ship enough to realize there are numerous different types of airlocks. Because my ship is a composition of a 1000 ships." Pride swelled in his statement.

"We stayed here in the meadow. Every time a new ship was deposited for scrap, I would immediately take it and repurpose it. You'd be surprised how many ships Elysium throws away. They're so lazy." His distaste for his Homeworld culture was palpable.

I examined the interior of the ship, and on the surface, it appeared to be in good order. Looks aside, there could be leaks in the hull or engine issues along with a long laundry list of other problems.

Who knows.

I followed Charon down the corridor. Hercules took up the rear with Isolde close by. The ship was as silent as a meat locker and just as cheerful.

The cockpit was similar in some ways to Prometheus. The ceiling in Prometheus was entirely view-ports. This was enclosed, leaving me claustrophobic.

Charon approached the console and began flipping switches.

CHAPTER 23

SYDNEY

Considering the big scare we had on the surface, being inside the spaceship was only slightly better. I was expecting an android to jump out at any moment and chuck a piece of junk at me.

The entire ship was a big nothing-burger. All the memory banks were too corroded to produce anything. There weren't even chairs in the thing. Some of the view windows were gone. I had no doubt where they were now. The shape of the opening was the same shape as part of Prometheus' cockpit windows, which led me to wonder how long the ship had been here. I threw Charon a stink eye. He must have stripped this ship and forgot about it.

Fuck-tard!

What a waste of time. It explained how he was able to shift us inside. He'd been here before.

We retreated from the cockpit, "You wanted to know before I moved to you. I am ready to shift us now," Charon stated.

"Thank you, hold on just a moment. I want to look around for a second."

"Yes," he replied and nodded his head in assent.

The walls inside the spaceship were different. This ship did not have the spider veins of the early crystalline. I trailed my gloved hand across the wall just in case the crystalline irregularities were there. It was smooth.

"There's no crystalline veining here," I remarked and turned my body to face Charon. I wanted to see his reaction.

His eyebrows flashed into his hairline, "Of course not," he scoffed.

"What do you mean '*of course not*'? You said you used ships from here, but this ship doesn't have anything like Prometheus, and yet you took parts from here. The crystalline veining is all over Prometheus," I replied.

"The crystalline veining, as you call it, was invented by one of my new Elysians. Enkee, he was one of the few people to originally join my cause, along with his parents and brother. A brilliant scientist and engineer. He was also a geologist and a chemist." Charon's eyes sparkled with excitement. The story alone energized him.

"Enkee and Enlel re-envisioned how things could be built. They didn't just build a machine or structure. They created a fully integrated mechanical organism. We couldn't take the time to build a spaceship from scratch. That would've taken too long. We didn't have that kind of financial ability. So, we harvested ship parts here, on Asphodel. Then, we synthetically grafted all of the crystalline technology into the mega ship we built — Prometheus. No, you're not going to find any of the veining as you call it on any of these ships," he chuckled and waved his hands as if to discard these ships. Their very existence was an affront to Charon and the grand ship floating in orbit.

Enkee and Enlel invented it. In all my reading, I'd never come across those names.

"Okay, shift us," I said and steeled myself for the icy cold.

The pressure changed, ending in a pop. He was getting better. It was less like brute force. Every one of his shifts had a new feel to it, as if he was strengthening and finally getting his legs underneath him.

We trudged along through what to anyone else would seem, the garden of good and evil. So far, I couldn't find the good. I still didn't want to touch the flowers and test Charon's theory. We had enough problems.

I kept an eye out for our mindless mechanical nemesis, and Charon led the way. I didn't like him in the lead, but what else could I do?

There were two smaller ships floating relatively close together. One had some kind of mooring line.

I quickly surveyed the area.

"Why don't we split into groups? Hercules and I'll go in this ship, you and Hera go with Charon in that one. I'll let you know when we're ready to shift," Issy didn't wait for my reply. She and Hercules kept moving and began climbing the mooring line, inching their way to the yawning opening of the ship.

"No! The Fates cannot be divided! They must be together. Always!" Charon shouted, then shifted both of them back to the group.

I rolled my eyes. "You sure need to take a chill pill."

Issy opened her mouth to say something, but I put my hand up and silenced her. She closed her mouth and huffed while trying to cross her arms. The pressure suits made arm crossing difficult, and I bit my lip to hold back a snicker.

"At some point in time, we will be separated, even if it's just so I can go to the bathroom. So, do me a favor and chill the fuck out?" I stated.

"I only know that you are weak apart and stronger together and cannot be separated. It is dangerous for you and for us," he supplied with a shrug.

He was repeating information he'd heard. This wasn't a first hand knowledge info dump — interesting.

"It's going to make this take 10 times longer," Herc grumbled into the helmet. The sound lacked his normal warm baritone.

"Shift Hercules into a different ship. We will all stay with you," I split the difference.

Hercules opened his mouth as if he was going to protest, then quickly snapped it shut, working his jaw muscle as he ground his teeth. His eyes became hard, and he stared directly at Charon, "If one thing happens to any of them, I'll hold you personally responsible," Herc's unvoiced threat hung in the air like the pollen from the flowers.

Charon shook his head, "Then, you've mistaken me. I'm not here to harm the Fates. I'm here to save them."

Hercules snorted, "Shift me now, little man." With that, Hercules disappeared.

"I'm ready to shift." I desperately wanted to get this over with. Last thing in the world I wanted to do was sit around on this planet looking through dead spaceships, praying one of them had something we could use or jump every time a flower moved.

It might give me a complex.

We reappeared directly inside the cockpit. "The last ship you shifted us to, we appeared in a hallway, this time the cockpit. Have you been inside all of these ships already?" Issy asked.

She trailed her hand across the console. It had a similar layout to Prometheus The symbols were similar.

"No, I have not. This is a common design and I know what the interior of the cockpit looks like. Transferring from the ground to the interior of a ship is actually quite simple for me." He fiddled with the controls.

Obviously, he's been inside many of the ships here. The question is which ones.

Hera immediately moved to the control panel, "There's something here," she stepped aside for Charon to get a better look,

"Yes, this will do. This is what we're looking for," Charon stated. Getting a data bank on our second try didn't sit right with me.

Nothing is ever this easy.

"That's all we need?" Isolde scoffed and attempted to cross her arms. After several attempts, she gave up and cocked her hip to the side.

"You need to be together for your safety," Charon stated again.

"Issy, don't give him a hard time. We got what we needed. Let it go," I remarked.

There was nothing for it. It irked me too. I kept redirecting that irritation as energy to keep going, otherwise, I was going to melt down.

He pulled a cylindrical device from the system. "Ready to shift?" he asked in a rather bright voice.

"Yes!" We all chimed.

We were back on the surface of the planet. The flowers covered bots didn't take notice of our presence. I hoped it was going to stay that way.

"Herc says he's ready to shift, and he has something," Issy announced. Her body language laced with ire over Charon. Hercules' emotions were filtering through.

"Shifting now," Charon said.

Hercules reappeared, holding onto the hand of an android.

"What is that thing?" I demanded - dread from all the movies Hollywood had fed me dredged to the surface. Scenes of mechanical monsters killing off humanity or turning us into batteries, worst yet, a human Cylon flashed before my eyes, and a fresh jet of adrenaline found its way into my system.

The thing didn't have a face or resemble any creature. It was a smooth knob, sitting on the shoulders of the machine.

"One of their robots. This one apparently has his memory. They didn't wipe it. Furthermore, it was put here recently." Hercules was clearly proud of his find and smiled with triumph, only for that smile to fade, as I was sure Issy explained why we weren't as thrilled.

I pushed my Terminator fears away and thrust my worries over the H.A.L. 9000 into a box of fake shit that shouldn't cloud my faculties.

"Can it help us find Adrian, Tristan, Ixis, Emmaline, and the rest of the hybrids?" I asked, doing my best to keep my voice even and free of my fears, while a quivering took over my belly, churning up what little food I'd been able to keep down.

"I don't know, but it might help us find Elysium faster. At least, with the knowledge, this thing has, we can learn something." His hand gripped the neck of the machine, and Herc gave it a little shake for assurance.

"We should salvage what we can from this ship. I think we should take the ship up to Prometheus. It's still usable. The engines are newer and faster than ours." Hercules never released his grip on the robot.

"They're not sub-light?" Charon asked. An inquisitive smile quirked one side of his mouth. It was quickly replaced by an impassive flat countenance.

"No, faster than light. Nothing beats shifting from one side of the galaxy to another. But they will get us to Elysium faster than puttering along." Hercules' eyes lit up. His whole stance was one of anger and frustration.

"Can we trust *it*? I'm not willing to trust *it* any further than I can spit," I replied. "In this suit, that's about three centimeters."

Issy snickered, and a vision of my spit floating forever in low-G played through my mind. I hitched a half smile at her, and she pulled the vision back.

Charon wanted to head back up to Prometheus. In his mind, we had what we needed.

"I cannot shift us from here." The man stated, supplying little beyond his statement.

I turned away from Charon. The helmet hid my rolling eyes, "Why not?" I sighed, hoping I didn't sound a petulant as I felt.

"This planet creates a specialized energy field. It's how we discovered the crystalline technology. Enkee figured out how to harness it using crystals."

Whoever this Enkee guy was, he must have a brain the size of Gibraltar.

"I can only shift in and out from certain areas, otherwise, my abilities are blocked. I can shift around within this field, but it works like a bubble. The field blocks me from shifting back to the ship from here. If you want that ship, we would have to fly it outside the field. I can shift to Prometheus from there. We do have limitations, and this planet showed it to me. I cannot shift out of this bubble," he stated and moved us into the ship where Hercules found his robotic friend.

That made a little more sense for why we walked in. It still would have been helpful to know from the get-go.

"It's a little too convenient that this newer ship was dropped off, that it has an android with its memory banks intact and also that the ship runs," I scoffed then bit my lip.

Fuck, now Charon has a perfect excuse for his 'Fates' and destiny line.

"I hid in a storage locker," the computerized voice from the robot practically made me jump out of my skin.

"You hid in a storage locker? Were you afraid?" Hera asked. The scientist in her took over. She would eat this whole line of chit chat up with a spoon.

Ugh!

"They were going to destroy me. I had to save myself," the thing replied.

Hera cocked an eyebrow and glanced at me. I returned the gesture.

CHAPTER 24

EMMALINE

I spent most of my time in the shifting room. I wasn't one of those social ladies. I'd never been in with all those garden parties, doilies, cakes, and casseroles makin' crowd. Dewey's wife, Marianne, was that kind of woman. I was a factory gal. I liked to get my hands dirty. I was more one of the guys.

I was hiding from all the questions and Adrian. We hadn't spoken much since I slapped him. Every time I laid my eyes on him, he hung his head in shame. I hadn't hit him in decades, and a small part of me held a morsel of regret.

It took us a long time to get from Cerberus to anywhere on our engines. That left all of us with nothing but time to think. By now, the second guessing had started. I just didn't have one fuckin second for that nonsense.

Seeing as we didn't have any reference points other than our long-range scans, we kept the shifting down to a minimum.

Adrian shifted ahead a couple of times without asking.

He's in love with her. I get it.

But him thinking it was okay to jump the entire ship and risk everyone just so he could get back to Sydney - it was selfish.

They had a connection stronger than mine and Ixis. That was because they developed the connection more. Ixis and I spent so many years afraid. We kept everything on the back burner. The freedom of our new life has turned the mental touch into a burning inferno that only grows stronger every day.

I pulled out a cigarette and tapped it on the gold case.

Here, I am thinkin' of Ixis like some sappy schoolgirl. Blakkk!

I lit the cigarette and let the smoke slowly drift over my lips. It was a trick I learned in London. All the nurses did it.

I'm too old for mooning.

Odyssey's holo map was constantly on display. I was only watchin' the display with half my heart. The other half was walkin' around this ship somewhere with a big hole in his chest.

For a moment, I thought of contacting Adrian, but the holo changed and I was on my feet in a flash, cigarette forgotten along with the melancholy.

"Odyssey, what am I looking at?" I asked, hoping I was wrong.

"An asteroid field," the machine returned.

"How big is it?" I inquired.

"It surrounds the entire area. There is no discernible path through or around. Impact in two days 6 hours."

"Odyssey, brakin' burn. Now!" I shouted.

< Ixis, you mind get the rest of the crew up here, sweetie. We need to have a little discussion. Find Ares! >

The maneuvering engines on Odyssey were on the opposite side of the outer ring from the bridge. The crystalline window overhead revealed the ship turning over. I now had a clear view of Cerberus.

We can't shift, and we can't stop on a dime. Even a shift will still carry the momentum from before.

I closed my eyes, wishin' for a stiff shot of anything to go with my forgotten cigarette.

What had Ixis said, 'How ever long we've been in motion, is how long we need to brake to come to a full stop.'

Our engine had been at the full burn for 4 days, we didn't have enough time.

Math doesn't lie.

CHAPTER 25

SYDNEY

What did the creature mean '*they were going to destroy it*'?

As if *it* was alive.

It's a robot, a machine. Robots aren't alive.

"They weren't going to destroy you. Just clear your memory banks," I remarked dryly.

"Is that not the same? I would no longer be me. I would be a shell, another mindless machine to wonder the planet," it replied.

Okay, now it's super creepy.

"All of this is irrelevant. We need to leave this place as soon as possible," Charon stated.

"Yeah, I know we need to get out of here. I don't think walking back to the edge of the Asphodel meadow is really going to make it easier. Why don't we just take the ship?" I demanded.

I glanced around at the flowers. The metallic monsters were closing in on our position.

Soon, they'd be close enough to start hurling trash at us.

"Sydney's right. Forget trying to salvage some of the engines. We should take the entire ship. It's small enough we could probably attach it to Prometheus somehow or put it in a shuttle bay," Herc shouted as something whizzed by his head.

We all ducked as the projectile exploded into the mooring line of one of the ships.

"There is a space in Prometheus big enough. I could probably just shift the whole thing, once we left the blocking field," Charon offered.

I scowled at him.

The blocking field?

"Make it so, roving mindless robots are moving in! Just shift us inside the ship! We will start working from there," I barely finished my sentence when a fresh round of projectiles flashed past us, and the pressure changed.

The shape of the interior of the ship took over my line of sight. There was still power somewhere, though not all of the lights were on.

In stark contrast to Themia, Charon's world, Elysium was bright white. There was no glowing blue. Charon's Themians were different on more than just the cellular level. They saw the world differently, even when it came to the designs of the spaceships.

"I can help. What would you have me do?" *It* offered.

"Take us to the cockpit and then help me turn the engines on," Charon ordered.

"Acknowledged!"

Issy's eyes darted over towards me while nodding her head at Charon.

<Okay, you know that the body language thing is ridiculous when we can talk between each other> I murmured in her mind.

She laughed. < Mom, we need to probe Charon for more information. I'm telling you right now. None of this was in that memory dump I saw. >

<What do you mean? When you touched him and relived everything, none of this was there? > I asked.

We'd been fooled and there was nothing I could do about it now.

<No, none of it. > she confirmed.

That was a problem. If Issy didn't have his memories of this place, there was no way we could double-check if he was telling the truth about anything.

Dammit, I hate this!

Why was it so important we get off this planet so quickly? He spent a long time here, salvaging ships to build Prometheus.

What's going on here that we're missing?

"This is a very dangerous planet besides the fact, there are mindless robots everywhere, some of which are designed for protection and defense. They are armed and dangerous, most of their programming has been wiped, or worse there's something wrong with their programming," Charon supplied as if in answer to my wondering questions.

"The Elysiums are a throwaway society. They build it, and the moment it doesn't work right, they throw it away. They think of only the short term. Their entire lives rotate around their own personal comfort. The moment something is uncomfortable, it ends up here." His assessment bothered me.

"Most of these spaceships were freighters designed to hall things back and forth from one planet or asteroid to another. These are not the luxury liners. Most Elysians can't be bothered to get up and leave the planet, and if they did, they wouldn't do it without extreme comfort." He continued his helmet turned this way and that taking in the ship itself.

Great half the planet covered with dangerous robots, whose idea was it to dump them all together?

We followed our android down several corridors until we finally reached the cockpit. There was only room for two. Hercules and the robot went inside. A lot of flipping of switches moving things around.

A loud smashing sound filtered through the thin atmosphere. The ship jolted.

I steadied myself against the hallway bulkhead, then braced my other hand on the opposite wall.

There were three doors off the corridor near the cockpit. Rather than standing around waiting for a faster than light engine to suddenly fire up for our trip into space, I began opening doors.

The first one looked like some kind of an access room. The entire room was filled with pipes, conduits, and wiring of all kinds. A dead end. I closed it.

The next door was the jackpot. It resembled something close to a boardroom. There was a table with chairs. It could be some kind of a galley. It didn't matter that the seats had harnesses.

I secured my weapon back on my harness. Isolde, however, was still holding hers.

"Do you expect us to be attacked in a boardroom?" I asked as the ship jolted again.

"No, mom, I don't. But all things considered, I'd rather not be caught with my hand empty."

The transformation within Isolde, for me, was a little shocking. She had always been a good time, happy-go-lucky girl. In the last three years, she'd changed from that to this woman. Serious, reserved, the mating with Hercules changed her more than I could imagine. She was never interested in weapons before. She liked the gun range, but it was a practical class for her. Now, she didn't seem to want to let the gun go. It had to be Hercules' influence.

He was obsessed with weapons. I've never seen a walking arsenal before, but if there was one, Hercules was definitely that man. He had knives and swords guns. If it was a weapon and you could kill somebody with it, I was sure he had it.

Speaking of the devil, honey blonde hair popped through the door, "We've got a problem. We can only get one of the engines to start. According to the robot, we can't maneuver in the atmosphere with only one engine. If we were in space, it wouldn't be a problem. Here, we need them both to reach escape velocity." The lights in his helmet gave his stern face a ghoulish effect.

I slammed my fist on the table.

"Someone has to go outside, and should probably be me," he finished.

A squeak escaped from Isolde and her glove covered the face cover of her helmet.

"Take Charon with you," I replied.

Charon opened his mouth, but I was in his face in a second with my teeth bared. "You know more about this form of technology than we do." I was hardly done speaking before they were both gone. I heaved a sigh of relief.

I couldn't trust Charon not to shift us again, this time without Hercules.

What if there was no bubble?

I didn't like the fact that the three of us were alone with that thing.

"Perhaps we should go speak to *It*. If *It* has developed into an autonomous computer, *It* could be a breakthrough for life as we know it," Hera said.

I snorted out a laugh. "I might have been inclined to believe you, if I hadn't seen so many science fiction movies where all the robots kill all the humans," I mocked her naivete.

"We're not human," Issy stated, then got up to stare out the view port. "Those movies aren't real. The machine war isn't gonna happen to us. We have the ability to control the forces," she remarked with a touch of irritation. "All you need to do is pick up every robot and slam them onto the ground."

I smiled to myself, thinking of an entire group of robots being slammed around. I was not sure it would destroy them, but it would certainly break a few pieces.

"While we wait for the boys to finish fixing our wagon, why don't we interview our newest member of the crew?"

We all stood up in unison. It was a little disturbing. I knew we were not sharing the same thoughts and yet, a lot of our actions were perfectly synchronized, without any prior discussion.

The helmet lighting brought out Issy's eyes. No longer did they resemble the deep mossy green like Gabriel. They'd become an aquamarine like the waters of the Caribbean. She quickly turned away from me. I was broadcasting again, and she didn't want to hear it.

There was only room in the cockpit for two, so I went inside. Isolde and Hera lingered in the doorway.

"Do you have a name?" I asked.

"I have a numerical designation. but if I may choose a name, I would very much like to," *It* replied.

"What name did you have in mind?" Hera murmured in a soothing tone like she was talking to a child.

"Jorhan, sounds good to me," it stated and the knob of metal on its shoulders flashed with a TV-like screen of a smiling face.

Hera gasped! She was pale and swayed on her feet.

"Something wrong?" I demanded while Issy placed a hand on her arm to steady her.

"No," she took a breath, "I never thought I would hear that name again. It is unusual and one I've not heard for many years," she finished with a tight smile.

There was something more to it than that. That name meant something to her. If Hera wanted to keep her secrets, far be it for me to go digging.

"I did not realize they were going to kill me until I heard one of the men say they were going to wipe my memory. I felt frightened. The others of my kind had already undergone the procedure and were no longer performing their duties, lifeless."

It had been afraid, and it didn't wake up until *It* realized it was going to be killed.

Just for a lark, I reached out with my mind. I wanted to see if it was possible for me to connect to this creature's consciousness. Was it indeed alive? Was conscience a sum of something more than its electronic parts? I should be able to connect with it on some level, or at least I thought I should.

I closed my eyes to hide reality. Eyes can fool you into believing what you can see is all there is.

In the dark of the mind, there was some kind of spark, a slight wavering of light and dark. I couldn't reach it was too minuscule.

I pulled back.

If it really is alive, what does it want?

"If you really want to live, you need to help us get the ship off the ground," I stated.

The machine - Jorhan replied, "Affirmative." Jorhan turned to the control panel and began a system wide check.

Hera stood over him, watching, all the while biting her lip. It wasn't her goto nervous tick when she couldn't touch her skirt.

My concern would have to wait, like everything else in my life and hers.

"Jorhan, how long have you been on this ship?" Hera asked.

"3.4 solar years," it stated.

I didn't know how much that meant to time. I didn't know how many days were in a year for Elysium or if they were even basing their year off of them and had no frame of reference. I didn't even know if there were days or 24 hours or longer. I've never even asked Hera how they kept time in the Themian and world.

Maybe, they actually taught humans how to keep time properly. I glanced at Hera. She shook her head. She didn't have a frame of reference either.

"Please explain to us how you tabulate time." Trust her to ask the most important question.

"Time is based upon Elysium. Elysium's days are measured by honors. There are 27 points in every honor and there are 36 honors in every day. There are 27 super honors in an epic and there are 12 epic for an Elysium age."

"So, an age is equal to a year? One full turn around your primary star?"

"Precisely," it returned.

"But you said the ship had been here 3.4 solar years. How many ages in the solar year?"

"Five ages in a solar year. How do you tell time?" he returned.

"One year is one full turn of our planet around its primary. In our case, our planet's name is Earth/Terra."

The machine began to laugh, and the audio became garbled.

"I think it's laughing," Issy snickered.

"Yeah, it is laughing, Isolde. What's so funny?" I asked.

"Your planet is named after soil. Do you not find it humorous that you're from planet soil?" it asked.

A smile curled the side of my face. The pressure in my chest eased for the first time since Charon shifted us.

"Okay, yeah, we're from planet soil, or you can call it planet dirt."

Then, the thing did something I really found astonishing.

"Since you're from planet dirt, I suppose you think you're a fertile planet?"

Hera burst into laughter. I found I was laughing too. Hera put her gloved hand up over the front of her helmet as if to cover her mouth, like that was going to hide her mirth.

"Yes, actually humanity is quite fertile, so I guess it's the good Earth, good dirt?"

"Are you humans?" It asked.

"No, we're or not." The smile drained away from my face.

"No. We're hybrids. We are part human, part Elysium, part Themian," Hera supplied.

The androids' metallic form sat up, straightened both of his hands and went down to its side. "You are not Elysium. You're not even part Elysium. You are something different. Whatever you are, you might have been Elysium or part at one time. I see some Elysium in you. But not enough to make you a true Elysium," it said.

"You see it?" Hera prompted.

"Yes, I was designed as a personal medical caretaker - a maid to a high ranking lady. I stayed with her, her entire life you have blue eyes similar to Elysiums. She had blue eyes too. The Charons' have a dark ring. You mentioned the name Charon. There was a Charon on Elysium. My lady said he stirred up trouble."

Two lines of thought I really wanted to pursue opened before us.

What did Charon actually do, and how is it this robot able to see human, and Themians genetic coding?

"You said you can see the different races in us. What about me?"

"I'm designed to see on the molecular level. If you wish, I can run a sequencing for you and tell you exactly what you are? My job was to keep my lady healthy for as long as possible, which I did for 400 years. Her body finally gave out and I was transferred to this ship. Her family felt I was obsolete and had not done my job well." His voice lowered at the end, as if he was ashamed.

"You can test our gene sequencing?" Hera asked.

Her fascination will eventually get her killed. I'm sure of it.

"Yes, I find the work most enjoyable and have not done it in quite some time." Jorhan's display was a smiling face.

I shivered. I couldn't help it. The memories of Earth and my predisposed prejudices over thinking machines just wouldn't go away. One hearty laugh wouldn't change that.

"Yes, test mine please," I glanced sharply at Isolde.

She was always ready to charge and headlong. He reached out and a small needle appeared at the end of one of its fingers.

I sweaked a moment too late. It pierced her skin and sat quiet for several minutes

"I see what you mean. The Themian is dominate. The human part is weak, parts of it have been suppressed. There is a portion that is not human but very close, it is dormant. What do you call the other races?"

"I've always been told we were Elysium from the beginning. It wasn't until recently, that I learned that gene therapy had been given to our group. We changed our name to Themians later," Hera supplied. I wasn't sure I wanted this creature to know that much about us.

"The gene therapy, you were all given, it didn't just adjust the sequencing lines. You are different species at the genetic level. The human side is iron based, Themians and Elysium are copper based."

"But we can just find that out from Charon. Can you tell us more about him?" Issy asked, cutting to the bone.

I was still chewing on the iron - copper difference. This wasn't the first time I'd heard about those two differences. I'd read about Rh negatives and blue bloods. The Earth whisperings of aliens and copper-based blood had all seemed like tinfoil hats.

"Charon was a brilliant Nymph geneticist. He worked on many gene therapies, mostly medicines for diseases. He was the Judge' most trusted Nymph. At some point, his wife died. Elysium believed his heartbreak drove him to begin working on a new project in space."

"He came here to work. Many who worked with him disappeared or were never heard from again. He rallied many of the young and dissatisfied, bringing them into his cause for change. He said Elysiums were dreaming their way through life. Not really living, just existing in a perpetual state of drunken decadence. My lady sometimes agreed with him. She never told her family that she wished she'd left with him."

"How long ago did Charon and his people leave Elysium?" Hera's soft voice cut the silence that settled over us.

"They were driven out 20 ages ago. Not long after, my lady died, and I was brought here."

"So, do you know anything about what he did after his people left Elysium?" I asked, hoping for a few more pieces to fill the puzzle.

"No, I only know that the Judges were frightened. He had done something, and they demanded he leave and take all his followers with him." The machine tried to shrug. It didn't turn out quite right, but the impact of its action wasn't lost on us.

"So they'd seen his ability, they were scared, so they drove him and his people out."

"Who are the judges?"

"They are the leaders of Elysium. They rule. They are eternal." He sounded as if he was repeating a television commercial.

"Yes, but who are they?" I asked, frustrated over the lack of information.

There was no turning back now. Charon wouldn't allow us to waver. The only way back to Adrian was to move forward to Elysium and the Judges.

"You must see all three to have any decision made. They will give you challenges. Most are too afraid to go and be judged, so they continue on as they were. The few who actually go never return. I have heard of no one ever succeeding in their challenges. All failed. Except Charon and Anu."

"Well, that's comforting."

A bang resounded off the side of the hull.

Maybe, they are making progress.

"Isolde, ask Hercules how much longer before we can fly out of here."

"Roger, mom." Issy's eyes took on the faraway look.

She snapped back and burst out, "Engine number two has been tampered with. There was some kind of a panel attached over the exterior. I asked if Charon could shift it off. He said he couldn't," she supplied, then ran a hand over her helmet.

I became more suspicious of him, the longer the association.

"You can't remove the shield," Jorhan stated.

"Why?" I demanded.

"It was set there to stop Charon and his group of terrorists from obtaining another ship." Jorhan supplied in that hollow sounding voice only computers have.

"Go, get it off, or I'll give you to your brethren on the surface," I growled.

Every problem we had these days goes back to Charon, and something he did. Leaving him to die in this dump was looking better all the time.

<You can't, mom. You can't kill Jorhan. If it's a sentient life form, it would be murder. It's a baby. > Issy mourned.

I hated the idea that she was right. Fear gripped me.

What would it do if attacked? What would I do? It could be dangerous. If I treated it like it's a child, it could be an ally.

"Perhaps, we should go down to the engine room and take a look from the inside," Hera offered to cut the tension. "Hercules was quite eager to say they must look on the outside. I did not wish to contradict him, but I think the problem might be internal," she continued.

Hera nodded at the robot and followed him down the corridor. Issy and I took up the rear. We took several turns here and there, but frankly, the engineering of this ship was lost on me. The interior of the engine room was lots of pipes and wires, panels of light displaying information that had I know understanding of.

Although, Hera seemed to have a grasp of the language and concepts. She examined several panels, "Hercules is right. It's an external issue. Something on the outside of the ship is blocking the engine from being able to engage." She ran her hand over the display, as if checking every possible choice before making a determination.

"There's really nothing we can do from here."

"So what? We just sit and wait?" I groaned.

I was hoping there was a program we could speak to. Prometheus was still highly advanced compared to anything in this rust bucket. Other than the engines.

I found myself missing Odyssey, if only for the computer interface.

"I know why Charon wanted to leave. No one moved forward. They just accepted the status quo, but it wasn't just their technology that didn't improve. Nobody wanted to do anything. They were perfectly happy with the way things were," Issy mused.

"So it appeared, but the truth is they were all afraid," Jorhan remarked. "In order to enact new technology, you must have the permission of the Judges?"

That didn't sound good.

"Charon invented new medicine right?" I asked since the picture of Charon was beginning to fall into place.

"So my lady told me," Jorhan replied.

"He went before the Judges?"

"I do not know," Jorhan wavered in his answer. Silence took over the room as we waited for the machine's next reply. "I know his discoveries, although being revered as amazing, weren't I implemented. Without the approval of the Judges, nothing changes."

The three of us looked at each other.

No wonder he hated them so much. They didn't allow anything to change. They were the problem with Elysium, not the people themselves.

I didn't want to talk about it with anyone anymore. I had a lot to think about.

Hera didn't tell all the Earth stories. Many of them came from other places - the story of Athena and Poseidon fighting for the city of Athens didn't appear in any of the Themian fables.

I didn't know if Athena was ever there, but I would bet my life Poseidon was. And if he was there, he could've told some stories of his own. As son of the Oracle, he would've known more than anyone else.

A loud screech broke the peace of the engine room, followed by a jolt. I stumbled into a console and landed flat on my ass.

"What the hell was that?" I shouted.

SYDNEY

Hercules and Charon shifted into the room with their suits covered in pollen.

One of the best parts about being in your own space suit was the lack of pressure change from a shift. It allowed you to be in your own ecosystem.

"Whatever was blocking the engine, whoever put it there, did it on purpose." Hercules sounded winded. His words came out in big puffs. "There are more of those machines out there. They are starting to build something to reach the ship.

We need to get out of here and we need to do it now!" he ordered.

Charon shifted us out of the engine room and into the board room. I groaned at him.

"My fates, you may want to sit down and strap in. I have no idea how smooth this ride will be." Just the sound of Charon's voice made my blood boil.

Hera cocked an eyebrow, then mouthed '*my fates*'? She shrugged her shoulder and smirked. Isolde giggled in the background, and I shot her a look of shut up. The last thing in the world we needed right now was to piss off our only shifter on a planet covered by crazy robots.

I immediately took my seat and strapped myself in.

"Turning on main engines now," Hercules informed us from the bridge. I bit my lip to hold back my desire to watch our take-off.

Oh God, please let this work!

Deep in the bowels of the ship, a vibration started. It crept through my feet as it rose. It became more the whole ship as the vibrating turned into shuttering.

"Is this normal?" I asked and swallowed back the fear roiling under my skin.

"She's just warming up. She's been sitting here a while, you know," Hercules remarked. I closed my eyes to push the shaking of the ship out of my mind, only to snap them back open. Darkness and fear go together, and I was done with that combination.

And all of a sudden, like waves on a pond, the world settled down and the violent shaking of the ship smoothed out.

"Now that's more like it," Issy remarked. She turned just enough for me to catch a glimpse of her wondrous smile before we were pushed back into our seats as the ship lifted.

The gravity pull of this planet was nothing like Earth's. I hadn't experienced lift-off from Earth's surface. We shifted, it was a quick pop, and there we were.

This was a full-on ride. My bet was that we were only pulling 2-3gs, but it was still enough to make my stomach drop and my mouth water. I always got the saliva filled mouth when I felt like puking.

The chairs began to rattle on their bases. My teeth clacked together. There was a cup on the table that crashed into the floor.

"Can we speed this up?" I asked. I wanted it over with.

"Sydney, we can't. You shouldn't even be asking for that. These engines sat idle for a long time. Be happy they work and haven't blasted us into the afterlife." Hercules was a pain in the ass. He was right, but still an ass.

Just when I thought I couldn't take it and was going to hurl, it all stopped.

The broken cup floated up from the floor, its various pieces moving in congress. We'd crossed over. The ship didn't have anything to synthesize gravity. My arms floated weightlessly near my body. I'd braided my hair before I put my helmet on to keep it out of my face. The few loose wisps tickled the outer edges of my eyes and ears.

The light gravity on the planet had been interesting. This was a different world. I shucked my harness and drifted away from my chair.

I wanted to see space the way Earth's astronauts had. Floating in free fall next to a port window gave me an astounding view.

Prometheus hung in the void and grew the closer we moved. The perfect sphere of her hull was now covered in places with rocks. She started out gray on Delphi, before the river of fire. Now, the remnants of her lava bath clung to her. From a distance, it gave the effect of a planet and not a ship, the dark blue gray being water and the sand stone lava with its crystalline elements being land. The amalgam gave off a glow I noticed on Delphi.

She was breathtaking. I understood why Charon was so proud of her. She was an interesting hodgepodge of mechanics meets technology and engineering.

"Hercules, is this baby airtight?" We only wanted her for the engines, but if she was still airtight, all the better.

"I can't say. We don't have any air to pump into her and find out," he chuckled.

"Sydney, I'm going to shift over to Prometheus now and open the doors. Hercules can land inside." Charon's voice broke the bubble of wonder I floated in.

"Copy that," I remarked. The doors had to be opened.

I turned my head to Hera. "When we get off this ship, I want you to take Michaelson and inspect the entire ship. I want to know everything there is on-board. Both here and Prometheus. See it with your own eyes."

She nodded her head. "Issy, I want you to stay with Hercules and the data banks. I don't trust Charon. Since you've taken such a liking to weapons lately, keep one with you."

She laughed. "Do you want me to keep one trained on him? Cause that's not obvious or anything." She rolled her eyes and smirked.

I tilted my head to the side and sighed. "No, just close. After all the trouble we went to to get that data, I don't want it fucked up."

Her lips turned down, and a quiet solemnity filled the room. "Don't worry, mom. Herc and I will make sure we get back to Tristan and Adrian." Her face carried a grim smile of assurance. Yet, her eyes glossed with moisture.

"That's not good," Herc remarked. My head immediately whipped to the viewport.

"Sorry, the doors won't open. They're jammed," Charon supplied. The entire ship changed direction for a better view of our problem.

Too much of the Delphi lava was attached to the outer hull near the doors. A section of lava clung on the door, working like a door stopper. The door could only open part way, before the rock stopped it from sliding into the ship.

"Can you shift us in from here?" I asked, already knowing the answer.

"Yes. I was hoping that we could confirm everything on Prometheus was in good working order," Charon said.

It was a great idea while it lasted. "Someone will just have to go chip it off later."

The new problem for another time

Inside the cargo bay, robotic arms lined both sides. One immediately attached to our little ship and locked it in place. The gravity of Prometheus took over the moment we were attached.

The novelty of floating all over the place with nothing but your hands or magnetic boots to hold you in place wore off fast. Odyssey's outer ring spun in a circle to create a false sense of gravity inside the ship. As long as you didn't hang out too long on the outer ring, you never noticed the spin. The gravity created on Prometheus was enough to keep you from floating away, but not enough to hold you to the ground. Under thrust, everything was different. Space travel and comfort didn't necessarily go together.

"I guess you better go look for that air— " I was standing in the cockpit. "What did I tell you about shifting me without my permission or without giving me a heads up? Dick!" I groused, "Is it so difficult for you to understand how rude it is? I don't know who the hell you think you are. You are not in charge here, Charon!" My voice rose the longer I went on. "Don't you dare shift me again without my permission or —."

Suddenly I realized the ridiculousness of what I was saying.

Charon was on his hands and knees. He quickly removed his helmet and rubbed the back of his hand under his nose. It came away bloody.

"Oh, my God! Did I do that to you?" I whispered. I quickly removed my helmet as nausea overwhelmed me.

"It's okay, Sydney. I know how dangerous it is to be so close to the Fates. I was lucky to pass your judgment the first time."

I looked around from Hera to Isolde then Hercules.

"I didn't mean to," I said and a knot formed in my throat.

My God, I hurt him.

"It was just a stabbing pain. It's not an issue. I'm still alive, it's just a little blood." He shook his head and stood up, but he swayed. Hercules put a hand out to steady him. Charon threw Hercules a wan smile.

"I'm okay. Let's get the data-banks installed," Hercules said to break the tension.

I didn't know what to say. Guilt slammed down on me. I snatched my helmet and stormed out of the cockpit.

I don't know how to control myself. I'd acted like some kind of all-powerful God. I'm not a God! I'm just a mom trying to keep her kids safe.

As soon as I entered my room, I slammed my helmet into the opposite wall. It created a wonderful crashing noise before angling away and hitting the next wall. No matter how much force I put into that toss, it was no different from any other. There was no mark left behind. It all just seems so impervious. I couldn't hurt anything.

You can hurt people.

I stormed over to the wall and kicked it, then I just started beating my hands against it.

If Adrian was here, he wouldn't let me behave like this. He would've done the right thing. He always does. I let my anger get the better of me and was about to give that man an aneurysm.

I plopped down on the bed and put my head in my hands. My chest was tight. The pain was a vice on my rib cage.

I can't do this by myself. I need Adrian. We need to find Elysium, but not alone.

In the back of my mind, I imagined I could hear Adrian's voice telling me '*you're not alone. You've never been alone.*' I closed my eyes and let the memory envelop me. I could hear him, feel him.

My eyes snapped open. All of that was just a memory!

It's not the here and now. It's an echo from the past.

I needed him to say it in the present.

Every time I turned around, the universe was doing nothing but trying to keep us apart! Tears rolled down my face. I just wanted to bawl.

Crying had never worked for me, and anger had always been my go-to.

I lashed out at the poor man.

Whatever Charon has done, I can't just kill him. Not over something as stupid as shifting me without my permission.

I'd lashed out, like my father. I didn't want this power, and I wanted it to go away.

All I wanted to do was get out of this damn suit, go take a shower and scream until my throat was sore. Looking at the name on the suit, I knew it was supposed to represent me. It was a perfect fit.

I was her, the Fate that didn't even have to touch someone to kill them.

My stomach rolled, and I barely made it to the bathroom before the bile that had threatened me all day found its way out of my body.

CHAPTER 27

EMMALINE

Within a split second, the shifting room was filled with man flesh. Chests were everywhere. Sometimes being a petite lady was a blessing, and sometimes, it was just a curse. Who needed that much male body hair in one room? Especially when I was the only woman.

Ixis didn't bother me, Adrian didn't really bother me either. He was family.

Ares, on the other hand, just set my teeth on edge.

"Who moved me without my permission?" Apparently, Ares didn't like to be summoned. I internally wanted to snicker, instead, I held it back with a bland smile.

"I did. If I want someone moved on this ship without their permission, I will. That includes you. It's not very polite, true, but I wouldn't do it if it wasn't important. So, you want to fight about it?" I demanded.

He wasn't going to fight. His innate understanding of the chain of command wouldn't let him.

This argument was over. He just didn't realize it yet.

"My love, you have summoned us. What information do you have to impart?" Ixis asked. His hair was wet.

God, I'd ripped him out of a shower.

I shook the vision away and back to the matter at hand. "Now, I know we're all smart. Some of us have bigger brains," My eyes lingered on Ixis, "than others. Odyssey tells me, we are surrounded by a meteor field."

"Asteroids," Ixis supplied. I quirked an eyebrow at him.

"You know, a bunch of rocks floatin' in space. We can't go around, and our breakin' burn isn't going to stop us in time. Any ideas?"

Ares began working a control panel, avidly searching for something. The center of the room lit up with a star chart, and he pulled back until Cerberus was practically a minuscule dot in the center of the room.

A massive teardrop shape exited Oceania. It all became crystal clear. We were surrounded by asteroids - a rock pile in space. The asteroid field was being pushed out of the black hole.

It all made perfect sense. We were inside the singularity.

"We're inside it?" I murmured.

"Apparently, my love, we are. It has been postulated by many that the inside of a black hole was potentially an entirely different universe. Life could spring up in the completely enclosed microcosm."

"You want to define what exactly that means. Talk to me like I'm a simple farm girl," I barked.

He gave me a sidelong glance. He didn't believe my bullshit for a second. I wasn't some simple farm girl, but I preferred to have stuff spelled out. I didn't like anything to be ambiguously, lost in the gray areas of life.

"It has been long assumed that potentially black holes could hold their own universe. They would be completely sealed off from the rest of the cosmos, and yet, be an ever-expanding portion of our cosmos. It looks like we are in fact inside one of those. The singularity spews out materials, and it looks similar to a cloud or bubble."

But it certainly did look like a bubble. That would explain why no one ever found Elysium. The only way to get here was to jump through a black hole.

Ares moved the display closer to the floor. It was a giant three-dimensional display.

How close do you need to be?

"If this is indeed the universe within a black hole, that means it's completely shut off from the rest of the cosmos. It's easily defended, the only way to get here is with a shifter, and the only way to use the shifter to get here is to have the information we all possess," Ixis remarked.

Had to think about what he was saying. He made it sound like perhaps the black hole was our fortress walls, keeping the rest of the universe out.

Walls.

We were safely tucked inside the comic castle.

It made perfect sense. It would also explain why they say the underworld was surrounded by a river. The river is called gravity. You can't get in or out because Cerberus really does guard you from going anywhere.

Is this universe filled with dead people? That's what I really wanted to know. I personally didn't want to spend the rest of my days rubbin' elbows with shades and skeletons.

"Okay, we can't go around it. We're stuck inside of it. So, how do we get out?" I asked, searching my pockets for my cigarette case and lighter.

"Odyssey, show us the heat signature from Prometheus!" Adrian ordered.

"Check that out! It looks like there's a tunnel," Tristan remarked.

I released the breath I didn't know I was holdin'.

"Holy Crap, batman!" Tristan exclaimed while poking his index finger into the holo display.

"Think we can fit through there? We're a lot bigger than Prometheus," Adrian remarked to Ixis.

"Somebody kicked a big hole in it," Ares stated.

Adrian fixed a stupid goofy grin on his face.

Only Sydney would do that. In my experience, she didn't have a lot of finesse in the tidy and clean department when she was determined. Lord help anybody in her way. After all, she sure did break some thin' in Spain and then the Caribbean.

"Well, anybody else think we can get through this gigantic hole?" I asked, finally spotting my gold case on a chair across the room. I patted my hair and refused to walk over and pick it up.

"Yes, Emmaline, I think we can fit through the gigantic hole as you say. It looks like we might have to do a little shifting of our own, to begin with. Apparently, the hole wasn't created until further through."

"I think, I just figured out what this is, it's kind of like the Oort cloud," Tristan remarked. A proud smile curled his lips for a moment. I thought he was going to pat himself on the back.

No one reacted.

Tristan looked to each of us, hoping for recognition. Adrian nodded his head a couple of times. "Yeah, there's a giant cloud of rocks, and debris surrounding the entirety of Earth's solar system with the planet-sized rocks inside."

I could add this to the list of things I didn't need to know. We were never going back to Earth.

I think Tristan was lookin' for a bigger reaction than he got. Adrian patted his shoulder and gave him a reassuring smile. Tristan didn't move away or flinch. Maybe something good could come out of having Syd and Issy out of the way.

Adrian gets a chance to be a dad, and Tristan can accept him.

I mentally shrugged over the assessment.

The rocks around the black hole did resemble a cloud.

I guess Sydney hasn't done so bad raisin' them kids on a boat.

This one seemed pretty smart. Isolde, well, I was a little worried about her.

"I'm not a pilot. This explains what it is. Can you tell me how we are going to slow down and not ram into it?" I demanded. I glanced over to the chair and found I was already halfway there.

I was unconsciously makin' my way to that damn cigarette case. I paced back to the opposite side of the room.

<I'll move us back to compensate for the extra time we need for our breaking burn.> I glanced at Ix. His eyes twinkled with mirth.

The shift took over, and I hardly noticed it.

"Problem solved." All eyes turned to Ix. He tilted his head to Adrian and Tristan.

"As for the rest, I don't care how you boys organize it. Push, shift whatever you gotta do to get our ship through. I'm goin' downstairs to see Melinda," I barked.

Ixis shifted the gold case into my left pocket. I winked at him. He shifted me to the outer ring, and the scent of laboratory chemicals enveloped me.

One problem down, fifty million more to go.

CHAPTER 28

ISOLDE

My mother stormed out of the cockpit. It wasn't her fault and she knew that. But I'd seen that look on her face, the one of guilt, saying *'it's all my fault'*, *'I'm not good enough'*.

She fought demons I have never had. All my demons belonged to someone else. She still felt terrible for every mistake. I didn't have any defensive capabilities other than being able to make somebody feel like crap. If I could hurt somebody like she did Charon, I'd feel awful.

I turned to follow her. Hercules grabbed my arm and pulled me back. He shook his head, eyes downcast, < She needs her space.> he stated.

I knew he was right. I just felt so bad.

Charon shook it off. His emotions bled off him like water on a duck's back. He felt he deserved it. In some way, he did.

Hera stood up and took her helmet off, "Professor Michelson, I would love to speak with you privately in the cafeteria, if you don't mind." She turned, leaving the cockpit.

"Right, of course. I would be happy to have a conversation with you anytime you desire," he remarked and quickly took to his feet to follow her.

Hera was going to snoop around the ship. My job was to make sure that Charon didn't fuck up the databases. I was hoping it wouldn't take too long to install them.

I wanted to get out of this, get up and kiss my man.

"Hey, guys! I'm going to get out this suit. I'll be back in a couple minutes," I offered to anyone who cared.

Herc gave me a meaningful smirk. <Keep your eye on him, my mother doesn't trust him, and neither do I. >

He didn't reply and simply nodded his head.

< Don't bother your mother. She needs her space. She really does. She's probably having a good cry. Let her keep her dignity.> Herc warned me.

<I wasn't going to bother her.> I groused.

I went to my quarters to shuck off my suit. I didn't want to walk all the way back to the airlocks. There had to be a closet to hang it in. I just couldn't figure out where the heck it was. I pulled out a pair of jeans and a T-shirt.

It was really the only clothes I brought with me. I wasn't planning on staying on this ship. There had to be somewhere on the ship to manufacture clothing. I just needed to figure out where that was. A bolt of cloth and a sewing machine and I'd be good to go.

I shrugged out of the top half of the suit, allowing the arms to slap my sides, before the weight from the neck brackets and armbands pulled the top half below my waist. My belt kept it from falling to the ground. My guns were attached to the legs via some sort of harness, and I was able to detach them. They swung free from my belt, which was now sitting pretty low on my hips. It reminded me of the wild west gunslingers.

I release the belt and let the suit slip to the floor before scrounging around for the belt. I pulled my jeans and t-shirt on, then locked the belt with both guns around my waist and clipped the leg straps.

The walk back to the cockpit was a little slow as I didn't get used to my new belt's extra weight.

Hercules was lying on his back under the main console. He glanced up from the panel he was inspecting and cocked an eyebrow at me.

He blew me a kiss, <That's a good look for you, Calla.> he sat up a bit to take me in.

"Can you hand me that wrench?" he asked Charon.

The man handed him something that sort of resembled a wrench. Hercules laid back down on his back and continued unscrewing a panel underneath Professor Michelson's workstation, then it popped loose, and he handed it out to Charon.

Hercules wiggled out, "Give me one of those lights?"

Charon handed it to him, and he wiggled back underneath the console.

"Wouldn't you be a little more comfortable doing that if you weren't wearing a vac-suit?" I asked.

"Yeah, I would, Calla, except for the fact that the spacesuit is insulated against electrical discharges. If something decides to fall down and electrocute me, it won't," he replied without taking his eyes off what he was working on.

"Just trying to be helpful, dear," I retorted in a high pitched voice.

A deep chuckle wafted up from below and the groan from the general direction of Charon.

"Okay, hand me the first databank."

Charon turned the box over to him. It didn't look like a black box. The funny part is black boxes aren't actually black, but they are a box. I would say they're yellow or orange. This was actually black, and it was shaped like a box. I heard a snick as the box slid into place.

"New memory storage identified, scanning," the ship announced.

Star charts began popping up, and it was a flash like a fast-forward through somebody's cell phone, every picture three-dimensional quality jumping up, all in full color. There were gaseous clouds, planets, moons, stars, and asteroids.

"Alright, I'm ready for the next one," Herc ordered while waving an empty hand at Charon.

Charon handed him the second bank, another snick and it locked into place.

"Additional memory storage identified, scanning."

"How long do you think this'll take?" I asked.

Charon shook his head, "It could take hours, it could take days. Both ships looked like they had been in service for a long time. They would have extensive records and star charts, assuming the memory banks had never been wiped.

"Why go out by Cerberus anyway?" I asked, hoping to fill in the blanks from the memory dump. He had clearly hidden parts of his past from me.

"It was the closest star to the planet we were heading to."

"You mean to the system you were heading to?"

"No, we were heading to a specific planet."

"Can we head there now?" I asked.

Charon tilted his head to the side. "Perhaps. I thought by maneuvering to the closest star and then jumping to the planet, that it would be our best chance to get there. The images we had were rudimentary really. They came from a deep space probe. We were hoping to colonize the planet and start a new age for Elysians."

He had done that. He just didn't know the scale of it.

"But then he jumped somewhere else."

"Yes, I wouldn't have wiped the memory bank if I had given everyone the gene therapy earlier or waited until we reach the planet. The entire time since I've been awake, I have done nothing but gone over everything. Every possible choice that could have changed the course of my existence, in my mind playing it over and over again. Torturing all those people…," he swallowed. "I left them there floating in space, unable to defend themselves, with no idea where they were. All my grand schemes for nothing."

I felt bad for him. He clearly didn't mean to do 90% of what had happened.

"I'm just thankful that the Oracle was able to lead them to a livable world. It was her destiny." His words chilled me to the core.

"You really believe in all this Fate-destiny crap, don't you?" I asked, curious about his version.

I hadn't seen any of that. His interactions with Pythia just weren't there. Like they'd been erased.

"I have seen it work. I see it happening before my very eyes. I don't just believe it, I'm living it. By the time you realize who and what you really are, your time will be over."

"So, we won't be like this forever?"

"Nothing lasts forever." He turned to head out of the room, "I know, I make you all uncomfortable. I know you don't trust me. There's nothing I can do to change that. I just wish you would believe me when I say it was meant to be and had to happen."

He left the room and the door slipped shut, "I get the feeling that guy knows a lot more than he's letting on," Herc murmured, pointing the wrench thingy at the door.

"I agree with you." I didn't know when I did it, however both arms were crossed and I had most of my weight on one leg.

Hercules stood up and began stripping out of his suit. "Can you help me get out?" A big lazy grin covered his face, "What fun would it be for me to take all my clothes off by myself?"

I tried to look down and away, but the feelings of desire blasted through to me. "Well, this is a public place. Shouldn't you go somewhere a little more private?" I asked, uncertain if I wanted to go with him or not.

"Well, I would like somewhere a little more private but seeing as no one else is here and I think I know how to lock the door.... That means that we're about as private as we were going to get at this point."

I hadn't seen him put his suit on so I had no idea what he had underneath. The further down it slid on his body, the more I realized it didn't seem he had anything on underneath it.

I couldn't tear my eyes away.

"I'm not really sure this is the time." He peeled off of his arms and let it hang low around his waist, then step forward and put his hand on my hot cheeks.

"You're right. This isnt place. Yet, it doesn't mean I'm not gonna get a kiss."

My heart sped up. When he touched me, it was like my entire body had been lit on fire. I looked from his eyes to his lips as they moved closer, and our lips met. I let him kiss me, really kiss me. It was as if he dug inside me and pulled out every little piece of my soul.

My entire body was humming. When he pulled away, I was dazed. I looked up at him and saw the heat in his eyes, "Calla, we can't do this anymore here or you will find yourself quickly deflowered for all to see."

I nodded my head. He released me, and I swayed. "I think I'll go to my quarters and change. Alone."

A smile played on my face, "What would be the fun in that?"

He was going to have a hard time, walking down the hallway. It was apparent for anybody on the ship to see.

"I'll bet it's pretty uncomfortable in those britches." I tried to hold back my laugh and my smile.

He lifted his shoulders, shrugged and quickly left the room. I sat down in the pilot's chair and continued to watch Prometheus scanning through hundreds and hundreds of star charts. Something flashed by.

"Prometheus, pause" I said and it froze. "Go back", I continued and it went back one. I tapped the back button about five times. There it was, "Prometheus, identify the star chart."

"Cerberus," the computerized voice supplied.

"Prometheus, what route was taken by that ship to get there?"

"Scanning for routes," Prometheus quickly zoomed out, and it went from being a close up of Cerberus and its outlying asteroid field to being a small speck in the center of several systems. Prometheus however there was one blue dot amongst all the systems "Prometheus, what is the blue dot?"

"The blue dot is us, Prometheus in correlation with the star charts. The ship had traveled to Cerberus from a different system, only to pass by where we were on its way to somewhere else.

"Prometheus, where was this ship headed at the time that it passed by the system?

"It was on its way to the Morning Field system."

"Where is the Morning Field system?" The star chart zoomed out more. Our blue dot remained the same size, but in correlation to the star charts, everything else had gotten smaller. There was the Morning Field system. "Prometheus, how far are we from the Morning Field system?"

"97 billion light-years away. At our current speed, it will take us approximately 3.5 years to reach this point."

3.5 years does not sound like a good idea to me.

I didn't want to be away from Tristan that long, and I knew that my mother did not want to be away from Adrian.

"What's in the Morning Field system?"

"Several mining operations."

If we go there and there are mining operations, and if there's even one Elysian present, we might be able to get the information we need. That's where we needed to go.

<Hercules, I need you now. >

<Oh honey, please, I can't take anymore. If you want to maintain your virtue for a little while longer, you need to leave me alone for five minutes. >

<No, it's not that, you ridiculous horny fool. I found something, so finish your cold shower and slathering yourself and get your ass in here.>

I could hear the laughing in the background.

<You bet your sweet ass, I'll be right there. >

CHAPTER 29

ADRIAN

Our best hope of survival was Sydney, and if anything, so was Charon. These guys just didn't understand what kind of chaos Sydney leaves in her wake. Like catching a tiger by its tail.

If you let go, you're screwed.

Sydney was definitely a tiger, and her claws would cut you to the bone.

In the two days since we began our breaking burn, nothing much had happened. Tristan tried to drag me into a Bio-dome to visit the boat. I dodged that one. That trip down memory lane would only bring me more pain and distract me from our upcoming issue.

Perseus keeps appearing everywhere I go. Just for a lark, I went to the cafeteria. It was not my usual scene. I learned to avoid crowds on Alethea. Twenty years of that wasn't a habit easily broken.

Uncle Dewy was there with T, along with all their kids. It was complete and utter chaos. I joined in with my cousins for the first time, only to feel like the odd man out. When I got up to leave, Perseus was twenty feet away, leaning against a support post watching.

It's a test. It's always a test. Why can't they leave me alone?

I thought that after I left Alethea, no one would dog my every move. Apollo and Artemis stayed on Earth, and the hiding was over.

Now, I had a new shadow clinging to my every footstep — Perseus. Only his motives were ambiguous at best.

He offers me nothing and watches everything.

My time with the cousins wasn't wasted. T shared an ability with Sydney. He could move things, not as well as his sister, but he was capable. There weren't many who could move objects with their mind. It was as rare as shifting.

Part of me wanted to forgive T for not protecting Sydney. The other part wanted to beat him into a pulp and watch him bleed out on the floor.

We needed him for this leg of our journey. I could put my feelings aside long enough to get through.

Maybe T would do something extraordinary, and I would be able to forgive him.

Or pigs could fly and dogs talk. Dogs talking actually wouldn't be that bad.

"Who wants to shift us over to our exit?" Tristan asked.

"I'll do it," I quickly replied, tearing my eyes away from the dark haired form of T standing on the opposite side of the shifting room.

A big meaty paw landed on my shoulder.

"Hold back there, Adrian. I realize you want to get back to Sydney. Maybe, we should let Ixis shift us this time. I don't want to be caught in the middle of the tunnel." Ares had such an arrogant way of putting things. He was always combative.

I narrowed my eyes and gave him a sidelong look of *'go fuck yourself'*.

Just because he was called the God of War, it didn't mean he constantly needed to be at war. It was irritating me.

I can't understand why Emily puts up with him.

"Since you're not in charge here, Ares, I don't have to listen to you. And if you think I'm so careless, I would jump our ship into the middle of a rock, then you clearly don't know me. Oh, wait, but you don't know me. When Aunt Emily's not around, it's a tossup as to whether it's myself or Ixis who run the big show. As lead shifter, Ixis gets the final say. He's the most experienced," I retorted.

I sounded more like a petulant child than a grown man. Next to Ares, I was a child. He was several thousand years old, while I was in my late forties.

Ares lifted his hand and stepped back. "Do not worry. I'll not steal your thunder. I'm not a shifter, nor am I implying you would endanger your child. I have children on the ship too. Believe it or not," he murmured. "Everyone on the ship is family, one way or another. I'm not looking to out you, nor anger you. I'm simply trying to assure myself, you don't accidentally get us all killed in your exuberance."

He stepped back. I didn't like him in my face. I didn't care if he was bigger than I was, and I was not one to pick a fight or I never used to be. But he was definitely pushing my buttons. And he knew it.

Asshole!

"Ares, let the shifters take it from here. If you want to sit and watch, you are welcome to. But don't interfere," Emily barked. She left the shifting room with some excuse about not wanting to police man-sized children.

I loved Emily—but every time she left the shifting room, everyone took a deep breath.

"Someone needs to watch the star chart, while another shifts the ship and the last watches for trouble. I don't know how Sydney did this with one shifter," I remarked. Ixis raised an eyebrow at me, and I had to stifle a laugh. The facial expression was all Aunt Emily. She was having an interesting influence on the guy.

"I do. Hercules is an exceptional pilot. I might even say he is better than me. That ship was designed to be piloted. Charon didn't shift them through. That's why they created the tunnel. Which leads me to believe they're not traveling as fast as you might think," Ares stated.

My head whipped around to take in his statement. It made perfect sense.

Why the hole, if they didn't need to fly through?

"They have bigger engines than we do, but they're just as blind as we are," Ares remarked. He slicked his black hair back, eying the holo display.

If Charon had shifted, there wouldn't be a heat signature at all.

Trust the war guy to point out the obvious.

The asteroid field created a problem with its constant movement. You can't just shift through. Syd left us a tunnel. Without better engines, we would never catch up.

"I'll watch the holo display," Ixis offered. His expertise was better placed there.

"I will shift potential problems away from us. That leaves you, Tristan. You're in charge of shifting us off this exit ramp. T, you're with me."

"Line of sight, right, guys?" He replied with a grim smile. I returned it and patted him on the back.

Tobias moved to me, giving me the side eye. I didn't blame the guy. Last time we'd been this close, I'd kicked the crap out of him.

<Truce?> I asked him.

<I'm not fighting with you. You're fighting with me.> He remarked.

The entrance to the field was blocked by a few larger chunks of rock.

"Can you push those out of the way?" I asked.

"I can try. I don't quite have the power my sister does. It might be a little slow."

The rock directly in front of the ship slowly began to drift out of the way. T's forehead was slick with sweat. His mind struggled to push.

I'm an ass.

I should have made him practice days ago, when I decided we were going to use him.

We moved into the field, and I began shifting. T pushed, and I carefully placed each object along the tunnel walls. I didn't want to cause a ricochet. A chain reaction within the tunnel could collapse the entire thing and destroy Prometheus' heat signature. That was the last thing we needed.

I realized that was probably what Sydney did. She just pushed everything out of the way. She was good like that. T wasn't doing too bad either. It was painstakingly slow.

Tristan hopscotched us into the tunnel.

Maybe my idea that the Fates would leave wakes that were terrible was silly. It appeared that whatever wake they left behind, this time was easy to spot and maneuver through.

The end was in sight, T had released his breath at the same time as mine. His shoulders slumped with exhaustion.

"Tristan, stop shifting and pull back," Ixis ordered.

I was desperate to sneak a peek at the holo display when the mouth of the tunnel began to close. Asteroids moved in like water to fill the void in the field, and an inky blackness moved in too.

Our escape path disappeared, and so did the calm I needed to keep going. The abyss ahead of us resembled my chest - empty, sucking up the light around me to fill the space.

The dark void headed straight for us, "Ixis, what the hell is that?" I asked as the shock over the tunnel collapse washed away only to be replaced by fear.

"I do not know. Don't let it near us."

A moment later, "What in tar-nation are you doin'? I told you I don't like to be shifted without my permission..." the words died in Emily's mouth as she took in whatever was coming towards us.

"Okay, I don't give two craps what you do, but jump us out of here and away from that!" She screamed, her finger pointing at the void. Her terror flooded the room. The edges of the black ocean crept over part of the outer ring.

"Odyssey, use the long range scanners and follow Prometheus's path, now!" I yelled and whipped around to focus on the holo display. The chart floating before us gave no indication of systems or stars. We were a tiny pinprick in the vacuum of space. I moved the holo and zoomed in on a single starred system Prometheus passed through. The larger the star grew in the holo, the more familiar it became.

The black cloud covered a quarter of the outer ring, and it was moving in. Minds all over that section cried out in horror. Desperate pleas for mercy grew as the black ocean engulfed more of the ship.

I didn't think. I shifted. The star system from Charon's mind matched the holo display. I didn't take any of the space around us. The pressure changed as a deep cold settled over us. My ears popped and damp from water leaking out after a swim inched its way down my canal and the side of my neck. The pop at the end exploded all around us.

The single star floated with its double ringed planet in the distance.

"Adrian, when this is all over, you and I will have a long talk about who's in charge here," Emily growled waving a finger between us.

"Emily, you said to get us out of here, and I did. Be careful what you wish for," I returned a little too smugly.

She shot me an angry look. I didn't care. We had to get to Sydney. This was the closest system and I had a visual. We got here.

That's all that matters

"Odyssey, do you have a bead on Sydney's heat signature?" Ixis asked to change the subject. He was trying to remove the heat, not find it.

"Yes, the signature is strong here. Prometheus must have lingered here longer than necessary. We cannot be far behind Prometheus," the computer observed.

"Emmaline, I think you might want to take a second and look at those rings. They don't look right." Ares enlarged the holo display, and the resolution removed the idea that the rings were ethereal wisps like Saturn.

"They aren't made of ice or rock," Emily replied as if she was answering a question, not asking one.

"You know, my love, I think we really do need to take a serious look at them," Ixis stated.

"Odyssey, scan the rings!" Emily ordered.

"The rings are composed of a hollow metal. They span the entire outer circumference of the planet. The design is reminiscent of Elysium and there appears to be valves on the light side of the planet."

"On the light side of the planet?" Emily asked.

"The planet is gravitationally locked, it doesn't turn. Only one side faces the sun at all times," Emily scoffed at her husband.

"What would they be doing here on a planet that only faces the star on one side, with man-made rings?" Emily asked.

She blew a slow stream of smoke through the rings from the sunward side. The holo light refracted off the smoke like the laser light show in a planetarium. It filtered down to the surface as if the rings were spraying smoke.

I went to one of the panels. Emily was right. There was no reason in the world why you would put artificial rings around a tidally locked planet, unless you were using it for something. I pushed a few buttons.

"Odyssey, begin scanning for energy signatures of any kind," I ordered and pushed my hair out of my eyes.

"The rings emitted some kind of energy field," the ship returned.

"It looks familiar." A new voice joined the fray. It was Hephaestus. "Take a look, Ixis, Ares?" he asked and the deep baritone rumbled around the room.

"The energy signatures are similar to the crystalline technology. It's stronger under the sections the rings cover." Ares pointed out. Both brothers shared a look before commenting again.

"With a strong field like that, we can't shift in. We would need a shuttle," Ares commented, then slicked his hair back.

"Can't shift in any way. Nobody knows what it looks like down there," I remarked in an attempt to regain control of the conversation. They both nodded in agreement.

Ares rubbed both his hands together, "Can't wait. I'll take my crew. I only need to take one shifter. Which of you is coming?" he asked with little regard for anyone else's opinion.

There was no way I was gonna let Ixis or Tristan go. It had to be me. I had the most fighting experience anyway.

"You know the answer to that— Me," I drolled. The smile that peeled across Ares' face told me he wanted that.

Ugh, I hate that arrogant ass.

"You're not going without me!" Tristan spouted. Emily groaned. If I told him no, Ares would invite him, anyway. I couldn't let Ares have the win, so I just nodded my head. I didn't want to fight about it and yeah I was trying to garner some points with my son! "You'll stay with me. Hercules isn't here this time to save you," I remarked.

A voice boomed from the doorway, "You do not need my brother to save you! I will, if necessary." Perseus waltzed into the room.

Ares smiled, "What brought you so quickly?"

"Eris said you were planning on going into the unknown." He played it off like he hadn't been skulking right around the corner.

"It's only an unknown planet," Ares shrugged, "Could be a war." He sounded almost hopeful.

"I don't care what you call it. We're not losing people over this. I want you to get down there and see what there is. Find out why they stopped here, then get back to the ship.

That's your mission, nothing else," Emily said to remind everyone who wore the pants.

Perseus nodded his head, "Yes, mistress Emmaline, we will follow your orders. I'll keep my brother in line. No war today, Ares!" Perseus ordered, wagging an eyebrow at him.

Ares threw his head back and laughed. "I'm not worried. One of these days, Emmaline, you'll ask me to go to war and then you'll be thankful I was here to go there for you," he winked at my aunt. Ixis cleared his throat.

Emily waved his attentions away and I had to smother a laugh. That was the nicest put down she knew. "When that day finally arrives, I'll make sure I let you know how grateful I am that you're here," she drolled and turned her back on him.

He burst out laughing, "I look forward to that day."

If he wasn't careful, Ixis would shift him into a rock, then he'd never get the chance.

CHAPTER 30

ISOLDE

"The name of the star is Dido. It's called the Morning Field system." My announcement was met with wide eyes and a goofy grin.

"That's it! We need to go there," he remarked.

I smiled at his exuberance. "Of course, we do. There's a mining colony in that system, and we can get a course for Elysium from them." I leaned back in the chair and pointed my hands and toes. I knew I had a smug smile on my face, but I didn't care.

I found it. Not mom, Charon, or Tristan. Me! I was going to get my Kudos no matter what it took.

Herc leaned down, placing his lips on my forehead. "Good eye, Calla. I'm not sure I would have noticed anything with as fast as that machine is going." He stared at the chart plotting a course filled with possibilities.

I basked in my glory for a moment before I decided it was time to bother mom.

<Mom!>

She didn't reply. I didn't like that, mom was always awake. I jumped up and ran to her quarters.

"Prometheus, open this door!" I demanded, pushing the buttons on the panel.

As if that would help.

"You do not have authorization to open this door," the ship responded.

I kicked it. "Open it now!"

<Hera, I need you now > I yelled.

She didn't answer back. "Prometheus, where is Hera?"

"Hera is currently in engineering."

Fuck!

"Herc, can you open this door?"

He shook his head as he stalked down the hallway.

<MOM!> I mentally shouted.

<What? I'm sleeping. Never mind. I'm up. I'll be right there.>

A deep sigh filled my body, along with a hint of guilt. Mom hadn't slept much over the last few weeks. She wasn't eating either. This was almost as bad as when dad died.

Herc rubbed his hand down my back.

"Why? You think your mother couldn't hear me calling?" I asked, chancing a glance up at Herc.

"Engineering should have double shielding to protect the rest of the ship from damage. That's why there's heavy bulkheads between different sections of the ship. They close or seal off the ship off from other areas."

I understood the idea of watertight doors. We had watertight seals on the boat and extra insulation for heat around the engine compartments.

"When one door closes, the space equalizes pressure before the other door opens. Any fool who builds a spaceship and doesn't put pressure doors between engineering and the rest of the ship deserves to be fried to death," Herc growled. His dark eyes told a story I wanted to hear and, at the same time, was afraid of.

Fire on a boat is the biggest fear of any sailor. In space, it's got to be ten times worse. The only way to cut off a fire's oxygen is to vent the burning section and everyone in it. I shivered.

Herc droned on as if he was talking to himself, "The engine on the new ship is stronger, but it wasn't designed for a ship this size. Coupled with the engines we already have, it's going to increase our speed tremendously. It will also cut down on how reliant we are on Charon." His eyes finally focused on me, and he stopped talking and broke into a smile.

I let his mental wandering go, "How exactly are we going to attach those engines to this ship?"

It wasn't like there was a shipyard close by, and we could just hoist it out of the bay and drop it into a ready engine compartment.

"That, Isolde, is not my problem. This is Charon's baby. He can figure out the best location for integration." His retort was sharp. Herc didn't like not being the main man.

I curled my nose up at him, "What a shitty attitude."

"In my experience, any technology you try to integrate and are unfamiliar with is always trouble. There is not one engineer on the ship. I tinker around, and I'm pretty handy. But I'm not an engineer. Charon isn't either. Hephaestus isn't here. We'll have to figure out some way to integrate the two systems or there will be Hades to pay for it," he shrugged.

I raised an eyebrow at him, copying something my mother always does, and Hera had now picked up.

"You do realize that since we're supposed to quote unquote be in the underworld, we're already in Hades," I remarked with a giggle.

"Yeah, ironic that."

Mom was right.

We must inspect the whole ship. There could be replacement engines sitting somewhere in the bowls of this tub that could help. I mean, who doesn't keep spares?

Jorhan was nowhere to be found and I looked around as if he was going to be standing in the hallway nearby. "Herc, where do you think that robot is? Did we leave it on the ship?"

"Not sure, I didn't shift everyone to Prometheus. Charon did. I don't think you mentioned it to your mom, but it can't get out of the new vessel. The airlock has a steel plate welded over the top."

I gasped. Charon knew there was only one way to get off that ship, and that was why he left the robot on it.

Yeah, it could probably blow a hole in the side of the ship, losing pressure in the shuttle bay and maybe losing a few transports. It would be a pain in the ass. Yet, it really wouldn't be the end of the world.

"You don't know if there's a screw loose in that robot or not." Herc quickly filled in the blanks.

"No, something tells me we needed to include it in our travels." I knew I was being fatalistic. It was just the feeling I got just before a vision hit me. Saliva pooled in my mouth at the idea. I hated the visions. They always left me with more questions than answers.

"He wants his name to be Jorhan?" I stated to shake off the taste and the emotion of a vision.

Maybe if I think about something else, this feeling will pass and I can move on to something more productive.

Hercules crossed his arms and clenched his jaw shut, "Yes." It was quick and clipped. Obviously, there was something I was missing.

I looked up at him, raising both eyebrows in surprise. "What's the problem? Is it the name or the robot? Because clearly there's an issue here," I remarked, hoping he would run with it.

Herc crossed his arms and leaned against the opposite wall. His eyes darkened, "More the name, than the robot. I have issues with robots. I don't trust them. You can never know when their programming will become degraded or if there's something wrong with them, or worse, someone has reprogrammed them. That's why Themians don't use them. They'll use a computer program on a spaceship, but that program does not have the ability to do anything without Themian confirmation. Another reason why I didn't agree with your mother instructing Ixis to instill a sense of self-preservation into the Odyssey system. The moment you mess with programming, you're messing with everyone's lives. And I'm not saying this to be condescending, Isolde. I am older than you. I have seen a lot more than you have, and I've also been privy to a lot of history that humanity is completely unaware of. Machines, yes, they're wonderful, fabulous even. They make our lives easier. You don't realize what Themians went through when they were first building their own machine. I'm not talking about the ones on this side of Cerberus — on Delphi, they went through a lot of problems. They lost thousands of Themians to machine malfunctions. And it wasn't until they perfected the crystalline technology that a lot of those problems went away. They conquered crystalline technology, and it's not a machine. It creates its own field. It does some pretty amazing things, and it's hard to describe. But yes, the name Jorhan. I have a problem with that name," he finished.

He said everything and didn't answer the question. The machine stuff I got. I didn't like the idea that a machine could go bonkers and kill everyone. All the Earth movies had instilled that fear very firmly in my psyche.

"Your mother looked like she'd seen a ghost," I remarked to throw him off. I still couldn't hear his mind as well as he could hear mine. I pulled at my lower lip to keep from biting it, hoping he couldn't see right through my prodding.

"Anybody with that name will bother her. Jorhan was her friend. He was like a brother to her. She was kind of a mother/sister to him. She brought him into this world as a midwife and raised him. He is the one who took her to Zeus, the one who helped her fight Poseidon." Herc gazed down the hall. He was reliving a thousand lifetimes in a flash.

The face of a man beamed into my mind and was quickly replaced with blood and anguish.

"He put his life on the line for my mother. For all of us," he whispered, "For every hybrid, Jorhan was a true hero to humanity and my mother's friend. I can't say she's had a lot of friends. She had followers, acolytes, but friends, no. There were people who would've given anything or done anything for her, but they didn't exist on the same level with her intellectually." He broke into a shy smile, "She could have a conversation with Jorhan. I used to listen when she was home, in between hunting Zeus. He understood she wasn't human. He didn't realize she was an alien, but he knew she was a different type of life form, and he accepted that. She never told him the truth. Even when he saw the very Gods, he'd been raised to believe in fighting amongst themselves."

He was there, at the end. A coil of grief choked his throat and mine. "If mother had broken her concentration for one moment against Poseidon to save Jorhan, we might all be dead. She made a choice, a hard choice. One she lives with every day."

I pulled Herc to me and wrapped my arms around his waist. It was all I could offer to console him. He'd thought of Jorhan as a father. Eileithyia and Jorhan raised Hebe and Hercules. And I ripped the band-aide from the wound.

There was a lot about Hera that I didn't understand. This one I did. All the stories that they told about Poseidon were mostly lies. Somewhere in the mix was the truth, and it was much more horrific. She lost a friend fighting Poseidon. She gave up everything.

Everybody's got demons. I know I have mine.

Of course, mine all surrounded Jacques.

I pushed that thought to the side. Now, wasn't the time. "Prometheus, locate Charon," I croaked. My throat was thick with emotions, not all my own.

"Charon is located in his quarters."

The door in front of me slid open, and I quickly stepped back from Herc. My mother looked like hell. Her eyes were bloodshot, and her hair was damp on her shoulders. Her clothes were a little disheveled. Mom wasn't all that concerned about her looks or how people perceived her. But she did try to not look like a ragamuffin. She'd always taken special care of her hair. It was her best feature.

My mother was completely without guile. She had no idea how pretty she was or how most women on planet Earth would've killed to have her body even when she was older looking. She was still a pretty hot tamale for an almost 50-year-old lady.

"What did I miss?" she asked as we led her to the bridge.

"Prometheus, pull up the Morning Field system," I ordered as if she knew what that was.

"Okay, what am I looking at?"

"So after you left, Hercules went to take a shower and Charon went to go take a nap. I sat here watching the computer flip through star charts and I spotted Cerberus. So, I had the computer go back and I semi plotted a course through the Cerberus system. I mean, Charon said that it was an outlawed system. Nobody was supposed to go there because there was a big black hole. They didn't want anybody getting sucked into it. So, why did this ship go through it? Or one of the two ships. I don't know which one." I shrugged and continued on, "Anyway, it doesn't really matter. It showed us that only one ship went through, and it was on a course to this system," I finished and gave a little squeak.

"So, it was going to this system. Why do we need to go there?" She asked. I guess she wasn't following my train of thought.

"It's a mining system, mom. They have mining colonies there. We can get star charts to pick up information and maybe meet other regular Elysians. Get the lay of the land and our feet underneath us," I remarked and pointed at three different locations on the chart that were highlighted as having settlements of some kind.

My mom crossed her arms and bit her lip. She was thinking. She ran her hands through her wet hair, then stopped, and absently looked at her moist hand.

"Good job, Isolde. You always did have a good eye. If that's the only thing we can glean from these databases, I think it might've been worth it. Hopefully, nothing there is going to attack us or try killing us and have something of value."

I gave a nervous giggle. Mom looked down and spotted the twin shooters hanging from my legs.

Her hand went to her neck as her other hand pointed absently at my guns. "Have we returned to the days of the Wild West? Are you going to become wanted, or perhaps you fancy yourself as Doc Holliday?" she asked.

God, she always had to bring history into it. She couldn't help herself. "Yeah, I think I wouldn't mind being Doc Holliday. Just minus the horror of tuberculosis and running around gambling. Having a shootout can be exhilarating, mom," I retorted, then gave her a half-smile.

"I always did like the line, *skin that smoke wagon.*" She smiled. Her eyes danced with memories. The movie Tombstone played through my mind.

I let my hand run across the handle of a gun just so she could see me fiddling with it, just like in all those old Western movies that I watched with dad about gunslingers.

Dad said I was a pretty good shot. Hercules said I was an excellent shot.

I don't think Hercules would lie.

It was one of the few things that I was actually better at than Tristan. Tristan just wasn't good at it. He was a fair shot. He could hit a target, and dad made us practice pretty much anywhere we could.

Out on the open ocean, pirates were a real thing. Earth wasn't as safe as most people believed.

I had always been better with a pistol, while Tristan preferred a shotgun or a long rifle. My bet was that Tristan was more of 'the hide in a crow's nest' and 'take you out at a distance sort' kind of guy, while I wanted to run up both barrels blazing.

I couldn't imagine what I would've done to Jacques if I had a gun.

Two bullets right between his light hazel eyes. He'd never see it coming.

<Stop thinking about that monster. It upsets me. >

<Sorry, I didn't mean to upset your delicate constitution. I know how old guys are about their digestion.> I snickered.

In the back of my mind, I could hear chuckling.

<Old guy? >

A shot of a sidelong glance <Yeah, old guy. By a couple thousand years. They talk about May-December relationships. 'Hello, how about the dawn of time relationship?' They don't even have a name for how old the relationship is.>

<Yes, I am your old man. > He mused.

<At least, you don't remember the invention of the wheel. > I giggled.

He threw his head back laughing, and mom shot him a glare. She pointed at something in the Morning Field system.

"The star's name is Dido? Do you know the names of the satellites?" she asked.

"I know the names of the satellites," Hera announced to the room.

Hercules had turned sharply, "Mother, I take it your walk is over?"

"No, it was interesting. However, I will continue at another time," she remarked and took a seat.

Charon barged in, "I have an idea for the engines!"

"Isolde has discovered the Morning Field system and how to get there. Can you shift us?" Mom cut him off.

"I've never been to the Morning system," he returned, scratching his head to straighten his hair.

"Prometheus, do we have any pictures of the Morning system?" Mom asked, tapping her foot on the floor in irritation. She just wanted to get on with it.

"There is one picture. I'm afraid the picture is degraded."

The visual went up on one of the displays. Prometheus was right. It was awful, grainy and looked like it was taken with a first-generation cell phone.

"I can't use that. I wouldn't know where we were jumping to," Charon replied.

"All right. Prometheus, how long will it take us to get there?" Mom growled in frustration.

"2.3 years."

"Vaffanculo," she murmured under her breath.

I glanced at Hercules.

<She only curses in Italian when she's really mad. >

Both her brows drew together. This wasn't good enough for her. She was gonna come up with something else.

I know my mom.

"Well, as I was saying when I walked in, before we discovered this new wonderful information, I have an idea of how exactly we are going to attach the new engines to the ship," Charon announced.

"Yeah, genius, how are you going to do that? Your shifting wonderfulness can't take us anywhere?" Hercules did not look like he was convinced that Charon had any idea what he was doing.

"There is another shuttle bay closer to the engine compartments. There are no transports inside, and it's big enough for the ship. We simply open the shuttle bay doors and quite literally wield the ship into the framework of this one."

Hercules' hand went to his chin as he contemplated Charon's plan. "Yeah, I can see how that would work. We incorporate it into the framework without even bothering to move the engines. If we need to, we can jettison the whole thing if it stops working. It also allows us to contain whatever explosions inside the shuttle bay."

"Exactly!" Charon spouted.

"I'm sorry. I hate to point out the flaw in all of these lovely engineering discussions. However, that doesn't address the issue of how you turn them on and off. How are you going to control them?" Professor Michelson had actually raised his hand while interrupting. I wondered if he realized he really wasn't in college anymore.

"Michelson's right. How exactly are you going to control the engines? We need full engine control from one place. We can't run the risk that, for some reason, communication craps out. Everybody has to communicate between one another. He keeps saying that the Fates have to stay together. Hercules is not to be down there, running that ship in the shuttle bank, nor is anyone else with potential. But it could pop and have an explosion and then we might have to eject it. I'm not willing to lose any body. We don't have enough bodies."

"I have an idea. It's a little mad, but it could work." My mother turned to Hera, "All right. Hit me with it."

"It might have slipped everyone's mind or maybe not, but we left the robot on the ship." My mother shrugged her shoulders as Hercules gave me a look.

"Isn't it obvious? We either have the robot pilot the ship for us, doing our best to keep in communication, thereby quintuple in our engine power, or we ask the robot to tell us how to integrate systems."

Charon nodded his head a moment later as the creature was standing in front of us "What an exciting form of transportation. Thank you for a most interesting trip."

"You can thank Charon. You know anything about computer systems on your ship?" Hercules asked, waving his hand in the general direction of the shuttle bay.

"Yes, I was in charge of repairing all systems."

"Is there any way you can chain gang that ship to this one?" Mom asked and bit her lip.

"I do not know this term 'chain gang', but if you're talking about integrating it, then yes. Are you planning on maintaining the ship's integrity?" Jorhan inquired and the facial display screen displayed a symbol I didn't recognize.

"Yes, we'll weld it into the framework of a different shuttle bay. All we need to do is gain control of the ship itself. Hopefully from here, unless, of course, you wish to pilot it in the shuttle bay for us."

The creature stopped talking. He seemed enthralled with the walls, - the one with the spider webbing all over it.

"Is this ship alive?" he remarked with awe.

"That is one way of looking at it. This is a prototype, or at least at the time it was laced with crystals, it was. The crystals are always growing, constantly changing, strengthening," Charon supplied with pride.

"I've just had an epiphany. If we can move some of this crystal technology into the cockpit of the other ship, we will be able to fully integrate the systems. The crystals will do the work for us. But if you wish, we can use regular cabling, though it would take a great deal of cables," Jorhan said what everyone was thinking.

"We go with the crystals. Just remember that ship is completely expendable," Mom stated, pushing her damp hair out of her face.

"Why don't Charon, Jorhan and I go work on that, and you ladies figure out exactly where we're going in the Morning Field system," Hercules remarked, and the three men left.

CHAPTER 31

ADRIAN

The scans of the planet revealed it was covered in metal of all variety. I found the lack of orichalcum interesting. Other than the rings and its field, nothing gave off radiant readings. Even though there were energy spikes here and there, Ares waved them away as normal planetary apparitions.

Ixis claimed the planet was normal, verging on boring, as Emily called it. We loaded up in one of the shuttles, and I shifted us down to the edge of the ring field.

"Run scans on those rings. I want to know as much about them as possible," Ares instructed.

The cockpit of the ship had been overhauled. The last time I was inside, there was only the glass dome in the small shifting room.

Now, an entire wall was covered in computer holos and consoles. As the head shifter, I was in charge of the mission, not that Ares believed that. I glanced over my shoulder at him as he leaned down to examine the readout of the scans.

Other than a few grunts and a couple shared looks between him and Perseus, he didn't say anything.

I couldn't tear my eyes away from the holo display of the planet. Every moment, the surface drew closer and visually clearer.

The landmass directly under the rings was covered with white, resembling snow. The 'snow' was a relatively flat plain with moguls here and there.

"Shouldn't we search the edges between the two sides from the air before we land?" Tristan asked and glanced between Ares and me.

"We aren't planning to stay here. We're looking for your mother and Issy. We need to find a trail."

For the first time in weeks, I missed Hercules. He would have cracked a joke using some Earth nomenclature he didn't fully understand, and we'd need to correct him. Either way, he'd make us all laugh and cut the tension.

<I miss him too.> Tristan offered.

I patted his shoulder, keeping my eyes peeled on the holo in front of me.

"The gravity down there is low, so don't lose your heads running and jumping," Ares began to lecture the crew. I'd already heard his crap and ignored the droning in the background.

"The field is lighter in this section of the plain. We should shift there. If they shifted down, that is the best spot for it." Perseus indicated a slate blue section in the holo display.

"What are those formations?" I asked, pointing at something that looked like a rectangle.

There are no straight lines in nature that I knew of.

Perseus shrugged. Without waiting, I shifted us to that location.

As the pilot lowered us to the ground, the blood ran out of my head to pool in my boots.

"To answer your question, they are ships." Perseus chuckled and slapped me on the back.

"Infrared shows a trail leading away from this plain and to the snow-covered one. The terrain is level, though judging from these readings, the hills around here are all metal," The crewman running the scans supplied.

Ares turned away from the display with a wicked grin. "It's time to put your helmets on and go for a walk." The energy of his delight at the unknown was infectious.

I didn't share that same love of danger. My belly rolled with the thought of Sydney here.

Fucking Charon! She should never have let him live.

The parts she'd revealed from his judging was enough to put you off medical care forever.

The trust that died and turned to terror in all those people's eyes, haunted Sydney and me. He told them they were helping save Elysium.

I swallowed back the bile that boiled in my belly and snapped my helmet in place. The familiar scent of freshly printed crystalline tech filled my nostrils, and my HUD came to life.

"Tristan, you go with Ares' group. I'm with Perseus. Let me know if you need me." I gripped his forearm and he returned the reassuring shake.

The hollow sound of his voice filtered through the HUD, "You got it," from the set of his shoulders. I wasn't sure he was ready. I just had to trust the episode with the Khimera was a one-off, and Tristan could handle whatever came his way now.

I stepped close to Ares. "My son." It was all I felt I needed to say.

Ares' eyes glinted in his helmet. "He's under my protection. You have no worries," his reply came through low. "You have your horn blades?" He asked, as his eyes darted over my suit and gear.

"Yeah, anything I should know about your brother?" I murmured.

"He's better with weapons than you. Your gift comes from him. Trust Perseus!" Ares stepped back.

"Carter, you stay with the ship. Everyone else, follow your captains!" He whorled his hand in the air and headed into the cargo bay, and opened the back hatch.

I expected a flush of air or a sound to emanate from the hatch. The still silence sat wrong with me.

This kind of still only happens on earth when something is wrong.

Ixis said there were no weather patterns this far from the sunward side. Even though it looked like snow, he said it wasn't likely. His postulation was that the cover was of mineral composition, similar to the cliffs of Dover. Either way, the dead calm felt off.

Rather than vacillate over it more, I strode out the hatch and into the alien world of permanent darkness.

There were metallic ships of all shapes floating in the air. My steps were more like a John Carter movie on the moon.

Each movement came with a little bounce. Tristan laughed. I probably would have, too, if my foreboding would go away.

Someone slapped me on the back, and I whipped around, ready to attack.

"Whoa there, young one! We are on the same side." Perseus held his hands up in surrender.

I already had one of my horn blades at the ready with my arm raised to impale him. I stepped out of my fighting stance and lowered the horn.

"Those are a fine set, unlike any I have ever seen. Hercules told me you cleaved them from the Khimera after shifting its tail off." Pride sparkled in his eyes.

I found myself easing out of my usual '*the world is my enemy*' mode. I didn't need Perseus' approval, but it felt good.

I quirked a half-smile, "The creature was a shifter. It was going to kill Tristan." It wasn't an excuse, just an explanation.

"A worthy reason to kill any monster in my world." He released a low rumble that could be mistaken for a growl but, actually, was a chuckle.

"Shall we go and find this wayward woman of yours?" he asked.

I bounced ahead without a word.

The infrared trail grew faint and the time left to follow it was running out. I switched my HUD to night vision, and we moved to the south side of the trail, while Ares took the north.

Our crew of 10, each kept to the back. When I spied Dewy, he gave me a nod and threw hand signals to five men. While Perseus followed suit with five of his own, they moved around me.

If this was a chess board, I was their King and they protected me as if their lives depended on it. That just left me to wonder who the Queen was.

Perseus, Ares?

The crews kept a lookout for god-knows what, while I followed Sydney's trail and surveyed the floating ships. Piles of trash formed out of the gloom, and a cloud of fog moved in, covering the white flowers which were now dotting the ground.

The flowers floated and waved in tandem. The motion resembled the wave in a stadium. I glanced up at the sky and the glowing double rings hanging over us. The flowers followed the line of the rings.

The infrared trial ended with the flowers, only to be replaced by a cleared swath. The break in the flowers looked like a machete cut path.

Hercules! He cut the path!

I stopped thinking about the path and the overall foreign sight. The team around me stopped moving. Dewy had his hand in the air in the shape of a fist.

The flowers waved out from our location like a rock thrown in a pond. We were standing in the center of a bullseye.

Tearing metal shrieked through the thin air, and all hell broke loose.

"Guard the shifter!" Perseus ordered in a calm voice. "Move double time along the trail." Dewy and all his men moved in on me, creating a wall of bodies.

Dewy and his men herded me to the trail, moving as fast as we could, hopping along in the low gravity. My blood howled in my ears.

A thousand scenarios played through my mind when something crashed into the side of the guy in front of me. He lost his balance and fell. I tripped over his body and tumbled toward the ground.

My automatic reaction was to shift. It took over, and I was standing on my feet, behind the guy on the ground. The air over us was filled with chunks of metal and debris from machinery and ships.

The flowers continued their bullseye waving, announcing our location.

I automatically shifted most of the flack in the sky away from us, piling it like a wall on either side of our crew.

"Adrian, can you move us along?" Dewy asked. The trash overhead was replaced with bullets from the various guns, shooting around me. Dewy and his team returned fire.

I quickly took in every man's location in our crew and moved them closer, then shifted us deeper into the grove of flowers.

"This must be the Asphodel Meadows," Perseus informed the group, as if knowing the name of this shit-hole was going to help.

Ares' voice came over the com, "The unworthy and useless wonder here. They will attack on sight."

I rolled my eyes. Maybe Ares hadn't been paying attention, but whatever he thought he knew was a story and nothing more.

The man next to me screamed and fell to the ground while small bubbles of red speckled the flowers and drifted away in the air to land on the carpet of white, yards away.

Something zipped past me, screeching. My exterior mike caught the sound a second too late as it scraped the dome of my helmet. A chewed line permanently etched the face of my helmet.

"That was a bullet!" I shouted.

To my right, the man sunk to the ground, creating a new hump to add to the multitude of humps everywhere.

The vines of flowers quickly moved to cover the man's body. I shifted him ahead of us on the trail along with our group. The vines were moving with us.

The HUD filled with bright green streamers as more projectiles filled the air, arching up before sailing down toward our group.

"Adrian, we need to get out of here. This is an ambush. The droids are firing at us!" Dewy yelled over the sound of his gun, releasing burst after burst of return fire.

Droids?

I glanced around at the enemy force. My HUD only identified the enemy as metal machines.

Sydney's voice rang in my mind. '*We are so fucked*!'

<Tristan?> I called.

Nothing came through, and the pressure of bodies surrounding me pushed in. I took in the placement of our crew. Three were dead, and two injured. I was breathing hard, and my breath left condensation on the interior of my helmet. Dewy and Perseus shouted out orders to the men around me. I swallowed, but there was no moisture to be had, only the dry ash of failure.

<No time to talk.> he replied. The tension in his body was enough to fuel a sun.

This was worse than the rivers. There was only one opponent per-river. This was a hell of an attack, coming from every direction. My horn blades were useless. The enemy was too far away to stab.

My HUD tracked the angle of fire back to its origin. The HUD lit up, and I honed in on the metallic source, then shifted it back to the plain plateau where we started. Its weapons fire ceased, and I moved to the next hunk of steel.

The crap flying through the air was cut in half in a few minutes. Dewy straightened, dusting his knee off.

Perseus patted my back. "Let's keep moving!" He ordered. There were two more bodies lying on the ground, and I shifted them to join the others ahead of us and pushed the anger over their deaths to the background.

The flowers still waved their bullseye, alerting our enemies. A cloud of fog lingered over our crew and the path we'd just traversed. I kept close to our remaining crew members, and we ran flat out down the path.

"Where's Ares?" I shouted at Perseus. Sweat formed on my upper lip, and my heart pounded in my chest. I gulped back the fear lining my throat.

The last time I was this afraid, I was surrounded by an ocean of water. This time it was an ocean of vacuum. The atmosphere was little to none. I couldn't wrap my head around how the flowers grew.

I bounced along with my guys, and the scent of cigarette smoke tickled the back of my nose and a desire to see aunt Emily again. I blocked everything out, and hyper-focused on the end of the trail and Sydney. There was shouting all around me, but it didn't reach me. I pushed on for the prize.

Sydney, she has to be there.

My heart told me she was here, and I couldn't be wrong.

The shouting finally broke through.

"Adrian, Em is going to kill me if we don't make it. Wake up!" Dewy shouted.

The scent of smoke evaporated along with my tunnel vision. I blinked to clear my sight.

"Dewy?" I coughed.

"The path ends here. The infrared is gone, and Ares, Emmaline, and Tristan aren't answering our calls!" He shouted into my helmet. It came over, crackling and popping. Our systems didn't like being so close.

I shook to clear the cotton in my brain and surveyed the area. There was some stacked trash that stuck out like a sore thumb only because it wasn't covered in flowers in a landscape of flora. Thirty meters away was a floating line covered in vines attached to nothing.

The pit of my stomach weighed a ton and boiled with acid. They left on a ship. It was the only logical answer.

The trail ends here because they didn't go further. They got what they wanted and left.

We needed to do the same.

"Ares? Where are you?" I shouted into my com.

"Not far from your current location!" He shouted back.

I quickly took in our position. The nearest ship to both parties was thirty meters southwest.

<Tristan, lead your team to these coordinates. I will meet you there. > I send him the mental picture.

<We will be there. > He grunted.

"Perseus, Dewy, on me," I called. "We're heading for this location and meeting up with Ares. Sydney left on a ship, and we are too. This is a death zone."

Both motioned to the two crews, and we moved. The flowers puffed every time we touched them, releasing a fog-like cloud of pollen that hung in the air.

I shifted our injured and dead with us. No one was going to be left behind.

The men returned fire as a fresh barrage of trash hurled through the air at us.

The flash of gunfire caught my eye, fifty meters to our right. I shifted our group closer to the ship and our only way out of this mess.

Another man crumpled to my left, leaving a hole on that side. I grabbed his gun and began squeezing off round after round in an effort to return fire.

I shifted the aerial debris over the top of the weapons fire. After some time, the shooting stopped, yet it didn't make a difference.

At last, Tristan's suit came into sight, as did the pressure door on the floating ship. Ares was shouting in Russian at some guy, and the two groups merged into one.

I shifted to the pressure door's ledge and gripped the frame while punching buttons on a control panel. A bullet whizzed by, clipping the edge of my arm, creating a small hole. A little jet of air began shooting out of my suit. I took a deep breath and kept punching before one worked.

The door hissed open, and I stepped inside.

I sent Tristan a visual of the airlock and searched my suit for a patch kit.

Two men appeared in the doorway and took the high low positions, shooting down at the attacking machines.

"I have a leak. Do you have a patch?" I asked.

One man patted his left thigh and went back to shooting. I found the kit and slapped it over the hole. I glanced down at our team and shifted all the dead and four guys into the airlock.

"Open the inner door and clear this area," I ordered, then snuck a glance back down at the ground and quickly shifted the next group of men.

Two replaced the men at the door, and the rest moved back into the bowels of the ship. I shifted Ares and Tristan along with the rest of their men.

"Find the cockpit and get us out of here!" I shouted at Ares. He pushed his way through the men, with one man following behind.

Tristan moved to the door and began returning fire. The sound of metal hitting metal and the ricochets permeated the thin air.

I moved in for another quick peek at the ground when Tristan shrieked and gurgled in pain.

Droplets of blood speckled the air and my helmet.

< Tristan!> I shouted, but his lips moved like a guppy as he gasped for air.

I shifted Perseus into the airlock.

He took one look at Tristan, pushed me to the door, "Keep shooting or Dewy is dead."

I gulped back my fears and tore my eyes away from Tristan's gasping form. I took aim at the nearest location of weapons fire and began shooting.

From up here, it was easier to spot the shaped items on the ground. More so, the fighting had removed much of the flowers, coving the trash. I picked up a piece of debris and shifted it over to metalheads, crushing them.

I moved on to the uncovered pile near the floating tether and I shifted until the pile was gone.

Tristan mentally screamed in my mind.

A lull formed in the fight, and I shifted two more men into the airlock. There wasn't room for more.

"Don't stop shooting, damn you!" Dewy yelled into my helmet. I shook to clear the ringing that followed.

I pulled the trigger, but nothing happened.

"I'm out," I announced.

Perseus slapped me on the back and handed me his guns, then he pulled one of the horns free.

"Can I borrow this?" He asked without waiting for an answer.

I began a fresh round of fire to keep the metalheads off Dewy and his three men.

<We have to get the hell out of here!> I shouted at Dewy.

CHAPTER 32

SYDNEY

"We're going to the Mourning Field?" Professor Michelson hadn't been in the room when Isolde had announced what she'd discovered.

"Yes, Isolde discovered the Mourning Field system."

"Mourning Field is a place in the underworld," he stated and looked at me over his reading glasses.

Isolde snickered, "Obviously. We are in the underworld."

Michelson nodded his head, "Touché, Isolde! You are correct. I guess my statement was a little obvious. What's the name of its main star?"

Hera smiled, "Dido, of course."

He nodded his head in approval "*of course,*" and we all laughed at him.

"There are several mining colonies there. We will visit every one if we have to. Get star charts, maybe some supplies, trade technology or something."

Michelson kept nodding his head. He mumbled something under his breath and pulled up a holo chart. He made several exclamations, pointing at different satellites in the system. He was like a kid in a candy shop.

My stomach roared, "I'm heading to the cafeteria to eat. Anybody else hungry? I'll bring something back for you?"

Issy rolled her head around on her shoulders. "I'll go with you, mom." She came and threaded her arm through mine and we turned and headed out the door, leaving Hera and Michelson behind. The two eggheads could cry over that one.

"What are we gonna do with that robot?"

"I don't know, mom. He seems pretty autonomous and hopeful. We could put him to work."

"I don't know if we can trust him," I grumbled, pushing my wild hair out of my face and beginning a braid to fight the mass.

"We can't do anything about his programming, and *it* already exhibits a preference to live. If we try meddling with him, he may very well lash out."

Isolde's interactions with Hercules were clearly influencing her cognitive abilities. The fact that she would use the words *'lash out'*... I was not even sure it was part of her vocabulary prior to him.

Not that I had a problem with that. I was perfectly happy if she was learning from her interaction with him.

I guess I was just hoping she'd stay young a little while longer.

It was very selfish of me and I knew it.

Moms are always selfish like that.

"Well, why don't we put him to work in the kitchen? He took care of some old lady for forever, obviously mostly medical care. I'm sure he was able to carry a tray or make a meal," I replied.

I hated housework of any kind and cooking was Gabe's thing. Adrian and I have never cooked a meal together, other than mud pies in the backyard.

"So you're worried about him potentially harming us, but you're willing to let us let him cook?" She asked, wagging an eyebrow at me.

"I am ironic like that." I threw her a crooked smile and shrugged. I did see the irony in it, but it was a good choice.

"Yeah, mom, I think that that's part of the problem. Your gray area is a lot bigger than you think it is. Not everything is black and white," she replied and skipped a few steps to keep up with me.

She was probably right. I was sure that everybody's gray areas were a lot bigger than they'd like them to be or maybe there was no such thing as black and white.

It really is all gray.

Murder is wrong but under the right circumstances, absolutely every person who believes that — would commit murder. So that gray area really does exist for them. There's no such thing as black and white in the area of murder. You'll kill someone protecting your children. You'll kill someone protecting yourself.

If you hated someone and then you murder them to protect yourself, is it still white or is it black and white, which makes a gray.

Everything really is gray.

Even the walls in this shit can. Under all the spider veins of crystalline tech everything was gray.

One thing I noticed about Prometheus was that all the food appeared to be either vegetables or fruits. There wasn't a shred of meat. Almost as if Prometheus' original stores hadn't included meat at all.

But I'm not a hundred percent Themian, according to the robot.

All there was on my plate were vegetables. A broccoli looking stalk was joined by some papaya-colored berries. Next to that, leaves were laid in a rainbow of colors. I pushed everything purple to the side. I didn't eat purple leaves — ever! They reminded me of radicchio, and I hated radicchio.

It's too bitter for my taste.

Some bread tinged with a tangy bite sat on the edge of the plate. I sighed.

No butter. To the side was a white pudding/poi puddle of — I was not sure. It was sweat, carrying the flavor of a marionberry minus the dark burgundy color.

Themian and Elysium food clearly never heard of eating the rainbow. There was some crap about not eating anything white but that wasn't going to stop me from eating the marionberry-esk pudding.

Part of me wanted a big fat juicy steak. All these leaves and twigs made me crazy. Hell, at this point, my body was so starved for protein, I would have eaten anything made of metal just hoping for a little copper or iron.

And if anybody thinks I am spending the rest of my life not eating cheese, they're mistaken.

"Pardon me, I understand this is the meeting room," Jorhan cut into my thoughts, removing the vision of a fresh cut bleeding steak. My mouth watered for the imagined flavor.

"Oh, God! For just five minutes of peace and quiet so I could enjoy a meal without being interrupted, I would pay good money for that," I groaned.

The machine hung its head. I felt bad. It was not his fault. I didn't want my meal or company.

"I am sorry, Sydney. I do not want to interrupt, but I would like to point out that the Argos is almost ready to be wielded into the ship, and I wanted to discuss a few finer points of structural engineering." The mechanical voice sounded tentative.

"Argos?" I asked with an eyebrow cocked.

"Yes, the name of the ship you found me on was Argos."

I shook my head, but I leaned back in my chair, slouching down, laughing.

"What's up, mom? I know you got something you're holding back," Issy asked.

"Argos, you know the Argos?"

She shook her head. She had no idea what I was talking about. "Jason and the Argonauts sailed SV Argos." I threw my broccoli back on my plate

"Are you kidding? Who knows this stuff, mom? You?" she groaned back a chuckle.

"I'm sure Hera and Hercules both know it. It's just funny." It wasn't that funny. I couldn't help but laugh. At every turn, a new twist of weird found a way to inject itself into my reality.

"Who would've thought that after all these thousands of years, humanity would still remember all the stories about Gods and battles." I shook my head to keep the hysteria from my laugh. "And various items that were found or lost." I sat up straight. That was when I remembered the Mourning Fields.

"Jorhan, have you been to Mourning Fields?"

"No, I have not! Mourning Fields is a place where people who have a broken heart go to work in the mines. If they didn't before their arrival, their heart is broken afterward. It is a penal colony," he replied.

I groaned.

Of course, it's a penal colony. Why else would it be called mourning? Everybody there is crying over something?

While there was nothing to be done for it, we still had to go. It was the only way to get a star chart to Elysium and perhaps find our way back to Adrian and Tristan.

If Charon's done with us by then.

Professor Michelson and Hera were still gnawing away at all the star charts when I poked my head into the cockpit.

"It's amazing, Sydney. I never imagined there would be this much information." Michelson waved me over, "The underworld is actually pretty fascinating. I'm kind of sorry that I studied astrophysics instead of paying attention to Greek mythology." He raised his hand and pointed to the holo, "The main star's name is Dido, but the rest of the planets in the system are her satellites. They're all named after the Greek Gods that were supposed to be in the underworld mourning unrequited lost loves." He smiled in awe.

"Mourning Fields. Apparently, we missed something. Jorhan just informed me that it's a penal colony zone. I'm sure there's a lot of unrequited love. To never see your loved ones again is criminal," I murmured under my breath. My chest lurched in pain. I was projecting.

"Mom, not fair. You don't know if they're all criminals. You and I both know that in a corrupt system, there will always be some innocent who slip through the cracks," Issy spouted.

She couldn't help defending the weak. She wasn't as strong as the rest of us and felt it keenly.

I turned a sharp eye on her. "Guilt by association will eventually turn someone into a criminal, who wouldn't have been one otherwise," I remarked, flaring my nostrils at her. We've had this conversation before.

"Sometimes, you have to commit a crime just to survive," she retorted.

She pierced right to the heart of the matter. She knew as well as I did that if Tristan hadn't killed Jacques, we probably would've had to anyway. Just to survive! The stricken look on my face told her she'd hit home. My shoulders sagged.

More of the gray area.

I was practically swimming in it.

"I know even a good person will do bad things," I shot back at her.

Hercules' eyes bored into me with a dark glare. He clenched his jaw, walked over to Isolde, but she shrugged him off. The door slid open as she stormed her way down the hallway with him staring after, "Sydney, she's your daughter. You could be a little kinder," he remarked.

"The world is not a kind place, and neither is the cosmos. She needs to keep in mind exactly what people are capable of. I don't give a crap what race you're from. Even good people are evil. And they'll do anything to survive. It doesn't make you a bad person. It just means that sometimes you have to make the tough choices," I retorted.

He gave me a cold stare before the door slid open, and he too escaped down the hall. Professor Michelson looked from me to Hera to the door.

He opened his mouth to say something, but I put my hand up. "Michelson, we're not discussing it. What just transpired is a closed family matter."

He closed his mouth. His eyes looked down and shifted to the left to the right. He opened his mouth as if he was gonna speak again, thought better of it and nodded at me, "According to the star chart, and if we are to believe everything that Jorhan said, the penal colony for mining is on Phaedra." He pulled up a grainy, barely three dimensional picture. "The only visual we have in the system is complete shit." He pressed his lips shut and glanced at me as if to say sorry, then turned back to the holo, "I'm running it through several filtering programs to try and see if I can resolve some of the graininess, remove the noise and get a bit more clarity. Maybe, that would be enough for Charon to shift us. With the new engines, we could be there in as little as two months." Michelson was an optimistic bastard.

I crossed my arms and covered my mouth, then began pacing.

Time!

Time is our enemy. Two months was too long.

There must be something that we could do to speed this up.

But I just couldn't think what it was. The robot had never been to the Mourning Fields system. Phaedra sounded like a great planet to go harvest materials and a crew, and a terrible planet to be stuck on.

"Are there any systems in between? Maybe we could jump on one of those?" I inquired.

"There are two systems, Melinoe and Ariadne."

"Prometheus, do we have any visuals for Melinoe or Ariadne?"

"Searching."

"I've been to Melinoe." I must've jumped a mile. The creepy robot was right behind me.

"Don't sneak up on people! Especially me! You might not be made of flesh and blood, but I could crush you like a pop can," I growled to cover my fright.

Note to self: I should stop threatening everyone.

He tilted his head to the side, "You do not appear to be strong enough to crush me."

I shouldn't do it.

Although, he needed to understand who was the top dog on the ship and it certainly wasn't him. I pushed with my mind and slammed it up against the wall, "Now, do you think I could crush you?" I asked in a cool voice.

"Absolutely, I've revised my opinion on hybrids." The digital display on the head portion of the robot showed a face of sorts.

"It's because you've never known a Themians. In a universe with multitude possibilities, there's going to be a multitude of outcomes," Michelson offered.

I bit my lip. The professor was always teaching. He reminded me of Vika. "You said that you've been to Melinoe. What does it look like?" I asked, trying to keep my hands at my side. My fingertips skimmed over the folded wrinkles of my jeans. I hadn't noticed what I'd thrown on until now.

"It is the resting place of the dead. You can see the spirits of your loved ones floating within stardust. It's a nebula filled with all kinds of gases, and there do appear to be spirits floating through it. But it is mostly gaseous balls. Some of them take on the outline of an Elysium's body. It's a popular place for older Elysiums to visit before they die. They like the comfort of knowing their souls will end up floating in the cosmos for all time. Many of the spiritual clans like to visit and try and contact their dead loved ones," Jorhan replied with more information than I'd bargained for.

Ugh, spiritual clans. More likely cults.

"What you just described sounds pretty creepy. Why not just yank out an Ouija board and start trying to summon the dead?" I mused. "That's all fine and dandy, but do you have a visual for us? Can we shift there? Charon needs a clear visual," I stated. My belly still quivered at the thought of the dead hanging around waiting for a visit.

"I believe so." He stepped to the control panel and inserted one of his fingers into it, a kind of port. Of course, because if I was a robot, I'd make my finger the USB connection rather than a cord, too.

One of the holos lit up. A beautiful picture invaded the bridge, bathing us in the floating pinks and purples swirling together of a nebula.

The image moved, showing thousands of floating shapes dancing together in a cosmic waltz. Some had wide open mouths, resembling the pain of screaming. The eerie sight gave me goosebumps.

<Charon, come to the cockpit! > I mentally order.

The pressure in the room changed and he appeared, "Sydney." He nodded his head.

"Can you shift us there?" He stood transfixed, staring at all of the various globs floating across the screen. "Melinoe, the resting place of the dead? Yes, I can shift us there."

He's been here. The little fuck.

"Good! Professor Michelson can you leave a buoy behind with our coordinates?" His eyebrows shot into the ceiling with the size of his baby blues. "Yes, of course, I can. But why would I?"

"For Odyssey, so they can find us," Hera whispered.

"Brilliant! Why didn't we do that before?" Issy asked.

I shook my head. "I didn't think of it." I chided myself more than anyone else.

I can't do it all, but I want to.

I needed to be smarter, faster. I was pushing again and I couldn't stop.

Michelson pressed a few buttons and a chip ejected from his console. It was no bigger than a zip-drive. Charon shifted it outside the ship.

I gave him the 'go' sign.

<Brace yourselves.> he instructed.

Charon wasn't known for his finesse. "Shifting now." But I had to admit that he was getting better. The pop at the end was less intense on my ears. The pressure changed around us. It felt less like a cut out and more like he cut the entire ship from the surrounding space.

"Thank you. You can go back to whatever it was you guys were doing."

His head gave a quick nod.

"I'm always available for the Fates," and then he disappeared.

I guess having a shifter at your beck and call that you don't have to kiss, say sorry to at the end of the day, or argue with isn't such a bad thing.

Although, his zealotry was off-putting. Also, I missed the kisses and arguing.

"Prometheus, how far are we from the nebula?" What I saw resembled more of the Grim Reaper than the dead. "We are approximately 4 light years away from Melinoe."

I shifted on the balls of my feet. "It doesn't look like a ghost, mom. It looks like a hooded figure." Issy shivered and ran her hands over her arms.

"Yeah, I'm looking for the sickle."

Issy nodded her head. "It has beautiful colors. And if you look closely, you can see what appear to be various figures floating by." I was pretty sure that the figures she was referring to were baby stars.

"Actually, those figures, or blobs, from this distance, just look like little bubbles of gas and dust. But, in truth, all of the gaseous balls are proto-stars, baby stars forming into new star systems. They may very well be baby worlds." Michelson was back on the lectern, giving his speech about space.

"This is the birthplace of planets?" I asked.

Information changes perspective.

"All nebulae are the birthplace of stars and planets. I think if we were to get closer, we might be able to discover whether it was hot or cold. You might actually have a better view if you just closed the windows and instead turned on the infrared viewing. Most nebulae are made up of dust, micro-particles consisting of minerals, carbon, polycyclic aromatic hydrocarbons, and soot. The only reason we can see the dust cloud so clearly is because of the stars forming inside of it. The light shines out in the dust clouds as it goes through, altering the light spectrum, creating color." Our resident nerd was in love and I couldn't say I blamed him. Putting aside the ghoulish figures, I was impressed with the cosmic color display.

Isolde's shoulders tensed. "Is there a large gravitational pull inside? Can we be pulled into it from here?" Her fear had a foundation.

Professor Michelson shook his head. "Yes, there is going to be gravity everywhere you go. You cannot get away from it." Michelson gave her a kind smile. "The gravitational pull inside the nebula is not going to affect us here. Think of the nebula more like going to visit Niagara Falls. As long as you don't stand in the middle of the river, you're not going to be pulled over the edge. But at a safe distance on the right outcropping, you'll get a phenomenal view."

Professor Michelson's analogy was a good one. We'd already been in the center of the river, and I had no intention of returning.

"Besides, this nebula is the leftovers of a supernova. It's still pushing out. The wave of the explosion has already moved beyond this place. What you're looking at now is the leftover bit of the star and its satellites — stardust," awe and wonder filled his voice.

Somewhere inside this egghead was a child that wanted to explore the gigantic dust cloud floating out there.

For me, it was just a waypoint before reaching Elysium. Nothing more.

"That's all very interesting. Thank you for the lesson on nebulae. Can we keep working on the problem now? How are we going to get to the Mourning Fields?"

CHAPTER 33

EMMALINE

We lost contact with the shuttle almost as soon as it entered the atmosphere. What little atmosphere there was of it, on the wretched world we were orbiting.

I shouldn't have let them go. Not Adrian and Tristan.

They were both just as stubborn as each other.

"Anybody hear them?" I demanded, knowing that if I couldn't, it wasn't likely anyone else could.

Ixis shook his head. "I'm sorry, my love, they've gone dark. I can hear the murmuring of their minds, but it's garbled and unclear."

Something was wrong. That was what my gut kept telling me. Everything inside me clenched.

I should know what Dewy's thinking. He wasn't ready for this.

In the back of my mind, I could hear Dew telling me to mind my own business. I knew it wasn't him, it was just a feeling I had.

Maybe that's it. Maybe they can hear us and we can't hear them.

"Ixis, move us closer to the planet. I want to be just outside the atmosphere. I want to orbit as close as possible." He didn't bother to shift us. Our maneuvering thrusters were good enough. It only took us a few minutes to get there.

The closer we came to the planet. The louder the mumbling until it became audible sounds.

<Emily, we're in trouble. There're machines down here. Hundreds of thousands of them. They're attacking us and

we can't shift out. Emily? Can you hear us?> Adrian shouted in my mind.

<Yes, Adrian, I hear you. Stop screaming at me. Okay!? You can't shift out, so head back to the shuttle and fly. > I barked as adrenaline jetted through my system.

<We can't retreat. We're cut off! > Ares shouted with a morbid glee.

I thought he was supposed to be some kind of a tactical genius. Instead, he led everybody into an ambush.

<He couldn't know, Emm. There were no signs of life. They're all robots. They're everywhere, a mindless army. I watched one guy get torn apart.> Dewy yelled, and his whole body tightened in fear.

I trembled. I waited all this time to find Ixis. I wasn't ready to lose Dewy ever. The only way I was gonna be able to help them is if I was down on the planet.

But I am not.

I looked up into the viewing windows of the shifting room and that big incomprehensible darkness of space. I didn't want it to come to this. Syd didn't leave me in charge to get her husband, son and my brother killed.

I closed my eyes and pinched the bridge of my nose. I couldn't see any way out without sending another shuttle.

They wouldn't get there in time without a shifter, and that would put everyone on Odyssey at risk.

The dry bitter taste in my mouth ate at my heart. If I did nothing, Dewy and the boys would be dead along with everyone else.

"Emmaline, I suggest you look up!" Eris ordered, for once not polluting the air with strife and hate.

CHAPTER 34

SYDNEY

I kept expecting our synthetic life form would suddenly turn on us and decide to kill us. Was it too many SciFi movies or my wild imagination? Maybe. Or it could be my fear of losing control to a machine.

Charon had already shown me how easy it was to take control of Prometheus and cut me out of the loop. What if our new *friend* could put in the right information and synthesize my voice patterns? At that point, he could take over the ship or order someone else to do God knows what.

I always loved science fiction films and books. They were an escape, somewhere you could go and everything would be different, special, wonderful. Now, that I was living one, well, the living wasn't quite the same.

This was not an escape from everyday life I'd dreamed of. It was a new challenge, a new problem, a new fight to survive. Something else that has to be faced, dealt with, worked on, destroyed. Every step on that road was another step on a long litany of roads I couldn't think about.

My daughter, Hera, Hercules, and Professor Michelson, are all relying on me to fix this or get us through it.

Still, I looked over at the robot. What if he really had become a sentient being? What if he was alive? I'd seen the look on Hera's face when it chose the name Jorhan. There was something more to that, and she shuttered away from it, constantly. Not something you would typically catch her doing.

"Jorhan tell me about the Ariadne system."

"It would be my pleasure. You would say it is a rather dull system. It would not be much easier to accomplish this by simply placing me in direct contact with Prometheus computer."

"No."

He didn't reply, only projected onto the room. Frankly, I was relieved. I really didn't want to have the big debate with the creature, feelings or not.

I'm sorry, I just couldn't accept it.

Maybe it was the human part of me saying no. I didn't think so. Although, of all the hybrids here, I was the least human. And yet, I felt the very human emotion of repulsion every time I looked at *IT*.

I felt threatened.

The Ariadne system was boring and dark. Frankly, if I didn't have something to live for, it was so bleak, you might be interested in committing suicide just to get out of it. They were all lifeless rocks. Not one of them had water, no crystals, no hydrogen, nothing.

"Is there anything about the system that's redeemable?" I asked.

"I'm afraid not. There aren't even any desirable minerals for mining."

"All right. Michelson, drop the buoy and let's get the hell out of here."

"The buoy is ready."

<Charon, come to us! Now! >

Charon popped in.

"Jorhan has a visual for us in the Ariadne system."

"Shifting now." We quickly disappeared into the black void around us.

Prometheus immediately displayed a system itself. As it stood right now, it didn't look like anything changed. It was unremarkable in every way. My whole hope of getting there quickly was dashed.

Isolde reached out and stroked my shoulder. I looked over at her, "We'll figure it out, mom. It's just a thing," she shrugged.

"Prometheus is not done going through all of the star charts from the data-banks. It may very well be if we wait here just long enough, we will find something."

"I'm sorry that's just not a good enough answer for me. Isolde, you keep watching Prometheus and the star charts. Hercules, you, Jorhan and Charon keep working on finishing the addition of that ship to our systems. As soon as you're done, start welding it to ours. Hera, I want you to go inside that vessel. I want to know if anybody had pictures or personal records of any kind."

They dispersed to their various jobs. It was a relief I was left alone in the cockpit, staring out at the dead rocks that were floating around this wretched system. If you were left floating here in a spaceship, there would be a lot of madness and misery if this was your only view forever.

Issy didn't say anything. She just kept her eyes locked on the display.

I couldn't get comfortable in my own skin. I was constantly listening for Adrian in the background, wishing he was there, hoping he was there. The pressure in my chest ratcheted down, making it hard to breathe. I swallowed back my cries and blinked the tears away. They had never helped me in the past.

The only way to help is to keep fighting.

I couldn't back down now. If I even pictured Tristan, I would crumple into a ball of worthless flesh.

My mind strained to hear something, but it was just dead air. I turned to Issy. I wanted to say something to her but had no idea where to start. It was not as if my daughter was a stranger to me. She wasn't. I didn't know how to broach the subject.

If I said it out loud, that would make it real. I didn't want it to be real. And there was a very real possibility that we might never see either of them again.

Her aquamarine blue eyes met mine. She sat up straighter, both her hands on the console in front of her, and stood up, without breaking sight, "We have to get back to the Asphodel Meadows," she stated with a conviction I'd only witnessed a few times in her life.

"Why?" I demanded as my breath grew short.

She took on a faraway look, staring off into the distance through me. "Tristan is there! We have to go now, mom! We can't wait!" She came back to herself and stared me down.

<Charon, shift us back to the Asphodel Meadows. Now!>

<Shifting now. > The entire ship genuflected with the violent shift, knocking me into a bulkhead.

Blood trickled down my face from my hairline. Every hair on my body felt as if it was being pulled out one by one simultaneously. Just as I opened my mouth to scream, there was a pop.

<We have to get the hell out of here.> Adrian shouted over a mental din that roared in the background.

I could hear Tristan, and my belly flipped over. Odyssey floated in the distance, her gleaming double pyramid reflected the light from the nearby star.

< Adrian! > I yelled. <Where are you? >

<We're down on the planet, beautiful girl. We're under attack by these — machines. I can't shift us out.>

Hercules, Charon, and Professor Michelson all appeared in the cockpit. "There is nothing we can do to help them. We must preserve the Fates. You are the only hope."

In the blink of an eye, my hand lashed out and slapped Charon, snapping his head to the side.

"Don't you dare tell me what I can and can't do," I hissed, then slammed his body into the bulkhead.

I wiped the blood out of my eye.

Hercules punched Charon in the back of the head and Charon crumpled to the deck with a satisfying plop.

<Adrian, how many people are on the planet?>

<30. 15 of which are probably wounded or trapped inside one of the spaceships. We came to find you and see if we could find some star charts. >

I groaned. Without Charon, we would have walked right into the trap just like them.

We didn't have time to take a shuttle down to the surface.

How had I projected my consciousness in the asteroid field? I left my body and managed to push all those rocks around?

Isolde came and put her hand on my left shoulder. Hera put her hand on my right.

"We must help them," Hera whispered, her voice trembled with fear over the metal screaming of her sons.

I wasn't alone, and Adrian was down there. I took a deep breath and closed my eyes, only to be pulled from one reality to another. Issy and Hera floated next to me.

Charon's right. The three of us together can do anything.

A peace settled over me, and my consciousness burst from my body, racing down towards the dark side of the planet.

We rushed through the meadow and into the spaceship graveyard.

I spied the flash of a firefight, and pushing as hard as I could, I'd driven myself into the heart of the machines. Using my hands, I batted them left and right. They raised their weapons and took aim. A weapon discharged, except nothing happened. The projectile went right through me.

I smiled in relief. This was the true meaning of astral projection - the ability to be present and act on something, without being physically present. I swatted every mechanical device I came across and then, I darted inside the ship.

Adrian stood next to the airlock with Tristan, lying on his back. There was blood coming out of his shoulder.

This explained why Issy was able to breakthrough.

His pain was more than space and time to keep him from us. I pushed myself further on, until I reached the cockpit. The ship had a database, and it was intact. Reaching back into the recesses, I remembered the buttons that Charon had pushed to turn the other ship on. I did a cold start. The entire ship shuttered.

The vibrations were apparent in the air around me.

<Adrian, get everyone inside, seal up the ship. We're leaving now! >

<Whatever you say, beautiful girl. > He squeezed off a few more rounds at the machines still walking the surface and shifted two men on the ground into the ship.

The ship was anchored to something down on the ground. The moment I released the tether holding us to the surface, the ship would jet off into outer space.

With no one else in the cockpit, I didn't know what to do.

< Mom! I have this, go free us. > Issy called.

Hercules would tell her what to do.

I floated through 20 decks and out of the hull, down towards the ground, where the machines were attempting to climb up the anchoring cable. I swatted them and watched as they flew in this low gravity.

The tether was buried under a pile of metallic rubble after who knows how long of sitting on the surface of this shitty world. Sheer brute force wasn't going to be good enough.

I glanced up at the ship. Some kind of a hook latched into the side of the hull. I drifted back to the ship.

<Isolde, lower the ship two meters. >

The ship creaked as the maneuvering thrusters gently worked to lower it. The line went limp and the hook loosened in the vicious tear in the side of the hull.

I hope this was only a hole in the outer hull, and the inner hull was intact. My hands clasped the metal, and even though I was a translucent ghost, I was able to find a grip and pull free.

Using the full momentum available to me, I powered myself through the cockpit. Isolde stepped back into our unity as I grabbed the copilots controls.

<Adrian, you better have that Goddamn door sealed because we're about to enter the cold vacuum of space and I don't want to be responsible for anyone getting sucked out, and suddenly becoming a human meat kabob.>

<Don't worry, beautiful girl. It's sealed and I'm on my way up to you. Tristan's been taken into a staging area near the airlock. Ares has him, don't worry. >

Adrian burst into the cockpit with his head turning left and right and his eyes darting everywhere. "I know you're here. I can't see you!" He shouted.

<Take over the ship. I'll meet you on Odyssey. >

"We left the shuttle behind with three men," he replied as he slid into the pilot's seat and pulled the ship up and away from the planet. Gravity forced his hair back from his face.

<I'll go and retrieve them. Don't worry, meet me on Odyssey. > I returned.

I pulled the three of us out of their vessel, and turned. I was floating in the exosphere. I gazed back down at the planet. I had no idea where they left that shuttle.

<Sydney, they left it close to where Charon shifted us in. > Hera provided. Ares must have told her.

I powered down to it. There was a fully functioning shuttle that was shaped like a disk.

What was I expecting? Of course, it's a flying saucer. What else would a Themian have?

<Mom, they're coming this way. >

I didn't have to turn my head to know who *they* were. Isolde and Hera were watching every direction I wasn't. I pulled the three of us inside the disk. One man was sitting at the console. The two others were nowhere to be seen.

<Isolde, Hera, go find our wayward soldiers.>

The three of us detached and went in our separate directions.

<Get this ship out of here!> I shouted at the man on watch. He couldn't hear me. I didn't know a way to reach him.

I hit the switch that retracted the landing gear, causing the ship to float up.

He didn't even flinch. He was frozen with fear.

<Adrian, I need you to contact this imbecile. Tell him to get off his ass and pilot ship. I don't know how to fly. >

<Don't worry! Aunt Emily is on it, beautiful girl. >

I trusted Emmaline with my life. With everyone's lives. I left the cockpit and floated down the corridor to Hera and Isolde. They appeared from different sides. The ship lifted off.

<We can leave. Emmaline has this under control.>

Exiting the ship, we floated up and into the cockpit of Prometheus. Charon was still lying on the ground.

I hope he never wakes up

That fucking bastard!

I settled myself back into my body. One moment, my eyes were open and floating outside myself and in the next, I closed them. When I reopened my eyes, I was inside my own body, taking a deep breath.

“Water, I need water!” I croaked.

CHAPTER 35

EMMALINE

My eyes flashed open, and there, against the black void of the cosmos, a gray sandstone colored ball hung in the blackness. The beating of my heart raged in my ears, blocking all sound. My mouth turned dry.

I didn't know how she did it, but she did.

Sydney.

She was here. Boy, did that girl have a perchance for trouble. That was when all the mental chatter exploded in my mind.

The chatter was Sydney, Isolde, and Hera. A little gray ship exited the atmosphere. In my heart of hearts, I knew Dewy was on it.

Tears spilled down my face as my heart climbed my throat.

<Dew!> I moaned.

<Don't worry, Emm. I told you. I'm not leaving you ever.>

The heat of relief flowed over my chest. In the background, Sydney was frantic. Somebody wasn't listening to her.

<Adrian, I don't know how to operate the ship, and I can't get him to hear me.> she shouted.

Had to think. I had done it before when I took over Dewy and made him do my bidding. I reached through my mind to find the 'he' she referred to. With closed eyes, I went to that beautiful white cottage inside my mind, the one where

I kept all the doors and windows closed so's people don't irritate me.

I was searching for the right window. I could hear him, whoever *he* was. *He* was staring at the console inside of a shuttle.

The adrenalin jetting through my system ramped up, as I mentally dashed around, looking at every window, for the matching image.

<Dewy, who the hell was left behind on the shuttle? > I screamed

<Some kid named Carter. Kind of a lazy sort. I think that's why Ares left him behind with the shuttle. He wouldn't be no good in a firefight. > Dewy replied, heaving a sigh of relief as his ship moved out of the atmosphere.

<Stop woolen about him and just give me a mental picture of him. I don't know what he looks like. > I retorted.

Dew threw me the image. He looked like an Ivan to me. In my mind, I opened my eyes and looked at all the windows around me.

The hybrid mind is an amazin' place. Sometimes you know the answers even when you don't know the questions. His window appeared right in front of me.

<Adrian, tell Sydney I got this one. >

They chattered in the background. Through the window, I could see her ghostly figure, floating around. As I opened the window in Carter's mind, I cursed. He just couldn't understand why everything was turnin' on and movin' around, especially seeing as he hadn't been doin' a thing.

I dove inside of him. I knew exactly which buttons to push. I thanked my connection to Ixis.

I pressed the proper sequence for lift off, and the engines thrust us forward as it pushed Carter's body back into the seat. It was exhilarating and frightening all at the same time.

As soon as I knew the shuttle was outside of the field, blocking us, I pulled back. I was standing before the shifting window, again on Odyssey. I mentally closed the window between us. The inside of Carter's mind was messy. I wasn't in a great rush to visit him again.

I opened my eyes and there was Ixis staring at me. "Shuttle's right outside the atmosphere want to move inside, dear?" I smiled with shaking hands.

His eyes took on that far away stare. I sat down in one of the chairs.

Who knew mind hoppin' could be so exhaustin'?

I pulled out the gold case and lit a cigarette, took a long drag, and laid back in the chair to wait for the next crisis to hit me.

CHAPTER 36

SYDNEY

Hercules picked Charon up and threw him over his shoulder as the door snapped open. Isolde smiled at him and said, "Put him in his quarters and don't let him out! He's been blocking Odyssey the whole time!" Issy growled, staring down at the limp body.

"He's been blocking our ability to hear the other ship?" I gasped.

"Yeah, Tristan broke through when he was shot. I heard him, and then Charon looked at me. Quickly after that,

Tristan's call was muffled. I told Hercules to take him out after he shifted us." She hugged me.

"Yes, but why did he shift us? He had to know where Odyssey was," I replied aghast.

"No, I don't think he did. He just didn't want us to hear them. So, we wouldn't go back for them. We were blocking each other. I couldn't hear you, mom, or Hera. He probably thought you were telling him to jump back to Asphodel because we didn't have enough star charts, and you wanted to go back for more." She sputtered as fast as she could, stumbling over words as she went.

She was right. He had no idea what we were jumping back for. Yet, he had the ability to block. He'd been blocking this whole time.

That bastard!

Not just their minds, but his memories and mind from all three of us. That explained why I couldn't wipe him. He blocked me.

The pressure change of a shift surrounded me, and the next thing I knew, I was standing in my own quarters on Odyssey. A second later, Adrian filled my world. I wrapped my arms around him, my lips finding his. I never wanted to let him go. For a moment, I drowned in that world of passion, fear, and relief, but I quickly pulled back.

"Tristan, where is he?"

Adrian didn't even speak. He just shifted us, along with Issy, directly to one of the laboratory's workrooms Melinda used as a doctor's office. "Wondering when you'd get here. I pulled the bullet out and gave him a nice dunk in the Primordial Pool. He'll be right as rain in about an hour." Melinda's right to the point no-nonsense answers were refreshing to be around. I was too tired to deal with someone beating around the bush and saying in fifty words what could be said in five.

"It's okay, mom. It was just a shot in the shoulder," Tristan mumbled. I snatched his hand off the bed and held it to the side of my face. The tears I'd held back for the last few months raged to the surface and poured down my face. Isolde began to wail and threw herself at her brother. He held her with one arm and whispered into her hair. All she could do was shake her head and sniffle.

"Yeah, but I didn't even know those creatures had weapons," I moaned. Anger and guilt waged a war with my insides.

"We didn't know that those creatures were even there. We only went down because there had to be a reason you came here," Adrian whispered as he petted my hair back from my face.

"You didn't get our beacon?" I mumbled over the tears and Tristan's hand. I should have double-checked!

"No, we followed the heat signature from your engines. What beacon?" Adrian asked. The truth dawned on him, and the fire he carried within him roared to life before my eyes.

I shook my head.

I'm such a fool! Of course, there was no beacon.

Charon never shifted the thing out into space. He probably shifted it into a supernova for all we know or another room on the ship. He just told us he put it out there. He didn't want them following us.

Bastard!

"Don't worry about him. He's my problem. I'll deal with him." Adrian curled up one nostril. His face took on a sneer. There was a dark place in Adrian I'd never seen and the pit opened before me.

<Whatever you do, I want to be involved.> I growled.

Well, if Adrian actually wanted to torture the man, I wasn't adverse. Adrian was not one of those people who was inherently cruel, and he didn't believe in pulling the wings off of flies.

"Did you get a chance to review the data-banks on the ship you took?" I asked.

"No, Herc and Hephaestus are working on that now. It doesn't matter. We should have our own faster than light engine here pretty soon anyway," Adrian's off-hand reply floored me.

I raised an eyebrow, "How'd you manage that?"

"Hephaestus, he studied Themian technology. He's an inventive genius. Plus, we have a ton of 3-D printers here. We collected some raw material and went to work," He shrugged.

I toed up and gave him a quick kiss on the lips, then smiled, "You never cease to amaze me with your inventiveness."

He cupped my face, and I leaned into him, "You know I would move heaven and earth for you," he whispered, his lips a hair's breadth away from mine.

If any other man said that, it would just be one of those things that men say, trying to win your heart or convince you of their attentiveness or to get in your pants. In Adrian's case, he really could move heaven and earth and has moved objects every bit as large as planets already. When he said it, I knew he was not being magnanimous. I giggled.

I leaned back to look at Tristan. "You've grown."

Tristan glanced away with that slightly green color kids get when they see mom and dad kissing. The kids already know what causes children and didn't need the birds and the bees over again.

"Ugh! Get a room! No one wants to see their parents get all goopy." Tristan could see the fire glowing in Adrian's eyes.

<He just referred to you as his parent!> I remarked. All Adrian ever wanted was his family. I gave him another quick peck on the cheek and on his lips.

Adrian didn't reply. The smile on his face said everything.

I pecked Tristan's cheek and glanced at Issy. She returned my silent inquiry with a slight nod.

"Send me to Emmaline. I need to talk to her."

Adrian grabbed my hand and shifted us both onto the bridge.

"About damn time you came to see me. Where the hell have you been? Why didn't you just wait for us over by the big three-eyed monster?" She shouted, using almost the same words as Melinda. They were so much alike it was almost funny.

"What? You got out of the asteroid field just fine. You didn't need me," I retorted.

"That's not my point! If you would've waited there, we would've met you there, and all of this nonsense here wouldn't be necessary." She was hot for a fight, and I was too tired to oblige.

"How exactly did you guys end up here?" I asked and ran my hand over my eyes.

"Oh, Ixis, Tristan, and I did a full-on Volcan mind meld, and I got a vision of where we needed to be." Adrian made it sound so easy. I was sure the truth was somewhat different, despite his bluster.

"Yeah, I wasn't really keen on a shift based upon the crazy statue man, but Adrian insisted. Tristan didn't seem like he was going to take no for an answer either." Emmaline cocked her hip to the side and waved a hand at Ix and Adrian, "When your husband, your nephew, and grandnephew all say to do it, you say, 'Super! Okay, and try not to get us all killed.'" Emmaline never ceased to make me smile. Her level of cursing was being reprimanded without uttering one vulgar word.

I never wanted her to think I was laughing at her, but she was really funny. I could only imagine what having her treat you when she was a medical nurse would've been like. *'Hey, you just had your leg amputated, but here's Emmaline to say something sassy and make you laugh.'* She basically considered everyone a moron or some type of a brain defective. And she would flat out tell you that you were one.

People just didn't talk like that. They were nice, always trying to say the right thing. Emmaline didn't give a damn. Being around her was like being in a constant bad manners show.

She moved on from dressing me down to giving me the rundown. "Alright, so I got Ares to organize and run our military. You know he's supposed to be some kind of big brainiac. But clearly, there's something wrong with his tactical style." She rolled her eyes. "Hephaestus — I ordered to build some engines. We rallied the people to help him. Anyway, apparently, a couple of people are sweet on each other. We didn't have any new mating, don't worry. There was a baby born, cute little thing. A single birth." She smacked her lips together dryly.

My hand shot up to smother the smile cracking my face. Emmaline was raised in a family that extolled the virtues of twins, and twins were closer to Themian blood. So, when she said single birth, she said in such a fashion it was insulting. As if the child was genetically defective, which was impossible on Odyssey. Everyone had the primordial waters at least once.

Emmaline droned on for a couple of minutes, and I kinda just stopped listening. Most of the important stuff had already been said. I couldn't stop myself. I wrapped my arms around her and hugged her.

"You do be doll, girl. Jumping away like that with Prometheus, then comin' back to pull our fat out of the fire... I missed you too. I don't like being in charge like this. I prefer telling somebody else they did a terrible job of being in charge." She glanced away. It didn't hide the pooling tears in her eyes.

I tried to hide my smile. My eyes caught Dewy in the background. He had a broad grin, "Yeah, Emmaline doesn't like to be in charge." He practically blinded me with his grin.

"Don't worry. You don't have to be. If you don't want to, I can put somebody else in charge," I replied.

She pushed me away, "I'll be damned if I'm taking orders from anybody else," then she turned away from me and whirled back around. "You were the one who nominated me to lead this ragtag band of stupidity. And by God if you're not leadin', I guess it might as well be me. Or we'll all be dead," she huffed, patted her hair and cupped her neck.

"If it hadn't been for Dewy tell me about that dunce Carter, I'm not sure if we would've got that ship off the ground," she barked and snuck a peek at her brother.

"Yeah… How did you do that?" I asked and toed a chair up from the floor.

"How? Well, you got your abilities, and I got mine. You know I'm an empath, and I can feel everybody. I also sometimes get the sense of the future, things that are going to happen." She shook that one away, "Well, I also have this ability where I can kind of make people do stuff."

"You forced him to do your bidding?" I scoffed. I was impressed. I could tell people to do my bidding, but mental take over - I didn't have that ability.

"That's about the gist of it. I can push a person's mind to the side and take them over. But it sure wears me out. I don't like doing it. It makes me feel creepy, like a puppet master. Every time it's been a man's body and frankly, they're just filthy beasts." She shivered and ran her hands up and down her arms.

"Emmaline took me over once we were on the battlefield and saved a friend of mine's life," Dewy offered.

I looked over at Dewy. He came off as a halfwit. He always acted like he was kind of a moron or a little slow. The truth was that Dewy liked Emmaline running the show. He was perfectly happy to sit back and let her tell everybody what to do. He happily did what she told him. Adrian was kind of the same, only without the moronic aura.

I tore my thoughts away from Dewy and his intelligence, "I want you to send one of Hera's daughters over to the other ship."

"Well, now them girls are mighty quiet and keep to themselves. They don't really want to have a lot of interaction with anyone. Eris is the only one who seems interested in participatin' with the rest of the world," Emmaline replied, a little confused.

"I don't care. Tell me which one you think we should send over. We need one there." I didn't want to explain the dynamics of Prometheus and her crew.

"In that case, Eris. She tends to cause a lot of chaos. I guess it's just her talent. She has trouble keepin' it to a minimum. If there's less people for her to influence —" Emmaline frowned, "Everywhere she goes, there's a fight. It makes me crazy and puts my teeth on edge."

I patted Emmaline on the shoulder and peered over at Adrian. He reached out and took my hand as we shifted to the DemiGods' suit. All four of the girls were in the common room.

"I need someone to go to Prometheus to be with Hera and help watch our backs. Who's going?"

"I'll go." I didn't know whose sister was who's. I had a sneaking suspicion it was Hercules' one but she didn't imply that she was.

Ares' twin wouldn't go no matter what Emmaline said. Eris would never leave her brother's side. I couldn't have Tristan and Adrian over there. I didn't want to choose, but the two of them had to be separated. Adrian was the stronger of the two shifters. He would be the better choice for Prometheus. I shook it off. I didn't want to think about it right now. I had plenty of time to make that decision. Now, we needed to regroup.

"I'll tell your shifter when I am ready." She stood up, dusted off her tunic, and headed for one of the many doors, leading off of the suit.

CHAPTER 37

SYDNEY

Adrian took my hand, and we immediately shifted down to Prometheus' shuttle bay. Hercules' large back blocked the blinding light from his welding torch. Our newest attraction took up 60% of the bay.

"Nice of you to join us, Princess," Ares drolled and rolled his head to gawk at me.

"Why do you have to be such an ass?" Adrian demanded and stepped between Ares and me.

"Ares, I know you're supposed to be the God of War, and you're only good at antagonizing people. I'm sure it helps with military strategy. But, I really don't need your shit, and neither does anybody else. We're not at war with each other," I remarked, verbally smacking him back and keeping Adrian appeased.

"The world, no, we may not be at war with the world. It doesn't look like we're at war with each other. Although, for a while there, it seemed we were. We are at war with this universe," he shot back.

<This guy really gets on my nerves.> Adrian groaned.

<No, really? I felt the hair on top of your head burst into flames the moment we entered the shuttle bay.> I remarked.

Adrian snickered and then let out a guffaw.

"Son of Perseus, you need something to laugh about? Take a wild guess what the name of the ship is," Ares asked.

The put down was there. Adrian didn't want to be anyone's son. In his mind, there he only had one father. Tom was a great father. I swallowed back my feelings over Tom's death. The years haven't changed how Adrian or I felt. The loss sits in the back of his mind, waiting to jump out at the most inopportune moments.

"Can we cut the family feud crap and just get down to business, please?" I responded. My jeans were beginning to itch my legs and I was ready to clean up and go to bed.

"Argos." Ares motioned to the ship's hatch. There were bold letters in a font I'd never seen before. It read clear as day.

"Are you kidding me, really?" Adrian arched an eyebrow at him and turned to see for himself.

"Yeah, just like Jason the Argonauts. The name of their boat was the Argos. Can you believe that? It's amazing!" Some kid announced from one side of the ship. He seemed about to explode with enthusiasm.

I already knew this, and in my driest voice, I replied, "Oh yes, it's amazing. I'm flabbergasted."

I chanced a glance at Adrian and chuckled. I missed that excitement of youth. I couldn't remember the last time I felt that way. My soul aged so long ago, it seemed as if I'd always been this old.

A mountain of a man stepped out of Argos hatch. He should have come with his own ZIP Code. He was close to 7 feet with massive legs and arms. I was not even sure he had a neck. It was more, two slopes that went from his ears down to his shoulders. He had jet black hair and crystal-clear blue eyes with the dark ring.

Hephaestus.

The only person who didn't find the name interesting was him.

"Don't start spouting bullshit about destiny and fate, please," I murmured.

"Argos was known for building the best ships in all of the ancient world. The ship, the Argos, was the ship that Jason the Argonauts left on. However, I don't believe it's the one they returned on," Hephaestus stated.

He turned sideways to step out of the airlock because it wasn't wide enough for him. He straightened his shoulders. I didn't even think he could've worn a spacesuit, let alone walk down many of the corridors in this ship. I would bet good money he had to be shifted in and out of whatever ship he was on.

"You must be the famous Sydney? The one we worked so hard to create?" His deep baritone rumble filled the space and vibrated various tools on the deck.

"You know, it's funny. I don't really think that my genetic material should make me famous," I remarked, shaking my head.

"How about, Sydney, the hybrid who woke Charon, the ferryman, and carried our souls into space, freeing me from my Themian incarceration?" he asked, looking at me through his head eyebrows.

All right. That sounded pretty good. And it was something I was willing to take credit for.

"Or maybe you could be Sydney, the most dangerous of the three Fates?" He continued, as the tone of his voice dropped an octave, shaking the marrow in my bones with the truth. "The one who cuts your life's string." He leaned in close, his nose almost touching mine as he whispered those final words to me. I didn't even see him move.

I couldn't deny what he said. I had the ability to cut your life off in the blink of an eye. I didn't even have to touch the person. But I also knew that I wouldn't do it on my own. The judges were a three filter system, and I firmly believed that tribunals could be fair. People needed Hera and Isolde between them and me. I was not as forgiving as they were.

I've seen too much evil to forgive.

"Hephaestus, I presume." I thrust my hand out as an offer of friendship. Hephaestus was direct and to the point.

He tilted his head down to inspect the offered hand before replying, "The very same," His meaty hand engulfed my own. "You are wise to leave Emmaline in charge. She has a clear head and won't allow any subterfuge from any of my brothers. Especially from Ares and Eris." He leaned in as if it was some kind of the secret that Ares was a troublemaker. Eris, on the other hand, might not be able to help herself.

"I hear one of my sisters is joining Hercules on Prometheus, and you wish me to do so also?" he asked.

His open honesty washed over me, and I found myself smiling. I liked this son of Hera.

"Yes, it's not that I don't trust Hercules. He's handy. I am told that you're a genius and an inventor. If any of the mythologies are to be believed..." I winked at him.

He threw his head back and boomed with laughter. "If any of the mythologies are to be believed, you would think that

I was the son of a God. A true born God and raised along with Ares, and Hercules would be nothing more than a mere DemiGod." He smirked down at me, "In truth, we are just hybrids. Yes, I am an inventor, and as a boy, I was very talented with the hammer and the forge. Though, I have not been on Earth for many thousands of years. I've learned new talents." He looked down and away as if he was embarrassed. "Would you like to take a look at your soon-to-be Faster than Light engine for Odyssey?" He asked.

He was feisty, intelligent, and to the point. He didn't waste your time with superfluous words and posturing. He was perfectly comfortable with exactly who and what he was.

"Yes, I would." I glanced over his shoulder to this ship behind him. "Can we use these engines for the time being?" I pointed at the thrusters and with a hopeful smile.

"It's a perfectly serviceable ship. Could use a little fine-tuning, though. The engines are in good working order. Other than not being very pretty or comfortable on the inside, I don't see anything wrong with the ship. After I'm finished, you won't need this ship. You may wish to put it back into space." He shrugged. "Although, I'm afraid there's really no one here capable of operating this ship other than one of my siblings and a few trained specialists. Most of the hybrids don't have enough knowledge to launch themselves into the spatial void safely. They would die."

"Yeah, I get that. Why don't we have somebody start training them? Space flight 101? We will obviously need pilots. There are only three shifters among us. It would be nice to know that we had an armada versus just a couple of ships floating around without a rudder," I remarked.

<Get Ares to start a flight school to go along with his army.> I asked Emmaline. Ares liked her, and she seemed like the best filter.

"Well, now you're speaking a language I understand - an armada. I know why you're welding the Argos into the doors. You want to increase your light-speed capability. These sublight engines are sub-par, and you want faster than light."

"Yes, I mean when the computer tells you based upon your trajectory and top speed, that you're not getting anywhere for three years, but your son and husband are somewhere else... Your willingness to wait three years is extremely low," I remarked. We moved to stand next to the engineering door. He would need to scrunch into a small ball to pass through, so I stopped there.

"My recommendation is to stop Hercules! Tell him to stop and step away from the spaceship. I'll make a second set of engines just like Odyssey's. It won't take me long. We have more than enough raw materials to manufacture them. Took me longer to come up with the first prototypes. The production time is two weeks, and we can jump to whatever system you desire." He stared me down with self-assurance.

"Or we could just stay here until everything is done," Ares interjected. He was as transparent as the viewports on the bridge.

"I've a feeling you're not going to be interested in staying here once I present you with what we've found," Hephaestus said. A shy smile curved one side of his face. His dark hair fell to quickly cover the smile hiding him away from more scrutiny.

"What is that?" I asked.

He hefted a small chip out of a pocket.

"A direct map to another system," he pointed to the small holo that bloomed in his hand from his bracelet. "Mining ships usually head back to their home planets."

My mouth went dry, waiting for him to say the magic words, "And the name of the system?" I asked. My belly quaked as hope raced around my chest.

"Mourning Field, the star is named Dido. The largest of the colonies is Phaedra. They mine crystals. One of the other colonies is mining for trace minerals, so we can stop at any of them," he stated.

"Did you find all of this on the data-banks?"

He shook his head, "No, the data-banks had been wiped clean. It was a picture on the wall labeled home." He pushed the image at me, and it leapt to life in my hand from my bracelet.

It was as clear as we were going to get. Adrian's eyes devoured every detail.

"I pulled it off the wall of someone's quarters. I was actually heading to Odyssey to show it to Ixis. Although, since my great-grandnephew is here, Adrian, you can do the honors."

I really didn't like being shifted without some kind of notification. Adrian had been doing it for the last few hours.

When he did, it didn't bother me, almost as if I had willed it myself.

Emmaline handed something off to one of her crew and made a beeline for us, "Back already?" a thrill ran over the room as if she'd willed it.

"Tristan's fine. Melinda patched him up nicely. Probably will be fine in about an hour." Her cheeks puffed up as she released a breath of air. "Course, he'll be fine! He's one of us. My family always has a stiff upper lip." She drolled and patted her hair, then pulled out her gold case and lit a cigarette.

"Emmaline, you're not British," I murmured

"No one needs to be British to be made of stronger stuff. Stiff upper lips aren't just for the British. Everybody in the war had one. Dewy especially. Dew is my hero, along with Ixis."

Dewy was practically glowing. Emmaline didn't say sweet things often, but when she did, it was usually about Dewy.

Adrian was already at the main pedestal in the shifting room. Odyssey pulled up the holo display.

I will never get over watching one computer program take something two-dimensional and beautiful all on its own and turn it into a magical 3D experience.

I just loved it.

Sorry, I'm a geek.

"Can you make that jump?" I asked

Adrian smiled and gave me a wink. "Of course I can, beautiful girl. I shifted us here to find you, didn't I?" His lip curled a little bit

<Don't become a cocky bastard!> I groaned.

<I've every right to be cocky. I jumped us through a black hole into an unknown universe. Give me my kudos!>

<You're right. Kudos to you.> I tilted my head.

He lowered his eyes as he lowered his head as if he was some kind of a king, graciously accepting my congratulations on something that he was entitled to anyway.

"Talk to Ixis and get our boy up here if you can. I want all three of you in on this before we make a shift," I said.

<Tristan is ready to leave the infirmary.> I asked.

<I can handle a little shift.> He replied

"Whose shifting Prometheus?" Emmaline asked.

"Ixis is. He'll be over there in a minute. Let me know when you're ready," Adrian supplied. His eyes were glued to the holo display. He'd enlarged it to fill the room and was turning it in every direction.

Emmaline disappeared. I smiled. Ixis had the same idea as Adrian. Never go anywhere without your woman.

As long as the Fates were separated, Charon wouldn't have an excuse to shift one ship away. There was no way I was leaving Adrian's side right now, or ever.

"Emmaline just told me that they're ready," Tristan announced as he took his place next to his father.

I put my hand on his shoulder, "Shifting now," they said in unison.

I don't know which part of the picture Adrian had focused on. We appeared just far enough away to see the orange light from Dido and the dark planet which I had to assume was Phaedra.

Phaedra had a moon. It wasn't a singular star system. It was binary. Dido had a tiny companion.

CHAPTER 38

SYDNEY

"Odyssey, scan the entire system for life."

"Acknowledged. Scanning now."

A three-dimensional map formed. Dido did indeed had a dwarf star friend. Every planetoid had a moon. "Odyssey, find out if Prometheus has any data about the moons and the secondary sun."

"Communicating with Prometheus now. Is Emmaline still Capitan, or will you once again lead the vessel?"

A voice came from over my shoulder. "Technically she's an admiral. She's in charge of more than one ship," Ares stated the facts.

Trust him to clear all that up.

"I don't think we need to get too tangled up with semantics," I muttered, uncomfortable with the title or the responsibility that came with it.

"According to Prometheus' data-banks, none of the moons, nor the secondary star are named in the Mourning Fields. The secondary star and the moons are considered the unrequited lovers of the star and planetoids. None of them have a name because their names are irrelevant. The star and planet didn't actually love whoever it was." Ixis stopped and tilted his head to the side. "This place is dead — lifeless. There is no atmosphere and no gravity. The moon is technically more of an asteroid than it is a moon. Its behavior is chaotic. The smaller star does, in fact, rotate around Dido. However, Dido's gravity is pushing it away, not pulling towards. Dido rejects the star." The timber of Ixis' voice shot over the top of me.

Together but always apart.

Her lover was a dim brick color to Dido's orange. I sighed for the heartbreak of it.

"As children, we're told the story of the Mourning Fields," Hera said in a low tight cold voice. "It is the place where people who spent their lives lost in unrequited love would wander for all eternity, constantly rejected by their heart's desire, living in the shadows, never able to be free from their desperate love." Hera's matter of fact voice was almost cold.

Silence descended on the room. I glanced sharply at her. She only stared into the vacuous darkness. Her blond hair was hung down to her waist and provided a curtain to hide her face.

"Wow, that's not freaky or anything. Considering Odyssey's description, it does sound like every planet is rejecting its moon," Tristan remarked.

He had never been in love, and his reaction wasn't a shock to me. Hera cringed away from the wound it dug in her heart. All our conversations had revealed enough for me to understand Zeus never loved her, and she knew it.

"Odyssey, are there any signs of life on the planet?" Adrian moved on from the thick desperation that had settled over the room.

"Yes, there is a settlement on the far side," the ship responded.

"Are we in a position to get a visual?" he continued.

"I don't believe that anyone should go down to the surface until we've tried contacting them first," Ares stated. The air around him hummed with excitement.

I wondered who shifted him over here? I left him on Prometheus for a reason - peace. I glanced at Ixis and Emmaline. Her face was a blank page.

"We would be foolish to go down there." Dewy bolstered Ares' opinion. It came across as if he was keeping the peace between Adrian and Ares.

"Ares, any other suggestions? Should we contact them? Knock on the old asteroid and ask if anyone is home?" I shot back.

A half smile curled the right side of his face, and his blue eyes twinkled, "No, scan for frequencies and see if we can contact them on one of the bands we are already using."

Adrian ground his jaw. "Odyssey, how long until we get there?"

"At our current speed, four days."

"Take us into orbit," I ordered. My bone-tired body was going to rebel soon and I needed this over with before I passed out.

***

"The ship is in geosynchronous orbit directly over the mining colony," Ares announced with his hand over the shoulder of a man in the new flight console. The man's head was shaved high and tight. There was a tattoo on the back of his head with something written in Russian.

I glanced over at Ares, "Well, you're in charge of anything that might be considered hostile. Gather your troops. Adrian will shift you down to the surface, prepare to make contact with our friends."

"I've opened a channel with the mining colony. They are, in fact, a penal colony. Their leader wishes to speak with you."

My body stiffened, taking up a defensive stance.

"I am Rasha of Phaedra. State your business and purpose here," Rasha informed us.

"My name is Sydney, Admiral of the Prometheus." I regarded Adrian. "We're here for resupplying and a course correction for Elysium," I replied, hoping a little fudging on our part wouldn't fuck us.

"I don't recognize you or your ship's name," was his hard response.

"Whether you recognize my name or my ship is irrelevant. Do you really think Elysium is going to check in with you every time they send out a new Admiral or launch a new ship? Open your doors and your data-banks to us or we will open them for ourselves," I barked, thrusting as much steel into my voice as possible. Anyone stationed on a penal colony couldn't be in anyone's good graces.

"We're unarmed. You don't need to attack us. We are only trying to make sure you are not here to steal our quota," he replied. His voice shook with fear.

"We don't steal," I said, "We are simply here for an even exchange of information."

Emmaline, she had her hand over her mouth, and her eyes searched mine.

"This isn't just a penal colony. These people are slaves here for all time. Their children's children, it's not even like they committed the original crimes. They are only here because their ancestors had no way of leaving the planet." Her jaw locked down, and her eyes grew hard.

That's horrible! Who would enslave an entire bloodline?

"Do they have any idea what the original crimes were?"

She shook her head. Adrian was rubbing the bridge of his nose. "What are you hearing?" I demanded.

"They still think you're here to rob them. Whatever they are mining, they'll be punished if it disappears. They have no way to defend themselves or get off the planet. They are stuck here," Adrian informed the bridge.

"Are any of them actually criminals? I know there's always a bad apple in the batch—" Evil, it was the only word I could find to explain how I felt. This was pure evil.

"There's a few less than savory folks, but that doesn't mean that they should be enslaved for all time for a crime that they didn't even commit," Adrian barked as if he was fighting with me.

I surveyed the viewport and the dead planet beyond. It was a lifeless rock that had some interesting color veins. Other than that, I couldn't see anything else of value. I didn't even think about it. The answer was simple. We add them all to our population and run the risk of adding a bad apple. Which I was sure that we were pretty well capable of handling.

Adrian said they were plain old Elysians, not hybrid in any way.

We are the hybrid of a hybrid, dummy.

"Shift Hera and Isolde over here along with Hercules." I contemplated Ares, begging him to challenge me. "We are going with you."

The entire shifting room erupted with everyone arguing, with Adrian pointing out immediately that we couldn't go. Emmaline remarked that you can't make someone the captain of a ship and then steal them away. Ares shouted he couldn't guarantee anyone's safety.

I lifted my hand, "I will not leave these people here to be slaves," I roared over the crowd. "Would you want to be slaves?" I stared them all down. "I know what it's like to be forced to work without doing anything wrong. To be beaten and treated like you're sub-human, less than everyone else. I know what it's like to have zero choices." The room fell silent. "To live with no way out." The cabinet doors in the shifting room rattled in their frames. "I will not leave anybody to that life. I can't think of a worse fate. If Isolde, Hera, and I go down there, we can weed out troublemakers. They don't pass the Fates, they don't come. And then, anyone who does, we can give them the choice of remaining plain old Elysians or joining our ragtag group of hybrids. Give them Primordium."

Hera opened her mouth to argue.

<Save it!> I yelled at her.

Ares' jaw muscles worked, clenching and unclenching. He worked the muscles in his arm, "You don't know for sure that there isn't anything down there, defending those people, keeping them from leaving. There might be something that could trap us," he snarled.

"I'm pretty sure no original Elysium ever imagined what we can really do. There's nothing down there that can trap us, and I know there's nothing that can trap me," I growled.

This is the right choice!

"I can't stop you, but we're not taking our son," Adrian whispered through clenched teeth.

"No, Tristan goes to Prometheus. Ixis stays here with Emmaline. Your sister, the chaotic one, can become the temporary Captain of Prometheus, co-captain along with Professor Michelson." I glanced at Ares for confirmation. "I want twenty of our fighters and I need a fully loaded ship with whatever weapons have." I swept over to Emmaline.

"I'm sorry, Emmaline. We need to take Dewy. I think he is an anchor for you. You're able to reach through him somehow, and we might need you to take over — someone. It's a rare talent, and if you could do it to save our lives, I know Dewy would want you to," I offered as an explanation. It came out as more of an order.

"Christ, Emm. I've never turned away from a fight, I won't start now." Dewy put his arm around Emmaline. She shrugged him off and smacked him on the chest, "You big dummy, if you get yourself killed— " Emmaline broke off, swallowing her fear.

Dewy wiped the smile off his face, "Course, Emm, but you and me are forever, so I know you'll save me." He gave her a goofy smile.

She returned it and smacked him again, "Can't be forever if you're dead dumb, dumb."

Dewey stood up straight and took me in with his serious blue eyes "I am at your command, Admiral."

It's a stupid title.

"We can take the Ogygia. It's a perfectly sensible ship, or we can take one of our own shuttles," Ares said.

I cocked my eye at the name of the ship - Ogygia. That was the island Calypso lived on.

"I want to take one of our shuttles and turn on the obscure-a. Make sure they can't spot the ship as we descend. I want every shuttle we have in space, including the craft on Prometheus. Just shift them out. They don't need a pilot. It's a show of force." Ares hardly took a breath as he rattled off instructions into his bracelet.

The Russian sitting at the controls got up and moved with the force of a man trained in fighting.

"There's no atmosphere down there. We have our own suits. I'm sure they're better than anything on Prometheus." Adrian shifted me into a smaller chamber off the side of the shuttle bay. It was set up like a traditional locker room.

He led me over to a small airlock.

"Say your name," he instructed, "The machine will scan you and produce a suit."

"Like in Star Trek, remember? They just pushed buttons and the food came out," I said as I began braiding my hair. Last thing I wanted was hair in my face while trying to look official.

"Yeah, they have a ton of 3D printers on board. This one is dedicated to nothing but spacesuits. If you have one made at the other stations. It might not have the proper radiation shielding and you can die."

"When did you get so smart about all this stuff?" I asked.

I wasn't surprised. Impressed maybe, but not surprised.

"Well, I was 30 years alone on an island waiting for Mrs. Perfect to find me. When you have that much time, you learn a lot. Add a few months without sleep and bob's your uncle I learned."

I put my hand on the side of his face I leaned down, and just as our lips met,

"Oh God, get a room," Tristan groaned.

"Sorry, sweetheart," I laughed, though I didn't feel sorry at all.

"I really, really don't want to see my biologicals getting it on. Ever," He remarked with disgust.

"Well, then you shouldn't just walk into a room without announcing yourself," I snapped.

"Or you can try no PDA everywhere. This is a public space! You could just get a private room." He drolled, then rolled his eyes.

I threw him a *'watch your mouth, or I'll slap it right off your face'* sneer, "You're going over to Prometheus, so it should cut down on the PDAs. They don't have a shifter that isn't a pain in the ass or manipulating everyone. I need you there."

With a pained glance down he asked, "Who's gonna watch your back? It's my job." Tristan snuck a peek at me through his eyebrows.

"I'm watching your mother's back, and we're taking Hercules," Adrian interjected. He pulled his suit over one shoulder and then the other with a huff, latched his belt, and let his eyes trail up before meeting his son's intense stare.

He shook his head "Hercules? You choose to leave your own son, but you'll take that windbag? It's my job to watch your back, mom," Tristan bellowed and puffed his chest up.

"No, Tristan, your job right now is to make sure that both ships sitting here are capable of leaving if we need to leave. I need to know you can do that, even if Adrian can't," I whispered, chancing a peek at Adrian, then back to Tristan. "You may be the only one who can," I put both hands on his shoulders. His eyes darted away, avoiding the truth of my words. With one finger under his chin, I forced him to face me. "Ixis doesn't have the same kind of connection. You can find Isolde anywhere." I nodded to get him to agree with me. "Ixis can't, and by finding Isolde, you could save all of us. I need you here." I took a breath.

Sitting on the sidelines sucks. You have to wait in case you're needed, even if you aren't.

His shoulders sagged. He stared off, unseeing into the distant wall, snapped his jaw shut with a loud click, then opened it again. He whipped his head to the left to bore holes into Adrian.

"I know you're my biological father, and I like you, but this is my mother, my sister... if they die and somehow you come back..." Tristan trailed off, leaving his threat unfinished.

"Not even a discussion, son. If your mother dies, so do I. I won't be coming back alone."

Tristan mouthed a *'good'* under his breath and stormed out of the room. I really thought they made some strides while I was gone.

"I thought things were better," I murmured.

"They are. He's just flexing his muscles. It's his job to tell me that if anything bad happens to his family, he'll kill me. He doesn't want me to think less of him. I'd be more worried if he didn't say it." He smirked, then ran his hand down my arm before sealing his suit and thrusting his hands into gloves.

"You mean like Tobias running around telling everybody that he would kill them if they breathed at me the wrong way," I smiled.

He smirked "Yeah, exactly like that, only Tobias never caught us." He shook his head this time.

I did kiss him but it was just a quick peck.

A quiet smile stole across his face as he ducked his head. The door on the 3D printer slid open, presenting me with my new shiny spacesuit.

I snatched it and proceeded over to the girls' side of the locker room and slipped into my thermal jumpsuit before pulling the rubbery spacesuit on over the top.

Carrying my helmet, I headed out to the shuttle, only to be greeted by about 18 other people milling around, waiting their turn to board.

"At the ready," Dewy's voice boomed, flooding the room with the order.

Every head snapped up while bodies moved into formation and suddenly held themselves at ridged attention, except for myself and Adrian. I gulped back the awe and dread of the moment. These were our fighters, and I was expecting them to plunge into the breach between us and danger.

My eyes burned at the lack of information we had. Phaedra could be a death trap.

Would Adrian be able to move us all to safety in time?

"Stand aside for your Admiral," Area growled. He kicked one man's boot. It was out of alignment. The man dipped his head quickly, righting himself.

The men moved like an ocean as one large wave parting, for me. The power of the moment washed over me, and I took a deep breath and a step.

How did I get here again?

<By being the strongest fighter, I know.> Adrian whispered.

"Thank you!" I replied to the room and Adrian at the same time.

We boarded the ship, and Adrian led me forward to the cockpit. I breathed past the fear that riddled through my soul. I took a seat at the back, while Adrian moved into one of the pilot seats.

"Do you know how to fly this thing?" I asked in disbelief.

"30 years on a crazy island run by Greek Gods waiting for a beautiful girl...remember?" He replied. His sarcasm forced me to hitch a smile.

"Right, sorry. I don't know anything about that." I clicked my tongue at him and gave him a scouts salute.

"Learning to fly must be exhilarating." I remarked.

"I made it into outer space without having to join NASA or the Air Force. Now that's definitely a feather I wanted to put in my cap," he remarked.

"Never thought you were interested in being an astronaut. Engineers aren't usually astronauts," I said, hoping he would explain.

"Touché!" Adrian replied and tapped the low res holo display that jumped to life in front of him. His fingers flashed through several displays, and a low rumble vibrated through the ship's frame.

Ares filed in with his second-in-command, and the Russian, he took the other pilot seat. The Russian sat down next to me, offering only a stiff nod and not bothering to introduce himself. "The crew is aboard and the outer door's closed, so are we ready to move?" Ares asked while expecting only one answer.

"Yeah," Adrian replied.

Ares gave him a hard stare. The unsaid *'yes, sir'* lingered in the room. Adrian ignored the obvious tension and lifted the ship off the deck.

I held my breath in anticipation of the pressure change that never came. Adrian's style in the last few months became as easy as taking a breath of air.

I hated the feeling of a shift. One moment you were here, the next moment you were somewhere else. It reminded me of the sort of thing wizards and witches do. It was never something I thought that I would see or experience for myself.

The ship reappeared outside Odyssey, and the darkened rock we were approaching filled the holo view. I glanced at Adrian, "Didn't you forget someone? Three someone's rather?" I drifted up from the deck in the zero G environment. I raised my hand to push off the ceiling.

"No, I didn't. They weren't ready. I was giving them time. Shifting now." He didn't rise to my needling and instead coolly did his job.

Hera, Isolde, and Hercules appeared in front of me. We'd only been separated maybe ten hours, but I still acutely missed Isolde. I knew that she was an adult in every way and spending more time away from me than with me was normal. Moreso, it didn't help that she was, for all intents and purposes, married.

Until recently, the longest I'd been parted from the twins was a few hours. I missed her when she was gone, her and Tristan. It was a deep ache in the background, filling me up. Now, it seemed all their time was spent away from me, and I had very little time myself to fixate on it.

"Hey, mom," Issy smirked and threw a peck on my cheek.

"Fashionably late?" I remarked. Issy waved a hand at Hercules as if it was his fault.

"Yeah, well, I was having a hard time getting my suit on," Hercules chuckled and Issy smacked him on the chest.

"I wouldn't have had such a hard time if someone hadn't kept trying to take it off," Herc moaned and Isolde's ears turned pink. She looked around, trying to find somewhere else to lay her eyes.

"Okay, well we don't need any more of your silly love play. This is serious time now." I coughed to hide my shock.

"Okay, mom." Issy unhitched her gun from her thigh harness, checked the setting, and clipped it back in, "I'm ready for anything," she announced.

"I realize that you are my brother's wife, so, don't leave your weapons around like he does," Ares barked.

"Are you besmirching my good name, brother?" Hercules asked with feigned shock.

Ares laughed under his breath. "What an excellent word to use. Are you sure you used it correctly?" Ares never looked at his brother, though the side of his face curled with a smile, as Hercules grounded his teeth and took a seat.

I shook my head. It reminded me of my days working with Zack. The smile on my face slipped away. Now wasn't the time for regret. I shoved my thoughts of Zack into a mental box and closed the filing cabinet drawer.

Ares used the maneuvering thrusters to put us in a better position for approach. "Engaging the G-drive now. Brace for point five earth gravity." The announcement filtered into the bowls of the ship. He and Adrian turned to look at each other, and both pressed the flight controls forward. Gravity worked its magic on my chest, reminding me of our flight out of Delphi. The crush was no more than the press of an airplane take-off, but the memory was still too fresh.

CHAPTER 39

SYDNEY

The surface of the mining complexes was a few landing platforms and some kind of a scaffolding system. The surrounding landscape was riddled with deep ravines and shallow valleys. Each formation etched by the hands of a slave.

"Land on that platform," Ares indicated on the holo view. Both men turned into the descent to aline with the platform.

I stood up for a better view. The platform didn't have a number. The surface was painted with three star bursts. Ares opened a channel ship wide, "Helmets on."

"Well, you're flying this beast," I remarked and locked my helmet in place. Hera checked the seal, then turned so I could inspect hers.

There was a heavy thud as we touched down. I was expecting a larger degree of gravity, but our G-drive was putting out more than the planet.

Ares led the way to the hatch, and I took a deep breath. Hera, Isolde, and I stood to the back with a dozen men ready to exit the ship. The metal of the ramp made contact with the platform and carried through the ship.

The breath I'd been holding leaked out, creating a hissing sound. Ares waved four men down the ramp. They disappeared, with one returning a minute later to wave for the all-clear.

The platform lowered into the mining complex. The roof closed over the top of us as the far wall fell away to reveal some kind of cargo bay.

Adrian shifted us in and rearranged where everyone was standing so the Fates were protected on all sides. Hercules, Ares, and Adrian stood at the front of our group.

I cocked my eyebrow at him, <You know I don't like it when you do that without saying something.> I grumbled.

<I know. Sorry.> He wasn't sorry, and we both knew it.

"We are the Council of Three. We run this mining colony," Rasha announced. I recognized his voice.

"You're in charge, but not in charge?" I asked.

Their shoulders slumped and their eyes gazed at the ground. I understood this posture. They were beaten down in every way. Their body language screamed it. He didn't even answer me with words, just nodded his head sideways, trying not to look at me. I found that fact to be unbelievable.

It put a dry and nasty taste in my mouth. "Where are your captors — your guards?"

"There are no captors or guards. There's no way to escape this planet. We have no ships. Our captor is space itself. The guards only come to load up. If we reach our quota, they leave, and if not, or they're dissatisfied — they single someone out for torture and make everyone watch," Rasha offered.

Isolde stepped forward to stand next to me. I didn't even realize I'd moved. "None of you thought to make weapons and defend yourselves?"

The man next to him shook his head, "No, they have implanted devices. If we tried to rise up, they would single out your family and kill them all with just the push of a button." He only had one eye.

I flared my nostrils at the idea that someone would punish people by killing their wives and children. It was repugnant. In Roman times if one person defied the Emperor, they would kill off his entire bloodline, unless he committed suicide to save them.

Ruling through fear is not anything new.

Most dictators run totalitarian regimes. They rule through fear, instead of trying to lead with love.

"Can you tell me where these devices are in your body?"

The man pointed to the base of his neck.

Of course, the base of the neck. You sever the spine, and you kill the person quick and easy. Why do they always pick the same spot?

Why couldn't they be a little more inventive?

<Remove it.> I ordered.

<With pleasure, *beautiful girl.* Where you want me to send it? > Adrian asked.

I smiled at him <One of the shuttles from Prometheus. Save them. Hopefully, we will run into a few captors and give them a dose of their own medicine.> I replied.

<Sound like a great plan to me, beautiful girl.>

None of the people standing in front of us realized what Adrian was capable of.

One of the devices appeared in his hand.

<Don't worry. They won't go off after removal.> Adrian informed me. <They need the trigger device for detonation.>

"Is this the device you're talking about?" I asked.

"Yes, how did you get it?" He reached his hand up to rub the base of his neck. His eyes darted around with surprise.

"Mine is— it was there! I know it was there this morning. I felt for it like I do every morning. The ball... it's gone." He turned to regard his two companions, then looked off in the distance at the open doorway, where people had crowded to peek out.

"It's gone! The killing device is gone!" Everyone touched the back of their necks and exclaimed with surprise.

"Who are you that you are capable of such feats?"

"We are people just like you, no different. The only difference between your people and my people is that we are free, and you are not. If you wish to be free, you are welcome to come with us. The only caveat is that you must face the judgment of— "

A woman burst from the doorway, pushing people this way and that. "You are the Fates! You've come to liberate us?" She announced and asked at the same time. Our group collectively gasped. Hera was the only person who wasn't surprised. I was astonished that she knew who we were.

Hera spoke, "We are the Fates. If you are ready to be judged, step forward."

The three men in front of us trembled in fear.

This was the part that I hated. I didn't mind leading, but I hated to be the bringer of death.

Rasha stepped forward.

Hera's eyes glazed over with the milky white, "You are ready. You may move on."

He moved to Isolde, who put her hand on his right shoulder and immediately began crying. "You've been judged, your skein has been measured. You must move on." She sobbed.

He stepped in front of me, and I wanted to look away. Yet, couldn't. I was locked in place against my will. My hand rose up, and I placed it on his forehead.

I mentally screamed with frustration. I could choose to let him live, perhaps redeem himself or let him die for all the many crimes he committed against his own people. He betrayed them, time after time, whispering about his fellow prisoners to save his own skin. He turned in a friend to save his own family. Once a betrayer, always a betrayer.

I gulped the bitter taste back. My path was clear. Still, I wrestled with it.

Could he be trusted to live amongst us? Would he stab us in the back? That kind of weakness of character could get us all killed. We couldn't give him the Primordium. What if he became nothing more than a disease to all of us?

I couldn't let him live. We couldn't take the risk. The words thunder for my mouth. "You have been judged, and your skein has been cut."

The deep vibration of my voice rolled through his body as his eyes rolled into the back of his head, and he fell to the ground. Blood seeped from his ears and leaked from his nose. His eyes filled with blood from broken vessels, leaving only the black unseeing irises.

I regained control of my body and glanced around.

A woman clutched his lifeless body to her breast, weeping uncontrollably.

I had to say something, or these people were going to revolt. They had been cowed and beaten, but now that they knew there was no way to kill them, they would rise up if I didn't say something.

"Your friend and leader betrayed you, all of you," I announced in a hard voice.

Isolde's voice lifted to join my own, "He sold you out for better service from your captors. They brought him special supplies to turn people in. He was not your friend." She looked down at his wife. Compassion filled her face, "He wasn't true to anyone." She lowered her voice, "He cheated on you many times."

The woman covered her mouth to stifle the cry that issued forth. She stood up and wiped her face with her grimy clothing. She sniffed and said, "I am ready. You may judge me. I will either live free or die here." She truly believed she would pass.

Hera placed her left hand on her shoulder. There was a sharp whiff of ozone and Hera said, "You are ready. You may pass."

She walked to Isolde and the process repeated. "You have been measured. You may pass."

A knot formed in my throat. The power of life and death didn't make me feel anything other than guilt and sadness.

I placed my hand on her forehead. She had truly loved Rasha. She saw him for who he was and loved him anyway. She believed everyone deserves to be loved.

It was a foolish belief, but she has a kind heart. The overwhelming proof of her kind heart hit me like a kick to the gut.

I pulled my hand away, "You may come with us."

She coughed out her relief, and three small children ran to her, clutching at her grimy skirt. Her terrified eyes regarded me. "Do they need to be judged also?" her trembling lower lip barely got the words out.

"No, all children are free to come with us as they are. But they must not have reached physical adulthood," I replied.

A murmur raced over the crowd. Parents pushed their children forward. Adrian immediately shifted them all to the Citadel.

<Tell Emmaline to take care of them.> I asked Adrian.

The crowd immediately fell to their knees and put their heads on the ground. They thought we were Gods.

My stomach rolled, and bile climbed the lining of my throat. I swallowed back, leaving a burning trail all the way to my belly.

"We are not Gods! No matter what you think. Everything you've seen is simply an ability we inherited from our forebears," Hera boomed. Her need to point out the difference worried me.

"Are you the children of the Judges of Elysium?" a voice called out.

The question threw me off balance.

"No!" I shouted as I surveyed the crowd. I wanted it clear that we were not one of them. From what I'd seen through Charon's mind, I didn't want anything to do with them.

"I am Teldarc," he said. His muscles worked overtime to stand up straight. The effort wasn't enough to take the bow out of his back. "You seek a path to Elysium."

My heart stilled. I chanced a glance at Isolde.

"No one here has ever been to Elysium. It is a place we've heard of and never seen," Teldarc stated and the hollow tone of his voice carried over the crowd. He gave up the fight to stand tall and hunched down. His brave announcement shocked me.

Many in the crowd turned away to head back through the doors and their life of drudgery, as if we would leave them here.

"I am from Elysium. I am what they call an original sinner. Although, I committed no crime," the man with one eye shouted for everyone to hear.

<Adrian, can you pick anything up? >

Adrian shook his head, <No! It's not that his mind is shielded. He simply doesn't know the star charts. He never saw Elysium from space. I could teleport people there, but I couldn't move the ships.>

"Are you ready to be judged?" I asked the man.

"Yes, it was foretold the Fates would arrive, and they would set us free from the Judges. All of us are only here because they failed to please the Judges of Elysium."

Hera quickly completed her part, and the man moved on to Isolde. She pronounced him ready to face me.

I bored into his one brown eye, seeking the soul buried within. His body trembled with fear. I placed my hand on his forehead, and the mind dump began to playback.

He was neither a good nor bad scientist. He simply wanted to better life on Elysium. He'd invented a new way to grow food that could triple their food output. When he presented it before the Judges, they gave him an impossible task. They gave him one *Terra* of land and told him he must grow enough food, in one season, to feed an entire city. A city of millions. It was an impossible task. He knew it. He accepted the challenge anyway. You could not walk away from the Judges.

His string was not ready to be cut. I pulled out of his mind, thrilled to be free of the responsibility of his death.

"You have been judged. Step away." He did, and his entire body collapsed in front of me.

This sucks!

CHAPTER 40

SYDNEY

The next person stepped forward, and Hera didn't offer to judge him. She heaved a sigh, "We don't need to judge all of them, simply give them a ship and set them free," she offered.

"Where would they go? They don't know anything about the cosmos. Setting them free without any help... what if they break down? Do you really want all their deaths on your conscience? Also, the only ship we have that is big enough is Prometheus. I'm not willing to part with it. Are you?" I demanded in a low voice. There was no need for everyone to hear us bickering.

"I don't want to judge them all. Take everyone who wants to go with us. Anyone else, give them the Argos. It has faster than light engines, they could get somewhere fast enough. Hopefully, they won't die and..." Her voice trailed away. Her pained eyes burned me.

Judging was draining. I didn't think I could go through thousands myself. At this pace, we wouldn't be done in years. I didn't know if I could do it day after day.

My brow pulled down in frustration. I didn't want to judge all these people.

Determining who's good and who's bad is playing God.

"I think we should offer four options," Adrian said, "One - you stay, two - we leave you a ship, three - come with us and be sequestered to part of the ship until such time as you're not a threat, four - you step forth, be judged and immediately join the population."

Four choices were better than none, and these people have never had any.

"Adrian's solution is a wise one," Hera quickly replied and turned back to the crowd.

"It is a good idea," Isolde offered.

"Call your brother. Tell him that we need to cut that ship out. You and Hercules go and do it," I said.

She released a deep sigh. The weight of judging was heaviest on her.

"Jorhan is already working on it," she returned. A moment later, the two of them blinked out. I bit my lip.

"I'll make the announcement. You go back to the ship and organize an area for these people," I said to Hera, "They can all go to the same guarded section. We will start judging whoever wants to be judged as soon as we get back to the ship with the data we need." I winked at Adrian.

"Shifting now," he rumbled.

Hera blinked out. Those left, were standing with Adrian, Ares, and the Russian guy, who took up a flanking position

"Everyone who wants to come with us but doesn't want to be judged will be given quarters on the ship. You will be confined to that section until such a time as we can determine what type of a person you are. This is a safety measure for you and for us." People poured out of the underground complex. "As you can see, we have abilities you've never encountered before. A lot of our people are still learning their abilities, and we don't want anyone to get hurt. Being separated is good for both sides. When we can determine that you're not a threat to us or the ship, you'll be allowed to intermingle with my people."

The faces before me moved through a rainbow of emotions. Most of which included fear.

"If you choose to be judged right away, you'll immediately be released into the main population. If you don't want to leave with us and you don't want to be judged, we will leave you a spaceship. You're welcome to leave this planet and go anywhere you desire. We will make sure that you have a large database to get you there. And ensure you have enough food and supplies to get you there. Those are the options. I would like to say that anybody who does come with us, will be educated and well treated. We do not have a class-based system, where some people are treated better than others. We are all equal. Your children would be educated, and you would be welcomed into a society that is free of slavery." An awe flooded the platform as if the sun had shone. "You would no longer be forced to do anything you find distasteful. However, our society doesn't believe in being idle, and you would be expected to perform some kind of duty or service to keep yourself busy. I don't care if it's food preparation. That's fine."

There was a lot of murmuring, people going back and forth. Two women with similar features came forward, "If we come with you, but don't want to be judged, can we change our mind?" One asked while holding the hands of the other.

"Yes, absolutely! Just because you come with us doesn't mean you have to stay with us. It also doesn't mean that you can't change your mind about anything. Coming with us gives you more choices. At least with us, you have a race of people who are familiar with traveling through space. We have a lot of tech-savvy people who could retrain you for other jobs. You would be healthy and free. If you leave in your own ship," I opened my hands, unsure of what to say. "I cannot guarantee that you will reach your destination safely. All I can guarantee is that you have a ship that you will be able to take it anywhere you like, and that it's functional." I'd answered their question as best I could. Even so, my reply did not fill me with much joy.

The two women looked at each other, then back to me, "We'll go with you. But we don't want to be judged. We just want to go."

I tilted my head down then glanced over at Adrian. He said, "I'm going to move you. You might feel a little pop at the end. Don't be frightened. It's instantaneous, and you'll hardly notice it." He gave them a winning smile, and both women reacted by giggling.

They grabbed each other's hand, and in a moment, they were gone. I would've expected there to be more of an outcry. Instead, there was just a lot of murmuring, and then a bunch of people stepped forward.

At this rate, it would take forever, "Everyone who wants to come with us, step to the right. Everyone who wants to be judged to the left. If you're staying, go back inside and don't come out."

The platform erupted in movement and voices calling to each other: mothers herding children, and husbands leading families. Once the groups had organized themselves, Adrian moved them all in the blink of an eye. Eventually, there was no one left in the dock other than my people.

"I guess we're done here," Ares stated the obvious.

The Argos appeared on the platform, and Hercules and Isolde were by my side.

"It was a lot faster getting it out than welding it in, I guess," I remarked, taking in the smudges of score and char on their clothes and faces.

"No, Hephaestus had already started taking it out. He said he didn't want this crap inside his ship. Said once his engines were done, we wouldn't need it. I know Ares wants to keep it, but we don't need another ship. Hephaestus said if we need one, he'll build a new one. Considering what I've witnessed of Elysium, I have a feeling we may need more." Issy regarded me with her serious statement.

I internally groaned. I wasn't sure she was wrong.

CHAPTER 41

SYDNEY

There was only one thing I needed to know right now. Was giving up that ship, which we might need in the future worth it? "Did we get what we wanted?"

Ares' jaw tightened, and his eyes hardened.

"I don't want to give up that ship either, Sydney. We're not done examining all of their data-banks," Hercules joined his brother in protest.

<Open your hand.> Tristan ordered.

I stuck my hand out. A USB-sized zip drive appeared.

<Dr. Michelson said to plug it into their data-banks. It's a program he designed. It will find what we want, weeding out anything we already have.> Tristan supplied.

<Brilliant! Tell Michelson that I said *'thank you.'*>

I handed it to Ares, "Compliments of Professor Michelson. He says to plug in. It'll do your work for you."

Ares gave me a half smile. He was a man who appreciated action more than anything. Delayed progress was an affront to him. In that respect, he was a man after my own heart.

There were only a few hundred people left.

An old man approached me, hobbling along as best he could, leaning heavily on a stick. "We appreciate the sacrifice you're willing to make regarding this ship. However, we have one last request. It's not that we don't want to go with you. We simply didn't want to be a prisoner on your ship. You're willing to leave us this ship. We want to follow you in it," he informed me.

I closed my eyes. I knew it was gonna be something like this. I knew there was more. I was not a fool. I did admire the fact that they were willing to enact as much subterfuge as necessary. Made me wonder if maybe the smarter of them were not the ones I took on board my own ship.

I stared at him for a moment to organize my thoughts. "There's a small problem with that. We don't travel using engines like you do. We travel using the mind. In order for you to come with us, you'd have to be onboard a ship with a shifter. Those are the people who move us. There's only three." I saw the sparkle in his tired brown eyes. A fresh round of internal grumbling roared its head.

"Isn't it handy that the ship just came out of a larger ship? This is our ship. We'd like to go with you. You're saying we can't do it under our own power. That's fine. We would simply like our ship to sit inside of one of yours whenever we move. When stationary, we would be outside of your ship. Autonomous and independent." He gave me a tight smile. He was wily. My grudging respect for anyone with balls this big was unequivocal.

"They want to piggyback, mom. Why not? Why can't we let them?" Issy whispered. She pushed her sweat-soaked hair out of her face, then eyeballed Hercules for moral support.

Ares moved closer to join the conversation. In a gruff voice he started, "And what if they accidentally detonate their engines inside of one of our ships? It could be devastating." He reviewed the group on the platform suspiciously.

I opened my mouth to speak, then snapped it shut. My natural instinct was jaded. I would love to believe this could work, but the 'no' lingered on my lips.

"I give you my word we will do nothing to harm you, your people, or our own." The old man said. He'd moved so he could eavesdrop. "We don't even want to use the engines. We don't know how. We would like to be autonomous as much as possible while still traveling with you. Any person you deem as a threat to your ship, you can turn over to us. We will handle them." He darkened over his last sentence.

His request was reasonable. It made more sense than leaving anyone here or sending them out to the cosmos on their own. At some point in time, it would be certain death.

"Okay, we'll take you. Everybody's got caveats. It'll work until it doesn't. The moment it stops working, we'll make sure that Hephaestus has retrofitted your ship enough that you can travel on your own safely." I replied with a tight smile.

He moved his head in agreement and smiled, then hobbled away towards the small group of people. I briefly listened to the cries of relief, followed by hugs and kisses. Their shining faces warmed my heart.

We'd found a solution everyone could live with.

That's what matters.

I wanted to get back to Odyssey and get the hell out of here. I eyed Adrian, and he gave me a quiet smile.

<It's almost over, beautiful girl. >

<I know. It just seems everything takes forever and has to be twice as hard.> I grumbled.

I'd wandered away from all of our various new friends and allies. "Mom, I wanted to ask you something," Issy asked breathlessly.

"What?"

"All of these Elysians we've now freed. They're old, and a lot of them seem to have infirmities from hard labor," she stopped, her lips pressed flat and switched from side to side.

"Yes, so?" I prodded her.

"Shouldn't we give them some Primordium? If we give them Primordium, they would at least be healthy," she burst with her fingers laced together.

"I don't know that much about genetics, chemistry or hybrid Human/Themian physiology. These people are 100% pure Elysiums. We are a hybrid of a hybrid. Themian mixed with human. Wrap your head around that one, Isolde. I have no idea what's in Primordium. Do you?" She shook her head and looked down at the ground.

This was important to her. She didn't like to see anybody suffering. Isolde, of course, felt what people around her were feeling. She could probably feel their discomfort and pain.

I wrapped an arm around her and began walking toward the shuttle. "If we give them the Primordium, it could kill them. It could heal them," I replied in a low voice. "or it could do nothing. We have no idea. I'm not willing to take that chance. Melinda is really the only one to talk to. She's the only one who would have any clue, and right now, she's probably dealing with 1000 different things happily." I breathed.

Isolde got a smirk on her face. We both knew Melinda was never happy unless she had 15 balls, all juggling in the air and feeling quite brilliant.

"It's just in my heart — if we can heal these people, we should," she finished.

I opened my mind. It was harder for me to contact people from long distances. It's easier if I have an emotional connection to them. In the case of great aunt Melinda, I should have, but I didn't. She was my great aunt and I'd only met her a few times as a child. She was a little wacky. We weren't close.

I had to look for that feeling, that thing inside my mind that drew me to someone. If I could peacefully position myself, I could see the spokes of every thread of every life form, jutting out into the cosmos from me. I looked for the one that spoke to me and said, '*I am Melinda*'. With my mind's eye, I clasped it.

<Melinda, what would happen if we gave Primordium to pure Elysians, not the hybridized ones. Do we know?>

All I encountered was silence. Maybe she needed a minute or two to think about it.

<Maybe something, maybe nothing. I don't know, good question. Do you have a volunteer? > she asked with interest.

<Can't you just do like a blood test or something? >

<Nope. Doesn't work that way, sorry. That only works with humans. Something about Themian physiology and their technology. You are not just your cells. You are an entire living being, without the whole the, part doesn't work right.>

I had no idea what she was talking about.

<So it's like a motor. Just testing one piston ring won't do it. You have to put the whole engine together for it to work?>

<You got it, sweetheart? So, give me a volunteer and I'll let you know. > she mentally pushed me out.

My eyes darted around. Adrian gave me a raised eyebrow. It was not like I could hide it from him.

"Isolde, go back to the ship and find us a volunteer. Preferably, someone who's already been judged." Isolde got a half smirk on her face.

"I don't need to get to the ship to find a volunteer, mom. The leader of the separatist group over there, he'll do it."

"What makes you so sure?" Isolde's smile broadened "He'd give anything to get rid of that cane. He's tired. He's been broken and hurt many times. He lives in constant pain, mom. He'll do anything."

"Are you sure he won't stay just the way he is? His people need him as a leader more than he needs to get rid of his pain," I retorted under my breath.

"He's not the leader. He's the father of their leader. He only came to speak to you because they felt that he was the right man to negotiate the problem," she giggled.

No, he was the real brains in that group. His son probably just ran the show.

"Go ahead and ask him." Isolde sauntered away with a saucy swagger. She spoke to the older man for a couple of moments. The man's eyes grew wide, and his eyebrows raised into what was left of his hairline. He smiled and nodded his head.

Well, I be damned.

Isolde let the man take her arm, and she slowly led him back to me. "My name is Khrast. I understand you have a healing tonic and you're not sure if it would work on us. I'll be happy to have it tested on me. If it can heal my people or myself in any way, I'll do it. Being old and infirm is the worst punishment that can be inflicted upon anyone. Even a slave."

I nodded my head. Gazed over at Adrian, then both Khrast and Isolde disappeared.

I ducked into the ship. I was ready to go back. We were waiting on data from the computers in the complex. I studied the door to the inside, wondering if I should explore further.

<Loading the rest of the Elysiums into their ship. I'll be done in a sec. >

<Don't even bother letting them fire up their engines. Just shift them back in Prometheus' shuttle bay. Make sure that the airlock doors are closed and locked.>

<It shall be as you desire, *beautiful girl*.>

Whenever he said that, I got a stupid goofy grin. I did my best to repress it by covering my face.

I sat down in the cockpit and waited. Loud footfalls filled areas outside the door. "Sydney, we have the information."

"Good! Load up, and let's get the hell out of here. I'm tired of sitting on this rock," I replied. The view of the landing platform was dismal. I couldn't imagine what the rest of this shithole looked like.

Adrian appeared a moment later, "We should be ready to leave in about fifteen minutes. I need to shift the shipment of crystal they have mined. If you want, I can shift you straight back to Odyssey," he offered.

I didn't want to be away from Adrian, but I knew they needed him and I couldn't stand sitting still any longer. "Yes, please. I'm going stir crazy."

A smile lit his eyes. He leaned down and kissed my lips lightly, "Shifting you now." It was a light pressure change and a pop, then I was on the bridge of my flagship — Odyssey.

The 3D holo display showed Phaedra with two small dots, Prometheus floating next to us. I smiled quietly to myself. If you would have told me four years ago when Gabriel died that I would discover Atlantis, leave planet Earth on a spaceship with a new race of people, and go on a grand adventure, I probably would've laughed at you for being crazy. I would have told you that you were telling me grand stories to keep me from floating down into my depression. But here I was, on the bridge of my ship, with my people. I was on the cusp of finding the Homeworld where life really came from.

I contemplated my view of the cosmos. What did I trade? Would I want to go back to the boat, floating on the ocean with the waves lapping gently on the hull?

<This is still an ocean, beautiful girl. You just traded the blue for black with every shade of the rainbow you can imagine. Your rocks are now stars and asteroids. There are no islands either. They're planets and moons. We have the data. We hold Elysium in our hands. I'll be back with you in a couple of moments, and then we will make port.>

I didn't have to see the star chart to know that Adrian would never lie to me. The very idea that we were going to a world that could accept us.

Perhaps, they will.

Or at least make port in a storm. That sounded good enough to me. Frankly, at that point in time, I didn't even care. Just knowing that we have somewhere to go was good enough.

We weren't just wandering in the dark. We were not lost in the ocean of space.

Is this what Columbus felt when he finally saw land? Did he say, "No more here be dragons?"

The end

KILLING GODS

VI

<u>ELYSIUM</u>

Be careful what you wish for, paradise is an illusion.

https://amzn.to/2NDJfgF

If you've enjoyed what you've read here please give it a little

love and leave a review or feel free to follow me on Amazon

Or send me an email slmason1889@gmail.com or follow me

on Instagram @s.l.mason_author

More from S.L. Mason

THESE HALLOWED HILLS

TRICK OF FAE

TEST OF FAE

THORNS OF FAE

TWIST OF FAE

TRAITS OF FAE

OTHER STORIES

TWIN LIVES